THE SECOND THIRTY-THREE

Stories from the Make 100 Challenge

DEAN WESLEY SMITH

PUBLISHING

The Second Thirty-Three: Stories in the Make 100 Challenge
Copyright © 2020 by Dean Wesley Smith
Published by WMG Publishing
Cover and layout copyright © 2020 by WMG Publishing Cover art copyright © by
SergeyNivens/Depositphotos

ISBN-13: 978-1-56146-244-5
ISBN-10: 1-56146-244-6

CONTENTS

THE SECOND THIRTY-THREE

INTRODUCTION

More and More Stories

As I look through and organize these thirty-three stories, I am surprised at how many I remember, and how many I do not. When you write as many stories and novels as I do, it is more of a surprise to remember a story than forget it.

So, this process of putting all these stories out has been great fun for me, sort of reintroducing me to a lot of work.

How did this all come about? As I said in the introduction in the last volume, from the start of the indie publishing movement, I have wanted to get my short stories into paper books of their own. Stand-alone books, short story paperbacks in other words. It has sort of been a passion, to be honest.

And for about eighty of my short stories in 2010, I did that as a challenge. But that was a decade ago now. Wow, time does fly. I just never had the reason to spend the time and energy to do the covers and get the remaining two hundred to three hundred stories into paper form.

Or for that matter, redo the covers of the eighty I did ten years before, rebrand them.

But now, after a decade, I really wanted to do more, and along came Kickstarter with their Make 100 Promotion. It dawned on me that with a lot of help, a bunch of learning curves for me, and some time, I could do one hundred paperbacks of my short stories.

The Kickstarter got more support than I had hoped it would, which was wonderful. But it turned out the learning curves I had to go through slowed down the process. I wanted to redesign a website to get the new branding on, completely rebrand collections, and redo covers from my *Smith's Monthly Magazine.*

And to do all that I not only had to learn better website design, but I had to completely relearn both InDesign and Photoshop. Not small tasks.

But now, after a year, I am working away at redoing *Smith's Monthly* covers, and am about halfway through the 100 covers and gaining speed. As the first part of 2020 goes along, the paperbacks will be appearing and now I feel I can put together the three anthologies of the one hundred stories that I promised in the Kickstarter.

In this volume are the second thirty-three stories of the Make 100 Challenge. Just as the first volume, these stories cover many of my series and many others are stand-alone stories.

The introductions ahead of each story will be basically the sales copy, with a few changes, on Amazon and other sales sites. So my name gets repeated a lot. But in these collections I wanted you to see the sales copy.

I hope you enjoy these short stories. I can say that not only was it fun to write them over the years, but even more fun to get them into a stand-alone paperback and in this volume.

Dean Wesley Smith
Las Vegas, Nevada.
December, 2019

AS THE ROBOT RUBS

Science fiction, action, adventure, lust, and a ton of sexual innuendo. This story hits it all and even more.

Mike Blackmoon, son of the famous story-teller, Howling Blackmoon, tells the story carefully following his father's instructions.

This story inside a story features Buckey the Space Pirate, but not the same Buckey as later stories with the talking oak tree Fred. Who know there were two Buckey the Space Pirates?

A very different version of this story appeared in the anthology Alien Pets back in 1998. I added in a pet to get the story into the anthology. I like this, the original version, much better.

MY NAME IS Mike Blackmoon. And I got this story.

It might be called a romance, but it's not a romance.

Some folks might call it a mystery. Nope. Wrong again.

If the story were printed, some stupid bookstore owner might stick it in the horror section. Slap that person with rolled up page proofs.

There's just no way this story can be anything but science fiction.

That's right.

Science fiction with sex.

Of course, in science fiction, all the sex is like a Norman Rockwell painting. But it's still sex, so what the hell.

My daddy, Howling Blackmoon, was the greatest storyteller to ever sit beside a campfire. He always said that if you want to hold a listener's attention, you gotta start your story right in the middle of the good part. So that's exactly what I'm going to do.

"Don't stop," she panted.

How's that for a start?

I'll bet right now your mind is skipping right along with pictures of a young, big-chested girl, a must in science fiction — breathing heavily as this young space pirate named Buckey nibbles on her ear while at the same time unbuckling his blaster.

Buckey is a real ladies man in his white tights, white plumed hat, and black boots. He also wears a sabre strapped on one hip and a blaster on the other.

Now, if you're thinking Buckey is going to take off his blaster, you're wrong.

Wrong. Wrong. Wrong.

Buckey is nowhere to be seen. What's really going on is that this woman named Sarah — who is an escaped slave from the horrid Alien prison camp — is telling her fellow escapee, Loreina, the main character of this story, to keep running toward the ancient hidden ship. Sarah has decided that she must stay behind and hold off the prison guards in the narrow desert canyon.

Loreina argues with Sarah for only a moment, then gives her one of those looks.

You know the look.

The same deep understanding look that every mother has when she sees wads of used Kleenex in her teenage son's garbage can.

You know... THE LOOK!

Loreina hugs Sarah.

Only a sparkle of tears form in their eyes. (It's the desert so they can't waste much water.) Then Loreina turns and runs up the canyon while Sarah faces the quickly approaching Alien guards who will for sure either (a) kill her, or (b) torture her, or (c) do whatever else mean and nasty Alien guards do to young women in science fiction stories.

At this point, it is a good story telling technique to jump forward in time. Or, sometimes back in time to explain the good time all the characters had getting to the present time.

Of course, anytime you jump in time, you must let the story listener know you're signaling time out.

In the movies, they do it with fade-outs. In fiction, they use white spaces. In this case I'm just going to pause.

(Pause)

Pause for effect, then hook the listener again, my old man used to say. (He could tell a whopper with the best of them.) So, being a good listener, I'm going to follow old Blackmoon's advice and jump back into this story right at the most interesting part.

"Don't stop," she panted.

I bet I know what you're thinking. Loreina is sitting in the copilot's chair (Right?) of this small space ship (Right?) while the handsome Buckey (the space pirate who rescued her from the prison planet) nibbles softly on her big toe and then starts working his way north.

Right?

Don't you wish.

Remember, this is a science fiction story.

What's really going on is that our heroine (An aside here in the middle of this sentence: My daddy once noted how close the word heroine is to heroin. Heroin is defined as a powerful sedative drug. He told me to think about it. End of aside.) is laying naked, face down, with only a towel over her butt (Don't want to get the story teller too worked up, now do we?) on a massage table back at Galactic Headquarters while a robot carefully works all the soreness out of her muscles.

3

Leaning against a post (yes they have posts in Galactic Headquarters) is Loreina's boss and possible future love interest, Jerome.

At least their love might be possible if they don't find out that they are really brother and sister later in the story. (Of course, you might stop and ask yourself why Loreina would be interested in anyone by the name of Jerome. But I wouldn't. It would just complicate the story too much. Trust me that Jerome looks like no Jerome I ever met. Besides, Loreina likes the fact that he doesn't wear underwear under his tight-fitting Galactic uniform.)

As the robot rubs, (Note how swift the title worked in.) Loreina tells Jerome all about how she and Sarah were captured when they were zapped by a Lomax Ray which shut down all their food processing and bar equipment, as well as their main Wild-Blue-Yonder Drive just as they were about to learn how the dreaded Aliens were managing to steal fruit off Eden, the most heavily guarded planet this side of the core.

Jerome just shakes his head, so Loreina goes on to tell him about how horrible it was in the Alien prison and how Sarah stayed back so that one of them could get through with the message and get a good massage.

Again, Jerome just shakes his head.

He knows Loreina likes the strong silent type in her science fiction.

He also read on her job application for heroine that she liked men who didn't wear underwear.

Loreina gives Jerome that serious stare, raising up on one elbow so that she can see him better — and he most certainly can see her better. (The robot doesn't notice. Stupid robot.)

She then tells him, in a very deep tone, that she must return to save Sarah if Sarah is still alive.

She (Loreina) just can't leave her (Sarah) there in that awful place (the Alien prison), she (Loreina) says.

Again, Jerome just nods, never taking his eyes off of Loreina's boobs. (Which means that while Loreina talked, he had moved his face right up against her chest and, as in all good science fiction sex scenes, it is now time to fade out, white space, or pause, and thereby miss all the good description that follows when Jerome removes his eyes from her chest and puts other body parts there.)

· · ·

4

(Pause...damn it anyway.)

"Don't stop," she panted.

Take your mind out of the gutter. I am not starting the story back on the massage table where Jerome and Buckey the Space Pirate have drawn a dotted line down the center of Loreina and are having a duel to see who can get their half the most excited.

I wouldn't do that in a science fiction story. Besides, Buckey likes his women whole.

But during all that white space around the last pause Jerome has done the regular man-like, middle class, try-to-take-over-the-story thing and told Loreina that she can't go to rescue Sarah. He has assigned her to a desk job in Galactic Headquarters where he can keep her under his thumb (as well as other parts).

Loreina didn't take kindly to that kind of shit from above, so, not really being a "company" girl or terribly fond of the missionary position, she captures a guard at the space port and is following the guard up a long, circular staircase in the launching tower of the new Bigger, Longer, and Taller spaceship.

The BLT has nifty screens that make the ship almost invisible to Aliens and block out the aliens Zapper Beam. That will allow Loreina to get close enough to the prison camp to rescue Sarah and still have lunch.

This part of the story opens as the guard stops suddenly in front of Sarah halfway up the huge tower. (There's a lot of stairs and they're both out of breath.)

Sarah keeps him going and then, at the top, once she has gotten into the ship, she stuns the guard. As he falls, she notices that he too doesn't wear underwear under his tight-fitting uniform. (The guard, who is a friend of Jerome's secretary, also snuck a peek at Loreina's application.)

Of course, at this point, Loreina is heavily occupied with stealing the ship and getting Sarah out, so, with only one mouth-watering glance at the guard, she jumps into the Captain's chair, straps herself in, and blasts off.

Blasting off should not be noted here with a bunch of noise.

She just floats up through the rain clouds quiet as you please. The drive on the BLT is very silent and doesn't need a match to light it.

5

Real advanced science fiction stuff.

Of course, out in space, she gets chased by the entire Patrol Fleet, which happened to be home on leave. She doesn't want to Atomize them (or even fire a warning shot across their bows) because she knows The Patrol is on her side, and that some men in those ships may have read her application.

Instead she does a few really nifty moves around the sun, looses about ten pounds when the inside of the ship heats up, then pops off through the Time Warp Instant Trajectory.

When in the TWIT, no one can follow, so she's safe.

Next she goes about getting herself ready for instant sleep to pass the sixty-four days it will take to reach the Alien prison world. She strips down to only her skimpy bikini underwear and a sweat-soaked tee shirt and crawls in.

The last thing you see is her breathing slowing as she passes out and her nipples get hard.

And again, you guessed it, it is time to...

(Pause)

Now where should I open the next part of the story?

My daddy said never let a listener down. If you've got someone's attention, don't disappoint him, especially toward the end of your story. So, following old man Blackmoon's advice once more, I return to the story at a "good" part.

"Don't stop," she panted.

God, don't you just love an exciting story?

I mean, imagine Loreina there with Sarah and Buckey, The Space Pirate on the filthy dirt floor of Sarah's cell in the Alien prison. The three of them are tied up, naked except for Buckey's white hat.

Buckey has one foot between Sarah's open legs and his other foot between Loreina's open legs. He's working on untying the girl's ropes with his toes.

Of course, his heels are making the escape a somewhat pleasurable experience for both women.

Now that you've imagined all that: dirt floor, moldy smell, low moaning, and all, I'm glad you got it out of your system because that's not what is going on. Remember... science fiction story?

I know, I know, I hate repeating myself, too. But sometimes I must, I must.

In the real story, Sarah wakes up after sixty-four days, crawls out, and does the classic yawn. Her little panties seem even smaller and the tee shirt still looks wet, but that's beside the point.

Without dressing, she runs to the cockpit of the ship and checks her instruments. (I won't say it if you don't.)

She discovers she is almost to the Alien prison planet. Now what is she going to do? She looks quickly around nearby space for the intervention-of-the-machine (sounds better in Latin) that will end the story quickly, but she doesn't spot one.

Failing that, the plot must thicken like overripe soup.

Loreina clicks on her screens and sneaks up on the Alien prison world. It just so happens that the entire Alien fleet is circling the prison planet. (Probably on vacation.)

Loreina decides it would be suicidal not only to her, but to her lust for men who don't wear shorts, if she went in alone. Probably get Sarah killed, too.

She thought and thought and wracked her brain trying to figure out what to do. That wasn't a pretty sight, even with her still in her bikini shorts and wet tee shirt.

A smoking, ruined brain is never fun to look at.

Finally, after two issues of Playmate of the Spaceways magazine and a good nights sleep, she realizes the answer has been right there in front of her in the story line all the time: Buckey, The Space Pirate.

She and Buckey go way back. Her first true love.

She loved his sabre.

Only she went corporate and he stayed in the private business sector and it had all ended with a net loss. Why hadn't she thought of him before? She used to think of him often, usually in the bathtub.

She sat there in the Captain's chair and thought about sitting in the bathtub and thinking about Buckey. Pretty soon she is thinking a lot about Buckey and her tee shirt is getting damper and damper and she is panting and it is right at this point, with her eyes closed, that Loreina utters the opening words of this section.

(Bet you thought I'd forgotten, didn't you?)

After a few moments more of thinking, Loreina slowly comes around and realizes (before her hands turn this into a romance) that she's not in the bathtub after all and that Sarah is still sitting down there in that stinking, dirt-floored, Alien prison waiting to be rescued.

Buckey is the only hope.

Loreina brushes her damp hair back out of her eyes, does a few quick calculations, and inserts the ship back into TWIT. Three quick days and she'd be with Buckey, The Space Pirate's fleet.

She did a few instrument checks, then headed for the bathroom. She wouldn't deep sleep this time.

She needed a long, long bath far more.

And, as the door to the bathroom hisses softly closed, this story again does the correct thing and...

(Pause.)

"Don't stop," she panted."

Nice hook to the climax of the story, huh? My daddy would be proud of me.

So, the tension builds. Where is Loreina now? Is Sarah still alive? Does Loreina get Buckey to help spring Sarah from the prison camp? Does Buckey wear underwear?

Tough questions that must be answered in this section because this is the last damn chance.

That's right.

No more pauses.

If this were a standard science fiction story, this section would have opened with Loreina in the bathtub thinking of Buckey when (suddenly) alarm bells go off all over the ship.

Of course, Loreina would have had time to struggle into clothes before facing the problem of one of Buckey's ships attacking her ship. She would have finally gotten through to Buckey who would have saved her in the last moment so that they could both go rescue Sarah.

Now that's pure pulp story telling.

But that's not the way it happened. This is a liberated world, remember? Loreina has got to do it herself or it just won't mean anything.

On the third day of Loreina's bath, she gets to Buckey's home base and discovers from Buckey's second-in-command, Fred, (who has a large nose, very white teeth, and a small part in this story) that while on a raiding mission on an Alien world, Buckey's ship blew a warp and Buckey had been captured and was being held on the prison world. (Wow! That explains the entire Alien fleet being around the prison world much better than them just being there on shore leave.)

Fred doesn't know what to do.

But Loreina, after three days in the bathtub thinking about Buckey, has a desperate idea.

She decides to give Buckey's fleet the secrets to the screening device in her BLT so that they can all sneak inside the Alien fleet. Buckey's ships can keep the Aliens busy while she rescues Buckey and Sarah.

Neat plan, huh?

Fred likes the idea (and why wouldn't he?) and so, for the next two weeks, while Loreina takes a lot of baths and she and Fred do a lot of careful rescue planning, the screening devices are built and installed in all sixty-plus ships in Buckey's fleet.

Finally, the fleet is ready, Loreina is well wrinkled, and the plot must go on.

At this point I could go into another pause, letting the three days travel back to the Alien prison world pass quickly. But remember, I still haven't got to the point where the story starts after the last pause. So, let it suffice to say that the three days do pass like a bowl of chili and Buckey's fleet, with Fred in command, sneaks inside the Alien ships and attacks them on their naked, exposed undersides, right where they least expect it.

I could go into long detail about the battle. Blood and violence are okay in science fiction, and in fact are currently fashionable as long as the violence occurs in the future and has a high-tech feel.

You can't make love to someone, but it's all right to kill them.

Even though my daddy was an Indian and my mother was a German, I don't like violence. I like sex.

Luckily, so did my mother and father.

So, if I can't tell all about the sex in this story, I'm not going to give any of the violence, either.

So there.

Trust me when I tell you that except for the loss of two of Buckey's ships, Fred and the crews were completely successful in blasting those mean and nasty Aliens out of the system.

Loreina flew the BLT right down to the prison, landed, and led a raiding party into the cells.

In the human section of the prison, they found Sarah sitting in one cell staring at Buckey in the next cell. Both Sarah and Buckey were fine, except Sarah was a little glassy-eyed from staring at Buckey all those weeks.

That all happened in the last pause.

The last part of the story opens finally with Loreina leading Sarah, Buckey, and the raiding party back through the narrow halls of the prison at a full run. (They don't know that Buckey's fleet is winning the battle out in space.) Loreina guards one side corridor as she tells them breathlessly not to stop. (Remember: great opening line of this section.)

They make it safely back to the BLT and as this story closes with the ending that of course will leave enough open for a trilogy, Loreina sits in the Captain's chair with Buckey kneeling at her right and Sarah standing beside her on the left.

Picture this:

Sarah's hand is on Loreina's shoulder.

Buckey's left hand is on his sabre.

Buckey's white hat is tipped slightly to one side. His right hand is on Loreina's knee.

Loreina's shirt is still wet.

All three are smiling like damn fools into the view screen in front of them, as if posing for a wedding picture.

Silently, the BLT leaves the nasty Alien prison world behind and inserts itself (with a rainbow of colors) into TWIT, going who knows where.

"Don't stop," she panted.

Loreina gives her last command and, as the story fades to a close, leans back, closes her eyes, and sighs. Buckey's hand moves softly on Loreina's leg.

Sarah glances down and licks her lips.

The end. Except for one loose end. Buckey does not wear underwear. (What do you think Sarah was staring at all that time?)

DREAMS OF A MOON

A Captain Brian Saber Story

USA Today *bestselling writer, Dean Wesley Smith, returns to the fan favorite universe of the Earth Protection League.*

Once again, Captain Brian Saber and Captain Dorothy "Dot" Leeds must leave their nursing home to fight for the very survival of the Earth.

This story first appeared in Fiction River: Moonscapes. *The story was also incorporated as a number of chapters in the novel last month,* Life of a Dream.

One

THE YOUNG, STRONG lieutenant gently nudged Captain Brian Saber in his nursing home bed, pulled back the blanket and sheet covering him, and then easily picked Brian up with strong arms. His name was Lieutenant Magusson, but he had told Brian one night that some people called him Big Ed.

Brian was going on a mission.

Brian could feel the excitement surge through his old body.

A mission, a chance to live again, to be young again.

He made himself take as deep a breath as he could without setting off a fit of coughing.

The Shady Valley Nursing Home room hadn't changed since Brian fell asleep at 10 p.m. Now his old clock on his dresser told him it was a little after one in the morning. If he survived this mission, he would be back in fifteen minutes. But he might be out there in space for a month or more, if he was lucky.

Big Ed turned for the room's sliding glass door. Behind him Brian saw Captain Dorothy "Dot" Leeds being carried from her room across the hall and through his room. The young woman carrying her was Lieutenant Sherrie and she followed Brian and Big Ed out into the cold night air of a Chicago winter.

The light nightshirt Brian wore to bed was no match for the biting cold air, but he didn't mind. He wouldn't be out in the cold long enough for it to matter.

Overhead he could see the full moon, bright in the night sky. He and Dot were both far too old to ever walk under that moon. But at some point they would be together, staring up at some moon, somewhere.

No one talked.

No one said a word.

They were on a mission for the Earth Protection League. Something had happened on the border a long ways from Earth, which is why the League needed Brian and Dot. The League needed their ships, needed the two of them young and willing to fight.

All over the country right now his crew and Dot's crew were going through the same routine.

Damn he was excited.

He always felt this way going on a mission.

The four of them neared the center of the courtyard of the nursing home. The frozen snow crunched under the boots of the two lieutenants and Brian could see his shallow breath in the dim light.

The full moon was so beautiful on a clear winter night. He hoped he would see it again tonight.

Then a yellow beam struck them from above and lifted all four of them up easily into the big intergalactic transport ship.

The warm air of the ship covered him and behind him he heard Dot say softly, "See you on the other side."

He would have answered her, but he couldn't talk louder than a whisper. He couldn't walk or even lift his arms much at all either. A stroke had taken most of those skills a few years earlier.

She knew that and didn't expect an answer from him. He was eighty-eight, she was eighty-seven. Both of them were captains of major starships for the Earth Protection League.

They had been friends in the nursing home and one night she had seen him being carried out to go on a mission. So the next day he got permission to recruit her, and she had risen quickly to the rank of captain as well, in just under twenty missions. She was that good.

And they were both very much in love. At some point soon they would get married and live out on the frontier, not ever having to return to earth and their old bodies.

But right now they were still frontline fighters. And clearly they were needed.

Big Ed laid Brian down in what looked like a coffin in a private cabin off to one side of the big hallway.

That coffin was a sleep chamber that knocked Brian out during the trip at Trans-Galactic speeds toward the frontier of the Earth Protection League. And during that sleep, because of the nature of space and time and matter, his body would regress to being young and healthy again.

He had no idea how or why it worked that way. A couple of people had tried to explain it to him once. Something about matter being at a fixed point in time and space, so if a person flew faster than light, everyone on board regressed in age in relationship to the distance traveled.

They had figured out a way to help the brain hold the memories of being old, and the experiences during the trip.

Brian was just glad it worked the way it did, because otherwise he would be stuck in that nursing home and in the stroke-damaged body just waiting to die. Now he could actually do something constructive, help defend Earth and its allies.

Big Ed stepped back and snapped off a salute. "Good luck, sir," he said.

Then he lowered the lid until it latched over Brian and the light went out.

Brian would have loved to salute the young man back, but he couldn't.

Instead he just lay there thinking of seeing Dot again in her young and youthful body.

And he thought of them dancing as they always did after a mission.

But first they had to survive whatever faced them in deep space this time.

A faint orange smell seeped into the coffin and Captain Brian Saber dozed off.

Two

CAPTAIN SABER AWOKE what seemed like just an instant later.

He reached up and easily pushed the coffin lid open. Then he levered his young body out of the sleep chamber.

He never got tired of that feeling after being trapped in that wheelchair and bed what seemed like just moments before. The magic of the Trans-Galactic speed had done it to him again; given him his young body back.

He had sure taken this body for granted when he had been young.

He quickly slipped off the old nightshirt and tossed it back in the coffin. He would need that for the return trip back.

If he survived.

If he didn't, his son would be called in the middle of the night and there would be a funeral for a body that was a fake of his. And no one but those in the Earth Protection League would know Brian Saber of Chicago died in space, fighting for all humanity.

And he didn't honestly care if anyone knew. He just loved doing this, getting a chance to be young again.

He quickly dressed in his tight brown pants and tall black leather boots over the pants. He put on a loose white-silk blouse and a brown vest over that with a logo on it that read EPL. He strapped his two photon blasters on his hips with a wide black-leather belt and then looked at himself in the mirror.

This trip they had gone a little farther out. He looked to be about twenty-five. Often he ended up closer to thirty on missions.

So that meant they were very, very close to the EPL border, more than likely the border with the Dogs, one of the nastiest alien races to ever exist.

And a race set on the destruction at any cost of the EPL and Earth.

He turned and left his room, turning right and heading for the command center. He was on his own warship, the *Bad Business*.

Dot would have been transferred to her ship as well, the *Blooming*

Rose. He wished he could see her now, kiss her, hold her with his young strong arms. But there would be time for that later.

Right now he had to focus on the mission they faced.

He got to the control room just a few seconds before his other two command crew arrived. Marion Knudson, a striking redhead from Wisconsin took her second chair. The two of them had been a team for a dozen missions now.

She was tough, all business, and smart as they came.

This time she had her red hair long and down over her shoulders. Usually she kept it up tight against her head.

Behind them Kip Butcher dropped into his chair with a "Damn this feels good."

Kip was from Southern California and lived in a nursing home there. When he was young he had been a surfer and now, even in his uniform, he still looked the part with his tan skin and blonde hair.

Back in Wisconsin, Marion lived alone, even at the age of ninety. As Kip had said once, she was too damn mean to die.

Marion had not argued with that, only smiled that smile that let Brian know that at some point Kip would pay for the remark.

"So any news as to the mission, Captain?" Marion asked, her fingers running over the board in front of her. "We are within striking distance of the Dog border. Much closer than normal, actually. No sign at all of Dog warships."

"And there are six other EPL warships with us," Kip said. "One is the *Blooming Rose.*"

Everyone knew about his and Dot's relationship.

"No word yet," Brian said. "But I suspect we don't have long to wait."

He pointed to the board and as he did, a red light started blinking, meaning an emergency message was coming in.

"You creep me out every time you do that," Kip said, shaking his head and turning back to his board.

Brian just smiled at Marion. The brass had a certain timetable that they allowed the crews to get into positions on their ships, and that never varied.

"Message on screen," Kip said a moment later.

General Dan Holmes's face appeared, his frown causing his middle-aged face to wrinkle even more than it already was.

"Captains," he said, nodding. "I'm afraid this is as bad as it gets."

Brian said nothing, as did the other captains of the other six warships, so the general went on.

"The Dogs have launched a moon at Earth."

Brian sat there hoping that General Holmes would take back that statement.

He didn't.

The General just kept frowning.

"The moon is accelerating from deep in Dog space and will be at the border at your position in about six hours."

"Fleet of ships with it, I assume?" Saber asked.

The General shook his head. "They don't think they need ships on this one. The moon they have launched is as big as our moon around Earth."

Brian sat back and tried to imagine what it would take to get a moon like that actually moving, what kind of power and how the moon would even hold together. And how they would even aim it from such a long distance through space.

And how many thousands of years at real-space travel it would take to get to Earth.

"I'm sending all the data we have on it through to you," the general said. "We want you to investigate the moon the moment it crosses into our space, pass on the data to our scientists."

With that he clicked off, leaving the screen blank.

"Why do I think there's something he flat omitted from that briefing," Kip said.

Marion's fingers flew over the keys as Brian sat there, waiting. He knew Kip was right. The General wasn't telling them everything. There was something more.

"Oh, shit," Marion said.

Brian looked over at her. She never swore.

She put up the report that made her swear on the main screen in front of Brian so that they could all see it.

"One hour after the moon crosses into our space," Marion said, "it reaches Trans-Galactic speed and will be protected by the Trans-Galactic shields. Nothing will be able to change its course until it plows into Earth."

"They built a TG drive big enough to power a moon," Kip said, shaking his head. "Wow! That's impressive."

Brian had to admit, it was impressive. But there was only one problem. Once something was in Trans-Galactic drive, it couldn't be stopped. It wasn't in real time and the shields that formed with the drive could plow through anything.

So they had to figure out a way to stop a speeding moon.

Or Earth would be destroyed very, very shortly.

Three

CAPTAIN SABER LOOKED around at his command crew, then shook his head. "Looks like we got seven hours to figure this out. Marion, make sure to get that report to the people on board who understand Trans-Galactic drive physics."

Marion nodded, her fingers moving quickly over the controls as Brian turned his big chair around so he could face Kip on his right and Marion on his left.

"Done," she said.

Brian knew that meant the other 40-some members of his crew all knew the score and were working on solutions as well. When you got that many experienced people working hard on something, results tended to happen.

And Brian knew that everyone on the other ships was doing the same. That was a lot of years experience focused on the same problem.

"Let me kind of think out loud here," he said.

Both Marion and Kip nodded.

"I assume TG space will power the thing once the moon reaches Trans-Galactic speed. But what's powering it now?"

Both Kip and Marion had the report at their fingertips and it was Marion that spoke first. "The moon has a hot core, so the engines spaced around the moon are feeding off the internal core of the moon itself."

"All TG engines," Kip said. "All shielded as would be expected. Nothing we have will knock them out."

Brian knew that and he nodded. He'd been in a lot of fights with Dog warships and knocking their engines out was never an option, just as Dogs knocking out a TG EPL engine wasn't possible either. It was the nature of Trans-Galactic engines and the shields that built up around them.

"Can we dig the engines out of the moon's surface outside the shields?" Brian asked.

Again both his command crew worked on the report, then both shook their heads at the exact same time. "Engines are buried thirty miles deep inside the moon. No dislodging them."

Brian looked at the big screen near Kip with the report and wondered how the EPL got all the information. More than likely a number of people had died for it.

"And I assume no blowing the thing apart before it enters Trans-Galactic speed?" Brian asked.

"They found the most stable hunk of rock I've ever seen," Kip said, and Marion nodded.

"It would take an entire fleet of ships," Kip said, sounding disgusted, "pounding it with all weapons, and I doubt that even that much would make more than a dent."

They all three sat there in silence.

Brian just kept looking around, looking at his young body, at his command crew's young bodies. Somehow they had made it out here, to this exact location in space.

He looked at Kip. "Who is driving the moon?"

"No one will be on the moon," Kip said.

"So who drives us when we come out here," Brian asked. "to exact coordinates, with our Trans-Galactic drives?"

Marion frowned and turned back to her board.

Kip did the same thing.

You don't just send a ship hurtling through more miles of space than Brian wanted to think about without something or someone driving. Even with top shields, you didn't want to plow holes through things along the way that didn't need holes in them.

So that transport ship from Earth had someone driving it, controlling it, from somewhere.

And that moon would have someone driving all the way to Earth. One planet that far away was far, far too small a target to hit from this distance without a number of course corrections along the way.

"Computers," Marion finally said. "Each transport we take out here is run by a computer to do course corrections."

"Through sensors, the computer is able to see the route ahead," Kip said, "and make corrections to avoid the transport putting a hole in a planet or moon or anything else along the way."

"So there is a computer on that moon somewhere?" Brian asked. "We know where?"

"Buried with the Trans-Galactic drive engines," Marion said.

"Damn," Kip said, clearly getting angry. "They thought of everything."

"Not everything," Brian said, smiling. "Is the moon rotating in any fashion?"

Kip and Marion both looked puzzled at him, then quickly checked.

"No," Marion said. "It couldn't rotate and maintain its TG drive thrust."

"So we blind it," Brian said. "Tough to hit anything without being able to see."

"The computer sensors," Kip said, laughing. "Of course, they would have to be hidden on the front side of the moon to feed the computer."

"And I'll wager those sensors are not hardwired into that computer," Brian said. "Not through that much rock."

Marion laughed, the first time Brian had heard that for some time. "What are you thinking, Captain?"

Brian sat back, his hands behind his head.

"How about we feed those computers in that moon some bad targeting information, something simple such as the location of a Dog military base."

"Oh, that will annoy them something awful," Kip said, laughing so hard tears were coming to his eyes.

Marion informed all the other ships of the idea and then all three of them set to work on exactly where on that moon those sensors would be planted and how to intercept the signal from the surface sensors to the moon's targeting computer.

Four

THE MOON WAS fast approaching the EPL border when Command gave the clearance to try their plan. It had been a scientist on Dot's ship who had finally cracked the Dog computer code between the moon targeting computer and the sensors.

And it had been a scientist on yet another warship who had figured out how to intercept the signals from the sensors.

They would need to have a ship in tight over each of the six sensors on the moon and the intercept signal would have to be sent at exactly the same moment to all sensors.

In essence, the control of the moon was going to be transferred to Brian. He and Kip and Marion were going to turn the moon just before it started into Trans-Galactic drive and fire it at a Dog military base.

And then destroy the targeting computer by feeding it a very nasty virus.

That moon would wipe out that Dog base and then head out into deep space at full TG drive. The engines would have to fail before that moon dropped back into normal space a very, very long ways away from this entire galaxy.

At least that was the plan.

But there was one major problem with the plan that Brian didn't much like. Six EPL ships would have to basically hover in close over the moon to intercept the signal from each sensor and relay the signal to his ship and then, in turn, take the new instructions and feed them back into the sensors.

Dot and her ship would be one of those in close.

And they would have to stay in close during the moon's turn and then somehow get a safe distance away when the moon jumped to Trans-Galactic drive.

It was going to take exact timing. Just a second or two of delay and a warship would be lost.

And if one warship didn't stay in close enough, all six sensors wouldn't feed the computer the right data and there was no telling what might happen.

Brian sat back in his chair, trying to keep his nerves under control as they waited the last ten minutes. He knew everyone was busy checking and double-checking the plan. He had talked with Dot privately thirty minutes before, telling her to be careful and that he loved her.

She just laughed that wonderful, young laugh of hers, and said, "Trust me, I'm not missing the dancing tonight for anything."

Dot loved to dance, more than anything in life it seemed at times.

And he loved to dance with her.

"Moon crossing the border now, Captain," Marion said.

Brian nodded to Kip who opened a fleet-wide communications

link.

"Move into positions now."

On the screen in front of him, Brian could see the six other EPL warships with their sleek noses and wing-like appearance move as one, turning toward the large moon and matching speed with it. EPL warships had been designed to look like birds not only to allow them atmospheric flight if needed, but because in so many of the cultures the EPL fought against, birds were feared.

Including with the Dogs.

Brian kept the *Bad Business* outside and above the group, moving with them to match the speed of the moon.

Then, almost as a practiced dance in space, the six ships broke away from each other and moved in over an area of the large moon.

The closer the moon got, Brian could see that it did look a great deal like their moon at home. It had no atmosphere and was covered with impact craters. And it was just about the same size.

Brian took the *Bad Business* in right over the center of the moon and matched its speed and acceleration to stay in position.

"Thirty seconds," Marion said.

"Signal when in position," Brian ordered the other ships.

Each ship had to hover no more than a football field length above the surface where the sensor was, and match the increasing speed of the moon at the same time.

Very, very tricky flying and a slight miss and the EPL warship would crash into the moon's surface, or be too far away to intercept the signal.

Brian could see the *Blooming Rose* turn and settle into its assigned position above the moon surface. Dot would be flying it. She had one of the steadiest hands at the helm of a ship that he had ever seen.

Three other warships signaled ready.

Then Dot signaled *The Blooming Rose* was in position and steady.

"Ready here," Brian said, checking to make sure his people were ready with the computer download and new signal into the moon's computer.

At the same moment the other two ships reported they were in position and stable.

"Hold and be ready to turn with the moon," Brian said.

"Intercept signal," Brian ordered the other ships.

As one all turned green that they had the sensor signal.

Then he turned to Marion. "Feed it."

Her fingers flew over the panel and the new programming for the Dog's computer was fed through all six sensors.

An instant later the moon started to turn off its course for Earth.

"Stay with it, everyone," Brian commanded to the other ships as he moved the *Bad Business* to maintain position and keep the feed to the other ships constant.

The moon kept turning and somehow the EPL warships held their positions.

"We got some swearing and close calls," Kip said, "but everyone's holding.

"Ten more seconds," Marion said. "And the virus will be loaded."

At five seconds Brian counted it down for the other captains.

"Five. Four. Three. Two. One."

Marion signaled cut.

"Get out of there now!" Brian shouted to the other pilots.

As one, the other pilots moved their ships up and away from the rough surface of the moon.

Brian had the *Bad Business* moving with them, pushing the ship as fast as he could to try to reach a safe distance.

Twenty seconds later the moon vanished into Trans-Galactic drive space, headed back into the Dog's territory and right for a large military base.

"Clear," Kip said. "All ships made it out of the wash zone from the drive."

Brian slumped in his chair, just smiling as both Kip and Marion applauded and laughed.

Somehow, Earth had dodged that moon.

Barely.

Five

CAPTAIN BRIAN SABER looked down into the wonderful brown eyes of Captain Dorothy Dot Leeds and smiled. "One more dance?"

She laughed, the sound high and wonderful and something he needed to remember in the long days and nights at the nursing home. "Our bus back to the home is going to leave without us."

"Let it," he said, pulling her close and enjoying the feel of her against him. Since they had turned the moon weapon back on the Dogs, the general had allowed all seven EPL warships to dock at Stevens Base for some well-deserved time off while in younger bodies.

Brian and Dot had spent the first night dancing, then in his room on the base. The next day they had spent in meetings with the general and others, then dancing more that evening, then back to her room for the night.

The General had approved their application to move to Stevens in a very short time, be married, and work frontline there with their ships and any crew that wanted to join them, based out of Stevens.

As the General said, it was about time they had a staffed base full of frontline defenders. He wanted Brian to lead the wing of fighters. The EPL would still bring many in from Earth when needed, but a number based out on the edge of the frontier would be a good idea.

But until that was fully approved, Brian and Dot now had to go back to Earth and the Shady Hills Nursing Home.

With one last dance, they kissed and walked hand-in-hand to the transport, not saying anything.

He kissed Dot one more time at her cabin door, then with a promise from her that she would help him with his applesauce at breakfast, he went to his cabin and took off his uniform, slipping back into his old nightshirt and crawling into the coffin.

The very next thing he remembered, he was being carried by Lieutenant Magusson from his sleep chamber.

His old stroke-damaged body now part of him again.

Dot and Lieutenant Sherrie met them at the transport chamber.

Brian so wanted to reach out to touch Dot's hand, but he could no longer move his arms hardly at all.

The cold air of the Chicago night hit him as the transport beam let them go in the nursing home center court.

Above him the golden moon was full in the crisp night air.

He stared up at it as the Lieutenant carried him toward his room.

"Not so pretty any more, is it?" Dot said.

She was right. It wasn't.

After this mission, he wasn't sure if he would ever look up at the moon in the same way again.

It was amazing how seeing the universe and defending Earth could change a person's perspective on things in such a short time.

Simple things, like staring up at the moon.

MUSIC IN TIME

"Music in Time" takes a look inside the mind of an artist when that art seems to have left him stranded on a space station.

First published many years ago in an anthology entitled Love and Rockets, *this story remains one of my favorite personal stories. Every artist, in all fields, hits bottom at one point or another.*

I find this great fun to bring back after all these years, now that I have gotten off the bottom.

One

THE BRIGHT LIGHT from the Benson Space Station sundeck made the inside of Scott's Tavern as black as the insides of an ore carrier. The thick musty smell of the bar, the comfortable herbal smoke, and the thick, rich odor of beer wrapped around me like a whore's arms, dragging me into the dark. It was cool inside, making sweat break out on my forehead.

A whole lot cooler than that stupid sundeck. Whoever thought of putting a station tube made out of mostly windows open to the closest sun on a space station should be shot. Idiots in bathing suits actually laid out on lounges out there, more than likely frying what little brains they had left.

I let the door slam behind me, closing out the sundeck heat, and stood there for a moment, fighting for my eyes to adjust, letting the cool air relax me. I knew Scott's Tavern wasn't really dark, but until my eyes adjusted, it sure seemed that way.

"Yo, Danny," a voice said from the shadows in the direction I knew the bar was. "Bright out there, huh?"

The voice was Carl's, the owner of Scott's tavern. Carl had bought the place after Scott died in a shuttle accident a few years back.

"Like walkin' on the damn sun," I said.

My eyes had adjusted enough for me to see the tables and chairs, so I started toward my normal bar stool. Carl was already sliding a beer onto a bar napkin just like he had done for me hundreds of times over the last few years.

I could see the shadows of a couple at a table, and one woman bent over her drink at the bar, two stools down from mine. Steve usually sat on that stool later in the night. Steve actually had a real job on the unloading pylons. Middle of the afternoon was too early for him.

I had no job, hadn't found a job in a year of searching, and had basically given up at this point. I was going to die on this stupid space station orbiting a star with a name I can't even pronounce. This morning I hocked my old guitar. I used to think I was going to take the Old Earth Country Music world by storm. I dreamed of selling millions, having fans want my autograph, be in demand by women, the whole deal.

Fat chance that was. I couldn't even find a damn job flipping burgers or cleaning up shuttles or mopping the stupid hallway floors.

I had used the money from the guitar to buy enough food to last for a week, and I had enough money left over to drink myself into a blind drunk tonight. What I would do for tomorrow's drinking money I would worry about tomorrow.

Damn I was going to miss that guitar. It had been like a best friend to me for twenty years. My first and only wife told me I loved the damn guitar more than her, and the bitch had been right about that toward the end of our marriage.

Man, how had I gotten so low as to hawk my guitar for food and drink money?

I shook the thought away, ignored the twisting in my stomach that I had made a fatal mistake, and climbed onto the stool. Coming to this stupid space station had been my fatal mistake. The promise of a gig here fell through twenty minutes after my ship arrived and I've been stuck ever since.

I grabbed the beer and held on for dear life. The glass was cool and wet and felt damned good after the hot sun on that sundeck. Actually, it felt good for a bunch more reasons than just the heat. I downed half, letting the wonderful taste wash away some of the regrets like I had taken a big-ass pill.

I then took out the fifty station credits I had on a chip and slid it across the bar toward Carl. "When that's gone, kick me out of here."

"You got it," Carl said.

He started to pick up the credits when the woman two stools over said, "Hold on a minute."

Both Carl and I glanced at her. Even with my eyes still not completely adjusted to the dim light yet, I could see her well enough.

She had on the traditional space wear business jacket, dark shirt, no tie. Her pants matched her jacket, and I could tell she spent far too much time on her short blonde hair.

I couldn't get the color of her eyes, but I was betting blue.

She was shorter than I was by a distance and looked to be athletic, not extra hyped up like some women were today. She seemed natural and aging normal, just like I was. I liked that.

She didn't look the type to be in Scott's place at this time of the afternoon, let alone picking up some loser like me. I hadn't had a real woman look twice at me in longer than I wanted to think about.

More than likely that was because I had nothing to offer any woman, hadn't cut my brown hair in half a year, and didn't have a non-wrinkled shirt to my name.

"That one's on me," she said, indicating my half-finished beer. "And you may not want another after what I've got to say to you."

Carl and I both just stared at her, then finally Carl just shrugged, as any good bartender would, took the price of my beer from the chip in front her, and turned away.

"And why would something you've got to say stop me from having a few drinks?"

The woman shrugged. "I got a job for you if you're up for it."

My stomach clamped tight at the idea of getting a job, earning enough to get my guitar back. Could something like that actually happen? Could I actually get so damned lucky?

I stared at the woman, her thin face and faint smile. I had never met her before, that I could remember, and I couldn't imagine what kind of job she might have. Or what type of job that would need a drunk from a bar to do.

But damned if she wasn't good looking. Even a loser like me could notice that I suppose.

I turned back to my beer and took another long drink, almost finishing it. My fifty credits still sat on the bar in front of the beer, waiting for me to drink it away. And I had no doubt I was going to do just that, even with a nut-case sitting two stools down from me. But it was nice of her to buy me the first one.

She scooted her stool back with a scraping sound, then reached down into the darkness below her and pulled up a guitar case. She put the case up on the bar between us. "I think you lost this."

I stared at the old case, the once-broken upper latch, the faded sticker from a trip I had taken to the New Mexico Star Cluster for a gig ten years ago. I had figured when I walked out of that pawnshop this morning I would never see it again.

My stomach felt like someone had kicked me.

"My guitar," I said, my voice soft. I wanted to reach out and clutch it like a long lost child, but instead I just turned to stare at the woman. "How did you get it?"

"I bought it out of hock for you this morning, on the assurance to the man in the shop I would take it to you." The woman laughed to herself. "I had to pay him a little extra to let me take it though."

She slid the guitar another few inches toward me. "It's yours. All I ask is you consider doing one job for me in return."

I looked at the case, then back at her. "A few answers first. How did you know I had hocked the thing? And how do you even know I want it back?"

She sort of shrugged and smiled, the smile of an insurance agent.

I was right. Her eyes were blue. I wondered if any of her appearance was actually real. It looked real, unaltered. But with enough money, looking natural could be bought these days and she looked like she had enough money to do just that.

"I happened to see you coming out of the pawnshop, so I went in

28

and asked what you had sold. When I heard it was your guitar, I knew you could help me."

"And how would you know that?" I asked, doing my best to not get angry at some woman who was trying to give me back my guitar.

She stared at me, then said flatly, "I'll be honest with you. Coldly honest if you can take it."

I nodded and looked her right in the eyes.

"No one with your talent, your former career, would ever give up their instrument," she said, not looking away from my gaze, "without being flat on the bottom, with no hope. And right now I need someone with talent who thinks there is no hope."

I figured right at that moment I had two options. I could let my normal pride make me turn away from this woman, ignore her, or I could laugh. And since my guitar, the special Earth-made guitar I had hocked just a few hours ago, was sitting on the bar in front of me, I figured laughing was the better option.

"Am I right?" she asked.

I finished off my beer and turned on the stool to face her. "Oh, lady, are you right. With the money from the guitar I bought food for a week and that money right there to drink tonight."

I pointed at my last fifty station credits.

"After the food and money are gone, I'm done. I'm about to be kicked out of my room in the workers section of the station since I haven't paid in three months. I've borrowed from every friend and some strangers, and more than likely I'll be sleeping in some station shelter in the outer ring in a week and eating handouts or from garbage before it gets recycled."

I held up my empty beer glass, caught Carl's attention, and motioned for him to bring me another. "Friend, I don't know about the talent part, but you found someone with no hope."

The woman nodded, then stuck out her hand. "Mr. Danny Kenyon, my name is Alexis Pierce. Just call me Lex."

I reached out and shook her head. Her grip was firm, like she had done a few years of good solid work. But at the same time there was a softness to her hand and I held the grasp a little too long as I looked into her eyes.

She didn't look away.

I felt disappointed when I let her hand go finally. I was sure attracted to this woman for some reason.

I stared down into my beer, now feeling embarrassed. "Lex, I don't know what to say."

Carl brought me another beer at that moment, and Lex, bless her heart, bought, indicating that Carl should take the price from the money in front of her on the bar. Lex was going to make my fifty credits last a little longer than I had hoped at this rate.

"Just listen to my offer," Lex said. "You don't have to say anything yet. And no strings attached." She shoved the guitar a few more inches my way. "Better put that under your chair before we spill something on it."

I picked up my guitar and slid it to the floor between my legs. I had sat in many a bar over the years in many a different solar system and space station with the guitar in its case in that same position.

Me and my guitar had seen a lot of bars and a lot of light years. It felt good to have it back.

No, better than good. It felt great. I was whole again. I decided right at that moment I'd head for garbage cans to eat and sleep in the hallways before I pawned the thing again.

"Thanks," I said. "I'd offer to pay you back, but I doubt I'm going to be able to do that any time soon."

"Just considering my job offer is all I ask in return," Lex said. "I'll call it even if you do that."

"Lex, I've been looking for any job for the past year. So I'm more than willing to listen. Fire away."

As I looked into her eyes I felt even more of an attraction. Was she drawing me in with some chemical or some special way she looked? I could see no reason why she would, but I had better be damn careful. Men have disappeared around the systems over far less than a good-looking woman with a fast pitch.

"I need you to play a series of concerts for me."

I laughed again. "For who? I haven't had a gig in three years."

"After I got your guitar this morning I made some calls about you," Lex said. "The information I got is that you're talented and could have made it all the way to the top, but drank it all away."

"That and a few other bad breaks," I said, stung by her words. What did this blonde bitch know about how hard it was to push ahead in the music business day after damned day, sleeping in tiny shuttles, playing in station bars for drunks? It wasn't until everything fell apart that I really started drinking.

Lex shrugged. "What happened in the past doesn't matter to me. I just needed to know you were good, that you could play, and I discovered you can. And that you can write your own songs as well."

I stared at her, then smiled. "You didn't just happen to see me come out of that pawnshop, did you? You've been following me or something."

Lex laughed. "No, not really. I just had some good contacts in pawnshops around the stations in this system. The pawn dealer contacted me."

"Why?" I asked.

"I'm sort of a talent agent," Lex said. "My job is to find talented people who have hit bottom, give them one special job, and a new chance in the future."

I kept staring at her, fighting the attraction, trying to not really ignore everything she was saying. Even with my eyes now used to the dim lights of the bar, I just couldn't get a read on her. She looked like an agent, she was sneaky like an agent, and she dressed like an agent. And she tossed money around like an agent. And over the years I had been around enough booking agents to know not to trust them with a mouthful of spit.

"Look," Lex said, scooting over to sit in the chair next to me.

Her wonderful soft smell shocked me. I wanted to lean away and get closer at the same time, so I just stayed centered, holding onto my cold beer like an anchor in a rough sea.

"I'm willing to give you a half million Intersystem Credits for ten concerts over a fourteen-day concert period. I need you to play about twenty or so songs per concert. I don't even much care which songs they are. Covers or your own originals."

"Lady, you are totally nuts," I said, turning back to face my almost empty glass of beer, doing my best to ignore her wonderful smell.

"You promised you'd listen to me," Lex said. "That's all I asked for the guitar."

I moved my right leg and bumped it into my guitar just to make sure it was still there. It was.

"All right," I said, "you're willing to give a washed-out guitar player a half million Intersystems to sing a few songs. What's the catch?"

"The catch is the location of the concert tour," Lex said, glancing at Carl to see if he could hear. He couldn't since he was down the bar cutting up limes for his fruit tray.

"So, I got to go out to the frontier or into the Farms or something like that?"

No way I was going into the Farms. They were the systems occupied by the only aliens humans had run into. The aliens looked like a cross between a black beetle and mass of mud shaped like a deformed cow, which is why humans called their systems the Farms. And from what I hear, they smelled like a sewer. I was fairly certain they had no desire for human country music.

"No, actually, your part of the tour will take just over two weeks each way, all done in a first class luxury cabin. But here in the human systems about ninety years will pass before you come back."

This woman was keeping me entertained, I had to hand her that. I hadn't wanted to laugh this much since I found a hundred credits on the sundeck on the way to the bar three weeks ago.

"I'm a talent agent here in this time period for this section of the Consolidated Planets," Lex said, talking fast and low. "In this time period the Consolidated Planets have not yet been formed, and except for a few high-ranking officials, no one here knows it will even exist in the future. There's a great demand for original old-style Earth music and musicians in the future and this is as far back in time as we talent agents are allowed to go."

I decided to play along with the nut case for a minute. "So how come you just can't beam me into the future and have me back for my next beer?"

"Space and time travel don't work that way I'm afraid," Lex said. "You'll be gone your time about six weeks total, but because of the speeds involved, and a whole bunch of stuff I don't really understand about time travel, about ninety years will pass here. That's why we look for musicians who have nothing to lose and very little family. Of course, it's a help that you are also very talented. Your talent, to be honest with you, is one of the reasons I can offer you as much as I can."

"Thanks, I guess."

"Look," Lex said, leaning forward. "I don't expect you to believe me. I wouldn't believe me if I lived in this time period. But I do want you to think about it. You'll play ten concerts, to audiences as human as I am a very long time into the future. You can stay in the future as long as you would like beyond the tour, maybe never come back."

"Stay?" I asked.

"Sure," Lex said, nodding. "You can stay for a week, or a year. If you stay a year it will be ninety-one years passing here. If you decide to stay in the future and make a career there, your money for this can be transferred forward. But if you do decide to return to here, you won't make it back until at least ninety years into this future."

"And a half million will be worth nothing then, right?"

"Actually, no, with some minor bubbles, money in the systems stays amazingly stable all the way up and into my time period in the Consolidated Planets."

"And I'll be too old to spend it when I get back."

"No," Lex said, shaking her head, "You'll only be six weeks older than the day you leave. Just ninety years will pass here. Again, I don't expect you to believe me, but at least think about it and meet me back here tomorrow."

Before I could say anything, Lex handed me five hundred station credits. "This should help get your rent caught up. Thanks for considering this."

I stared at the money in my hand like it was a snake that might bite me as Lex slid off her stool and headed for the door.

Five hundred station credits was about 50 Interstellar Credits. She was offering me a half million Interstellars. That was a lot of beers.

I watched her walk, wanting more than anything to jump up and follow her and never let her from my sight. But the money in my hand froze me to my stool.

When she opened the door to the sundeck, she was gone into the bright white light.

"Wow, she was a looker. Was she as weird as she seemed?" Carl asked, glancing down the bar at me.

I took another look at the five hundred station credits in my hand, then stuffed them in my pocket. "You have no idea," I said, finishing my beer and motioning Carl for another. "You have no idea at all."

Two

AS IT TURNED out, Lex's offer, my guitar, and the money in my pocket put me right off the idea of drinking the night away. I had one more beer, grabbed a take-home Old Earth style pizza on the way to my room, and then surprised the dump's manager with payment in full for all the back rent.

I was living in such a slum that even after the pizza and rent, I still had enough money left over to last for almost a month if I watched the drinking. Maybe by then I could find a job. A real job, not the crazed thing some good-looking woman had talked to me about. But at least she had bought me some time.

I dropped the pizza on the old scarred coffee table, then brushed some food wrappers aside and dropped onto the couch. I opened up my guitar case like I was standing at the door of a blind date. Inside was my guitar, just as I had left it this morning at the pawnshop.

I held it to my chest for a moment, just letting myself believe that it was actually back in my hands. Then after a few quick adjustments for tuning, I strummed a few chords before putting it back in the case.

How had I let myself get so low?

And why did some woman I didn't know go to the trouble of getting my guitar back for me, not counting the five big she had tossed my way. She couldn't be serious about the job.

There had to be something else going on.

I took a piece of pizza and worked at it, thinking over any possibility of a scam, which was unlikely since I had nothing to take in a scam. After a second piece of pizza, I still hadn't come up with anything that made any sense at all.

I was exactly what I seemed on the surface, a washed-out musician who liked to play in the style of old Earth country. I had nothing to scam. I was worth exactly the amount she had given me and not one credit more.

So, with a quick bite out of a third slice, I went out the door and down to the manager's office to use his com device. I used to know a guy who was one of the brainy types, read a lot, actually had a major education from somewhere. He had done soundboards on a tour I worked once, and we'd drunk a few nights together. He'd understood this time travel stuff and if it was real or not.

I had to give the manager the fifty station credits I had planned to drink earlier to cover any intersystem charges. I hoped like hell the call was going to be worth that.

"Steve," I said as he came up the com link. He looked about the same, maybe a little shorter hair, and he still hadn't had his lack of chin fixed. "This is Danny Kenyon, from the Country Old-Style Planetary Tour back a few years. Remember me?"

"Uh, yah, sure Danny, how are you?"

I knew he didn't remember me, I could see it in his eyes, but at this point, that didn't matter. At least I didn't owe him money, so he wasn't either cutting the link or asking for his money back just at the mention of my name.

"Sorry to bother you, Steve," I said, "but I got this dumb science question that a few friends and I have been arguing about, and I figured if anyone would know the answer, you might."

"Fire away," Steve said. "I took some science classes back in college." Clearly not talking music or money made him relax a little, even though he didn't remember me.

"Okay, promise not to laugh too hard," I said.

He laughed and said, "Promise."

"Okay, my friend was telling me that time travel is possible and in the future we might actually invent it. Does that sound stupid to you or what?"

"Not at all," Steve said. "Lots of scientists over the years, starting with Einstein back on Old Earth, thought that time travel might be possible. But a lot of factors would have to be solved and we're nowhere near that kind of major breakthrough."

"You're kidding?" I said, shocked. "It might actually be possible in the future?"

"Possible yes," Steve said. "Likely, probably not. Not in our lifetimes anyway."

"Well, damn," I said. "I lost that bet. Thanks, Steve."

"No problem," Steve said, "take care of yourself, Danny."

I shut down the com link and headed back to my room, thinking over what Lex had said. It was possible. How completely crazy was that?

By the time I had finished the pizza and played a few songs, I had decided to go back to Scott's tavern and meet Lex tomorrow. What could it hurt, as long as she didn't ask for her money back?

Three

JUST AS THE day before, it took my eyes a moment to adjust inside the dark bar from all the light in that stupid sun section of the station. I had managed to finally get some sleep and by the time I reached the bar I was slowly getting angry. I might be broke, but I'm not completely stupid, and Lex, for some reason, was trying to get me to buy a huge pile-of-shit story.

I just didn't know why.

As I headed across the dark bar I felt like I needed a beer more than just about anything, especially after the hot sun beating down on me in my walk through that sundeck ring.

I could see through the darkness that Lex was sitting on the stool beside my favorite, sipping on something. Just the fact that she was there again surprised me.

And actually made me happy.

I hated that I was attracted to a nut case. Just hated it.

My former wife had turned into a nut case, swearing there were aliens in every station, on every planet we visited, and that they were watching us every minute. *Invisible aliens.*

She blamed the aliens for our divorce. She was partially right.

Carl was behind the bar as always, and otherwise the tavern was empty.

"Danny," Carl said, slipping a beer onto a napkin in front of my stool. "Good to see you."

"Give my eyes a minute," I said, "and I might be able to see you back."

Carl and Lex both chuckled at my stupid joke, then Carl moved back down the bar to keep working on the evening preparations.

"Thanks for the loan," I said to Lex after taking a sip of the wonderful, cool beer. Again I'm not sure when I'll be able to pay you back."

Lex held up a beautiful hand. "No need to even think of paying me back. The money was like an option on your time. I wanted you to consider my offer."

"Well," I said, taking another sip of the beer. "I considered it. I even called a friend who confirmed that time travel at some point in the distant future would be possible."

Lex nodded. "It is."

"So how far forward would I be going?"

"A very long ways," Lex said.

"How far?" I asked.

Lex glanced at me, then at Carl to make sure he was far enough away to not hear.

"Fourteen thousand years."

"Not possible," I said, turning back to my beer. "Humans won't be around for that long."

"Oh, they very much are and have a real desire for Old Earth music like you play."

"So why not go back another six hundred years and get real Old Earth musicians?"

"Not allowed to," she said.

"So explain to me how it works," I said. "Since you're asking me to give up my life and climb into something that flies through time, I better know at least some basics about how it works."

Again Lex stared at me for a moment like I was some alien thing. Clearly other dead-end musicians she had offered this to hadn't bothered with any homework.

"I really don't know how it works," she said. "At least not the science of it. Something about folding space." She glanced down the bar to make sure Carl couldn't hear what she was saying.

Damn I just couldn't get the attraction I was feeling toward her out of my head. She had to be doing something to me. I hated agents and she was an agent. I couldn't want to sleep with an agent. That would be like sleeping with some mud-cow alien on the Farms. But I still just wanted to lean forward and kiss her.

Had to be the reaction to the money.

"The Consolidated Planets are a group of about forty thousand systems banded together for safety and trade. The Planets as an organization has been in existence about ten thousand years now."

I was too stunned at the number to say anything since there were only about fifty colonized systems now.

She went on. "Travel between my time and this time is done by only people who have no ties or family because of the time loss issues."

"Okay, that makes my brain hurt," I said. "So you have no family, no husband waiting for you back home?"

"None," she said. "If I did, they would be long dead by the time I returned from one trip. The time lag works both ways I'm afraid."

"Okay," I said, not liking the sound of that either, but deep down happy she didn't have anyone.

Lex went on. "Only two weeks will pass on board the ship, but decades will pass on the planets at either end of the trip, forty-five years on the trip there, forty-five years on the trip back here."

I finished my beer and held up my glass until Carl saw it and nodded.

"I see why you need someone with no ties to here."

Lex nodded and again I resisted the urge to just kiss her. She put her hand on my hand and the soft feel of her skin sent a shock through my system.

"Are you drugging me?" I asked, looking into her blue eyes.

"No," she said, smiling. "Not my style. Just trying to do a job."

"And this attraction I'm feeling to you is part of the job?"

She pulled her hand back and shook her head, looking away. "Never happened before."

I wanted to believe her but I wasn't sure that I did.

Carl slid another beer in front of me. Again Lex bought.

I stared at her, then decided I still needed a few more questions answered. "So, what planet were you born on?"

She smiled. "One named Small Five about two hundred light years from here. It hasn't been discovered or explored yet in this time period."

"So, how many trips have you made to this time period?"

"This is my second."

"Ninety years each?" I asked, staring at her. "How old *are* you?"

Lex laughed. "Actually, in real time just three years younger than you are. I'm thirty. Time passes normally on either end. I'm still aging just like normal. But if you took my birth date on my home world, I guess you would say I'm a lot older than you."

"We'll just leave it at thirty." I took a big drink out of the beer to try to give myself time to think and also not look at her. The attraction between us seemed to be growing by the minute, at least on my side.

"It's a job," Lex said, clearly feeling she needed to explain even more. "I meet interesting people like you and I do a service. In a few years I'll retire back to my time. There are some beautiful places in the future among the Planets."

"There are beautiful places here in this time, too," I said. "Granted I haven't seen many of them lately, but I know they're here."

"Take this job," Lex said, "live a couple of months like you've never lived before, see planets you can't even imagine exist, play ten concerts and then come back rich, with enough money to see the places you want to see and start your music career over under a new name."

"Ninety years from now."

Lex nodded.

"So why? Why me?"

Lex actually laughed at that. "Honest question. We want to hear you play concerts. That's all. The Consolidated Planets love any type of Old Earth music, and have gotten very little of the style of music you played before. That's why we're willing to offer someone of your talent so much money. Trust me, we'll make a profit on you."

"You've gotten people to go with you for less?"

"Oh, sure. One burnt-out rocker went out about two years ago with only the promise of a lifetime supply of food and drugs."

"And how did it go for him?" I asked, before it dawned on me Lex would have no way of knowing.

Lex shrugged. "He's still in transit."

"Still in his first day on the ship?"

"More than likely," Lex said. "He won't arrive for another forty-three years this time."

"Oh," I said. I was starting to catch on to how it worked.

"What I told you is the limit of my knowledge about this stuff," Lex said, her voice soft and sincere sounding. "I've been totally honest with you. I just fly in the ships and hope someone somewhere knows what they are doing."

"I know that feeling," I said, smiling at her. "I'm the same damn way with these spaceships that flit from system to system now."

"So you understand?" Lex asked.

"Not a bit of it," I said. "But what the hell difference does that make, right?"

"Right," Lex said. "So what do you say?"

"Give me an hour sitting here alone," I said, "and I'll give you an answer."

Lex nodded and slid off her stool. I really didn't want her to leave, but I had to be outside of her wonderful smell, those driving blue eyes, to think clearly.

A moment later the tavern was lit with bright light as Lex went out onto the sundeck

"The way you two were talking," Carl said, "it seemed important."

I shrugged and finished off my beer so Carl could bring me another. "She's just offering me a gig is all."

"Fantastic," Carl said, his face lighting up like someone had just given him a hundred buck tip. "It's about damn time you got back on the horse."

"Not even sure what a horse looks like anymore," I said.

Carl laughed as he slid another beer in front of me. "Man, I heard you when you opened for Baked Pie in the Princeton System in the Baseline Theater. Trust me, you know the horse."

I stared at Carl, actually looking at him for the first time in the two years I had been coming into this place. "You were at that concert?"

"Sure was," he said. "And I saw you over on Mercer as well, when you opened for Craig S. and the Princes. I even bought a hard disk copy of your first song collection."

"Only collection," I corrected.

"First," he said, smiling at me.

"Man, I didn't even think you knew who I was."

Carl laughed. "I let people in my bar do as they want. But I can tell you I was a huge fan of yours. You were just ahead of your time is all."

"Yeah, ahead of my time playing Old Earth Country," I said, sipping my beer. It sure seemed that time was an issue a lot lately.

"No man, honest," Carl said. "Things have changed, your original songs would take off now."

"I sure hope you are right my friend."

"Oh, I am," Carl said, smiling. "Take the gig, get back on tour. I'll miss your business, but I can buy the next collection and play it in here on busy nights."

It had always seemed that my songs, the only songs I really wanted to play, were just a little too "edgy" for most Old Earth Country fans a few years back.

"Man, this is exciting that you're getting back to playing," Carl said. "Just tell me when and where your first concert is, and I'll be there, right in the damn front row. I know a bunch of fans who will do the same."

"Well, right now everything's a little up in the air," I said.

Carl smiled real big. "Just let me know."

With that he turned and walked down the bar, going back to his prep work for the nightly crowd, leaving me to my thoughts.

I couldn't believe how much things had changed for me in simply a day. I had an offer for a short tour that I didn't really believe, yet part of me accepted.

And I had been reminded I still had fans, few as they may be, but they were still out there, and they remembered my work.

I glanced down the bar at Carl. I doubted he had any idea how important his comments were to me. Hell, any fan's comments to any artist, in any field were important. When the money runs out, the recording contracts are cancelled, all musicians have are fans to keep them going. Fans. They are everything.

I sipped my beer and sat there, remembering the concerts, the feel of making people happy with my music, the disappointments and setbacks on the business side, and finally all the loneliness, hitting bottom yesterday when I hocked my guitar for money.

Lex had been right. I had nothing to lose by taking her offer.

I glanced down the bar. Nothing to lose except fans like Carl, who still remembered.

Carl's dream had been owning a bar. He'd told me that right after he bought the place. He was scared to death, and at the same time as happy as a little kid at Christmas. It couldn't be easy running a bar off a sundeck on an old space station orbiting a star with a name no one could pronounce, but he was doing it, making it one day at a time.

I shook my head. Man, that was admirable. Maybe Lex was right, maybe I had given up and dove into the bottle a little too soon.

And now I was getting a second chance. Granted, no one like Carl would be around to remember me in ninety years, but it was still a second chance.

Maybe my songs would be dated by then, I would be dated. Wouldn't that be ironic, a musician who was ahead of his time coming back dated?

Again that time thing.

I glanced down the bar at Carl. I hated to lose my fans, even the few who still remained. I hated the idea of coming back and starting over and being dated then. For me it would only be a few months, but I wouldn't recognize most of anything.

There had to be a way to get everything. I was always accused of wanting everything, and I guess this time was no different.

I started to take another drink from my beer, then looked at it and set it back down on the bar napkin. I pushed it to the inside edge of the bar, away from me and said, "Hey, Carl, could you bring me a diet soda of some kind?"

Carl looked up, the smile on his face huge. "Coming right up."

Four

THIRTY MINUTES LATER, when Lex came back through the door and stood for a moment letting her wonderful blue eyes adjust, I had my plan pretty much worked out. It was going to cost me a pretty penny to pull off, but if it worked, I just might get the best of both worlds, Lex's and mine.

And if I got lucky, maybe Lex as well. As I said, I wanted everything.

Lex slid onto the stool beside me and Carl brought her a diet drink as well. I sipped mine, some sort of drink that tasted like lime only sweet.

After Carl moved down the bar, Lex pointed to my drink and smiled, looking into my eyes. "I see you've made a decision."

"I have," I said. "But hear me all the way out like you asked me to do for you. Okay?"

"Okay," Lex said, a puzzled look on her face.

"Your entire problem with finding people here on Earth to play out in the Consolidated Planets is time. Right?"

Lex nodded.

"And Carl said that my songs had been ahead of their time," I said.

"I think he was more than likely right," Lex said. "I listened to your first collection. It's amazingly good."

"So here's what I want to do," I said, plowing on and ignoring her wonderful compliment. "I want to take you up on your offer, but I want to postpone when I leave."

Lex really looked puzzled, but she didn't say anything, letting me go on.

"I want to try to make a comeback right here, right now, first, before I leave. And I want you to be my manager and backer with the money you'll pay me to leave to the future."

With that Lex sort of rocked back and got a distant look for a moment.

So I just went right on talking. "In exchange for you helping me get going again, right now, doing a little bankrolling, I'll help you recruit some top talent for your Planets tours. And if I don't make a comeback here, I'll take less than what you offered me now in a couple of years."

"And if you do make it big?" Lex asked.

"We both get rich and we'll just fake my death when I get as far as I can here, and then head out to the Planets together to make some real money. But the key is time."

"A win-win situation for you," Lex said, staring at me, a slight smile creeping into the edge of her perfect lips.

"For both of us," I said. "Think about it. You get me cheaper if I don't make it, we both make money if I do, and I get not one, but two chances to make a comeback. Now and in ninety years. All that is lost is a little time on this end."

Lex laughed and nodded. "You know, that sort of makes sense."

I looked her directly in the eyes and reached out and took her soft hand. "Eventually, my songs won't be ahead of their time."

"Timing is everything," Lex said, nodding, squeezing my hand softly in hers. "You've got yourself a manager and a bankroll."

While keeping one hand in hers, I held up my glass with my other hand and offered a toast.

Lex picked her glass up, smiling at me.

"To time," I said, "the real solution to everything."

"To time," she agreed, tapping her glass against mine.

Then she put her glass down and with her free hand pulled me close and kissed me.

And for me, right at that moment, time just stopped. And I had no desire to restart it.

THE TRAGIC TALE OF A MAN IN A DUSTER

Lost in deep space, Reeves knew rescue would never happen. But around him the Western, a supply ship full of a lifetime of living, could keep him alive.

Fresh fish from the hatchery, fresh meat from the stored animals, fresh fruit and vegetables from the botanical gardens. Completely alone, no boss, no one to tell him what to do. What more could a cowboy from Idaho want?

First published in stand-alone paper and electronic book form with a very different cover.

One

REEVES KNEW HE shouldn't be frying fish over an open campfire in the ship's botanical garden, but the smell alone was going to make up for all the problems he might face if anyone ever found him. The fire crackled in a rock ring in front of him, the flames casting strange shadows on the trees and brush ringing his little meadow. He didn't care about the extra oxygen consumption and the fire repellant system being shut off. All he cared about was the two fish in the skillet, and how wonderful they were going to taste.

Reeves still had on his deep-sleep jumpsuit. It didn't feel right wearing it out here, while cooking trout, but it hadn't occurred to him to change clothes since he woke up. That would be next, right after dinner. Besides, there wasn't much reason to stay in uniform when there was no one to dress up for.

He kneeled and picked up the skillet, studying the fish for any sign of them being overcooked, then quickly replaced the skillet on the fire before the hot handle burned his hand. His dad back on Earth had showed him how to do this when he was a kid, and he had watched it done a dozen times since. His dad always used to say that fish were never meant to be baked or broiled or steamed. Only fried.

Reeves had to agree. Cooking fresh trout in the ovens they had on this piece of floating space junk would be a crime. No sir, fish were born to be covered in corn meal crumbs and fried quick and hot in a half inch of margarine in a heavy metal skillet while the flames licked the sides of the blackened pan.

And right now the two Rainbow Trout he'd caught out of Danny's stream over in the hatcheries section of the ship were being cooked in exactly that way.

The rich, wonderful smell was almost more than he could take. It covered the faint odor of the pines around him, filling the small meadow with a mouth-watering aroma. He just wished that when the builders had designed the botanical garden they would have made it possible to open some sort of portal so he could sit beside a fire under the stars. He glanced up hoping to see stars, but the roof was black, the light low, simulating night. Maybe at some point in the future he'd go up there and paint some fake stars on that ceiling just to make the feeling right.

He glanced around at the darkened meadow and the trees and brush beyond. He had to do this cooking at night. No other time would be right for cooking fresh-caught trout over an open fire.

The smoke from the fire was swirling upward around the skillet and then on toward the ceiling, lost in the darkness. He had no doubt the garden was going to smell of smoke for months to come, but he didn't care. Hell, if this worked, and these two fish tasted anywhere near as good as they smelled, he might even fry a couple more fish tomorrow night.

And a couple more the night after that.

Maybe he might even fix up a tent and bedding to sleep nearby. What could it hurt? There was no one to stop him out here in the deep space between stars and jump stations. There was no fixing the ship.

He had determined that an hour ago. And if he did happen to get lucky and live long enough to finally reach Jump Base Perry, he'd deal with the consequences then. But in the meantime, he was going to eat freshly-cooked trout.

Two

"BLAME IT ALL to damn!" Canny said, her fingers running over the smooth surface of the tracking board, bringing up images on her screen faster than Fergason could follow.

Canny was in charge of tracking what they called the "pink sector," officially call the "P" sector, following ships and anything else that might be jumping through hyper space in that area. Fergason had never heard her swear in the three years he had worked with the tiny and very competent woman.

Canny was from a colony world around Devan Six, and claimed she was five foot tall. She had typical Devan red hair and light, fair skin. She also had a laugh that sounded like a chime and made him smile.

Today Canny wore a white blouse, dark black pants made out of some new material, and flat-heeled shoes meant for comfort.

Fergason was Canny's immediate supervisor and her exact opposite in just about every way. Where she was short, he was tall, slouching at six-five. Where her skin seemed to glow white in the lights from the screens, his skin was dark, his hair pitch black and short. And he came from Stevens, a planet that had been waging an economic war with Canny's home planet for decades. Yet somehow, over the years, even with the differences, they had become close friends.

And were getting closer every day.

Around them the large General Hyper Drive control room felt hushed as a few of the other controllers glanced at Canny's direction with a look of surprise.

Fergason stood from his supervisor console and moved over beside Canny, glancing at her screen. "Transfer to the wall screen," he said.

She nodded as her fingers moved over her board almost faster than Fergason could follow. He knew she was one of his best, but he had never seen her work at full speed before.

Suddenly she stopped, sat back, and just shook her head.

"Dropped out," she said. "Twenty-six hours ago real time."

Fergason stared at the wall monitor filling a section near Canny's station. It showed three-dimensional representation of the "P" area of space Canny had been monitoring. She had put up a line starting at Jump Base Peanut and ending about halfway to Jump Base Perry.

"What's the ship?" Fergason asked, stunned that he was seeing what she was indicating. He had never had a drop-out on his watch, and the last serious drop-out that had occurred was two years before. Ships, with all the fail-safes, and the nature of the hyper-space tubes between jump points, just didn't drop out of hyperspace in the middle of nowhere.

Yet one just had.

"It's a supply and research ship, a big one called the *Western*. Headed for the lower edge of the "D" section to help supply a new colony there."

Fergason nodded. Nothing unusual at all.

"Seventeen jumps successful, Canny said, "thirty-six more to go."

"So any signal from the ship?" Fergason asked, following procedure.

"Nothing," Canny said. "One minute it was fine, the next it had dropped out of hyper."

"Can you pinpoint its location?" Fergason asked, still following the questions he was supposed to ask a controller in this situation.

"I did," Canny said. She reached forward and tapped her board, changing the image on the screen on the wall.

Fergason just shook his head. The area shown on the map where the ship would have dropped back into normal space was a sphere of over three light years in diameter.

There was one more question on the list that he had to ask any controller in this situation, just for the record. "Could you get a reading on the real-space speed of the ship as it dropped?"

"Fast," Canny said. "Ninety-one-point-three percent of the speed of light."

"Damn," Fergason said.

"You can say that again," Canny said, shaking her head. "The poor guy. He probably isn't even awake yet, with the difference in time factored in."

"Only one crew?" Fergason asked. Usually freighters had two or three. The *Western* must be one of the newer model ships, only needing one man to take the chance on the deep sleep and the hyper jumps with the cargo. And all that one man did was wake up at each jump point, run diagnostics of the systems, then give the all-clear for the ship to make the next jump.

She leaned forward, tapped a key on her board again, and then sat back. "His name is Reeves, from Earth actually."

"What part?" Fergason asked, as if that was going to make any difference at this point.

Canny again glanced at her board. "Idaho region."

One of the old United States areas. Fergason had never been near it on any of his visits to Earth. Maybe next time.

"Alert rescue," Fergason said, glancing at the other controllers who were watching the event. "Tell them to get a ship headed to the center of his possible drop-out area. Make sure you feed them all your data, including his likely speed."

Canny glanced back at him, her green eyes showing surprise and maybe a little something else. "Sir, you know they will veto you. It's not worth risking the lives of a rescue team and ship in an unscheduled hyper-drop."

Fergason knew, but he said nothing.

Canny went on. "Plus the percentage chances of finding one ship in that much area are close to zero, even if the thing was equipped with a newer emergency beacon. The rescue ship would have to stumble within light-days of the *Western* to trace-hear it."

"I know," Fergason said. "But I'm not going to be the one to make the decision to let that poor man die out there alone."

She looked at him harder than she had ever done before. There was a caring and understanding in the look that he hadn't seen before. Finally she nodded and turned back to her board. "Alerting rescue," she said.

Later that night, she asked him to join her for dinner. It had been fantastic, a special baked-trout dinner with all the trimmings. That night she told him how much she admired him and his heart.

And later that night they kissed and kissed and finally talked about being together for the rest of their lives.

The next morning he learned, as they had both expected, that Rescue Control had declined to send a ship.

Reeves from Earth was on his own.

Three

REEVES KNEW, WITHOUT a doubt, that he would grow tired of fresh-caught, freshly-cooked trout, no matter how good they tasted.

He had set up camp with bedding, a tent, and a change of clothes in an area of the botanical garden near where he had cooked the fish the first time. After dinner that first night he had changed into some western-style clothes he had found in supplies for the colonists. Then with the addition of a cowboy hat, cowboy boots, and a duster he felt almost at home. He could almost imagine he was back in the mountains of Idaho, especially when he was near his fire.

He had reset the lighting in the garden so that there was more night, because that was the time he didn't have to think about where he was, and what had happened to him.

After finding the clothes he had gone to a mirror in one of the bathrooms. The hat hid his white forehead and receding hairline, and the duster swung loose and free, giving his body a lean and mean appearance. He had been lucky that the colony this ship had been packed to supply was for a western-based group. He hoped they survived the loss of these supplies long enough to get more.

Too bad there hadn't been something he could have done about saving the ship. He had been in cold sleep, as anyone was going through jump space, when the ship had malfunctioned and dropped out of hyper-space. His last readings before the jump had shown no indication of any problem at all.

The moment he had woken up to the sounds of the alarms filling every inch of the cold sleep chamber, he knew he was in trouble.

Deep trouble.

It had taken him a long time to check all the ship's systems and discover everything was just fine, except for the fact that he, the ship, and all its cargo were no longer in hyper-space. He had no idea what had gone wrong, and didn't have the skills or the desire to find out.

He had set the rescue beacon just in case someone came for him, and actually found him, and then he had sat for hours just staring out of the control room's viewports at the stars and the blackness of space. He had no idea where he was, or even exactly how fast he was moving, or where he was heading.

Hyper-space travel used jump stations, connected to other jump stations. Only close-in system travel used actual real-space movement.

It just took too long and had too many troubles with the differences in ship-board time and real time.

While he sat there staring at the stars and feeling sorry for himself, he started thinking about never seeing Earth again, and just generally considering his future death alone in deep space. Then, as if hit by a sudden blast of realization, he really understood his situation. He might die alone out here, but until he did he was now a really free man.

No more worrying about money, or jobs. The ship had more than enough supplies to last him for a very long life.

He no longer had anyone to answer to, to be chewed out by.

He was on his own, in a seven-mile-long space ship full of everything he might need.

With the realization he had laughed out loud, staring at the stars. The entire thing was sort of a glass half-empty, glass half-full sort of thing. Yes, he was trapped in deep space with almost no hope of rescue, yes he had known this possibility might happen, but now that it had happened, he could live any way he wanted.

He could cook fish over an open campfire.

He was a free man who loved fresh-caught fish.

Finally, on the third day of staying in the meadow near his campfire, it became clear he was going to need other fresh foods beside fish. So after finishing a wonderful breakfast of trout, he made a trip through the seven mile-long ship to the embryo stores near the nose of the giant ship.

He felt odd walking in his cowboy boots down the wide halls, his duster swirling around his legs with every step. And his duster was a little warm for the environmental settings, but he didn't care. He was living on a new frontier, just like his ancient ancestors had done when they had gone west in the old United States. There were hardships on the frontier, the least of which was heat and cold.

They had been alone, in a wild and dangerous place.

He was alone in a wild and dangerous place.

They had survived in their way, he would survive in his.

It had taken him hours to finally reach the right area, not wanting to use the ship's directional systems to help him. His ancestors didn't have directional systems to help them out west.

After only a few wrong turns, he found the storage area he was looking for. It was where the animals that were scheduled to be born and raised on the new colony were kept. He pulled up on a screen the animal cargo list and smiled when he saw it was as he had hoped it would be. Cattle, horses, sheep, pigs, chickens, and so on. And there was enough feed on the ship as well to keep the animals well-fed for many years.

And another thing that worked in his favor. The ship was carrying an Accelerated Growth Lab that could take an animal from embryo state to full grown in three or four days.

He studied the list of his choices. He didn't want to raise too many animals too quickly, mostly because he only needed as much as he could use over a few months time, and he wanted to make their feed last as long as possible. So he did some calculations as to exactly how long the feed would last for a certain number of each animal, then went to work taking out a few of the animals and putting them in the Accelerated Growth Lab chamber.

Then, as almost an afterthought, he picked out a horse and put it in the chamber as well. His ancestors rode horses, so could he.

He spent three days there in the lab, eating rations while wishing for trout, sleeping in a bunk room, growing the animals to a decent size. He used that time to set up sections of the ship for each group of animals to live.

The chickens he put in a large storage area with old-world furniture they could nest in, then set the timer on the ship's computer to remind him every three days that he needed to replenish the chicken's food and supplies, and with luck harvest the eggs.

His mouth watered at the idea of eggs and bacon, cooked over a camp fire. What a perfect life he was setting up.

He worked out similar environments for the cattle and pigs, then prepped a slaughter area and then used it to kill a calf, using a colony butchering-machine to package and refrigerate the meat all in one process.

Tonight, back in his meadow, over his campfire, he would cook veal. And then tomorrow he would start changing a few of the areas in the gardens for fruit and vegetable growing. Maybe in a few weeks he might have corn-on-the-cob with a great New York steak. His mouth watered at the thought as well.

Finally, after everything was set up, and his saddle bags were packed with the veal and oat feed for the horse, he led the big, brown mare he had raised into the hallway and back down the miles of corridor to the botanical gardens.

On this trip he felt better walking the halls in his duster, the horse's hooves clopping on the hard surface behind him. He now felt like a true pioneer going into the unknown.

Four

FERGASON SAT AT his desk in his living room and stared at a picture of Canny, his wife of over sixty years. He missed her more than he wanted to admit. Their children and grandchildren were good company, visiting him often, but nothing could replace the closeness that he had had with Canny.

They had had a great life together, happy, and had recently been planning trips back to their different home worlds to visit family. Then, without warning, a few months before she had died of a heart attack at the young age of only 104. He had another thirty or forty years of life expectancy these days, yet he couldn't imagine living those years without her. It was as if everything inside him had been ripped out.

"Grandpa?" a voice said from behind him.

The voice was from his youngest grandson, Steph, standing respectfully in the door to the study. Steph was going on thirty, and was already making a name for himself in Space Rescue Corp.

Fergason took a deep breath and slowly swung around, looking up into the green eyes and pale skin of his grandson. The kid was about the same age as Canny had been when they had started working together. Steph had her eyes and her good looks and fair skin.

"You all right, Grandpa?"

Fergason shrugged. "I guess as good as can be expected."

There was no other answer to that question. Of course he wasn't all right. He had lost the love and meaning in his life.

"Thought you might be interested in this," Steph said, stepping forward and handing a report from Rescue Central to him. "It came into control today after one of the test runs of a new search system."

Fergason glanced at the paper, not really seeing it. Then suddenly a name caught his attention. *Western.*

He quickly scanned the sheet, stunned at what he was reading. They had finally found the cargo ship *Western,* over sixty years after it had dropped out of hyper-drive and vanished.

He glanced up at Steph who was smiling. "This is the ship that was lost on your grandmother's watch. I was supervisor that day."

"I know," Steph said, smiling. "You and grandma decided to get married that night, didn't you?"

Fergason nodded as he stared at the report. He couldn't believe the *Western* had been found. He hadn't thought of that ship for decades.

"There was a man on that ship," Fergason asked, trying to find the information on the report that he was looking for, but failing. "What happened to him?"

Steph snorted. "His name was Reeves. Shipboard time only had two weeks passing. But the guy didn't manage to survive that long."

Fergason shuddered. He couldn't imagine the loneliness the man named Reeves must have thought he was facing. Deep space did that to people, sent them over the edge and into insanity, often far quicker than two weeks.

Fergason knew he was facing the same type of loneliness without Canny.

"What did he do, kill himself?"

"No," Steph said, shaking his head. "He broke his neck."

Fergason glanced up at his grandson. "How?"

"From what the investigators could tell," Steph said, "he fell off a horse."

"A horse?"

"A horse," Steph said. "And he had grown cattle, pigs, chickens and who knows what else in an old Accelerated Growth Chamber. He even had a campfire going in a botanical garden. He had reverted to being a cowboy from the old west region of Earth."

Fergason shook his head as his grandson went on, not really understanding how a spaceman could become a cowboy on a hyper-drive jump freighter in less than two weeks.

"You ought to see a picture of the guy. He put on the cowboy hat, duster and all."

"You're kidding?" Fergason asked, knowing his grandson wouldn't joke about something like that."

"Nope," Steph said, "it's the truth. And what's even more amazing is that he'd only been dead for less than an hour when they found the ship. There was even burnt fish still cooking over a campfire."

"Fish?" Fergason asked, remembering the wonderful fish dinner he and Canny had had the night the *Western* vanished sixty-three years before. The dinner that had changed their lives.

"Fish," Steph said. "Burnt fish. I doubt they're ever going to get the smell out of there."

"Fish," Fergason repeated softly to himself, shaking his head and remembering the dinner that night all those years ago.

The dinner over which he and Canny had decided to spend a lifetime together.

He glanced up at his grandson. "He fell off a horse?"

His grandson smiled. "Broke his neck while cooking a fish dinner over an open campfire."

For the first time since Canny had died, Fergason laughed, knowing without a doubt that Canny would have laughed with him.

BRYANT STREET

A Bryant Street Story

I fear Bryant Street more than anything on the planet. Honestly, when in a standard subdivision, I always get lost, turned around, and slightly panicked. Not kidding.

In a writer's workshop someone challenged me to write a story with the first line "The Wolves Were Howling on Bryant Street." I knew instantly what the wolves represented. As a fiction writer, doing battle with the wolves never ends.

When starting this magazine, the wolves howled and nipped at my heals more than once. Now at issue ten, they have calmed some.

One

THE WOLVES WERE howling on Bryant Street.

Duncan nudged the orange slice closer to the edge of his plate of ham and eggs and tried not to listen. He forced himself to concentrate on the loud clanking of pans in the kitchen of the Denny's Restaurant, then the loud, constant chatter of the large-thighed waitress.

It did no good.

He could still hear the wolves.

The waitress had started it all. She'd asked him why he never ate the orange slice that came with his late-night breakfast. She'd said most of her regular customers ate it, why didn't he?

Simple. He hated fruit with ham and eggs. Just the thought made the grease curl up into a ball in his stomach. But for some reason, every restaurant had an orange slice with ham and eggs. Stupid custom.

He had been about to tell the waitress, in so many plain words, that it was his business what he did with his orange slice when the wolves started to howl.

The wolves of Bryant Street.

Bryant Street was after Duncan.

He flipped the orange slice over and thought back to the first and only time he had been on Bryant Street. It had been a warm Friday afternoon two months ago, shortly after he graduated from college with his degree in electrical engineering. Road construction blocked the main street past the mall and he had been forced to turn his VW Bug onto Bryant Street.

Right away he had known he was in trouble.

The perfect houses all looked the same.

Each had lots of shrubs outside, two bedrooms inside, and an attached room for two cars.

The further down the street he got, the more uncomfortable he felt, like he was listening to the music in Jaws before seeing the shark.

He glanced first left, then right.

Perfectly spaced trees planted exactly correct distances apart fought to hypnotize him with their monotone swaying.

The green shutters on all the houses closed in around him and the evenly cut lawns beckoned to him like a soft bed to a man without sleep. He gasped for each breath.

On both sides front doors opened, ready and willing to swallow him.

The smooth driveways sucked at his little car.

Sweat dripped into his eyes as he fought to keep the Bug in the middle of the road.

He glanced back.

He'd only gone a hundred trees.

Five more trees and he couldn't take it any more.

He gunned his Bug into a u-turn between two Pintos.

Bryant Street now seemed to stretch for miles down a dark, forbidding tunnel of jagged branches.

He jammed the gas pedal to the floor, his mind racing with the fear of a flat.

Or engine trouble.

The trees slashed at him.

The street rolled, pitched the car from side to side.

He fought his way down the road tree by tree, the entire time keeping his gaze locked on the faint light ahead.

Finally, after what seemed to be all afternoon, he reached the detour, ducked between a Caddy and a Datsun, and headed back downtown.

He had never gone near Bryant Street again.

Now, it was coming for him, sending the wolves to round him up like so much mutton.

Damn it all, anyway. It wouldn't get him without a fight.

"Mister? You all right?" the waitress asked, popping her gum.

Duncan shook himself and looked up at her. He must have looked a little funny, sitting there, leaning away from the window. The wolves were still howling.

"Can you hear them?" Duncan asked.

"Yeah. They're awful, aren't they?" The whine in her voice reminded Duncan of a smoke detector going off. "Someday they're going to get a good band in that bar and fill the place. I keep telling Craig—he's the boss—that if he would just—"

"No," Duncan said. "Not the band. The wolves. The wolves from Bryant Street. Listen. Don't you hear them?"

She popped her gum once more. "Can't say as I do." She flipped his ticket upside down near his plate and walked away.

He should have known she wouldn't hear them. The street wanted him. He'd have to fight his own battle.

He picked up the orange slice and ate it quickly. He'd give them this first battle, but nothing more.

The wolves quit howling.

He finished his eggs, but left the ham. His stomach was upset enough without putting ham on top of an orange slice.

Two

FROM THAT NIGHT on, the fight with the wolves from Bryant Street became intense.

Every time Duncan got one step out of line, Wham-o, howl-time. And each time the wolves got louder and louder. It drove him crazy. It got to the point he felt they could hear his every thought.

For example, one month after the wolves started howling, on a Wednesday night, he had a date with Constance, a tall blonde with a high laugh and large features.

Constance was the lady who cut his hair while rubbing her large features against his back and arms. He loved the way her fingers massaged his scalp and had dreams of her massaging other places, including her large features.

By eight in the evening they had stormed and occupied a dark, lower booth in a plush hotel bar. One of those places where the backs of the booths were planters and the seats a form of fake leather.

They were getting down to the point of being real cozy, when suddenly, an old woman in the booth behind them looked through the plants and then whispered to her toothless old man, "Is that Constance's husband?"

Duncan turned around slowly, pushed one large bunch of plant leaves aside so he could see the shocked look on the old woman's face, and then looked the old bag right in her gray eyes. "Of course I'm not. What fun would that be?"

The wolves started howling their thing.

Duncan could hear them right over the music and the gasps of shock and indignation from the old woman. The wolves' howls were long and drawn out and sounded plain vicious. He imagined saliva dripping from their teeth as they threw back their heads and ruined his evening.

And, for the first time, they sounded close.

Almost right outside.

By this point he knew better than to ask anyone if they heard them. "Look," he said to Constance. "I just remembered that I have this appointment. You understand. Maybe another time, huh?"

With one last longing look at those large features, he stood.

Damn it all. He loved those fingers.

He'd fix those wolves for this.

He patted her hand like a father consoling a child, moved his scotch with reverence to the center of the table, and headed for the door of the bar. He had packed his father's deer rifle in the trunk of his car. He was going to bag himself a wolf tonight.

The wolves weren't in the parking lot or anywhere else around the side of the hotel. But the level of their howls never diminished. It was as if he were surrounded.

They didn't stop howling until the police arrested him for scaring hotel guests by stomping through the flowerbeds outside their rooms with a rifle.

Three

WITH THE WOLVES hounding him, life became one big bore.

Time after time they stopped him from one activity or another. He always looked for them without luck. Each time they sounded close, but somehow he knew they were still over on Bryant Street. And no way was he going back there.

No sir.

No way.

After a while he tried to convince himself he was making them up. Didn't work.

Their howls froze him, made him stop whatever he was doing. They were too real sounding.

But there were a few things in Duncan's life the wolves didn't seem to mind. One was his work with a small company downtown. They also didn't seem to mind baseball or Debbie.

Debbie was short and cute in a plain sort of way. She had shoulder length brown hair, perfect teeth, and tiny feet. She was also a complete take-her-home-to-meet-mother prude.

He had met Debbie the week before the wolves started their terrorist action. She worked in a downtown department store in the small-appliance section. He had gone in for a new toaster. The night before, while drunk, he had used his old one for a football. He had thought he was Joe Willy and threw a perfect pass through the window while fading back behind the blocking of his couch.

For the first month, Duncan wasn't sure why he kept asking Debbie out. Possibly for the challenge. He figured she finally agreed for the same reason.

That and the fact the he had what she called "big potential."

After the war started with the wolves, dates with Debbie were the only peaceful ones he had. For a while he suspected it was something she or her rich father was doing. But after searching a hundred places for speakers, he gave up trying to figure out how.

Dates with Debbie were boring, plain and simple. The same kind he'd had back in high school: movies, hamburgers or dinner, and a lot of talk about everything but the real subject on his mind. Every night, after he dropped her off, he went downtown and got drunk. The wolves didn't seem to mind that much either, as long as he kept his hands to himself.

One night, after six months of dating Debbie and fighting the wolves by alternately running from them or searching for them, the battle shifted.

For some unremembered reason, Duncan had promised Debbie to take her dancing. Debbie was having so much fun, she even had a few drinks. It must have been the drinks, because they started dancing all the slow dances and Debbie kept getting closer and closer.

By halfway through the night she was rubbing up and down and up and down real slow like she was carefully sanding a fine antique. It drove him crazy.

He kept waiting for the wolves to start their howl, but they didn't.

Later, after he was rubbed raw, they ended up at his apartment. That was the first time he had talked her into going up there.

She'd had four strawberry daiquiris and looked dazed. She didn't say a word about the three flights of stairs, but her face looked pale by the time she got inside.

"Bathroom's there," he pointed.

"Nice place," she lied, and headed for the door he had indicated.

He went into the kitchen and poured them both another drink of scotch. He didn't even know if she liked scotch or not, but it didn't matter. He used his best Goodwill glasses and only put one ice cube in hers so it wouldn't be too watered down when he drank it later.

He'd only taken a sip when the toilet flushed and she came out. She staggered straight up to him, pulled his head down, and kissed him with strawberry breath.

He set his scotch down quickly as she started hoeing his mouth with her tongue, planting strawberry seeds with drunken skill.

Fifteen minutes later they had worked their way to the bedroom and removed all their clothes.

"Careful," she said when they started.

He said, "Yeah," and she rubbed and he rubbed and the pace picked quickly up.

Then the wolves started howling.

Major battle time.

Tonight they sounded loud, closer, and extra mean, but there was no way he was going to stop. It was about time he learned to ignore them.

"I love it," Debbie said softly as she twisted her head from side to side. She started rubbing faster and faster. "I love it... I love it... I love you..."

He noticed the word change, but didn't stop.

Nothing was going to make him stop.

No word, no howl, nothing.

Debbie kept saying she loved him and the wolves kept howling and Duncan did his best just to keep up.

Finally, the situation was to that critical time which marked the boundary between thinking, "Why not?" and wondering "Why?" when the wolves stopped howling.

This time the silence made him pause.

"Oh, don't stop," Debbie said. "You feel so good."

A low growl came from near the door.

He tried to ignore it and go on with Debbie's request when a second mean-sounding growl stopped him in mid-rub.

He glanced around.

The wolves were no longer howling from Bryant Street. The battle had moved into his own bedroom where they now circled his bed.

On the left, two were crouched, ready to spring.

Another stood, hair on its back on end, growling. Saliva dripped from its yellow teeth and formed a wet spot on the rug.

He turned to the right. Two more were there.

He was dead for sure. He closed his eyes and waited for the first rip of his flesh. He was going to die in the missionary position without a fight.

What a way to go.

"Duncan, dear. Are you all right?"

"I don't know," he said and opened his eyes. There couldn't really be wolves in his bedroom. Why didn't Debbie see them?

How could they harm him and not her?

Made no sense.

He must be imagining things. That was it. If he ignored them, they would go away.

"Don't stop," Debbie said, her voice almost pleading. She started to move again and without thinking, he did too.

Out of the corner of his eye he saw the largest wolf take a step toward the bed and crouch to spring.

Duncan stopped again, bare essentials cruelly exposed to the pack.

The wolf stopped.

Standoff. Duncan looked both ways. They had all moved closer.

What the hell did they want? He'd been nice to Debbie. This had been mostly her idea. He didn't know what they wanted him to do.

He looked into the pale blue eyes of the largest wolf. It growled real low and angry-like.

Suddenly, what it wanted was clear to Duncan.

He glanced down at Debbie. She was watching him with a look of concern. The wolves wanted him to tell her that he loved her. He might be able to do that.

Maybe.

She was a nice girl. He sort of liked her. Telling her he loved her was the right thing to do and the wolves always left him alone when he did the right thing.

"Debbie," he said, "I... I..."

He turned back to the largest wolf hoping for one last chance. The wolf bared its teeth and growled.

"Debbie, I love you," he quickly said. That should do it.

It damn well better.

Debbie pulled him down into a hard hug that pressed his ear into her right breast. "Really, Duncan? Do you mean it?"

She kissed him with her mouth open and her orthodontist teeth showing. Then, without hesitation, she started to move again. He didn't know if he should join her.

The wolves were still there.

But his body won. He couldn't help himself and he slowly joined her rhythm.

Two of the wolves snarled again and the largest wolf stuck its cold nose against the side of his leg.

He jerked and rolled away from the wolf, pulling Debbie over on top of him.

"Oh, Duncan. You're so much fun."

She pulled her legs up under her and started practicing her belly dancing moves on his stomach. She was a fine belly dancer, he quickly discovered.

He lay there and looked from side to side at the wolves. He hadn't imagined that cold nose. The wolves might be invisible to everyone else, but they were real enough to his touch.

And they still weren't happy with him.

They were in close all the way around the bed. He could smell their stale breath. He had to do something and do it quick.

The biggest wolf again touched him with its cold nose.

Duncan jumped and Debbie gave a little squeal of joy.

"Debbie! Stop!"

Debbie pulled her hair away from her face and looked down at him. Her cheeks were flushed and she had this hungry look in her eyes.

The same look the wolves had.

"I need to ask you something." He checked the wolves on his right and then on his left. He could imagine his bloodstains on their yellowed teeth. They weren't giving him a chance.

They had him surrounded.

They had won this battle and the war.

"Debbie," he said as softly as he could, his mind racing for any other way. Anything. But this was what the wolves wanted. They had him naked, flat on his back, unarmed.

"Debbie, would you marry me?"

"What?"

The wolves all took a few steps backwards. It worked. He couldn't believe it.

"What did you say?" Debbie asked.

"Oh, nothing," Duncan said. The wolves started toward the bed again, all growling.

"Would you marry me?"

"Do you really mean it?" Debbie asked. "You know I've loved you since the first day we met."

"Would I have asked if I didn't?"

Damn the wolves anyway.

She kissed him hard and again started to rub, already trying to polish his rough edges.

He glanced around. Only the largest wolf remained. It curled up and went promptly to sleep in the corner.

After a short time, Duncan started rubbing back.

They were married seven months later in a big church wedding. He was the perfect groom.

Everyone said so.

They moved into a house her daddy bought for them on Bryant Street and he went to work for her daddy's corporation.

People only thought it just a little odd that he built a dog run in their back yard, even though it matched all the other dog runs on Bryant Street.

They don't have a dog.

No one on Bryant Street has a dog.

EYES ON MY CARDS

A Doc Hill Story

Way back in 2005 I wrote a thriller with the name Dead Money. *It starred Doc Hill, a professional poker player. I had every intention when I wrote the thriller to continue to write more Doc Hill stories, but because of the strangeness of publishing at the time, I put the novel in a drawer and pretty much forgot about it.*
Fast-forward to 2013 and a meeting with the publisher of WMG Publishing, Allyson Longueira, and my wife, Kristine Kathryn Rusch. Kris brought up Dead Money, *the long-stored thriller, and suggested I take it out, dust it off, and sell it to WMG Publishing.*
After rereading Dead Money *and coming to remember and like the characters again, I decided to write a new Doc Hill story for* Fiction River Special Edition: Crime. *This story is the first of many to come.*

One

I PUSHED BACK from the table and stood, disgusted.

I needed a break.

I left my chips in my spot indicating to the dealer I would be back. I wasn't down any of the five hundred I had bought in for, but I sure wasn't up either.

But for a change, winning money wasn't the reason I was at that table.

Around me the noise and lights of the Grand Casino and Hotel on the Las Vegas strip seemed muted and flavored by the slight smell of popcorn, like I was walking in a carnival instead of a casino. I moved between the empty poker tables, away from the no-limit game, and toward the larger part of the casino and the gaming tables.

To my right three tourists in shorts and bright shirts stood, laughing at something, and beyond them Webster stood in his dark silk suit, his hands crossed over his chest, his eyes missing nothing on the gaming floor around him.

B. B. Webster, the head of Grand Casino operations was the man who had hired me. He was the reason I was sitting in this mid-level no-limit game in his casino. He had asked a favor and I had agreed to help.

He had a suspected cheater working his poker room, a guy in a dark golf shirt and Reds' baseball cap. Webster wanted me to tell him how the guy was doing it.

And after an hour at the table with the cheater, I had no idea.

Not one, which had me totally frustrated. I had spent all that time at the table and couldn't spot a thing. Yet I too was convinced he was cheating.

I walked past Webster without even a nod and headed to the left of the gaming tables and toward the huge, ornate front lobby of the hotel and casino. Giant marble pillars dominated the lobby and it never seemed to be empty or quiet, no matter the time of day. And the popcorn smell faded in the big space as well, replaced by the faint smell of lilacs. Over the sounds of the people talking I could hear the fountains that lined two walls, water flowing over rocks and into pools.

A dozen tourists stood along the large front desk on the left, talking with smiling front desk clerks, clearly checking in. Suitcases were scattered behind them like deer droppings along a trail in a forest.

Right now it was just after midnight on a Thursday night.

As I went around the corner to my left and out of sight of the poker room, Annie Lott joined me, tucking her arm in mine and matching me stride for stride.

She had on a black pants suit with an open-neck white blouse and low heels that clicked lightly on the marble floor. Her long brown hair was pulled up tight on her head. She looked stunning and just having her walk with me, her steps matching mine perfectly, made me calm down a little.

We had been together now for over a year, living together for the last six months, and I had loved every minute of it.

And sometimes, like tonight, we worked cases together as favors for friends. She had been a former Las Vegas detective before becoming a full-time poker player. I saw things on poker tables she didn't see. But she saw things in the real world I never noticed. It was one of the many reasons we made such a good team.

Since our first meeting while investigating the death of my father, we had become known for being able to figure out some darned strange crimes in and around casinos. We didn't take every request for help that came our way, but if the friend really needed help, or the problem was weird enough to get our attention, we would try to help out.

"He's cheating all right," Annie said. "I can see that from beyond the rail. You figure out how?"

I shook my head. "Not a clue and it's driving me nuts."

"Yeah, me too," she said.

Poker was a difficult game to cheat at in a monitored casino. But it did happen, usually with some sort of collusion between a dealer and a player. This guy clearly wasn't working with any of the MGM dealers, since three dealers had gone through the table in the hour I had been there. And Webster had made sure the dealers tonight hadn't worked or dealt to the guy last night.

And two of the dealers had actually looked at the guy funny a couple of times, as if they were picking up on something being wrong as well.

We walked in silence past the front desk and down a very wide hallway that headed toward the parking garage. A few paces down the hall we went through an unmarked door on the left and into a reception area with a large desk.

We moved toward a lounge area on the right that had bottled water and soft drinks in a fridge and tea and coffee on a counter. The room was comfortable, with three overstuffed couches on three walls that seemed to be from an earlier MGM Grand décor. A very red one, including strange red paintings of desert landscapes on the walls. It seemed like it would have been too much, but oddly, I found the room comfortable.

I grabbed a bottle of water and dropped onto one couch and Annie worked to make herself a cup of black tea.

We didn't say anything. There was nothing to say until one of us came up with an idea as to how this guy was cheating.

The door opened and my childhood friend and business partner, Fleetwood Korte, entered, followed by Webster. Fleet's silk suit rivaled Webster's and together they looked like they belonged on Wall Street, not in a Vegas casino.

At six-two, Fleet was two inches taller than me and thicker around the waist than I was. His hair had thinned since our college days ten years earlier, but he made up for that with a huge handlebar moustache. Every time I kidded him about how Carol, his wife, liked his moustache, he would just smile and nod, a distant look in his eyes that told me far, far more information than I actually wanted to know.

"You got anything, Doc?" Webster asked, his voice deeper and filled with a sound like gravel being washed together. He clearly had smoked far, far too many cigarettes in his day.

"He's cheating all right," I said.

"That much is clear," Annie said as she moved over beside me and sat down with her tea. "I could see that just watching from a distance."

Fleet took a bottle of water and sat on another couch while Webster sort of stared at the three of us.

"Doc, I think he's got spotters," Fleet said.

I glanced at Fleet and nodded. I had thought the guy had spotters as well, but I hadn't been sure. That's why both Annie and Fleet were here, to scout around the table and the poker room area. "Guy in the blue tee-shirt who is pacing the hall?"

Fleet nodded.

"What about the woman in the green sun dress and long black hair," Annie asked, "sitting in the room to the back reading?"

"Possible," I said. "But she came in with the big guy who called himself Big Ed two seats to the right of our target."

"And what good is a spotter going to do him?" Webster asked. "They can't see your cards or anyone else's cards. I've watched some security videos and everyone is playing down on the felt, no flashing at all."

I shrugged, because I honestly didn't know.

Webster shook his head at our silence. "Strangest damn thing I have ever seen. And that's going some considering how long I've been in this damn business."

He headed back out the door and left the three of us sitting and thinking.

Finally, I broke the silence. "Let me lay out what I've got and see if we can put any theories together before we go back in there."

Fleet and Annie nodded, so I went on.

"He's a decent player. Nothing fancy, like he has played a lot of hours in a low-level casino somewhere in a three-six game."

"He doesn't know how to bet in a no-limit game," Annie added.

"That's right," I said. "But somehow he knows the cards in other player's hands."

"Or he's manipulating his own cards to make sure his cards are the best," Fleet said.

"He's not a mechanic," I said, shaking my head. Beside me Annie shook her head as well as she sipped her tea.

I went on. "The guy can barely hold his cards at times. And he's not playing hands when he doesn't have the best cards. But when he does play, he almost always wins. Or drops when his hand gets beat on the last card."

"Maybe he can read minds," Fleet said, shrugging.

"That would explain a ton of things," Annie said, laughing. "But my guess is that this is some sort of very ornate scam we just can't see yet."

"I agree," I said, the frustration coming back. "The guy played for five hours last night and didn't lose a hand he played to the end. And tonight he has kept that streak up, at least for the hour we've been watching."

"You know, if he were better at hiding what he was doing," Annie said, "Webster or any of the rest of us would never have picked up on this."

I glanced at Annie and smiled. "I think you might have given us a clue. He's a mid-level poker player, so this winning and high-stakes game is unusual to him. He flat doesn't know how to hide what he's doing yet."

Fleet shook his head. "And that's going to help us how?"

I ticked off three items on my fingers. "He can't manipulate cards, he isn't working with dealers, and he isn't used to these levels of games. What's left?"

Both Annie and Fleet shrugged.

"Mechanical," I said. I pointed at the ceiling.

"He can't be working with anyone in the security room," Annie said. "I doubt that would be possible. And Webster would have checked that first, before even calling us."

"The guy's not working with anyone in the casino staff," I said, standing. "I'm sure of that now. But I've got an idea how to take this guy and expose him."

"And how are you going to do that?" Annie asked, as she stood to join me.

"If he's not used to this level," I said, smiling, "I bet he's never dealt with a blind player."

Annie laughed, the sound wonderful to my ears while Fleet just looked puzzled.

"I'll show you," I said to my best friend. "You just keep on eye on the spotters. Especially that black-haired woman in the back."

"Got it," Fleet said, looking even more puzzled. "I think."

Two

I WAITED UNTIL Annie and Fleet got back into positions so they could see the table, then I joined it again.

The cheater with the Reds' baseball cap had a stack of chips in front of him that looked to be a few thousand large and there were two new players in the game.

I glanced at my cards a few times, tossing away garbage, then when the button came around to me, I decided it was time to really see what was happening.

One guy in early position made a slight raise, the cheater called, and I re-raised just enough to not scare anyone.

Big Ed folded quickly as did others.

I had not looked at my cards at all. In fact, I hadn't even touched them.

And I knew for a fact that the cheater hadn't noticed I hadn't looked at them.

The guy in early position called my raise, but the cheater was looking puzzled, shaking his head slowly.

Finally he folded.

The flop came and I pretended to look at my cards again, then folded to another bet from the player in early position.

The next hand the cheater limped in again with just a call and I raised. Again I had not looked at my cards. I was playing blind.

By the time the other players folded around to him, he looked very, very confused. Since I had not looked at my hand, he didn't know what I had either.

This sort of made sense if he was reading minds, but I doubted that was what he was doing.

Finally he again folded and I knew I had him.

As the dealer was washing the deck and putting the cards in the shuffling machine imbedded in the table, I pretended to play with my chips as I felt the underside of the rail in front of me. It took me a moment to find them, but I did.

Very slight bumps just under the rail in the leather.

My guess was that they were very, very tiny cameras, no larger than the size of pins stuck into the leather of the rail.

I looked around at the other seats. I honestly couldn't see the tiny camera heads at all, they blended in so well on the underside of the edge of the table.

I was impressed.

In major tournaments there were what were called "button cameras" to allow television viewers to follow along with the play. This guy and his team had cameras so small and perfectly matched with the table that they couldn't even be seen. At least three per spot to make sure that no matter where a player looked at their cards, the camera would pick it up.

This must have taken him and his partners a long time to set up. Days carefully installing the tiny pin cameras without seeming to do anything strange at the table.

Webster would have to go back over a lot of footage to catch the people who had installed the little pin cameras.

I just shook my head in disgust. Even a monkey could win at poker if he knew what everyone else held for cards. The idiot in the Reds' baseball cap was worse. I hated cheaters, almost more than anything else.

I made myself calm down and sit back and try to think. I had found the cameras, but how was this guy getting the information relayed to him?

I played the next hand normal, looking at my cards and playing them like a normal mid-level player. When I did that the cheater seemed to relax again and I studied his face when he didn't know I was watching.

I couldn't see a thing.

I could read the best players in the business and this guy was a blank slate. I doubted he had a good poker face. He just didn't think he needed to hide anything from anyone.

In other words, this guy was not trained well and I was starting to doubt he was in charge of this.

It took someone smart to figure out how to do all this.

People had always tried to cheat casinos. Over the years, people had put in signals in their shoes, small electrodes on their arms, and so on to help them count cards in blackjack or get information from spotters. But this guy didn't seem to have any of that and the Grand Casino's normal security systems were designed to block most electronic signals, or at least spot odd ones.

And from what little I knew about tiny cameras like these, they didn't have a very large broadcast range. In fact, they were so tiny, I couldn't imagine them broadcasting much beyond the edge of the table, which would guarantee that the signals from that many small cameras would not be picked up by casino electronic scanning.

The dealer took the cards out of the shuffling machine, cut and started to deal.

I glanced over at the woman with the long black hair sitting in the back of the room. She was reading on some sort of tablet and she had it turned so no camera over her could see what she was reading.

Suddenly I knew I had it figured out. And I had a sinking feeling it was a lot larger cheating scam than anyone had first figured. A lot more than one bad player winning too many hands.

I mucked my cards without looking at them and stood up. "Back in a second," I said to the dealer.

Then I again turned and headed out of the poker area and toward the casino. Again the popcorn smell filled the air and shouting from the direction of the craps table seemed to cover almost everything.

Out of sight of the table, Fleet and Annie and Webster caught up with me.

"So that's playing blind, huh?" Fleet asked as we stopped near the hotel lobby.

Annie laughed. "Doc drives people crazy doing that in tournaments when he spots someone who really cares too much."

"He drives a lot of us crazy like that," Fleet said, shaking his head.

"Well, Doc?" Webster asked.

"I got him," I said, smiling. "When did you switch out those shuffling machines?"

Webster looked puzzled. "A month or so ago, if I remember right. But they are carefully checked."

"I know," I said, nodding. "That's why this is so amazing, more than likely there's more teams involved in this working other casinos right now."

"Oh, crap," Webster said.

Annie squeezed my arm and smiled.

Fleet just shook his head as he often did when I said outrageous things.

I just smiled. "Get security to surround the entire area and hold that woman in the back with the tablet as well. She's the spotter, so you had better take that tablet away from her quickly before she erases anything. And my sense is that the guy who calls himself Big Ed is also in this, since he never played against the guy in the cap. He's just a better player is all and harder to notice."

"You're sure about all this?" Webster asked, his voice sounding even more full of gravel than normal.

"Positive," I said, smiling at the frown on the casino manager's face. "I'll show you. It's actually pretty damn smart system. Just get your people in place and keep a lid on this until you can warn other casinos."

Three

IT TOOK WEBSTER five minutes to carefully put his men into position around the poker room without anyone seeming to notice. His guys were good.

"Introduce me when we walk up to the table would you? I want to see their faces."

He laughed. "Gladly."

"Just make sure your guy gets that tablet quickly."

Webster nodded at his guy standing behind the woman and I smiled. She wouldn't even see that guy coming.

Fleet and Annie followed us a few steps back.

As we neared the table, Webster signaled for the dealer to stop play.

"Folks, I'd like to introduce you to Doc Hill, the top ranked Texas Hold'em player on the planet."

I did a slight bow, smiling at how the guy in the Reds' baseball cap had gulped and his face had gone white.

The guy named Big Ed just shook his head and muttered something about how he thought he recognized me.

Webster's man had taken the woman's tablet and was holding it and blocking her escape.

"I asked Doc to join this table," Webster said, "because it felt like something was wrong with the play."

I reached forward, under the edge of the leather near my chips, and pulled out a tiny pin and held it up.

"Camera. Three at each spot," I said to the table. "Pretty nifty, huh?"

All the regular players except Big Ed and the guy in the Reds' cap started feeling under the edge of the table in front of them and pulling out camera pins.

"The cameras all relayed their data to a small device inside the shuffling box," I said.

With that the dealer looked shocked and actually moved back from the box like it might bite him.

"The shuffler then sent the image of all our cards as a phone signal to the woman in long hair sitting back there."

Everyone looked around at her and she just sneered.

I went on. "She would then relay the information about the cards to our two friends here also by phone signal, which is not blocked in a casino or monitored."

I turned to Webster. "You'll find tiny ear bugs in their ears set to receive the phone signal from the woman's tablet."

"You can't prove that," the idiot in the baseball cap said.

Webster only snorted and motioned for the guards to take them away. Then he had the dealer split the cheater's chips among those of us at the table and broke the game.

"You had better be informing the other rooms around town and up in Reno," I said to Webster.

"I'm going to, as soon as I take that box apart and figure out how we missed the phone device in there. But I know you are right. This is a big ring and these three are going to suddenly vanish into some deep parts of this casino for a short time so that we don't alert everyone else."

He stuck out his hand. "Thanks, Doc. Fleet. Annie."

"Check's in the mail?" Fleet asked.

Webster snorted. "Not so much a check, but a lot of free dinners from here and I'm betting other casinos in town."

"Sounds even better," Fleet said, laughing.

"Come to think of it," I said. "I am hungry. That popcorn smell has been driving me crazy."

"It does that," Webster said.

"Steak?" Annie asked.

"I love steak," Fleet said, smiling at Webster.

"Maybe I should write you a check. Might be cheaper."

Then in his gravelly voice he laughed. "Head on over to the steak house and I'll tell them you're coming."

He turned and walked away.

The three of us laughed as I tossed the small pin camera on the table and racked up my chips. Then we turned and headed for a late meal.

It felt great to help protect the game I loved. Poker is a game of skill, but there will always be those who look for shortcuts in anything that takes skill.

I just hoped Webster kept these three "lost" for a very long time before turning them over to the police.

And that thought just made me laugh, so I told my friends what I hoped Webster would do and they laughed as well as we headed for dinner.

Even Annie, the former Las Vegas detective.

"In Vegas," she said, "casino justice can be much worse than police justice. Always has been, always will be."

"Especially for cheaters," I added and they both laughed again.

SKIING THE GRAVEYARD OF SOULS

I used to waterski early in the morning when the surface of the lake seemed like a mirror. Looking down into the water as the boat pulled me across the calm waters, all I could see was a reflection of myself flashing over the surface.

But to me, there always seemed to be something beyond, behind, deeper than just my own reflection. Those moments cutting over the water felt magical.

So years later, remembering those times, I wrote this story about Benny, who needed something special in his life, who needed to do something special with his life.

Benny's father found the magic before he died. Could Benny stand to face his own life, his own reflection, as he skied?

Or would his own soul join the graveyard flashing past below him? That's a question we all face at one point or another.

One

"HIT IT!" THE vagrant stood near the front entrance shouted to nothing in particular, then went back to staring out the window at the city spread out below the Penthouse Bar.

His words brought a faint ripple of a memory, but I ignored it and glanced over at my only two "real" customers, a guy about thirty and a younger-looking blonde with, from what I could tell, a real driver's license saying she was twenty-four. They huddled over their strawberry daiquiris and talked in lovers' whispers. Nothing short of this twenty-story building tipping over was going to bother them.

The bar had everything, from plush dark-leather seats in all the booths, the tables, and on the couches to one side of the small dance floor. Dark oak bar and pillars accented everything else with a tan carpet that helped ground the place along with the indirect lights tucked along the walls and in panels in the low ceiling. And around three sides of the room there was more glass looking out over the city than I could ever imagine trying to wash.

The huge room's lights were kept low everywhere except the center circular bar so that customers could enjoy the fantastic view of Boise spread out below them. That's why everything was dark wood and leather, to not distract from the view. I didn't much notice the view anymore. But everyone who came in from the elevators sure did.

The room could hold two hundred people, but at this late hour on a Tuesday night, there were only the two lovers, the vagrant, and me on the entire top floor high over the city.

The vagrant stood, moved over closer to the window and eased himself down into the ten-person booth. Behind him was a wall that divided the big room from the back area and restrooms. It was covered with autographed pictures of famous stars who had visited the hotel.

Somehow it felt odd to have him sitting there. How he had gotten past the hotel security I would never know.

I studied him while he stared out over the lights.

His hands looked red, stained by the cold night air. He wore a rolled up blue stocking cap, a dark blue, naval-style coat, and shin-high mud-waders over the tops of the cuffs of his pants.

He kept his eyes averted as if not looking at me would keep me from throwing him back out into the cold.

Maybe it would. I didn't much care at this point. I had slowly come to hate this job, the snobby college kids who thought this place was their own world, and the businessmen and women who didn't even notice the "help" as I was called.

One more person snapped their fingers at me and I would be gone. There had to be more to making a living than dealing with these people.

I went back to restocking the beer and pretended to ignore him.

He kept gazing out the window and didn't say another word.

Twenty minutes later I had finished all the stocking and was cleaning the well when he decided to break his silence. He stood and moved closer to the bar.

"You ever water ski?" he asked without taking his gaze away from the city, standing with the side of his head in my direction. His voice was hard and deep, but his words were clear over the soft, background music.

I wiped off my hands and studied the strands of brown hair jutting from the side of his stocking cap. "Sure."

"Ever single ski?"

"Sure. My dad taught me."

He nodded, but still didn't turn around to actually look at me directly.

I glanced out over the city with all its lights sparkling in the cold winter air. I couldn't see anything in particular he was staring at.

Why the hell was this guy talking about water skiing in the middle of February? Maybe thinking of warm things was one of the ways he kept himself warm.

More likely he was completely nuts.

"You ever ski early in the morning," he asked, "right after sunrise, when the water is glassy smooth, undisturbed by wind and the waves of boats? So smooth that you can see your own reflection?"

The memory of those mornings flooded back.

I could feel the rope pulling me through the crisp morning air.

Back and forth, back and forth, my cuts across the waveless surface so effortless it felt like flying. The difference between water and sky a line I crossed at will.

I had skied those early morning runs many times.

Every year, on the last day of our week long vacation to Driscoll Head Lake, Dad would wake me up real early. It would be barely light and the dew would still be on the pines and the path down to the dock. I always complained.

Then he'd fire up the boat, toss me the rope and life jacket, and in a few quick minutes I would be out on the lake making wide, deep slashes across the mirror-like water.

Then I'd remember why Dad loved it so much.

Every year Dad let me go first and we'd go north up the lake. I always skied hard, at times my shoulder almost skimmed the surface.

Then I'd take Dad on a long run down the lake to water I hadn't disturbed.

He'd make his long, lazy swings behind the boat and I'd watch him smile like I never saw him do any other time.

Looking back now, I think Dad put up with Mother's constant bitching about vacationing in the same place every year because he wanted to make that one run. Maybe making that one run was what kept him going during those long graveyard shifts at the plant.

The summer of his last year, when he was so sick, he wanted me to take someone up to the lake and make that early morning run for him.

And for me.

He said I should do it every year. It would give my life balance.

I had promised him I would. But I never had.

Not once.

I had always been too busy.

But I still remembered the silence of those early morning runs, the feeling of something so special that a crazy vagrant's question triggered ten-year-old memories at two a.m. in a smoky lounge.

I shook my head to clear it as the vagrant slowly turned and moved the few steps to the bar.

His face was as red and weather-beaten as his hands, but his eyes were deep blue and as clear as any spring water.

He stuck out his hand. "My name's Craig. Edward Craig."

I took his rough hand and tried to match his strong grip. "Ben Hodges. Benny to everyone here."

The vagrant nodded and seemed to laugh. "It's nice meeting someone who knows. Would you like to make a run? I'll steer for you if you'll steer for me."

This guy was totally nuts. Of that I had no doubt. I was suddenly very annoyed at myself for not calling security and getting him out of here when I had the chance.

"I'd love to," I said. "But I don't have a boat and it's February." I shrugged and gave him my best bartender "You're-out-of-luck-so-go-the-fuck-away" look.

The vagrant smiled and for a moment I thought he might laugh out loud. His gaze held me and I could tell he wasn't laughing at me, more enjoying the moment with a deep understanding, like a parent watching a child open presents on Christmas morning.

"Look at this city," he said, waving his hand at the windows.

"Imagine it as a lake. During the daylight hours it's choppy with human activity. Rough. Hard to stay on the surface. But in the late-night hours everyone is asleep and the souls of the world are smooth like a surface of lake at sunrise. Wouldn't you like to ski that?"

He looked at me as if I should understand his ravings. Hell, I wouldn't know what he was talking about if he stuck it up in neon.

I glanced out at the city and then back at him. My favorite time was between two and six in the morning. No one around, no waiting in lines, no stupid drivers, no loud noises.

But I had no idea what he meant by skiing it.

"So just how do we go about doing that?"

Again the vagrant smiled as if explaining an obvious answer to a child. And after a bitch of a long, slow night bartending, I didn't much feel like being treated as a child.

"Benny," the vagrant said. "If you simply stood on a water ski, you would sink. Correct?"

"Of course. If a jetliner stops in midair, it falls. I know the physics involved with lift. What's that got to do with skiing on a city?"

"Right now," the vagrant said, indicating the bar around him. "You and I are stopped. We are, for lack of a better way of putting it, dead in the water. We can't even see the surface. But it's there."

"Yeah, so?" I said. For some reason this guy had me so irritated, I wanted nothing more than to show him how stupid he was being. "And what kind of boat floats on this surface of yours? And what kind of engine are we going to use?"

This time he actually laughed. "We don't need much of a boat to ski among the souls. In fact, this stool will do nicely." He dropped onto the bar stool, adjusted himself, and continued.

"For power we use the mind and the force of change. But as with flying, it is the movement that is important. Remember that. The movement is the critical part. Now, are you ready?"

"For what?"

"Why, to take the first run. I'll steer for you and then you steer for me. What will it hurt to try?"

Now I was beyond irritated and starting to get damn mad. "This is nuts, you know that? And your scam isn't going to work. You're not going to get a free drink just by spouting a wild story about skiing."

The vagrant's smile disappeared and his eyes dimmed, as if he had aged ten years in a fraction of a second. He shook his head slowly. "He said you wouldn't believe."

"Believe what, for God's sake?"

He shrugged, the coat draping like a huge weight over his shoulders. "It doesn't matter. Your father warned me—"

"You knew my father?" I must have shouted it at him because the two daiquiri customers looked over at the bar and then went back to whispering.

"Of course," the vagrant said, his voice barely carrying over the soft music. "We worked every night together for thirty years. For the last fifteen of those we skied the graveyard of souls. That is, until your father died."

My head was spinning. "What was my dad's name? Where did he work?"

The vagrant sighed. "Carl Hodges and he worked at the Lane Lumber Mill. You see, I never had a son and I wanted to show someone what we used to do. But your dad said you'd never be a skier. He said he'd tried to show you every summer, but you'd never let yourself believe, just like some don't let themselves believe that a plane can stay in the air."

Some of the strange things my dad had said while getting ready those early summer mornings came flowing back.

"The surface of that lake, Benny, is no different than the surface of life."

"Benny, to do anything, you must first believe you can do it."

Then I remembered even more of his words.

"Don't fight the surface, Benny. Move along it. Feel it. Always remember there is more than one surface."

My dad's voice echoed in my head as the vagrant said, "I think I'll be going now."

"Wait," I found myself saying.

The vagrant looked up at me and I could tell the hope and some of the life was gone from his eyes. I struggled for a question to ask. Anything. I didn't believe the water-skiing bit, but he obviously had known my dad. For some reason I wanted to hold on to that. Besides, he had found me.

"How did you know where I was?"

"That was easy. Your dad told me. It's not important, really. I was being foolish."

"I've only been here seven months. My dad has been dead for ten years. So I don't think that's exactly possible. Why don't you just tell me what you really came here for?"

The vagrant closed his eyes and sighed. "When you look out those windows, you see buildings and lights. Am I right?"

I nodded and motioned for him to go on.

"When I look out there I see a graveyard of souls. Oh, the people all still walk, talk, eat, and sleep. But a surprisingly large number of them are dead. People who haven't taken a chance or done something really new in years. And who never will. They are content to sit and watch life, without ever touching. They are dead souls whose bodies haven't stopped yet."

Again I motioned for him to go on, even though my anger was slowly returning.

"Twenty years ago your dad and I were both dead. Oh, we worked and we ate and we did all the things we were supposed to do. But, in reality, we weren't alive. Then one night, when you were still fairly young, your father came back from his vacation and started talking about that special morning run. He described it over and over and we began pretending on the really boring nights that we were skiing over the city, on the surface of the dead souls. We'd describe it to each other, the colors, the feelings, while one steered and the other skied."

The vagrant laughed and looked up at me. "And you know, one night we found that we really were skiing. We had found the surface of the dead souls and enough motion to stay on top of it."

"Motion?" I asked.

"The power we used wasn't an engine, but more our belief that we were alive and could see the surface and ski it without falling into it and being lost. After that we skied every night until your dad died."

I shook my head, finally having enough again. "Come on, you really don't expect me to buy all this shit?"

"Your father was right," the vagrant said. "At this moment you are as dead as most of the souls of this city. You are afraid to believe in anything beyond the shallow surface of your own reality. I was wrong to come, to think that you might be able to ski with me."

The vagrant stood, turned, and walked down the hall toward the elevators. I wanted to shout out for him to stop, but somehow I was frozen by his words until the elevator doors closed behind him.

Two

"THIS IS STUPID, you know?" Carla said. She carefully picked her way down the dew-slick path that led to the dock through the tall pine trees.

The morning air was crisp, almost too cold for a July day, even though the temperature would reach the eighties by noon. But it smelled wonderful. Clean and crisp, with that hint of pine filling up everything.

Carla wore her down ski parka, tight Levis and tennis shoes. Her long blonde hair was pulled back tight and it was the first time in the four months we had been going out that I had seen her without make-up.

"I warned you I wanted to do this every morning," I said. "And it won't take long, I promise."

Carla didn't answer. She reached and crossed the narrow beach, dropped the life jacket on the wooden dock and stood there shivering, hands jammed in her coat pockets, staring out over the smooth water.

The sun wasn't quite above the ridge of mountains and the lake was as glassy as any mirror. Clouds of mist hugged the blue-black surface and in the distance a bird broke the morning silence with a sharp, echoing call.

Everything was exactly as I had remembered it when Dad and I skied. Only this time I carried the ski and Carla did the bitching.

I jumped down into the boat, dropped the engine into the water and fired it up, just like Dad used to do. So powerful was the silence of the mountain morning that it dampened even the sound of the engine.

I made sure the yellow ski rope was hooked up right, then tossed the coil up on the dock and got out. "I'm going to jump start off the dock, so do exactly what you did yesterday afternoon. Okay?"

Carla nodded and got in the boat without a word.

She'd been all fun yesterday when the sun was hot and she could lie on the dock in her bikini. She had found it exciting to learn how to drive a boat. She even wanted to learn to ski because it looked like so much fun. But she hated it at this moment.

I remembered how she felt.

I unhooked the lines holding the boat and nudged it away from the dock. "Head down the lake and watch for my signals."

Carla nodded and kicked the boat quickly in and out of gear so that it drifted slowly away from the dock as I had taught her.

As Dad had taught me.

I pulled off my sweater and put on the life jacket, then dipped the ski in the water, laid it flat on the dock, and stepped into the cold shoe.

I'd been waiting for this moment since Edward Craig had disappeared into the elevator of the bar in February. I'd tried to find him in the lobby, but no one down there had seen him.

And for the past five months I had looked for him in records and in shelters and everywhere.

I found out very little.

The day my father died Edward had quit his job and simply disappeared. No one had seen or heard from him since.

I had no better luck.

I grabbed the slowly uncoiling ski rope, made sure the handles were untangled, and moved to the edge of the dock.

"Get ready!" I shouted to Carla. She sat up on the back of the driver's seat and nodded, her hand poised on the throttle.

I watched and waited as the drifting boat gradually pulled the rope closer and closer to the right amount of slack. The cool morning air gave me goose-bumps.

The fear that I wouldn't make the jump right twisted my stomach.

The anticipation of cutting back and forth across that smooth surface, scattering the morning mists with my body, doing what very few others had ever done, made me feel alive.

More alive than I had felt in years.

Was that what my dad and Edward Craig had meant?

The rope was at the right length.

It was time to start finding out.

It was time to really start living.

"Hit it!" I shouted, and stepped out on the smooth surface of the water.

Three

EDWARD CRAIG WAS waiting on the dock as Carla swung the boat in close enough for me to drop off.

I had pushed the run a little too long.

My arms ached, my legs were made of rubber, and my face stung from the cold wind.

But I was alive.

I had tried to memorize every detail of the run, every sensation, every thought.

By the time I motioned for Carla to turn around and head back up the lake toward the dock, I understood a lot more of what Dad and Edward Craig had been talking about.

But I was still surprised to see him standing there.

He was dressed exactly the same as he had been the night five months earlier. And he looked just as out of place on the dock at five in the morning as he did in the plush bar at two a.m.

He nodded to me as I sank slowly into the water beside the dock.

I pulled off the ski, stood on the sandy bottom, and handed the ski up to him. "You have this knack for finding me. How'd you know I was here?"

He laid the ski carefully on the dock and then smiled as I waded the last few yards to shore. He handed me a towel without a word and then we both watched as fifty yards off shore Carla finished winding in the rope and putting it on the back seat.

"Well?" I said.

His soft laugh seemed to carry up into the pine trees. "I hoped you might have heard some of what I said. This was the week your father always took his vacation. And this was the place he always skied. I took a chance you might come back here to try to discover for yourself. Nothing more. You ski very well, I might add."

"Thanks," I said. "It seems you hit it on the nose."

Again I felt angry at him. Who was he to spoil my perfect morning? Who was he to read me so easily?

Carla swung the boat in a little too fast toward the dock and it took both Edward and me to stop it from hitting hard. Carla looked Edward over with obvious distaste as she jumped out of the boat.

"Are we done?" she asked me.

I nodded.

"Good. I'm going back to bed. Excuse me."

She brushed past Edward and crossed the beach toward the path to the cabin.

"She doesn't ski, I take it," Edward said.

I laughed. "Not hardly."

"What does she do, then?"

I watched as she climbed the path and disappeared in among the trees. "She works for a dentist. Beyond that I'm not really sure."

Edward nodded, took the bow rope from its hook and expertly tied the boat to the dock.

Four

CARLA WAS FRIENDLIER after a few more hours sleep and after I told her that Edward was an eccentric millionaire who didn't talk about his money.

Edward spent the morning telling me of his times with my dad at the plant and in the bars. Not once did he mention skiing or the grave-yard of souls.

I cooked us a huge lunch of trout I had caught the night before, then Carla headed off to sun on the dock while Edward and I moved out to chairs in the shade of the pines.

It wasn't until we were both settled that I finally broke the silence about skiing. "So explain to me again exactly how you and my dad started skiing the graveyard of souls."

He laughed and went back over exactly what he had told me the first night in the bar. It had started with my dad coming back from vacation and explaining to Edward what it was like to really feel alive and had progressed to them skiing the surface of the dead souls of the people who inhabit the city.

"So did you actually leave the plant?"

Edward shook his head. "Not really. We would sit in the break room. We'd take short runs because while we were skiing our bodies would be frozen, like statues."

He laughed. "Got kind of embarrassing the few times someone walked in while we were skiing."

I shook my head in an effort to try to clear it. "You mean there was actually a physical effect involved?"

"Sure was," Edward said. "I suppose you were too young to remember the night your dad was sent home with what they thought was a gas poisoning?"

I vaguely remembered it. "Something about a leak that got into the lunch room and a few people were hurt."

Edward laughed. "We were skiing and old man Bridges came in and saw us. By the time we got back, they had your dad's body out on the floor giving him mouth to mouth and they were about to start on me, too. Gave your dad quite a start, let me tell you."

Edward's eyes glazed as he drifted back along the memory, smiling.

I gave him a moment, then asked my next question. "So what exactly did you ski on?"

Edward shrugged. "Just an old piece of pine your dad cut one night. Whichever one of us was skiing would put the board under our feet. Made us keep a mental picture of a ski and made the skiing seem easier."

I shook my head and looked around at the pine trees and the rough lake beyond, ruffled by a slight wind and a lot of boats crossing back and forth.

I couldn't believe all this. Here was a guy making a great case for the fact that my dad was an A-1 looney. And I was letting him, even helping him. It wasn't right for someone to make Dad sound so nutty.

"I have to be going, now," Edward said, and stood. "Got some things to do and I can see you need time to think about all this."

"Are you coming back?" I tried to keep my voice even and hold back the feeling of panic that was growing in my stomach. I wanted to be mad at this guy, not have him stick around. Yet I couldn't stand the thought of him going away for good like Dad had done.

"You planning on skiing tomorrow morning?"

I nodded.

"From the looks of it, you might need some help."

I glanced in the direction of the beach where Carla was sun bathing. "You're right about that. You want to drive the boat?"

Edward laughed. "I'd love to steer for you. But only if you'll promise me one thing. Tomorrow, while you're skiing, look down."

"Into the water?" I asked. "It's like a mirror."

"I know," he said, "Just look. I'll see you in the morning."

He turned and ambled past the cabin and toward the road.

Five

EDWARD WAS WAITING on the dock as I picked my way down the dew-wet path at shortly before five a.m. Carla was still tucked under

87

the blankets and had made it very clear she wanted no part of skiing before the sun came up.

Again this morning the lake was like a picture off a postcard, glassy smooth, with little wisps of clouds hovering along the surface. The air was crisp and cold and smelled of wet sand and pine.

Edward was dressed exactly as before.

"Morning," he said.

I nodded, laid the ski down, and looked out over the lake. "It's beautiful, isn't it?"

Edward sighed. "Yes, incredibly so."

We both stood for a moment gazing around at the pine-covered mountains reflected off the misty surface of the lake. Again this morning I could feel my heart pounding as I slowly came alive. The smell of the pines seemed sharper than any smell before.

The crisp taste of the air seemed more fresh than anything I had tasted.

The cold of the morning felt good against my face. I had never been alive all those years working in bars. I had experienced nothing sitting in front of my television. Was that what Dad and Edward Craig had meant? Part of me said it was. But I knew there was something more. Something I was missing.

I turned to Edward. "Would you like to go first?"

He laughed. "I'm afraid I never learned how to ski on water. But I can drive a boat. Are you ready?"

I nodded, pulled off my coat and put on the life jacket. Edward eased himself down into the boat, found the way to drop the engine in the water, and then tossed me the yellow rope.

I told him how to start the boat, then untied it from the dock and gave it a little shove. I was ready, with the ski on, poised at the end of the dock by the time he had the boat warmed up and in position.

He wore the biggest grin I had seen in years when I gave him the thumbs up sign and yelled, "Hit it!"

My jump off the dock onto the surface of the lake was smooth, even though my stomach clamped up in fear that I would go headfirst into the water.

I gave the boat time to get completely up to speed before I made my first cut to the right out onto the mirror-smooth water. Edward's smile never left his face as I cut back and forth, loosening up the tight muscles, letting the bite of the cold air and the spray numb my face.

It felt as if I was skiing over velvet, almost flying.

After a long minute, I finally let myself really look down into the water.

I had been thinking about what I might see since Edward had made me promise to look. And I had come up with no expectations. At this point I was willing to try to understand anything.

But there was nothing there.

No magic.

No sights.

Nothing.

Oh, I could see myself, blurred only slightly in the dark surface. And I could see the sky and the mountains above me.

But there was nothing else.

I held my position to the right of the boat and looked up at Edward.

He pointed down, indicating clearly that I should keep looking. So I went back to staring at myself in the reflection of the water as the surface slid past my ski too fast for me to focus on it.

Maybe it wasn't the surface Edward wanted me to see.

Maybe it was something down in the water.

I tried to stare beyond and behind my reflection, down into the black depths.

And as I did, blurred images formed.

I wanted to shout to Edward that I saw something, but I didn't.

Instead I kept staring as faint lights and dark shapes came into view. As I struggled to bring them into focus, buildings and streets and lights formed below me.

I was flying over them at a height far above the Penthouse Bar. Yet close enough to see the details.

Then, suddenly, there were colors. Rainbows of colors, in all shapes, flowing, merging into one another like the colors gasoline makes on water.

The lines of colors flowed in and around the buildings and over the streets, heavy and thick in some areas, light and airy in others.

Part of me wanted to discount what I was seeing, to look up at the boat and focus on the trees and the lake I knew.

But instead I let myself go, let myself ski back and forth and back and forth over the tops of the buildings, over the colors and the lights, staring down into the souls of the people.

And, as in the water, I again saw my reflection in the mirror-like surface of the dead souls. Only this time I knew it was a reflection of what I might have been had I let myself completely die.

My face was blank, my eyes empty and afraid.

The reflection cut at my breath, twisted my stomach. It was a reflection I had seen many times in the morning mirror over the last few years and it scared me.

I forced myself to look beyond it, deeper, until I found myself closer to the buildings and the streets, again skiing a new surface of souls, sleeping souls of people who were alive, people who enjoyed living and trying new and different things.

This time my reflection was smiling.

Behind and below the reflection I could see many surfaces left to ski and explore. Surfaces that I could only guess at what they were.

But for now I felt content to be alive, so I skied the rainbow colors until my arms began to ache and my legs felt weak and limp.

The end of the run was coming.

I desperately tried to memorize the feelings, the power of the run so that I could return. As the rope started to go slack and my speed dropped, I took a deep breath and looked up, following the line of the rope toward Edward.

I expected to see the boat, the lake, and the mountains beyond.

Instead, I saw the inside of the Penthouse Bar.

My dad was perched on a bar stool next to Edward and the wall of celebrity photographs was behind them. The yellow rope hung between us. They both held it.

And both were smiling the biggest damn grins I had ever seen.

I could feel my speed dropping. The rope between us almost touched the carpet.

"Nice run," Dad said. "Keep practicing. Keep searching."

Edward nodded in agreement.

The rope touched the floor and I sank into the cold water of the lake.

Six

THE BOAT WAS empty and idling in neutral.

I looked around, trying to figure out where I was. It looked as if I was about a mile down the lake from the cabin. I swam toward the boat, pushing the ski along the surface of the water in front of me.

"Edward," I called out, as I tossed the ski into the back of the boat and pulled myself over the side.

But the boat was empty, as I had half expected it would be.

The lake around me completely smooth, as if the boat had not crossed it, as if I had not skied it.

I stood in the back of the boat, feeling alive, gazing out over the mirror-like water and the reflections of the mountains and morning sky.

Dad had been right all those years ago. There was always more than one surface.

All I had to do was look for them.

I dropped into the driver's seat and turned the boat toward the cabin, letting it cut slowly through the mirror waters, just enjoying the moment and the memory of skiing over the city.

And enjoying the feeling of really being alive.

THE SONGS OF MEMORY

A Jukebox Story

I put this story in here because it is the start of the link between my jukebox stories and my Thunder Mountain series of books and stories with Bonnie and Duster Kendal. I haven't written the story yet with Bonnie and Duster and Stout, but I will.

In this story, as the owner of the Garden Lounge and the time-traveling jukebox, Stout faces a critical decision when the love of his life comes to visit him and the regulars of the Garden.

Many lives hang in the balance, including his and the future of the Garden Lounge. And only a trip through the jukebox might save everything.

One

I LOCKED THE front door of the Garden Lounge with a loud click and turned up the lights slightly so that it didn't feel like nighttime. Then I turned back to the six friends sitting on the bar stools, drinking and laughing, with their backs to me.

This was going to be very, very hard to tell them.

Outside, the July sun was beating down on the afternoon streets, sending the temperatures to almost a hundred. But inside the Garden, I kept the temperature at a cool seventy-two. But even with that, I was sweating and worried about what I was going to say.

The old jukebox that had changed so many things for all of us sat in the corner, dark as always, sort of tucked away behind a planter full of natural-looking fake plants. I seldom plugged the jukebox in and turned it on for anything but the special Christmas Eve gathering. The background music in the bar came from an old stereo system tucked under one end of the bar.

That old jukebox could take a person back through time to the memory associated with a song, and the last thing I wanted was to have customers playing songs that took them to memories that they changed and then not come back to be customers. I didn't have enough customers as it was.

But today I needed to turn it on one more time, just for me.

So as I walked toward the bar, I moved around the planter and plugged in the jukebox.

All six regulars turned as one, all stunned.

"Stout?" Big Carl said, frowning. "What are you doing?"

Carl was a giant of a man and as gentle as they come. He worked as a contractor and had skin as tanned and leathery as shoe leather. Of all my friends, he also worried the most about me.

Dave, my best friend, sat next to Carl on Carl's left. He was still in his airline pilot's uniform and he looked suddenly very worried. He had managed to get here by changing flight assignments this afternoon. It was the only time I had ever asked him to do something like that, so he already had a hint about how serious this was.

Sandy, his daughter, sat to the left of him. She was a private eye, one of the best in the city. Beside her, Fred stared at me as well, watching me like I was about to rip off the hotel for older men he ran down on the south side.

Next to Fred on that end was Billy, a rough-looking man with even a rougher past. Billy had moved into Fred's hotel about six months ago, and the two had become like a couple, always seen together and bickering half the time.

Closest to me and the jukebox on Big Carl's right was Richard Cone, a manager of a local factory and the only one of the group besides me who didn't drink. Richard also ran the bar when I couldn't make it or was out of town for some reason. He was the only help I had, and he only worked when I wasn't around.

My six closest friends.

All very different people.

And all but Richard had experienced the effects of the jukebox. Richard just kept declining to go back to a memory, stating his life had turned out just fine and he was happy with where he was. But he loved to watch others disappear back into their memories from a song and then come back with stories.

"So what's happening, Stout?" Richard asked, as I moved around behind the bar.

"Just a little announcement is all," I said. "But before I do it, I need to take a little ride back in time."

"Not to change anything I hope," Sandy said, clearly almost panicked.

I laughed. Sandy existed because Dave had gone back through the jukebox and saved his wife. Without the jukebox, Sandy would have never been born, and no way was I going to take a chance on changing that.

"Nope," I said. "Not changing a thing. I just need to go have a look at someone one more time. Then I'll tell you all what this is all about."

"Jenny?" Dave asked.

I nodded, took a quarter from the cash register, then passed out earplugs as I moved over to the very special Wurlitzer jukebox and dropped in the quarter.

"Stay focused on the bar while I'm gone," I said. "I don't want any of you jumping by accident."

They all nodded. They all knew the drill.

I didn't dare let myself hesitate. It had been ten years since I had taken this ride, ten years since I discovered the jukebox, and I didn't dare hesitate now or I would never do it. But I had to know for sure if my feelings for Jenny were still there before I made my final decision. And the only way to discover that was go be with her for a few minutes.

The length of the song.

I punched A-1, the place on the jukebox where the special song had sat since I found the jukebox.

"Have a good visit," Richard said.

All my friends looked very worried. The next two minutes were going to be a very long time for them, of that I had no doubt. I had done my share of waiting the length of a song while someone was gone, wondering if they would return.

Those two or two-plus minutes could be an eternity.

Behind me the jukebox clicked the 45 record into place. The first note of The Mindbenders song "A Groovy Kind of Love" started and the worried faces of my friends and the Garden Lounge vanished and I was facing Jenny across the hard, polished-Formica top of the table at the university student union.

Two

JENNY HAD BEEN the one true love of my life. She had long, brown hair, very straight, as was the normal fashion of the late 1960s. She wore jeans and a white blouse tucked in with a cloth belt.

We were sitting at our favorite table in the old university student union. She had just told me she was transferring to a university in Southern California and would have to leave in three weeks to get to a promised job and get settled before the semester started. It was the best school for her music degree, and was a great opportunity for her.

Now for the "us" that existed, the couple we had become and been for the last few years, not so good, and we both knew that.

The Mindbenders' song played softly over the student union sound system, which was why the jukebox brought me to this moment.

She had just looked at me and asked me what I wanted to do. And what I wanted her to do.

I had just stared at her and not said a word, and eventually in a day or so we decided she should go and take the job and get the degree and I would visit as often as I could from Eugene, Oregon. I just didn't want to leave the job I had at the moment. She had married someone else six months later.

Now I sat there in that student union once again, staring at her, my stomach twisting just as it had all those years before. My young-self and my old-self memories were all locked into the same brain.

When I was young, I hadn't been willing to give up a job to go with her, and I had lost her. Would I be able to give up the Garden Lounge and all my friends in Portland this time around?

That was the reason I had taken the trip through the jukebox, to try to get an answer for that question.

My young self loved Jenny more than anything. And it seemed my older self did as well. But not just the young girl sitting there, but the woman Jenny had become over all the years.

As I had done when I was young, I just sat there silently and stared at her. Then the short song ended and I was back, standing in front of the jukebox and the worried looks of my friends.

"You all right, Stout?" Dave asked.

I nodded, then unplugged the jukebox and went around behind the bar.

"Not really, huh?" big Carl said.

"Not really," I said as I refreshed everyone's drinks, then leaned back against the back bar with the orange juice on the rocks that I sipped during the summer.

The Garden was as silent as a tomb, so I moved over and turned the stereo back on for background noise. Music was so much of a person's life, it didn't feel right to not have some music playing while I talked with my friends.

I couldn't think of how to start into this, so as I moved back to my position leaning against the back bar facing my friends, I just decided to start from the beginning.

"You know computers can be dangerous things."

"I'll drink to that," Dave said. As an airline pilot, he had told us more horror stories about computers than I wanted to remember. Especially the next time I had to fly.

"About six months ago, I decided to see how Jenny was doing," I said. "So I looked her up on that Google-thing that Sandy showed me how to use when she installed that computer in my office."

Sandy laughed. "That computer was for bookkeeping, not surfing the web."

Billy just shook his head. "Stout surfing. Now I've seen it all."

"Hey," I said, laughing. "I used to surf when I was down in Florida for those jobs."

Billy snorted. "Yeah, thirty years and fifty pounds ago."

"Twenty-seven years and forty-three pounds," I said, laughing even harder. Amazing how good friends could make you feel better even when you were trying to tell them bad news.

Billy raised his glass in defeat.

"So you found Jenny," Sandy said, getting me back on my story. "What was she doing?"

"I actually didn't find her at first," I said, my stomach twisting. "I actually found an obituary for her husband. He died of cancer two years ago. She was mentioned as surviving him."

"Oh," was all Sandy said.

"I searched some more, and discovered she had an account on something called Facebook, so I joined up."

"The world has ended," Billy said.

"My hero is lost," Big Carl said.

Fred just shook his head, saying nothing, while Sandy looked proudly at me and Richard and Dave looked worried.

"So I contacted her and we've been in touch for six months now."

"No wonder you've been in such a good mood," Richard said.

I let them chatter about my mood for a second until Dave said, "Let him finish his story."

"Jenny has two grown kids and a couple of young grandkids. She's living just south of San Francisco and doing fine. Retired from teaching at the university there."

"Is she going to come up and visit?" Fred asked. "I could clean a room in the Golden Dream if she needs a place to stay."

Billy just smacked him on the side of the arm and everyone laughed.

"Thanks," I said. "She actually will be in tonight, and I've got her a room at the Comfort Suites down the street from here."

Now smiles lit up on everyone, and they all started talking at once about how they were looking forward to meeting her.

Finally, after the conversation eased, Dave looked at me and asked, "So, Stout, how come the trip through the jukebox?"

"I wanted to see if the feelings were still there just from the old memories, or if these new memories were building new feelings."

"Getting serious it seems," Richard said.

"Skype will do that for you," I said, smiling.

"The world really has ended," Fred said, shaking his head. "Our Stout is doing the nasty with a woman on the computer."

I just laughed. "Only talking. Honest."

Everyone but Richard laughed. "So what's the upshot of this, Stout?"

I took a deep breath and looked at Richard. "Remember when I had you run the bar for a week two months ago? I was down seeing Jenny and getting to know her family. And that went well, which is why she's coming up here this time. To see my life and meet all of you."

"And if this goes well?" Richard asked.

I smiled. Richard really, really knew me. He was one of the sharpest people I knew. And since he never took a drink, he often caught stuff others missed.

"We might get married," I said, smiling. "We've talked about it, but nothing firm yet. Waiting to see how this trip goes."

Everyone cheered and I quickly hushed them. "Jenny is looking forward to meeting you all, but not a word of that marriage stuff, all right? Promise?"

Six hands went up as one, promising.

"And if you decide to get hitched," Richard said, "you'll need to move down there with her. Right? She's the one with the grandkids and family."

Suddenly even the background music didn't help the dead feeling of the Garden. I made a note to hear the Beatles song playing on the radio to anchor this moment.

"Actually, we're planning on living both places," I said. "And doing some traveling. But it will be tough to own a bar and not be here six months of the year."

I glanced at all six of the sad faces on my friends. The Garden was as much of a home to them as it was to me. Just like I couldn't imagine shutting this bar down, they couldn't imagine being without it and all the friendships. And that's what they were all thinking at that moment.

No one said a word, so I went on with my plan.

I moved down in front of Richard. "Mr. Richard Cone, sir," I said, acting very formal. "I know you have a great job managing that plant, but I also know you have always wanted to own your own bar."

Richard's head snapped up and he looked me square in the eyes.

A Beach Boys song called "Good Vibrations" was now playing.

"If this works out between me and Jenny, which I have a hunch it's going to, would you be interested in buying the Garden Lounge and running it in any manner you see fit?"

I watched him swallow hard, his eyes slightly misty.

Except for the background song, the bar was dead silent.

Dave leaned over and touched Richard on the shoulder. "I'll back you if you need the help."

"Yeah, me too," Sandy said.

"Count me in," Carl said. "I got some extra if you need it."

"Me too," Fred said.

"Not me," Billy said. "I barely got enough to drink and eat and pay my rent to Fred here. But I'll buy drinks if you'll serve me."

Everyone laughed then, including Richard. Then Richard turned to them. "Thanks. But with my job and low expenses, I've been saving for something like this for a very, very long time."

He turned back to me and extended his hand. "Mr. Radley Stout, if things work out with your new girl, you've got a buyer — as long as that damned jukebox stays with the bar. We can't be changing traditions now, can we?"

We shook hands as everyone cheered, and it felt as if a huge weight had just lifted off my shoulders.

Three

JENNY FIT IN perfectly with the regulars at the Garden. She and Dave and Richard hit it off perfectly, and after just a few evenings, she told me she felt like she had always been sitting at the bar joking with everyone.

And at one point or another every one of my friends told me in private that if I lost this woman, I was dumber than a post.

I had to agree with them, even though Jenny sure didn't look much like the thin, long-haired girl I had fallen in love with all those decades ago. Just as I had done, she had filled out, and now her once-brown hair was short and silver. And she tended to wear dresses more than jeans. And she wore glasses, those thin kind that professors wore.

She actually had been a professor for over twenty-five years, teaching music theory and history before she retired to care for her husband in his last year.

Her husband had been a building contractor, so she and Big Carl seemed to sometimes talk another language that most of us just didn't understand.

After four days, it was clear she and I were going to be together for a lot longer if I could just get past one more hurdle.

Dave reminded me that I needed to tell her about the jukebox.

I had to agree with him. It was important that a future partner would know that I owned — and was about to sell — a time machine.

So once again I passed the word to my closest friends to come in early in the afternoon to help me out in case I needed it. And I asked

99

Jenny to come with me to open the bar. I said I had something I needed to show her.

"This sounds serious," she said, looking at me with those wonderful brown eyes of hers. Those eyes hadn't changed at all, and her ability to really see me hadn't changed either.

"It is," I said. "And I hope nothing serious. Just something you need to know about."

The night before we had talked about me selling the bar to Richard and how happy I was about that.

And sad at the same time.

She double- and triple-checked that I was telling her the truth. After the last few days, she could see just how special the Garden Lounge was to me, and how hard it was going to be for me to let it go.

I told her I didn't plan on leaving the Garden forever. We would be regulars when we were in town. And I told her that every Christmas Eve we had to be there, no matter what. We could fly back to her kids for Christmas Day, since Oregon and California were only a few-hour flight apart.

I told her she would understand why after I showed her what I had to show her at the bar.

Christmas Eve at the Garden Lounge was a special time for all the regulars. It was the only time I ever turned on the jukebox and let customers go back to their memories. Richard had told me that even though he had never gone through the jukebox, he planned on honoring that tradition, and hoped I would be back every year to run the party.

So as I finished getting the bar opened, everyone sort of showed up at once, laughing with Jenny. All of them knew what this was all about, and they were all determined to help if they could.

So with Jenny sitting between Dave and Richard at the bar, I stood against the back of the bar and had no idea where to start. I just sort of stood there as everyone looked at me. I hadn't bothered to turn on the stereo yet, so the weight of the silence made starting even harder.

"Tell her about the glasses first," Dave said, pointing at the case over the bar.

I looked into the eyes of the woman I loved and then said simply. "You are not going to believe most of what I'm about to say, but for now just trust me. Okay?"

She frowned, clearly suddenly worried.

"Trust him," Dave said. "He's not totally nuts, only slightly."

Everyone laughed and I took the key for the cabinet out of the register drawer and went to get the four glasses.

I took three down and left the other in the case.

Then I walked the fine drinking glasses down the bar, putting the one etched with the name Dave in front of Dave, another in front of Carl, and another in front of Fred.

"I made these glasses for these men ten years ago this last Christmas. I served them drinks in these glasses, and none of them remembers that night. Except Dave, who came back after I closed the bar. Long story, but what this is all about."

"If you are trying to explain something," Jenny said, "remind me to never let you in a classroom."

"Now that's a deal, Professor," I said.

I pointed at the old jukebox, dark and sitting in the corner. "You understand the power of music. Music can take a person back to a memory, to an emotion, to an experience."

Jenny nodded. "There have been many studies on the power of songs to trigger memories to try to help some patients with different forms of brain injury and diseases."

Everyone was deadly silent, which wasn't a normal state for the Garden Lounge, so I just blurted it out. "That jukebox actually takes a person *physically* to a memory associated with a song."

Jenny looked at me frowning. Then she smiled. "Okay, what's the joke?"

"Toss me a quarter, Stout," Dave said, climbing off his stool. "She's not going to believe you; no one does, until they see it. I'll go visit Sandy being born again."

I tossed him a quarter and moved around the end of the bar and plugged in the jukebox.

"Give us a minute to get earplugs in," I said.

I quickly dug out the earplugs and handed each person a pair. When I handed the pair to Jenny, I smiled. "You said you trusted me. Just hold on for one more moment and you'll understand what I'm talking about."

She was really frowning now, but she did as everyone did and put in the earplugs.

"Ready," Dave asked, smiling.

I nodded, and he dropped the quarter into the machine and after a moment hit the number to the song that would take him back to the moment when Sandy was born.

I looked into the eyes of the woman I loved. "Cover your ears," I shouted so she would hear. "And think of this moment right here and right now. Think of this bar. Okay?"

She nodded, and then the music started and Dave was gone and we were all still here.

"How?" Jenny said, but I could barely hear her through my earplugs.

I just held up my finger for her to wait and pointed toward the juke-box. Then I put my hand on hers, holding her solidly in the Garden Lounge.

The two minutes of the song stretched into an eternity.

Then, faintly, I could hear the song ending and Dave shimmered back into being, smiling.

We all pulled out our earplugs and Dave rejoined us at the bar. "You know," he said to his daughter, Sandy, "you sure were a damn pretty baby."

"You all right?" Sandy asked, just before I did.

Seeing his wife again had to hurt some. She had died a couple years back from cancer and we all missed her.

"I'm fine," he said, taking a drink.

"So what the hell just happened here?" Jenny said. "What kind of magic trick was that?"

"No trick I'm afraid," I said, pointing at the jukebox. "That thing really takes people back to their memories. You end up inside the body of the person you were, only with old memories. When the song ends, you come back — unless you have changed something."

Dave held up his glass. "One Christmas, ten years ago, Stout gave four of his best friends a very special Christmas gift. He let us go back and change something in our pasts we wanted to change. I went back and saved my wife from being killed in a car wreck; as a result, Sandy, here, and her sister were born."

"That's why we only turn that thing on for Christmas Eve," I said. "And why we're very careful. It's very dangerous and can change a person's life."

I stared at Jenny for a moment, then said, "You still don't believe us, do you?"

She looked me square in the eye and I could tell she was angry. A deep-down angry.

I wanted to throw up. This couldn't be happening.

"You have to admit this is hard to swallow," Jenny said. "And I don't see why you would play this sort of trick on me, Stout."

The silence in the bar could be cut with a knife, I swear. I could hardly breathe. Was I going to lose the only woman I had ever loved for the second time because of the jukebox?

"No trick," I said, softly. "That really is a time machine."

Again the silence became thick and smothering. I had to do something and do it quickly.

"Do you remember the song that was playing right after you told me about your job while we sat in the student union in Eugene?"

She nodded. "Longest song ever," she said. "I was waiting for you to say something and you didn't say anything."

"Do you remember the name of the song?"

"It was a Mindbenders song about love. Why?"

I took a quarter out of the cash register and went around the bar to her side. I took her hand to indicate she should get down off the barstool. "Let's go for a ride."

She walked hesitantly to the jukebox. "Earplugs everyone," I said.

Then I turned to the woman I love. "You can't change anything while we are there. Nothing. Our older selves will be in control of our younger bodies, and our younger selves won't remember our little visit. But change *nothing*, all right? Please. A lot of lives depend on it, including your wonderful children and grandchildren."

She glanced around at the people at the bar, then nodded, suddenly very afraid.

I dropped the quarter into the jukebox and once again punched A-1.

A moment later I was sitting again across from the young Jenny.

Only this time Jenny's eyes didn't stay focused on the table in front of her as they had done the first time. They looked up at me, panicked.

The older Judy was in there this time.

Then she looked around, listening to the song over the sound system of the old student union, smelling the greasy fries and smell from the two jocks sitting far too close to us.

Finally she looked back at me. "Is this real?"

I nodded. "Can you remember your life with Stephen? Your kids being born? Your grandkids?"

She nodded, still looking around. "How is this possible?"

"There's some kind of very advanced equipment in the jukebox I've never had the courage to touch. Somehow it lets the power of a memory from a song take the person listening to the memory."

"And our young selves won't remember this?"

"Do you?"

She thought for a second, then shook her head.

"This was our turning point the first time, wasn't it?" she asked

"It was," I said.

"If you had said you wanted to marry me, I would have stayed."

"But sometimes things work out the way they are supposed to," I said. "We weren't ready that first time around."

She nodded. "I would have been angry at you for making me stay."

"I know," I said. "And I would have been angry for you making me leave."

"You've sat here before from the future, watching me, haven't you?"

I nodded. "A number of times. It's how I discovered the power of the jukebox."

"And you never said anything? Never changed our future? Why not?"

"I loved you too much," I said. "And then, after a while, I knew if I changed my future, a number of people wouldn't be alive right now. And that was before I knew about your wonderful family."

The song was slowly nearing its end.

"You are a very special man," she said, smiling.

"Then will you stay with me this time? In the future, of course."

"I want to more than anything. In the future, of course."

I smiled. "Would you marry me the second time around?"

She looked around at the old student union and laughed as the song finished and we appeared back in the Garden.

She put her arms around me and said, "Yes, you stupid fool. Of course I'll marry you."

Then she kissed me in a way I knew I would never forget, song or no song.

And our friends in the Garden Lounge cheered.

This time, it was *my* life the jukebox saved.

CUCUMBER PARTY

A Buckey the Space Pirate story

At science fiction conventions, lots of very, very strange things happen. And considering that over the years, I've gone to hundreds and hundreds of conventions, I have my share of stories I would be glad to tell over a drink some evening.

Buckey the Space Pirate started life in a story called "The Sexual Voyage of the Starship Shirley" which ended up in OUI Magazine. That story was about an event at a science fiction convention, just as this story.

However, I want to be clear. I have never been on the Starship Shirley or been to a Cucumber Party. That's my story and I'm sticking to it.

I WAS DRESSED in my Buckey the Space Pirate costume sitting in the hallway with about twenty other people in costumes, my back against the wall in front of room 1212, when she handed me the cucumber.

"Pass it on," she said in a husky whisper.

Then she winked at me. She had the edge of her eyes taped back and black cotton glued to her eyelids in typical alien-cat fashion. The wink made her look as if she was closing her eyes from a bad migraine.

"Hell, thanks a lot," I said.

"Hopefully, it will be myyyyyyyyyyyyyyyyyy pleasure."

She tried to make the "my" sound like a purr, but it came out more like she was gargling.

Then, with one more migraine wink, she headed off down the hall with her tail with a big black fur ball on the end whacking people who sat along the walls.

"I can't believe it," my best friend Alex said. "You've been invited to a cucumber party."

I held the warm green cucumber up in front of me and studied it. I wasn't sure if I wanted to know where it had been or how it had gotten so warm.

"It is kind of hard to believe, isn't it?"

I'd heard of cucumber parties before. Hell, who hadn't? They were the latest "in" things at science fiction conventions.

The first time I'd heard of one had been two conventions ago at Biggerthanlife Con.

And at Biggerthanyours Con last week, there had been rumors that people were actually thrown out of the hotel for participating in one.

I stared at the cucumber in my hand. Now I was invited. Me, Buckey, a simple space pirate, at a cucumber party.

The very idea of it made my stomach churn and my mouth water from excitement.

And it was only Friday night. The convention was just getting going. This was going to be one damn good convention.

"Can I go with you?" Alex asked and reached to fondle the cucumber.

"Look, Alex. I don't—"

"It's Hoover," Alex said, demanding he be called by his costume character name. "And I don't see why I can't go."

I looked at the cucumber and then at Alex. He looked damn stupid in his Hoover, the Jovian Fur Merchant costume. He'd tacked two of his mother's old fur coats together and it smelled of mothballs something awful. No girl in her right mind would get within ten feet of him, let alone join him in a cucumber party.

But what the hell. This was a science fiction convention. Stranger things had happened. He just might get lucky.

"All right," I said. "You can come along."

Alex brightened right up and smiled a I'm-better-than-you smile at the guy dressed like Darth Vader sitting across the hall from him.

The guy just breathed a little louder.

"You got any idea how we can find the party?" I asked.

I twisted the cucumber in my hands. "There doesn't seem to be a room number here anywhere."

Alex's smile dropped into a frown as he thought about trying to find the party. In a hotel that had over fifteen hundred rooms, if you didn't know exactly where the party was, which wing, which floor, the only thing you were going to get was sore feet.

Alex shrugged, so I held the cucumber up for the other dozen people sitting along the hall to see. "Anybody know where the cucumbers are meeting tonight?"

All the people in the hall shook their heads and looked envious, except a young girl dressed as a flat-chested elf in green tights. "There's usually a map on the cucumber," she said. "At least that's how I found it last night."

All the envious faces immediately turned toward her like they were all on the same string.

I looked at her a little closer. She looked tired. For some reason, I took that to be a good sign.

Alex took the cucumber from my hand and studied it. "It doesn't seem to be a map of the hotel," he said.

"Of course not," the tit-less elf said and looked disgusted. "If you can't figure it out, then you don't belong at the party."

I took the cucumber back from Alex and held it up so I could see it better in the hall light. Its skin looked more like the back of a frog. Sure enough, there etched in very fine lines was a map. Or what someone might call a map. It didn't look so much like a map as a spider web made by a half-drunk spider.

Definitely not a map of the hotel.

Great. Just great.

"Come on, Alex," I said and stood. "I know where it's at."

I set off down the hall in the direction of the elevators, letting Alex scramble after me. I really didn't know where I was going, but I sure didn't want to sit there and admit it to that no-tit elf and the heavy-breathing Vader.

We took the cucumber back to my room and took turns trying to figure out what the map meant.

After an hour, I had a headache and no real good ideas.

Alex figured the entire map was a code for a room number in some alien language. Maybe Martian sanskrit or Antarian stone drawing.

Fat lot of good that was going to do us, but Alex figured it was either room 816, 927, or 1419. He wouldn't tell me how he came up with those numbers and I couldn't come up with any at all, even holding the map up to the mirror.

I figured if he was wrong, we could always just walk the halls until we saw someone else with a cucumber.

Room 816 did end up having a party going on in it. A two-person party in which the man, dressed like a Doc Smith Lensman, Lens and all, didn't like being disturbed.

No one was home in 927.

At room 1419, Alex knocked. "This is the place," he said. "I'm sure of it."

I just shrugged. If it wasn't, I was going to need to go to the convention suite to get a Diet Coke and some cookies. No wonder the no-tit elf looked tired. She couldn't find the party either.

A woman with only a towel wrapped around her answered the door. She had green eyes, light blonde hair, and toenails painted bright orange. I was in love at first sight.

I pushed Alex aside, took off my white-plumed hat and bowed slightly. "Excuse us. We seem to be having some—"

"Midge," the girl said, shouting back into the room. "They're here."

"Well, let them in," a voice said from deep in the room.

The girl stepped back and let the door swing completely open.

Alex nudged me. "I told you," he whispered, and pushed past me into the room, leaving a smelly trail of mothballs.

"Oh, God," Alex said as he got past the bathroom door and entered the main part of the room.

Orange Toenails motioned for me to come in, then closed the door behind me and let her towel drop to the floor.

I don't think I've ever had my mouth go so dry so suddenly as it did at that moment. I felt like the planet Dune had been transported to the top of my tongue.

Orange Toenails had a great body. Medium sized boobs with huge brown nipples, light colored pubic hair, and a small butterfly tattoo on the inside of her right thigh.

I must have kept walking as I stared at Orange Toenails, because I bumped into Alex who had stopped just inside the room.

"Oh God," he said, again.

I glanced around to see what he was oh-Goding, even though I didn't want to stop staring at the beautiful body of Orange Toenails and that butterfly tattoo in a place I so wanted to explore.

On the closest of the room's two beds was a long-haired woman without a stitch of clothes on. She had her legs slightly apart and I could see just a hint of Never-Never Land no one was going to have to fly to get to.

"Oh God," I think I said.

Or Alex said it. I wasn't really sure at that point.

All I know is that my Buckey the Space Pirate costume was suddenly very tight in the crotch.

Buckey Junior wanted out real bad.

"You're still dressed," the woman on the bed said softly to Alex and me.

Somehow I closed my mouth.

Swallowing was out of the question.

Orange Toenails reached for my belt and started pulling me toward the empty bed. "I'm so honored," she said. "I've never made it with a famous writer."

I started unbuttoning my shirt as she worked on my pants.

Out of the corner of my eye I could see that Alex already had his mother's fur coats off and was climbing on the bed.

"I've read all your books," Orange Toenails said.

She helped me out of my pants.

Buckey Junior saluted her.

Right about then I certainly didn't want to ask her just what the hell she was talking about. Hell, I hadn't written any books. I could barely write a term paper when I was in school.

But if this was the reception a writer got at these conventions, I was sure willing to learn.

She had my pants off and pulled me down on the bed with her. "Just let me do all the work," she said, kissing her way past my neck and heading down my chest.

I think Buckey Junior waved hello as she got closer.

"My pleasure," I think I managed to choke out.

On the other bed Alex was saying "Oh God."

Over and over again as the long-haired woman rode his mid section like she was riding a bull in a rodeo.

I hoped for Alex's sake she didn't have spurs.

Miss Orange Toenails swung her leg up over my chest and took Buckey Junior in her mouth at the very same moment she sat down on my face.

She tasted of a cross between hotel soap and Oolong tea.

I loved it.

I might become a tea fan after this.

She ran Buckey Junior in and out of her mouth with vacuum pump skill while at the same time moving her hips on my nose in a slight circular fashion.

I tried to concentrate on letting my tongue explore the strange new world and kept thinking about going for a five-year mission, but with the excitement of the moment, Buckey Junior just couldn't hold on.

She worked at draining him dry, not letting one drop escape while I managed to find a world I had never explored with my tongue.

Then she turned suddenly around and cuddled against my chest, pressing her boobs against my side and pressing her crotch into my leg.

"That was really nice," she said.

"Yeah," I said, trying to stop the light fixture on the room from spinning. "That it was."

On the other bed, Alex let out one last "OH GOD" that they must have heard two floors up, the long-haired women threw her head back, and from my viewpoint, they crossed the line in a photo finish.

"Would you sign one of your books for me?" Orange Toenails said, looking up at me and fluttering her big green eyes.

"I'd love to," I said, "but—"

"Oh, nifty-keen," she said.

Nifty-keen? Who said that?

She jumped from the bed, grabbed a stack of books off the dresser, and set them down beside me on the bed.

Then she sat down cross-legged on the bed facing me. I could see all of the strange new world my nose and tongue had just explored.

Buckey Junior twitched enviously at the sight.

I forced myself to look down at the pile of books.

The top one was "The Edge of Planet Ten" by Aaron Frost, Jr.

Oh, no, she thought I was Aaron Frost. That's why the reception. Alex had been wrong. This wasn't the cucumber party. Now what the hell were we going to do?

I flipped the book over. On the back jacket was a picture of Aaron Frost.

I had to admit, he did look a little like me. Only a bunch older.

What happened if he suddenly knocked at the door? Obviously he had been expected. That meant he was still on the way. The best thing Alex and I could do was hit the road quick.

"Look," I said, clearing my throat. "Since you both have been so nice to me, I've got a very special limited edition of this very book in my room."

I tapped the top book.

"You do?" Alex asked. He didn't understand what had happened, so I tried to give him the sign to be quiet.

"I do," I said. "And after this wonderful reception, I would love for both of you to have a copy, personally autographed by me. We'll just run and get those and be right back."

"You'd do that for us?" she asked, looking almost in tears.

"After this wonderful encounter, which I shall always remember, it's the least I can do. Then I can sign all of these and maybe we can have a rematch. All right?"

That sounded so weak, I couldn't believe she'd fall for it.

"Ohhhh…. That would be great," Orange Toenails said.

She bought it. I couldn't believe it.

"Why don't I just stay right here?" Alex said.

"No," I said. "I need you with me. To help me find the books. We'll be right back, ladies." I jumped off the bed, grabbed Alex's clothes, tossed them at him, then started putting mine back on. All the time I kept expecting to hear a knock at the door and it would be the real Aaron Frost with BIG friends.

I would be dead for messing with his date for the night. I had this clear image in my mind of me being stoned by Aaron Frost fans with his books as I ran naked down the hall.

"You promise you'll come back?" Orange Toenails asked.

I looked at where she was sitting cross-legged on the bed with all her charms exposed. "Of course," I lied.

Buckey Junior wanted me to take the chance and just stay for a second round. But somehow, I got my pants back on, Buckey Junior tucked safely away, and Alex out the door.

"What the hell was that all about?" Alex asked as I halfway pushed him down the hall toward the elevators.

"Wrong party," I said.

"You mean that wasn't a cucumber party?"

"Nope," I said. "They thought I was Aaron Frost."

"The Aaron Frost?" Alex asked, then shook his head. "No wonder. The lady I was with said she had a story she wanted me to give to you to read. Lucky I didn't ask her why like I was going to."

In the elevator, I punched the floor number for the bar. Damn, I needed a drink.

Two floors down, two large-chested women dressed in harem girl costumes got on. Both looked really, really nice.

Alex had grabbed the cucumber on the way out the door, so I handed it to the shortest of the two just before the bar floor.

"Room 410," I said, giving her the number of my room. "Midnight. Just the two of you."

She looked startled, then happy. "Thanks," she said and waved as I pulled Alex off the elevator before he could ask me what I was doing and spoil everything.

We'd be waiting for them with our own special cucumber party. And if this worked, I'd bring my own cucumbers to the next convention.

Maybe a dozen of them.

Maps and all.

DRIED UP

A Poker Boy Story

Asked in the middle of the night to help the dangerous race called Silicon Suckers,
Poker Boy faces a challenge like none other.
He and Front Desk Girl risk their lives to help the alien-looking creatures, but
then come face-to-face with what their bargain just might mean in the future.

One

I VERY SELDOM get the feeling that something is wrong while sleeping beside Patty Ledgerwood, aka Front Desk Girl. In fact, until that very moment, it had never happened. Nothing ever seemed to be wrong when I was with Patty and not on a mission.

I get the "something-is-wrong" feeling at poker tables all the time, usually when another professional player is attempting to bluff me out of my shoes and all my money. I have learned to pay attention to that feeling, almost as if it is one of my superpowers. By paying attention, I have saved myself a ton of money over the years.

Right now I was in Patty's apartment near the University of Nevada, Las Vegas campus. In her master bedroom, to be exact. I could hear her regular breathing beside me, which told me she was sound asleep. The wonderful smell of her rose perfume filled the air and the feel of her expensive, fine-cotton sheets against my mostly bare skin felt wonderful, just as they always did.

Patty had had the day off, and we had spent it together; first at a movie, then a nice dinner at the buffet at the MGM Grand, and then back to her apartment to cuddle on the couch and watch television before heading to bed.

It didn't get much better these days.

But now, even without opening my eyes, I knew something was wrong.

I eased one eye open without moving, and couldn't see a thing in the dark room. The only light came from a nightlight in the bathroom to the right of the room and an alarm clock on the nightstand beside me. There was no light coming under the heavy curtains over the patio door, so it was still dark outside as well.

I eased over to glance at the time, and a lightning storm went off in the sheets.

And that wasn't a metaphor for some sexual thing.

A real lightning storm erupted around me, as more static electricity than I could imagine let loose.

And each spark was like a kid pinching me. Let me tell you, the sparks hurt.

"Wow!" I said out loud as I sat up.

It was as if I had rubbed my entire body across a carpet and then was touching things.

My movement caused the sheets to explode with even more static electricity which woke Patty up, and she sat bolt upright in bed as well, causing even *more* sparks as she sat stunned at the light show going on around us.

And the tiny pinches of pain with every large spark.

Somehow, every bit of moisture had been sucked out of the room, and a very large, background, static electric charge had filled the air.

"Sit still," I said, as Patty moved slightly and the room lit up with a light show once again.

"Ouch!" Patty said, freezing in place. "That hurts."

I had heard of many reasons for friction in bed, but this was ridiculous.

But in the light caused by the sparks with Patty's last movement, I had seen the problem.

Two alien-looking creatures with large black eyes and oblong heads stood at the end of the bed, staring at us.

It was like a scene out of a bad alien-abduction movie.

The UFO conspiracy people called them "Grays," but I knew them to be members of a race native to Earth called the Silicon Suckers.

In fact, they had been around far, far longer than humans.

They hate water and could deal with very little if any of it. Clearly they took what water they needed right out of the air around them.

They lived in very dry caves in the desert. The caves were so dry, the air would kill a human after just a couple of days, even with enough drinking water, which wasn't allowed in the homes of the Silicon Suckers.

Their very presence in Patty's apartment had sucked all the moisture out of the room.

I had never heard of a Silicon Sucker being seen inside a human city. Something had to be very, very wrong.

I carefully motioned for Patty to look at the foot of the bed. The sparks from my slight movement bit into me again and lit up the room.

She saw them and her breath sucked in with surprise. She instinctively pulled the sheet up to her neck covering up her nightgown and causing a large electrical storm around her and me.

Damn those little sparks hurt. It was lucky we just didn't burst into flames right there.

"Sorry," she said, holding her breath against the pain.

I had dealt with the Silicon Suckers a number of times before, and been in their sacred caves they called "sand castles." I had always been welcomed in their world because of a couple of favors I had done for them over the last few years.

"Greetings, honored guests," I said, bowing my head slightly and hoping the movement wouldn't set the sheets on fire. "What do I owe this great honor?"

Both Silicon Suckers bowed in return. Both looked identical. The one on the right spoke.

"Poker Boy, Front Desk Girl, we ask for your assistance in a matter of importance to our people."

"Of course," I said.

Both Patty and I bowed slightly.

After the sparks stopped I said, "It will be a great honor to help our friends."

Both again bowed in acceptance. "Our leader will speak to you at sunrise."

"We will attend," I said, also bowing again and setting off even more sparks. This room was going to need a humidifier real quick or we would be calling for fire trucks.

Without another word, the two turned and went out through curtains covering the bedroom's patio door, setting off a huge wave of sparks. I knew for a fact that the door had been locked and secured when we had gone to bed.

I had no idea how they had gotten in, or how they would get from Patty's apartment near UNLV, across town, actually across the Strip, and back into the desert.

The moment the curtains dropped back into place in a shower of static electricity, I instantly transported us into the living room area of Patty's apartment. The air there felt dry, but nothing like the intense lack of moisture in the bedroom.

I loved my newly learned superpower of teleportation. I just never expected to use it teleporting out of Patty's bed.

Patty used a napkin to flip on a light, took one look at me and started to laugh.

Now trust me, a beautiful woman in a sheer blue nightgown laughing when she sees your almost-naked body does not do wonders for even my superhero ego.

But I had to admit she looked just as funny. Besides all the tiny red marks all over her arms and wonderful legs that showed under her nightgown, her long brown hair stuck out in all directions from her head like she had been attacked by a mad hairdresser. Her hair was spread so wide, I doubt she could even get through a door.

And her wonderful face looked like it had a bad case of measles.

I glanced down at my own legs and chest, also covered with hundreds and hundreds of small red marks, as if I had been attacked by a swarm of bed bugs.

Then I felt my brown hair, which was also standing straight out in all directions. And I could also feel my face was covered in the tiny red bumps from the electrical shocks.

Thank heavens I had worn my boxers to bed. The thought of electronic shocks to certain parts of my body just made me shudder.

Two

AFTER WE CAREFULLY opened the windows and doors to let in some of what now seemed like balmy and humid Las Vegas summer air, we both drank three large glasses of water.

Thirsty didn't begin to describe what I was feeling.

Then, when we both had extra-large glasses of water in our hands, I shouted at the ceiling. "Stan. Need help!"

I have no idea how he always heard me, but he always did. Stan was the God of Poker, and my immediate boss.

An instant later he appeared in Patty's living room in front of us, looking grumpy that I had disturbed him in the middle of the night. He normally wore brown slacks, a light sweater, and black shoes. He was a short man, not even close to my six-foot height, and I seldom saw him smile. His dark hair was cut very short all the time, and his eyes looked almost black.

But tonight he had on a white golf shirt and blue golf shorts and the shorts looked like they were on backwards. When the God of Poker can't even dress himself, he really was tired.

He started to say something, then took one look at us and started laughing. I had seen him laugh a few times, but when a god starts to laugh at you, it is always worrisome.

But I had to admit that we did look funny. There was no containing our hair and the red marks on our faces, arms, and legs were getting brighter by the second.

"You two go through a swarm of bees on a rollercoaster?"

"Nope," I said as he laughed. "Just an electrical storm in bed."

He started to make some joke, then looked at Patty, then back at me and couldn't say anything because he was laughing too hard.

"I'm not kidding," I said. "Two Silicon Suckers woke us up and asked for our help."

Stan's laughing instantly vanished and he went back to his normal poker face. His golf shirt and golf shorts instantly became his normal slacks and sweater and black shoes.

It seemed I now had his attention and he was very much awake.

"How in the world did they get here?" he asked, shaking his head. "And when are you supposed to meet them?"

"We are meeting their leader at sunrise."

"You are meeting the Great One?"

Now he was stunned and when he said it like that, it bothered me as well. Patty just looked worried under all the red marks and massive head of hair spread out three feet around her head. It was going to take her some real time once the static charge faded to untangle all that wonderful long hair.

"You ever heard of the Silicon Suckers coming into any human town?" I asked Stan. "Just to ask for human help?"

"Never," he said, shaking his head.

"Have you heard any rumors about anything going wrong in their caves? Or anyone having a run-in with them?"

"Nothing," he said, "but I might have missed something. Stay put, I'm going to go get Burt and maybe Laverne."

He vanished.

Laverne was Lady Luck herself, in charge of all of the gambling and gaming universe. Burt was her second in command. I'd been around Lady Luck a number of times now, and Patty and I and the team had actually saved her life once. But she still scared hell out of me.

If Stan thought this was worth waking up Burt and maybe even Laverne, then Patty and I really might be in over our heads. We were just lowly superheroes.

Really dry and marked-up superheroes.

I had just taken another drink of water and was about to suggest we get a little more dressed when Laverne and Stan appeared. Lady Luck had on a strict brown business suit with her brown hair pulled back tight in a bun. She did not look happy.

When she saw us she raised one eyebrow, but did not smile, even though we looked really, really silly. With a wave of her hand Patty and I were both dressed, the static gone from our hair and the red marks gone from our skin.

Patty in her normal black pants and white blouse. Laverne had put me in my normal jeans with dress shirt, black leather coat and Fedora-like black hat. That was my poker uniform.

"Thank you," Patty said.

I nodded agreement. "Yes, thank you. I feel much better."

I could also feel the extra power that my coat and hat brought to me from the nearby casinos.

"No idea at all what the Silicon Suckers want?" Lady Luck asked, all business.

"Not a clue," I said. "Has something like this ever happened before?"

"Never," she said. "I have only met The Great One once, a few thousand years ago. But I do know that he only concerns himself with matters of major importance."

"I wonder why he came to us instead of you?" Patty asked. "It makes no sense."

"He didn't want to bother you," I said to Lady Luck, knowing the answer to Patty's question. "This is something he feels Patty and I can accomplish."

Both Laverne and Stan nodded.

"That makes sense," Laverne said. "But it gets us no closer to what he might want. And we just don't have time to figure it out. You had better get going."

"We have one stop to make first," I said.

I turned to my direct boss. "Stan, could you get me six thermoses and two backpacks to carry them in, and meet me at The Diner?"

Stan nodded and vanished.

"Good luck," Laverne said. "If you need my help in any fashion, just call out. I will be standing by."

"Thank you," Patty said as Laverne vanished.

I glanced at Patty, who looked stunning, as always, in the dark slacks and white blouse that Laverne had dressed her in. Her brown hair was combed and under control. Only the worry showing in her dark-brown eyes flawed the picture.

"Ready for an adventure?" I asked.

"With you, always," she said, smiling.

I took her hand and jumped us to The Diner, our favorite restaurant and meeting place tucked off on a side street in downtown Las Vegas. It was a place decorated in a fake 1960s look and run by Madge, a superhero in the food service part of the world. Madge seemed to always be there and she made the best milkshakes on the planet.

Ten minutes later, Madge and Stan had us ready to go and we jumped to the outskirts of Las Vegas near a huge Las Vegas billboard.

Three

THE COOL MORNING desert air hit my face and I was glad to have the leather jacket on. Patty had over one shoulder a backpack with three thermoses of hot chocolate, and I had the other backpack on my back with the other three.

Hot chocolate was like an extreme drug to the Silicon Suckers. One single drop of the liquid would send a Sucker into a drug high that seemed to last for a long time.

I had learned a long time ago to never think of going into one of the Silicon Sucker cities without a gift of a thermos of hot chocolate. And since we were going to see the Great One, it made sense to carry even more of the gift.

We had arrived fifteen minutes ahead of our time to meet the Great One, but I had a hunch it would take us that long to get to where he was through the vastness of the underground city. The sun had already lit up the hills and desert with a golden glow and the air still had an early-morning chill to it that promised to be gone very shortly in the summer heat.

"You ready?" I asked.

Patty nodded, but looked very nervous. She had never been inside a Silicon Sucker "sand castle" as they liked to call their huge network of caves and tunnels in the sandstone and rock.

While the hot chocolate was being made, Stan had briefed Patty on all the rules of the Silicon Sucker city.

We could never touch a wall. We could never sit down unless invited. We had to always treat the Suckers with respect by bowing. We had to give our full and honest name before being allowed to enter. And so on and so on. They were a very rule-bound race.

I had us face directly east, then, to the seemingly open-air twenty paces from the big billboard, I said, "Poker Boy and Front Desk Girl ask for entrance into the great city of the Silicon Suckers."

The entrance of a large tunnel shimmered into existence in front of us. It seemed to go into the side of a hill that just didn't appear to be there. Very weird.

I slipped off my shoes, leaving them on the desert sand. Patty did the same, and we stepped forward into the tunnel that slanted downward gently.

About twenty paces inside we were met by a Silicon Sucker who bowed as we bowed and gave our full names.

"Welcome to our castle once again, Poker Boy," he said. "It is always an honor to have you as a guest."

He turned to Patty. "It is also an honor to have you visit our castle."

"The honor is all mine," Patty said, bowing slightly.

With all the greetings done, the Silicon Sucker turned and indicated we should follow him.

As I had guessed, it seemed to take a long time for us to reach the major cavern and work our way down one wall on sloping ramps. For a person afraid of heights, this path on the face of the wall would be pure hell. It was a long ways down and there were no guardrails and you weren't allowed to touch the wall on the inside.

The cavern seemed to stretch into the distance and the walls were riddled with paths and open tunnels. They seemed to be crawling with Silicon Suckers.

I had never seen so many out and moving at the same time before. I felt like I had been shrunk down and was walking in an anthill.

The floor of the huge cavern had hundreds and hundreds of buildings and I knew from earlier visits that the caverns and tunnels went deep under all the buildings as well.

Seeing so many Silicon Suckers moving at once, I suddenly wondered what all of them ate and how so many could be fed? No doubt I dare not ask such a question.

I glanced at Patty who was following me. She seemed to be doing fine on the wall face, even in the drying air. I could feel the moisture in my lips and skin drying up and the leather jacket I wore didn't feel so comfortable now in the growing heat. But I didn't dare take it off, not only because it would be an insult in the city, but it gave me extra power. And there was no telling what I might need to do in this situation.

The deeper we got into the city, the drier the air got. We could not bring any kind of water with us. Plain drinking water was forbidden in a Silicon Sucker castle.

These places were very, very dangerous to humans. I knew of one superhero who had managed three days in a Silicon Sucker castle negotiating with them on some land swap, but she had barely made it out alive.

We reached the cavern floor and headed toward the huge center building. There was nothing ornate about it and no windows at all. It seemed more like a giant mound of sand. But it was the largest building and it did seem to be in the center of the cavern, which I was sure had some significance.

We were led inside and into a large, domed room with no furniture of any kind. It seemed to be the very center of the large mound of sand that was this building.

The floor was nothing but hard sand, warm under my bare feet, and the walls were brown like everything else in these underground cities. It looked like the special rooms weren't any more decorated than any of the other rooms in this cavern.

The Silicon Sucker who led us into the room indicated we should stand and wait and then he left.

There was only one other door into the room, an archway on the other side. We both stood, facing that doorway, not talking.

I could feel beads of sweat forming on my face and then drying away almost instantly.

I always got scared inside these cities. After all, Silicon Suckers looked just like every alien I had seen in the movies. That fear was very deep in all humans, more than likely from centuries around this race.

Honestly, at the moment I was more scared than I had ever been before.

If Laverne had only met the Great One once in thousands of years, why were we standing here?

And how many ways could we make a mistake and never see the light of the desert above again?

Suddenly, in front of us, a Silicon Sucker entered the room completely alone. As with all of them, he wore nothing, but he moved slower than the rest, and as he got closer to us, I could see his bright red eyes. And his face looked longer than the rest. But otherwise, besides the red eyes, I would have never been able to tell the Great One from any other Silicon Sucker.

Patty and I both bowed to him and he returned the bow.

"I thank you for this audience," he said, his voice strong and commanding.

"It is an honor to be asked," I said.

Patty and I both bowed again slightly.

"We have brought gifts, if you would allow us."

He held up his hand for us to not move, and we both stood still.

"I thank you for the gifts," the Great One said, "but I must first talk to you about why I asked you here. My people find themselves in a problem of our own making."

Patty and I carefully said nothing.

"It seems that the gifts you have brought us in the past, and the regular payment for the land we have exchanged, has brought us to a crisis point."

He paused and then looked down as if embarrassed.

I knew he was talking about hot chocolate. Over the last few years I had brought his people six thermoses full. And for a piece of land they were getting ten thermoses every month. I knew that hot chocolate was a very powerful drug to the Silicon Suckers, but I couldn't imagine it becoming a crisis.

Then it hit me. *A powerful drug!*

Could he be mad at me for getting his people hooked on hot chocolate? Had I created a drug problem in his perfectly ordered world? No wonder he wanted to only "talk" with me.

But why had he also asked Patty to come along? Was it because she was special to me and he needed to take something special of mine for what I had done to his people?

I would not allow that.

The Great One looked up at me, the large unblinking red eyes clear.

"Poker Boy," he said, "I do not think you understand the value of your gracious gifts to my people. Your precious gifts give us life and energy. It gives us an excitement that we have not felt in many, many centuries."

I somehow managed to keep my mouth shut and just let him continue. I needed to be ready, if this turned very ugly, to jump Patty and me out of here quickly, or call for Lady Luck to come to our rescue.

The Great One continued.

"Your gifts have allowed me to walk out here without being carried and to stand here as a leader once again."

Now I was staring at him and my eyes suddenly felt like they were as wide as his were.

"Our problem is that our numbers are increasing with the new vitality from your gifts and land payments. And each cycle the payment for the land is not enough to supply my people."

Suddenly the fear I had been feeling turned to barely-controlled panic.

He wasn't mad at me for bringing the gifts of hot chocolate. This was much, much worse.

He needed *more* of it.

Oh, crap. I couldn't just offer it to him as a gift. I would insult him, and more than likely we would die where we stood.

I needed to find a way, and find it quickly, to get the Silicon Suckers more hot chocolate and let the Great One feel as if he was paying a fair price.

I nodded and somehow, keeping my voice from cracking in the dry air, I said, "A great leader worrying about the well-being of his people. It is an honor to be in your presence."

I took the pack from my shoulder and took out the three thermoses, holding them in my hands and not allowing even the pack to touch the ground.

Beside me, Patty followed my lead and did the same.

"For the honor of meeting with the Great One," I said, "the leader of all Silicon Suckers, we have brought this special gift. I hope it will help while we work out a more lasting solution and a fair and equitable trade."

"I can only thank you for your generosity," he said.

Without any indication of a movement from the Great One, six other Silicon Suckers came out and each took one thermos and carried them away like carrying gold from the room.

After they had left I spoke again.

"May I be so bold as to ask how much of the precious substance is needed to supply the great beings of the race of Silicon Suckers with their needs?"

He stared at me for a moment and I began to wonder if I had gone too far with my question.

Then he said, "We would need four times the amount of your generous gift every moon cycle, plus the payment for the land we are already receiving."

I tried to look serious. Thirty-four thermoses full of hot chocolate. "That is a large amount," I said. "But it is possible. But I must ask for something in return."

"Of course," he said.

I had an idea on what we might trade for, but I had to be very careful in presenting it.

"My people are also in great need in this area for…" I stopped and looked pained. "…I am sorry, I cannot use such language in front of the Great One."

He motioned for me to continue.

"We are in need of plain water. We are a very different people, with different needs. We must have plain water to survive. Is there an area in your lands which is not usable to your people because of too much plain water that we might trade?"

"Something important to my people in exchange for something important to your people," he said.

I only nodded. Thankfully he saw my purpose and I had not insulted him by asking for what was, in essence, poison to his people.

"Poker Boy, there is a reason my people sing your praises."

"Thank you, Great One," I said.

A map of the area around Las Vegas appeared in the air between us. Some areas were colored in gold for Silicon Sucker lands. Black for human lands. Gray for land that neither party controlled.

I knew the Silicon Suckers protected their own lands fiercely when needed, and no building was allowed within one hundred yards of any border to their property.

Of course, no humans in Las Vegas government knew that. The map had been formed by treaty decades before by the Gods of Land Use and the Silicon Suckers. The gods in that area made sure nothing was allowed to be built on the Silicon Sucker lands.

The Great One pointed to a small area colored red off to one side of the old Boulder Dam highway. It did not seem to be attached to any other area of Silicon Sucker lands.

"We were forced to abandon a growing castle in this area due to large pools of the evil liquid under the area. I would like five times your most recent gift every moon cycle in trade for the entire area."

He had upped the amount expecting me to bargain. Again, I needed to not insult him by giving in too quickly.

"Forty containers of the precious liquid every moon cycle?" I asked. He said simply, "Yes."

I pointed at the large area of red off the old highway. "My people will find much of what we need here?"

"You will find much of the poison there," he said.

I didn't want to tell him that the precious liquid he was asking for was based on the poison we called water.

"Twenty-eight additional every moon cycle," I said. "And if we find what we must look for on the land, we will increase the amount to forty total in twelve moon cycles."

He nodded. "Your terms are acceptable."

The red coloring of the land on the map turned to blue and then the map vanished.

"The first payment will be delivered tomorrow morning," I said, "to the area near the entrance to this castle at sunrise, and then at sunrise every moon cycle after."

The Great One bowed and Patty and I bowed also.

"This exchange has given my people a new beginning," he said. "It will allow my people to reproduce and spread and build many large new castles. You will both always be honored guests as long as I rule."

With that he turned and walked away.

For a moment I felt the elation that we had survived the meeting. Then his last words came back strong, like someone was shouting them in my head.

Hot chocolate helped these creatures have baby Silicon Suckers?

Wow, I had not known that. No wonder I had never seen any children. I had never thought of it before.

What had I just done?

Patty and I followed a guide out of the building and back up the wall toward the entrance above. All the paths and tunnels teamed with Silicon Suckers, far, far more than I had ever seen before.

Was all this population growth from just a few thermoses per month of hot chocolate?

Oh, man, what would forty every month do?

What had I done?

Was I setting up a future war between mankind and Silicon Suckers? I sure hoped not.

Outside, after Patty kissed me for a job well done and we put on our shoes in the already hot sun, I told her my worry.

She just laughed in that way she does that makes me relax. It's one of her very special superpowers I'm sure.

Then she said, "I could really use a couple glasses of water and a large breakfast."

"You don't think this is serious, do you?"

"They don't dare expand into our areas and fight with us."

"And why not?" I asked as I jumped us from the hot desert to our favorite booth in the air-conditioning of The Diner. I didn't want to call for Stan and Laverne until I understood what Patty was saying.

"There weren't that many of them moving around last time I was down there," I said as we slid into the booth, the cool vinyl seat feeling wonderful. "That's only after six months of regular hot chocolate use. Imagine after a year?"

Again Patty laughed. "Trust me, they have to treat us well."

"And why?" I asked as Madge headed our way with large glasses of water she must have had ready.

"Because if they don't," Patty said, patting my hand on the table top like I was two years old, "we just cut off their supply of hot chocolate."

"Oh," was all I could think to say.

MARRIAGE IN SIX FLOORS

I wrote this story back in what I call my "horror period" of writing. In fact, back in that period I was nominated for a Stoker Award a few times, which is the award given out by the Horror Writers of America.

I tend to think of this story as a mystery story instead. But honestly, it never occurred to me to send it to one of the mystery magazines.

So finally, it sees the light of day. Yet another side of my writing.

FIRST FLOOR

THE DRUG WEARS OFF.

Jagger Swayne finds himself standing, arms tied behind him. Cold metal presses hard against the full length of his back.

His jaw aches. Something soft and wet jams his mouth open, wraps around his head, and pulls the skin of his face painfully tight.

His vision slowly clears.

He stands in a small, dark, cement room that smells of mold and damp. It is a cold smell.

A smell that holds years of sameness.

The room is very small, not much larger than a closet.

His head misses the metal ceiling by less than a foot.

Through the dark, he can see lines of shadows on the opposite wall.

He pushes the haze of drug back into the corners behind his eyes and tries to think.

Jagger Swayne.

His name is Jagger Swayne. He is from Chicago.

Can he be crazy if he can remember his name?

No? Clearly, he is here.

But how?

Susan.

Dinner in their honeymoon suite.

The wine.

Her smile as she watched him drink.

Damn it, Susan.

If this is a stupid trick, it is not funny.

Six Months Earlier…

Jagger punched his finger against the up button and turned to the woman named Susan he had just met in a bar about four blocks away.

She had long blonde hair she kept pulled back and a classic face that had only a little make-up on it because she didn't need it. She wore a light sweater that clearly showed the lace bra under it.

She was exceptional, seemed to have many secrets, and yet laughed easily. She was from out east, she said, and was only visiting the beach for a short time.

He was on business in Seattle, and had never even been to this beach resort town or old hotel before, but he was growing to like it by the moment.

He flat couldn't believe she had agreed to go with him tonight from the bar. His friends back in Chicago would say she was out of his class and too old for him, and after his money and more than likely they would be right. But at the moment he didn't care.

She leaned against a section of the brass that decorated the old Lost Cove Hotel's main lobby. As he watched, her gaze drifted around the plush lobby, drinking in the lushness of the turn-of-the-century setting. Her mouth was slightly open, her eyes shining. He could tell that she liked what she saw.

He liked what he saw as well, staring at her.

"They say that every room has a view of the beach," he said.

"And I suppose you've had girls in all of them," she said, laughing, knowing that he had never been here before.

"Of course not," he said with mock seriousness. "The top floor is the honeymoon suite."

She tried to tickle him, but the door to the old elevator slid back with a clank and he ducked inside. She ran her hands along the marbled mirrors and polished brass of the interior as she followed.

"This is really something."

"It is, isn't it?" he said, staring at her wonderful body and smiling face and long blonde hair.

He pushed the first floor button on the brass control panel and then leaned back against the side wall, staring at her. "Beautiful."

"They say this takes forever to just go one floor."

She moved across the small space and into his arms as the door slid closed. "So we might as well make the best of it."

He laughed as the lift jerked upward and locked them together.

SECOND FLOOR

FAINT VOICES OVERHEAD wake him.

Jagger Swayne tries to yell, but the gag chokes off all but a low moaning sound.

He tries to kick, but his legs are tied as tightly as his hands.

Rope winds across his chest and over and under his shoulders, keeping him so tight against the metal bar that he cannot slide down into a sitting position. Another rope cuts into the skin around his neck and hangs down in front of him like a long necktie.

That rope ends in a large pile at his feet.

A loud jolt echoes in the small room.

Movement.

He tips his head back tight against the rope.

The ceiling is moving slowly upward. Light cuts bright gashes across the dark from cracks in the opposite wall. What were streaks of shadow suddenly become greasy black cables.

He is under an elevator.

The bar pressed into his back vibrates. It is the rail the elevator moves on.

In front of him, a thick rope hangs down the center of the shaft. It is tied to the bottom of the elevator and now slowly uncoils from the pile at his feet like a slow-moving snake.

The other end of that snake is his necktie-rope.

He frantically kicks and struggles against his bonds as the elevator slowly moves upward. The slight whisper of the rope uncoiling covers his muffled screams.

Finally, a loud thump echoes down the shaft as the old lift engine on the roof shuts down. The elevator stops at the second floor.

He tries to take a deep breath against the gag to calm his adrenalin-pumped heart.

Footsteps sound above.

Then faint laughter.

Susan will pay for this.

Four Months Earlier…

"You really like this old hotel, don't you?" Susan asked as she pushed the up button of the old elevator. The door eased open slowly as if the hotel was yawning.

Jagger set the suitcases down against the back of the elevator and leaned against the brass and mirrored wall. "It feels like home to me." He shrugged. "There's just something here."

He didn't want to say that what was special was her. And he loved meeting her here.

"Ever think you'd like to spend the rest of your life here?" she asked. "Never go back to Chicago?"

Again, he shrugged, staring at her. "If possible, I probably would. I don't know why. I just like it."

She pushed the button for the second floor.

The door slid closed and the elevator bumped slowly into motion. "Maybe it's this old elevator," she said, and then kissed him.

As the elevator plodded, he came up for air. "That has a lot to do with it."

She laughed, and they kissed for the rest of the ride.

THIRD FLOOR

MORE VOICES AND FOOTSTEPS.

Sweat stings his left eye. He blinks the sweat back.

The elevator rises.

The rope snakes off the pile.

The elevator passes the second floor. He doesn't know how much rope is in the pile. He fights against the bonds that hold him tight against the rail. He doesn't know if he is loosening the ropes or not. He cannot feel his fingers.

A loud thud.

The rope stops.

He stops fighting, shakes the sweat from his forehead and looks up. The elevator is at the third floor.

The old hotel only has six floors. There didn't seem to be enough rope left in the pile for three more floors. How often did they rent out the top floor honeymoon suite? Maybe he will get loose or someone will find him before then.

How much time did he have left?

An hour?

A day?

The elevator clicks and starts down, blocking out more and more of the light as it comes.

This had been their honeymoon night.

But how can she do this?

Putting him here seems even beyond her.

What had he done?

He had hoped to be a good husband.

She didn't give him a chance.

He glances up.

The elevator descends on him like the sky falling in a nightmarish dream. He tries to duck, but the ropes will not let him. The elevator rattles to a stop a foot over his head.

Damn Susan.

She will never get away with this.

Never.

He hears the door slide open. Footsteps shake the cage above him.

He calls out against the gag and tries to shake his body to make noise. The ropes cut deeper into his flesh.

The door closes.

Again, silence fills the tiny concrete darkness and lets the smell of the mold and the damp crawl back over his face.

Three Months Earlier…

"What do you really like about me?" Jagger asked as they waited arm in arm for the elevator to get to their third floor suite in the old ornate hotel. "My money or my smile?"

"Your money, of course," Susan said, and then giggled in her little-girl giggle. "But you kiss real nice, too."

"What happens when I get old and have dentures? What will you do then? You can't kiss my money."

She leaned against him as the elevator bumped past the second floor. "Don't worry," she said, smiling at him. "I'll find some part of you to kiss."

She always could say exactly the right thing.

FOURTH FLOOR

The elevator stops and he stops screaming into his gag.

He closes his eyes and tries to swallow the thick taste of fear in his mouth. He doesn't dare throw up.

He would drown.

He takes slow measured breaths, then tips his head as far back as the noose will allow. Above him, the light comes into the shaft from the cracks around three doors. The rope sways in the center of the shaft like a pendulum marking the last moments of his life.

He stares up the nightmarish length and tries to think.

Why had Susan done this?

She had been rich in her own right. She didn't need his money. Or at least he thought she didn't need it. Even though a friend had warned him, he hadn't signed a prenuptial. If he disappeared, she would have all his money.

And none of his friends even knew he came out here. And Susan had always insisted on paying for the room.

She clearly has planned this for as long as she has known him.

But how can she expect to get away with this?

His body will be found.

He studies the ground around his feet. It's dirt. And has clearly been dug up a few times in the past.

Are there others under that dirt?

Is that where other husbands are buried?

Other lovers? How many are down there?

He pushes that thought away.

How did she get him down here?

Did she have help?

Of course she did. More than likely she has a real lover as sick as she is.

A partner.

The man with the sly smile and dark eyes behind the front counter of the hotel desk.

Of course.

She always demanded they meet at this hotel, always.

The elevator bangs against the track as it starts down. He feels it through his arms and his back.

The ache in his jaw is intense.

He tries twisting his head back and forth to loosen the gag. His skin burns against the rope. Blood drips into his collar and runs down on his shoulder.

At his feet, the pile of rope grows.

One Month Earlier...

"You sure you want to be Mrs. Jagger Swayne?" he asked Susan as he set the suitcases down against the back of the elevator. He could not believe that in a moment of passion last time he had proposed to her and she had accepted.

She smiled and rubbed against him like a cat against a leg. "It would feel really nice."

"You know," he said, as he punched the fourth floor number. "The sixth floor honeymoon suite is the only floor in this hotel we haven't stayed on."

"Good," she said. "On our wedding night, we'll break it in right."

The door slid closed.

And he liked the sound of that.

FIFTH FLOOR

THE ELEVATOR STARTS up and he comes alive.

He measures time with the rope going up and down.

Up and down.

His remaining life is measured by the soft whispers of the snake coiling and uncoiling at his feet.

Stretching up, then back.

Up.

Down.

Up.

Down.

Up.

He screams through his gag.

She has everything planned. She has pictures of him walking along the rock cliffs above the beach, she has pictures of him taking out a fishing boat.

He will vanish and no one will know what happened to him.

And she will take his money.

One Week Earlier...

"Did you hear something?" Jagger asked, breaking away from Susan's embrace as the elevator started up.

"Just my mind thinking how much I love you and how much I can't wait for next week."

"I had this feeling," he said. "Cold. Really cold. And a muffled scream." He tilted his head, trying to listen over the noise of the old lift.

"Suddenly getting afraid of marriage?" Susan asked, using her lower-lip pout.

"No, of course not. I must have just imagined whatever it was. You know how I am when I get excited." He winked at her.

She giggled.

SIXTH FLOOR

FOOTSTEPS ABOVE AND he knows.

This is it.

This is the time.

It has been almost two days.

Maybe Susan had figured wrong. He watches calmly as the elevator pulls the rope past the second floor and keeps going.

He can almost hear her voice above him.

This is the one and there is not enough rope.

He spits Susan's name against the gag. He hopes she chokes on his money.

No one stops the elevator.

No one will.

He did this to himself. He hadn't been able to see the real Susan, all he had been interested in was the sex.

It seemed she had money. He never figured out where she got the money from. Now he knew.

He hadn't paid attention to all the signs, the rush to get married, the desire to always come to this old hotel, to not meet his family and friends until later, to surprise them later, she had said.

They would be surprised when he vanished without a trace and so did all his money.

He closes his eyes and waits.

At his feet, the rope slowly uncoils and measures him with a soft brushing sound.

Above Him...

"We should open the champagne while we're still in the elevator," Susan said to her new husband, Benson Stevens. "When we get to the room, I have other things in mind."

She rubbed against him, more turned on and excited than he had seen her before.

They had dated for about six months in Portland up until he asked her to marry him. She had said she needed some time to think about it and had vanished back to Seattle for a number of months, calling him to tell him she still loved him, but she couldn't decide.

Last night she had called and said if he wanted to marry her, they needed to do it tomorrow before she got cold feet. The wedding had been quick and easy in Reno, then they had flown back on his private jet to what she called "Their hotel," for the honeymoon.

He loved the old hotel. They had visited it often. The place always seemed to turn Susan on even more than usual.

Benson picked up the bottle from where she had set it under the control panel with its lit number six. "Always thinking," he said.

"I try," she said, rubbing against him.

He had the outside wrapping and the wire off the bottle by the time they passed the fifth floor. He planned to pop the cork just as they reached the top.

Two feet short, the elevator slowed.

Then it paused, as if it didn't want to go all the way.

He could hear the elevator engine straining.

Straining.

Until Finally…

The elevator jerks upward.

The newlyweds bump together.

The cork pops off the bottle with a much louder sound than he had expected.

Benson holds the bottle up while the champagne bubbles out and drips on the carpet leaving a dark, round stain.

Susan damn near climbs all over him, kissing him with more passion than he could ever imagine a woman having.

The door to the sixth floor slides open, exposing the huge honeymoon suite with its plush red carpet, red hearts on the walls, and huge tub next to a stone fireplace. A massive four-poster bed dominates the center of the room.

He pushes the hold button and pours the champagne.

First her glass, then his.

"A toast to us," he says.

"And marriage," she says, giving him that smile that he both loved and that scared him just a little.

Their glasses click lightly together.

He doesn't notice she doesn't drink a bit of the champagne as she lures him into the big room before the drug takes effect.

THE CASE OF THE INTRUSIVE FURNITURE

A Pilgrim Hugh Incident

Pilgrim Hugh solved some odd cases before, but an old, smelly couch sitting in the middle of a beautiful lawn seems to have full-blown strange written all over it.

With his friend and beautiful assistant, Carrie, he must figure out why the couch ended up there and what the woman living in the perfect home hid (besides a bad facelift and a heart of stone).

A very cold case on a very hot day.

One

PILGRIM HUGH HADN'T seen a piece of furniture so ugly since the night his first wife had attended an auction in a barn and mistaken chicken droppings for a French designer signature on a chaise lounge.

Just like that chaise lounge, the standard American couch in front of him on the perfectly mowed, perfectly green lawn could not have been given away, let alone sold. The once tan cloth had faded to a pale, dirty white and one of the three cushions had a very large dark spot on it that looked to be the remains of a cola stain from a distant time in the past. Even the stain had faded.

And he hoped it was cola. Safer to just think it was and move on.

The couch looked long, like a full adult could stretch out and not touch either end, but damned if he was going to test that. What had started as a decorative wood trim on both arms and across the front of the couch was now scarred and dirty and the cloth on both arms had worn through to the threads.

The entire thing smelled musty and of long storage. He had spent many hours through the years, especially while in college and law school, on couches he was sure looked and smelled far worse. Only difference was those couches were in dark rooms, not sitting in bright sunshine in the middle of a freshly mowed suburban lawn.

He nodded to the poor cop named Dennis, a young kid with freckles on his nose, who had been unlucky enough to answer this call. Dennis stood in the shade of a nearby small poplar tree as Pilgrim walked around the couch, studying it, but finding nothing more than an old couch.

It was the kind of couch you see sitting beside a road with a "free" sign on it and no one takes it for a month and the rain ends up soaking it and the city finally has to haul it away and try to find the owners who dumped it to pay the costs.

Over the last few years as a freelance private detective and lawyer, Pilgrim had gotten some strange calls, but this call on a rogue couch had to rank right up there on the strange meter.

After he'd gotten out of law school at the ripe old age of twenty-four, he had gone to work in corporate law and had managed to last in the law firm through the two years of his first marriage before becoming bored with both. Then his grandmother, a woman he barely knew, died and left him more money than even he could imagine or try to spend. He had become free to do what he wanted.

So after a year of drinking and traveling around the world and another even shorter marriage, which got boring faster than corporate law, he went back to school to become a private detective.

Most of the training was not like the books about private detectives he loved to read. In fact most of what he had done was learn how to track someone by computer and look up financial records, which was flat dull.

Finally, out of desperation to do something interesting, he set up his own law and private detective firm, hired a couple of associate lawyers to handle the boring stuff, and offered his services for free to the different city police departments around the Portland metropolitan area.

Hugh and Associates was born, the strangest law firm to ever have plush offices in a downtown Portland high-rise.

A few old corporate clients paid very well and kept a growing staff of associates busy and the police forces started to take him up on his offer to look for free into strange and odd cases that no one else wanted to deal with. Now, at the age of thirty-eight, he had been working to solve weird crimes and find missing people for almost a decade. And not once in those ten years had he been bored. Even now, staring at an old couch.

This couch was so out of place as to be funny in the middle of a well-kept lawn in the Portland, Oregon, suburb of Hillsboro. The three-story home seemed perfectly kept and no doubt a gardener did the yard. Pilgrim imagined the house inside to be as perfect as the lawn. More than likely the owners pretended to be just as well-kept, at least on the surface. This area was known for its pretend rich. He didn't want to think about the size of the mortgage on this house.

He shuddered at the thought of how close he had come to this life-style with his first wife, Karen. This would have been her perfect home. And he would have spent more time in Henry's Sports Bar than in it if he had stayed married to her.

Two

THE SUN BEAT on the old piece of furniture, making it smell even worse if that was possible. Clearly something musty and rotten was inside it as well. More than likely a number of dead mice.

Pilgrim stepped back onto the sidewalk and clicked his earpiece to talk to his driver. "Carrie, a couple Diets for me and the officer if you wouldn't mind."

"Shit," she said in his ear. "Too damn hot to go out there."

Pilgrim smiled as he watched her climb out from behind the wheel to bring him and the officer a couple of Diet Cokes. They both had figured this was going to be a quick stop.

She was right, it was hot. Portland didn't have too many really hot days, but today was promising to be one of the record-setters. The sun and warm June day was making him regret wearing a black Henry's Bar tee shirt this morning. He should have gone with the white Next Gen tee shirt and Bermuda shorts instead of the Levis.

He loved being self-employed and rich and able to wear anything he damn well wanted any time he damn well wanted. Sometimes dressing like an over-aged college student helped him on cases. People tended to talk with him more when he wore a tee shirt than when he had on his three-piece court suit.

Carrie went to the back door of the limo and retrieved from the fridge a couple bottles of Diet Coke and then grabbed another for herself. Today she had on blue short-shorts and a white tank top that left little to anyone's imagination of what was under it. Her short blonde hair framed her deep blue eyes and chiseled features perfectly. She never wore make-up and never seemed to comb her hair, yet she always looked perfectly put together.

She was a good six-feet tall, just an inch shorter than he was, and looked like she belonged on a runway modeling dresses and underwear, even at thirty-eight. She had been Pilgrim's best friend since high school in Bend, Oregon, and acted more like his partner than his driver at times.

She had helped him get through two wives and far too many girl-friends to count. And not once had they slept together. It just seemed wrong to him, like sleeping with his sister, if he had had a sister.

She felt the same way about him. Over the years she had managed to keep boyfriends to the sex-and-leave stage that she liked. Never married, Pilgrim doubted she ever would. Not her thing as she often said.

Carrie had only one more year of law school and she would be joining the law firm side of his business. She had spent eight years in the military after high school learning computer skills and other things that constantly surprised him. Then she had traveled the world for a few years. During that time he got letters and messages from her from just about every scary hell-hole on the planet. Now she was just finishing her law degree.

She didn't handle boredom any better than he did.

Until she passed the bar, she paid her way through school and for her Penthouse apartment by helping him with cases and being his limo driver when he needed one for clients or for police cases.

For some reason he really, really liked showing up at a crime scene in a limo. It had become part of his image around town and he and Carrie had turned the limo into a major office and computer center on wheels. Tee shirts and a limo. Pure Northwest rich geek.

Pilgrim watched as Carrie headed up the sidewalk toward him. She had a sharp eye for details about a case that seemed right, but looked wrong. Just last week she had helped him solve a very obese woman's murder when both he and the police thought it nothing more than death by natural causes. The way the woman had fallen in the kitchen was just wrong to Carrie's mind and she led Pilgrim to discover the dead woman had a boyfriend who wanted her coin collection and thought murdering his girlfriend for the money was a good idea.

Why Chief Benson from the Hillsboro police had called Pilgrim on this "couch case" was beyond him. More than likely it was just something he didn't want to waste manpower on on a hot day and figured Pilgrim could find a way to make the problem just go away with some legal language. For Benson and the city, Pilgrim was free.

More than likely the guy in this house had donated a decent amount of money in the last election and had Benson's direct phone line.

It didn't matter to Pilgrim. He owed Benson many favors from over the years, so handling something like a misplaced couch on a lawn of a political supporter was the least he could do for him.

Pilgrim took the Diet Coke from Carrie, rubbed the cold bottle against his forehead, then opened it and stepped back to just stare at the intruding piece of furniture. More than likely this was just a bad joke of some sort being played on the family.

The plastic and wood wrapping that had brought the couch to its present location had been tossed to one side leaving the old couch sitting like a bad nightmare on the mowed grass.

Someone had paid a lot of money to have this old couch delivered here. Why?

The shipping instructions were with the wrapping so he went and retrieved them as Carrie came back from giving Officer Dennis his drink. More than likely, with what Carrie was wearing, her visit just heated the poor officer up more than the Diet Coke would cool him down.

The plastic wrap the couch had come in was very strange. Part of the plastic was clearly very, very old and had just cracked and fallen apart when removed, while another layer over the top was new, more than likely put on by the moving company. Clearly this couch had been sealed in that original old plastic for a very long time.

"So figured out *The Case of the Intrusive Furniture* yet?" Carrie asked, as he came back with the shipping instructions. "This is one for the strange disclosures file."

"Not a clue," Pilgrim said, shaking his head at Carrie. She really loved to name all their cases like mysteries from a 1940's serial radio program and planned on putting some of them into a book she called "Strange Disclosures."

There was nothing on the delivery instructions but the house address for delivery, instructions to open the plastic wrapping and just leave the couch on the lawn, and a greeting from a man named Thomas.

Pilgrim read the note on the shipping label aloud. "You liked this so much, I figured you should have it now that I am dead."

"Wow, that's cold," Carrie said, shaking her head. "You think that's blood on the cushion?"

"I'm hoping not," Pilgrim said, but after the note he was becoming less sure of his cola-spill theory.

He handed the shipping label to Carrie. "Get on the phone and talk to the shipping company. Get an address and name of where this came from and any information you can find on this Thomas guy, even if you have to threaten a subpoena."

She nodded, looking at the label in her hands. "You talking to the homeowners?"

"You got it in one," he said. "Feed me any information you might dig up along the way. Get a couple people at the office helping on this as well."

"Got it," she said and turned for the limo as he headed past the couch for the house.

Three

AS HE RANG the bell to the McMansion, he realized he more than likely should have gotten a sports coat from the limo. Someone in a home like this would give him more information if he looked like an investigator instead of an overgrown and aging college student.

"Too late now," he said to himself as inside he heard someone's steps coming toward the door over a hard surface.

A woman who looked to be in her late fifties opened up the door and a frown managed to cross over her face even with all the plastic surgery holding her skin in place. She had short brown hair done perfectly around her face. She wore a white blouse with a black lace garment under it that looked far too hot for the day. A cool blast of air-conditioning caught Pilgrim in the face as she glanced at him, then at Officer Dennis standing under the tree.

At one point this woman had been very beautiful. Fighting to keep that beauty had not gone well for her.

"Yes?"

"My name is Pilgrim Hugh," he said, handing her his card that said "Hugh Investigations" on it and nothing about him being an attorney. "Chief Benson of the Hillsboro Police sent me to look into the issue with the couch. Can I talk with you for a moment?"

She nodded and indicated by stepping back that he should enter enough for her to close the door to the heat. But she didn't offer to take him anywhere but the stone entryway. And she didn't introduce herself.

"Her name is Alice Bluehaven," Carrie said in his ear. *"Wife of Dan, mother of two grown kids both in college out of the city."*

Pilgrim glanced around as Carrie fed him the information. He had been right about the house. It looked perfectly maintained and impossible to live in. More like a home taken right out of a picture in a magazine. Sterile and angry-feeling. Just as the woman in front of him felt.

"I wish my husband had never called the police about this," Mrs. Bluehaven said, clearly upset. "It should just be hauled to the dump."

"What can you tell me about that couch?" Pilgrim asked.

"It belonged to me and my first husband, Thomas Williams. We lived in Chicago when we split up in 1984."

Pilgrim was surprised at that information. He expected her to not know a thing about the old furniture on her lawn.

"Married to Thomas Williams in 1981, divorced in early 1985," Carrie said.

"I don't want to press charges against Thomas for doing such a thing. I just want it off my lawn."

"It says on the note that he's dead," Pilgrim said.

"Then the executor of his estate should be replaced for doing this. That is just embarrassing to have sitting out there and I plan on having it removed as soon as possible."

Pilgrim was stunned. The woman was colder than her house. She had just been told her first husband was dead and hadn't even flinched or cared in the slightest. Even though Pilgrim and his two wives were divorced, he still liked them and would be very upset to learn that anything had happened to either of them.

Whatever heart this woman had once possessed had clearly been removed with the plastic surgery to her face.

And honestly, Pilgrim was starting to like this Thomas guy. He must have known what his ex-wife was like, that she wanted everything to look and appear perfect, and knew how to torture her perfectly after his death.

"Before I can allow you to have the couch removed," Pilgrim said, "I'm going to need more history."

"Why would you need that?" she asked, her cold blue eyes almost emitting sparks.

"Your husband filed a complaint and thus this is technically a crime scene," Pilgrim said, lying, or actually just stretching the truth some. "To clear the scene I need background about the couch and your former husband. Paperwork. Otherwise the couch will have to remain where it was delivered until we get to the bottom of all this, and that might take days without your help."

She looked appalled and shocked to her very cold core. The idea of that couch staying on her lawn all day and into the evening for her neighbors to see was clearly more than she could handle.

"What can I tell you?" she said, her voice cold and low and very mean. How this woman stayed married to any man was beyond Pilgrim.

"Why this particular couch? Why would your former husband keep it for decades?"

"I had an affair on it," she said, her voice level like she was telling him about the weather. "Thomas walked in and caught us. I grabbed my clothes and ran out the back door and never went back. I never talked to Thomas again."

"Oh," was all Pilgrim could say.

They stood there in silence for a moment. The house like a tomb around him. At that moment all he wanted to do was run for the limo and get out of the icebox this family called a home.

"Oh, wow, is more like it," Carrie said in Pilgrim's ear. *"This is really going into the Strange Disclosures file."*

"What happened after that?" Pilgrim asked Mrs. Bluehaven.

"I honestly don't know," she said. "I stayed with a girlfriend for a night, then flew back to Portland and stayed with my parents. Thomas filed for divorce and stayed in Chicago and I didn't fight it. As I said, I never saw him again after that day, so I would have no idea what happened next. Our marriage was clearly not doing well."

"Clearly," Pilgrim said.

She stiffened even more if that was possible, but said nothing.

"But even after all the years you still recognized the couch? How is that possible?"

"I would recognize that trash anywhere," she said, so disgusted she almost spit as she talked. "I wanted to get a new couch, but Thomas was so cheap he kept saying we couldn't afford it and that tattered old thing was perfectly fine. I refused to sit on the couch."

Pilgrim almost said, *But no problem screwing your boyfriend on it.* Luckily he stopped himself.

"One more question," he said, "then I think I can have Chief Benson close this case and remove the couch."

She nodded, clearly relieved.

"What was the name of your boyfriend?"

"I don't see how that would matter?"

Pilgrim smiled. "Just making sure all the details are in order is all."

"Craig Marshal," she said. "Craig S. Marshal. He was a graduate student at Northwestern. I never talked to him again, either."

"Got it, on it," Carrie said in his ear.

Pilgrim nodded and turned for the door. "This should be over shortly, Mrs. Bluehaven."

As he stepped back into the heat of the front yard and she closed the door solidly behind him, he had a hunch this was far from over.

And his little voice on cases was seldom wrong. Carrie just might be right. This might end up being one for the book.

Four

HE NODDED TO Officer Dennis and headed for the limo with only one more look at the couch as he went past. The heat actually felt good after being with that woman. She was one cold human.

But on the other hand, the couch was starting to get a real smell to it. And not a good one. He knew that smell anywhere. Something inside that couch was very, very dead. And the hot sun was not helping the issue at all.

As he climbed into the limo, Carrie was working the computer station on the right side. It had two large screens that dropped down from the ceiling and a full desk and keyboard that slid out from under the wet bar. Her fingers were flying over the keys while at the same time she was talking into a headset to someone, more than likely an assistant at the office.

From their car they could get just about any information they wanted. He had had it outfitted better than most offices. And both he and Carrie were damn good at hacking into places they shouldn't be hacking into. He just didn't allow them to do it without darned good reason.

After a moment she finished her conversation, thanked the person on the other end, and turned to him.

"The boyfriend vanished completely on October 4th, 1984," Carrie said, confirming what Pilgrim had feared had happened. "No sign of him was ever found."

"I have a pretty solid hunch where we are going to find him," Pilgrim said. "Did our couch-sender actually die?"

"Yes," she said. "Liver cancer from a lifetime of hard drinking. The couch was removed already wrapped as per instructions from the garage of the home and delivered as instructed. His death triggered the automatic pick-up and a neighbor let the movers into the garage. He has no executor. And no family as far as I can find. And not much of an estate beside the house."

"Great work," Pilgrim said, taking his phone and dialing the private line to Chief Benson.

"You think we have a body?"

"The smell in the sunshine around that couch isn't getting any better," he said.

"The husband killed the boyfriend?" Carrie asked.

Pilgrim could only shrug as Chief Benson came on the line, but for some reason Pilgrim doubted that the husband had done it. He had no proof either way, or even a body yet, actually, but there would be shortly. That sun and heat on the couch was going to make it perfectly clear very quickly where the body was located.

Pilgrim told the chief about his suspicions that the couch was an actual crime scene. "A very cold case crime scene," he said, "that is heating up by the moment."

"Why the hell do you always do this to me?" Benson asked.

"You keep calling me," Pilgrim said before the chief could hang up.

Carrie just shook her head at his lame joke.

Pilgrim had Carrie move the limo down the street and out of the way before the excitement started.

Ten minutes later the rest of the police started arriving. A number of police took up stations around the entire house and in the back yard while others taped off the area around the couch, then slowly worked to figure out exactly what was in the couch before hauling the entire thing to the crime lab.

While they waited, both he and Carrie worked the computers and phones digging up every bit of information they could about the woman and the lost lover and the man who had sent the couch.

Pilgrim actually talked with three of Thomas's friends and the bartender where Thomas liked to drink. Thomas only told the bartender that one day his wife had just left him for no reason. But all of his friends said that when she left he had never been the same. He hadn't seemed to get over it even after twenty-plus years.

That fit her story.

But something still just didn't feel right to Pilgrim.

At that moment Chief Benson knocked and opened the back door of the limo, crawling in with a sigh as the air-conditioning hit him. He was a stout man built like a longshoreman who always wore a tie and blue shirt and jacket. Even in the heat he hadn't taken off the jacket.

"I got to get the city to spring for one of these," Benson said, then laughed.

Carrie offered him a regular Pepsi in a can, the chief's favorite, then went back to her computer search.

"Thanks," he said, smiling at her. "Nice outfit."

"Keep your eyes up," she said without glancing at the chief.

Benson laughed and turned to Pilgrim. "So what more have you dug up?"

"I'm sure that the woman inside will want us to think that the sender of the couch murdered her boyfriend. She's setting us up for that. Take a listen."

He replayed his conversation with the woman for Benson.

"Wow, cold bitch," Benson said when it was finished.

"With enough plastic surgery," Pilgrim said, "to keep a doctor in new golf clubs for a long time."

"Figures," Benson said. "You ought to meet her husband. Short little guy who chases every skirt he sees. So what's bothering you, Pilgrim?"

"That obvious?" Pilgrim asked.

Carrie snorted and kept her attention on the screen in front of her.

"Like an open book," Benson said, taking more of his Pepsi.

"Well," Pilgrim said, "first off, if Thomas had killed the boyfriend and hid his body in a wrapped-up couch, he never would have kept the couch this long. Too much risk."

"True," Benson said. "It would have ended up in a landfill a long, long time ago. You just don't keep the evidence of a murder you committed in your own garage for decades."

"Exactly," Pilgrim said.

"But I have seen stranger things," Benson said.

So had Pilgrim, but he kept going. "When she let me in she refused to even look at the couch on the lawn. Like she knew what was in it."

"Not enough to even get a warrant, counselor," Benson said.

Pilgrim suddenly had another idea. "Carrie, can you find what day the woman of the house flew from Chicago to Portland back in 1984? She said she went within a day or so, but I'm betting she hung around."

Carrie nodded. "Good thinking."

A moment later she said, "Got it. She left three weeks after the boyfriend vanished. Not the next day as she claimed."

"So you think she killed the boyfriend and got the husband to help her cover it up?"

"More than likely," Pilgrim said. "You just have to get the motive out of her. But either way she's involved with a murder. It would take two people to move that couch into a garage and wrap it with plastic."

"Looks like I had better go read someone her rights," Benson said, "before she sneaks out the back door."

"Take back-up," Pilgrim said as he climbed out of the limo with Benson.

"No worries there," Benson said, laughing.

"Well," Carrie said, climbing out of the limo to stand in the heat beside Pilgrim, "it seems like we solved *The Case if the Intrusive Furniture.*"

Pilgrim nodded. "I think the sun and heat helped."

"So what do you think actually happened?" Carrie asked.

"Not a clue," Pilgrim said, "and I'm not sure anyone will ever know all the details with the former husband dead. He protected her and himself for a lot of years, even though he wanted to pay her back once he was gone."

"You think he still loved her?"

"My guess is that he loved the idea of who she had been," Pilgrim said.

"You know," Carrie said, "it's not often we solve a cold case."

"Especially on such a hot day."

Carrie just moaned and Pilgrim smiled.

He glanced around at the neighbors now starting to gather and watch from a distance behind the crime scene tape. "At least now the world is going to know what was really inside that pretend shell she's kept up all these years. And that's going to hurt her more than jail time."

"So true," Carrie said.

Up around the old couch the crime techs had started to work at the back, but Pilgrim had no doubt what they would find.

The entire neighborhood would remember this smell.

Afternoon summer heat and a body that had been wrapped in plastic for twenty-eight years just did not mix well.

WELL, MAYBE NOT

"One event follows another." I remember saying that up on a writing panel one day and then added in "Well, maybe not."

That stuck with me and I went back and decided to start with an event and see what happened if I ended the event with "Well, maybe not."

This may well be one of the strangest stories I have ever written. Well, maybe not...

One

CHANNEL SURFING WAS Henry's life.

Click.

Jackie "Big Tits" Simpson slipped seductively up to the counter of Chucky Cheese and leaned forward just enough to cause her low-cut sweater to bag open the right amount. As the newest star of the famous soap opera "Eat Me," this was her big moment.

Her big break.

Her best shot at showing off her big tits.

"May I help you?" the fat kid with the pimples on his nose asked. He stood back a few feet as if he were afraid to get too close to Jackie, but in actuality it was to make sure all eyes remained on her.

"You sure can," she said and then slowly, oh, so slowly, she turned to face the camera...

Click.

Jill Bantor, bartender extraordinaire, flipped the bottle high into the air and caught it with her perfect right hand, the bottle's spout poised perfectly over the highball glass, ready to pour the perfect martini, not too wet, not too dry.

Harvey, her boss, the love of her life, watched from his usual seat.

Tonight she would get him to her pink, padded bed.

Get those tight pants off those wonderful buns.

Get him to....

Click.

Henry sucked down another handful of way-too-salty chips and clicked past five shopping channels. He loved to channel surf, loved to spend the evening just catching slight glimpses of other worlds.

He'd sit in his small two-bedroom-with-one-bath ranch house every night, seven days a week, surfing. Dishes would pile up in the sink and he wouldn't notice until the flies got too bad.

His laundry would go unwashed for weeks until he ran out of socks. Empty bags of potato chips would surround his couch until he couldn't stand kicking them out of the way.

He'd surfed for years and now that they had improved the cable channels he had even more choices.

"Cindy Slut, private dick, will return after a message from our sponsor Magic Hot Tubs."

Henry was about to surf on when on the forty-inch screen appeared a naked, sloppy, fat man with a very small penis. So small it took a close-up shot with a ground level camera focused up to even see it.

Henry watched, arm poised, special surfing control aimed at the set ready to move on as the fat guy huffed and grunted and finally shifted his bulk over the edge of the blue hot tub and settled into the bubbling water. Below the picture flashed off and on the words "Hidden camera view of satisfied customer."

Water splashed over the edge of the tub and after a moment the man's eyes seemed to roll up into his head.

Below the picture the words switched to "ten minutes elapsed time" and the picture shifted slightly as what appeared to be the same man shook his head, stretched and then stood up.

He was now slim, with a deep tan, a handsome grin, and a huge penis. So big the camera had to pull back to catch it all.

"Wow!" Henry said and scrambled for a pen to write down the toll-free number.

Henry was clearly overweight and his dick at its best was no longer than his little finger, even though he always thought of himself as just average. This Magic Hot Tub would be the perfect thing for him.

He would buy the Magic Hot Tub, soak in it for ten minutes and never have to diet again. And he could meet women and do things to them that he couldn't even see done on the Penthouse channel.

And then afterwards they could channel surf together, of course, with him holding the control.

He reached for the phone. This would be great.

Well, maybe not.

Two

DETECTIVE DANNY DOHICKEY stared down at the bloated, overcooked form of Henry floating in the steaming water. So far the flies hadn't started swarming, but it would only be another hour or so. They had been lucky to get the call from the meter man on this one. Sometimes these hot tub deaths went days without being discovered. Usually the neighbors complained about the smell after three days.

"Another Magic Hot Tub death?" his partner, Detective Walter Waker asked as he glanced at the body, his face showing the disgust he felt and the indigestion from too much pork at breakfast.

"Afraid so," Danny said.

"Why anyone would use these things is beyond me," Walter said. He leaned over the edge and looked at the special box on the side. "Penis enlarger again?"

"Afraid so," Danny said.

"Another one cut off?"

"Afraid so." Danny pointed to the shriveled, finger-looking thing floating near the filter.

"Medical examiner done with him?"

"Afraid so."

"Which means we've got to haul him out of there?"

"Afraid so."

Walter rolled up his sleeves, reached in, and grabbed a leg.

Danny grabbed an arm and they heaved and hauled and huffed and puffed and after a good ten minutes they had flopped Henry like a dead white fish beside the tub.

"You as wet as I am?" Walter asked, brushing water from his arms and pants.

"Afraid so," Danny said.

"He's all yours," Walter said to the woman from the morgue. "We got a report to fill out, don't we Danny?"

"Afraid so."

Betty Black, the woman from the morgue, put the cart beside Henry and gestured to the two cops. "Not before you roll him onto there." She pointed to her cart.

She wasn't going to do it and hurt her back. She needed her back limber for what she had planned later that night.

Walter grunted, but both detectives quickly had Henry on the cart and were walking away.

Suddenly Walter turned back to Betty. "Forgot to tell you. His penis is still in the hot tub."

"You're kidding!" Betty said.

This was her first Magic Hot Tub death and she hadn't heard about what really happened from reading the papers.

"Afraid not," Walter said, obviously enjoying her discomfort.

"And I have to fish it out?"

Afraid so," Danny said, slapped his partner on the back. Laughing, they walked off.

"Wonderful," Betty said in disgust, staring down at the naked, penis-less fat man on her stretcher. "And I'll bet it was a big one, too."

Well, maybe not.

Three

BETTY USUALLY WORE black to work. She felt it appropriate, since she worked with so much death. But at work in the morgue they always made her put on a clean, white surgical gown over her street clothes.

Betty was a pretty average woman, both in size and looks and the white surgical gown did nothing to help those looks. It flattened her chest and covered her best asset, her ass.

Betty had only worked at the morgue for three weeks, but her years of training were medical. And some veterinary. But that was much earlier.

Now she was in line for helping out with autopsies. That had been a dream of hers since the first time she had cut open her brother's dead dog to see how much damage the car had done.

"You want this one to be your first?" Brad, Betty's boss, asked her, pointing at the naked Harry with his small penis laying on the stretcher beside him. "You could do him this afternoon and I could watch."

Brad's face seemed almost flushed and he sounded breathless.

Betty almost clapped her hands together in excitement. Her first. She was really looking forward to cutting this one open, stem to stern, then talking into the recorder about what she was seeing, and then doing the report. It was what she had trained all these years for, the ultimate moment.

"That would be wonderful," she said to Brad, doing her best to keep her voice in control and totally professional.

Brad nodded and smiled real big. "Good. But lunch first. I know this great Italian place with the best red sauce and big glasses of wine. I'll meet you outside in five minutes."

"Wonderful," Betty said and watched Brad head toward his office. Too bad he was married, she always thought when she watched him walk away from her. This time was no exception to that rule.

As Brad left, she turned to face the naked form of Henry.

"Well, it seems you get to be the lucky one." She patted his fat, cold stomach and then walked around the table. "You get to be my first real stiff, not like those in school. You get to be the one who pops my cherry."

Henry, of course, didn't say a word.

"You know," she said, "I need something to remember this day. Maybe I should buy myself a special present. What do you think about that?"

Again, of course, Henry didn't say a word. He was just too dead.

"Or maybe I should keep a little something from inside of you."

She pretended to make a cut mark down the center of his chest.

Henry kept very still, as was his condition.

"But Brad will be here then. Maybe I should just take this."

She picked up Henry's small (and now-even-smaller-because-the-water-had-shrunk-it) penis.

She held it up in front of her face, turning it to look at all sides, studying the pattern of wrinkles. "I think this will be a wonderful memento, don't you?"

Henry would have objected, of that there was no doubt, but he couldn't and therefore didn't.

So Betty pulled off her surgical gown, opened her black handbag and dropped Henry's penis into her change purse. "Thanks," she said and patted Henry's arm. "I've got a wonderful lunch date, but I will see you this afternoon."

Well, maybe not.

Four

BETTY AND BRAD had three large glasses of wine each and both were feeling very, very happy.

Brad had suggested she do Henry in the private cutting room, with the door locked so that they wouldn't be interrupted. Betty had been so excited at that suggestion she almost wet herself.

On the way back, both of them breathless, both excited, both half smashed, they didn't expect a problem.

But they got one.

A big one.

The city bus with the bad brakes that none of the bus drivers wanted to drive, jumped the curb and gave both Betty and Brad a very quick ride into the side of a brick three-story building.

Blood splattered everywhere and the clean-up crew ended up having an awful time telling which part went with which body. However, a few hours later Betty and Bob were both beside Harry again, in body bags, smaller bags, and buckets. Not at all the way they had intended.

Betty's black handbag was tossed clear of the massive mess and mayhem, where it was picked up by a homeless young woman from Kansas named Dot. She held it for a time, watching the cops and medics clean up the mess, pretending all the time that she would give the handbag to the first person who asked.

She stood there for an hour, pretending.

But no one asked, so she decided she would turn it in later.

Back at her hot-air grate beside the dumpster, she opened the bag and found eighteen dollars in bills. She also saw a picture of Betty's apartment and in a secret place inside the lining she found a naked picture of Betty with her legs spread. Why Betty would carry a picture of herself doing that was beyond Dot, who was from a farm and had never really even looked at herself naked in a mirror. When she was growing up she even locked her dog out of the bathroom when she was taking a bath.

Inside the change purse was another eighty-seven cents and a strange-looking rubbery thing.

"Oh, yuck," she said and dropped the thing back inside the handbag with the picture of naked Betty.

She dug through the rest of the junk in the bag, but found nothing worth anything at all. She stuffed the money into a deep pocket in her cloth coat and held the bag at arm's length and looked at it. "Maybe I can get a reward for this down at the police station."

Well, maybe not.

Five

THE BIG GUY with a gray mustache behind the desk at the police station just took the purse after listening to Dot's story. He sort of grunted a thank you and then handed the purse to a young woman in a freshly ironed and washed uniform behind him. "Run this to the morgue to be put with the other personal stuff of that woman bus-crash victim."

The young woman named Officer Josepha Friday nodded her head excitedly, like a little puppy, then scampered forward and took the bag. "Yes, sir. Will do, sir."

The desk sergeant rolled his eyes as she ran at top speed for the back door of the station that would lead across the alley to the morgue.

But she didn't have to run far.

In that alley waited postal worker Ken Silverman, who was angry at his wife, his boss, and the fact that his best friend had been arrested by the police for the sixth time for drunk driving. Because of that, Ken's friend had lost his job.

So while sorting letters, Ken decided to do something about every-thing. He went home that afternoon, early, without telling anyone and immediately got in a fight with his wife, took out the pistol he had bought for her to protect herself coming home on bridge night, and shot her in the chest three times.

Then he reloaded, went back down to the post office and shot his boss, then calmly walked downtown to the police station where he waited in the alley until Josepha came out.

He told her to stop.

She saw his gun and reached for hers. She had just been trained last month to do the draw and she knew how to do it real well.

But she never really got to it.

He shot her.

Twice.

Two hours later Betty's handbag ended up in Josepha's personal stuff in a locker in the morgue. And there it seemed destined to stay.

Well, maybe not.

Six

THE NEXT MORNING Jill, Josepha's twin sister, arrived at the morgue with her husband Jack Hill. Jill had obviously been crying all night and it took everything Jack could do to keep her from tumbling to the floor in a pile as she looked at poor Josepha laid out there on the slab, two holes punched in her chest and a look of surprise stuck on her face.

After all the viewing and crying and stuff was over, the night guy at the morgue, who had suddenly been promoted to the day guy, handed Jill her sister's box of personal things. Jill thanked him and without even looking at what was in the box left the morgue.

At home that night, in front of a crackling fire, she got up the nerve to open the box.

Inside was Josepha's uniform with two holes in it.

Her bra, also with two holes in it, but these holes were designed by the manufacturer and Jill was shocked. She quickly hid the bra so Jack wouldn't see it. She didn't want him to get any ideas.

Little did she know that Jack knew about the holes in Josepha's bra, and much more, too. He had spent many a night peeking into Jill's sister's bedroom window when he had told his wife he was out jogging. He always came home sweating, so she believed him.

Jill found no underwear in the box, but some nylons and lace garters. There was an envelope with the contents of Josepha's pockets in it. Just some change and a wine opener.

So Jill opened the big black handbag and the first thing she pulled out was the picture of a naked Betty.

"Oh my God," Jill said.

"Something I can do, dear," Jack said as he came in from the kitchen and looked over her shoulder. Before Jill could hide the picture he too gasped. "Who's that?"

"I don't know," Jill said.

Jill dropped the picture on the carpet and looked carefully into the purse. And there she saw this finger-long piece of shriveled skin and meat.

With her fingernails she gently picked it out of the purse and held it up. "What is—?"

"My God!" Jack said. "It's a man's penis!"

Jill screamed, dropped the penis into the bag, and then fainted.

Jill had never seen a man's penis, not even Jack's, since they "did it" in the dark.

Twenty minutes later she still hadn't come to, so Jack called an ambulance and ten minutes after that they were speeding toward the hospital, forgetting a few things such as the handbag on the living room floor, Jill's own much smaller purse on the stand beside the front door, and locking the back door.

Outside Bad Boy Benny Burges, the fifteen-year-old neighborhood bully and drug pusher watched the scene as they rushed Jill from the house to the ambulance.

He smiled to himself and ambled slowly down the tree-lined street as the ambulance sped off. He went an entire block before cutting through to the alley and then back to the rear of Jill's house.

He smiled even bigger when he discovered the back door was unlocked.

And he broke out into an even bigger smile when he saw the handbag and the purse. He stuffed the small purse into the handbag without checking either, then went upstairs to look for more cash and stuff.

His smile almost hurt when he found the jar in Jack's shoe with a role of $100 bills that Jack had used to buy hookers. And when he found Jill's "mad" money in her secret diary behind the fake part of her top drawer he just couldn't help it any more. He started laughing.

Now, anyone who really knew Benny knew he never laughed. In fact most of Benny's friends had never even seen him smile.

But on this night he laughed all the way to the alley, swinging the black handbag like it was a toy.

He laughed and even whistled a little down the three blocks to the back of the Safeway grocery store where he was going to go through the purses and toss them in the dumpster. Every time he thought how much money he had found and how easy it had been, he laughed. He reached the dumpster and opened the handbag. He was set for the next two weeks. He didn't have to worry about a thing.

Well, maybe not.

Seven

KEN THE POSTAL worker was still mad and still at large. And at the moment he was sitting beside the trash compactor behind the Safeway grocery store wondering who he should kill next and who he was the maddest at.

He saw Benny walk up with the woman's handbag in his hand and open it over the dumpster, smiling and whistling. And because Benny was smiling so much Ken just shot him.

Benny, being a big strong boy, dropped the handbag into the dump-ster and staggered back.

Ken followed him, pointing the gun at him.

Benny choked a little because the bullet had hit his left chest, nicking his lung. But somehow he had enough strength to keep moving away from Ken.

And Ken just followed him.

Right down the side of the grocery store.

Right across the parking lot.

And right into the street, where a cop named Roger spotted what was going on and yelled for Ken to halt.

Ken shot Benny again, twice.

Then turned to shoot Roger. But Roger had been around a few blocks before and he fired first, twice, killing Ken.

While all this was going on out front of the grocery store, it was trash day around back. The huge dump truck manned by Jerry and Tom picked up the dumpster and emptied it, handbag and all.

Then, since the Safeway was their last stop for the day, they headed for the city landfill not realizing what they carried, or the fact that they had run over blood stains from a recent shooting. To them it just looked like V-Eight Juice.

They dumped their load in the smelly landfill and left.

Henry's penis was buried under a truck-load of garbage and bad lettuce. It would never find its way to Henry now.

Well, maybe not.

Eight

THE NEXT DAY a plow driven by ex-lawyer Carl pushed the pile of garbage into a hole to move it out of the way so more trucks could dump their loads. Carl, like the justice system he used to play with, was mostly blind, so he never paid much attention to what he pushed around with the plow. He just moved it around to make room.

Constance Poe, a perky blonde with a good attitude and a lousy ex-husband, drove her Datsun pickup up to the edge of the landfill. She had been planning to move and was searching for a small house to buy and make her very own. But while she was searching, she figured she might as well be cleaning out her apartment and she had filled her Datsun pickup with junk to take to the dump.

She opened the door, wrinkled her nose at the sour smell, and choked back down the instant breakfast she had had earlier. She hated the smell of garbage.

Her big black dog Shep jumped out and went sniffing around. He, on the other hand, loved it.

"You be careful," Constance yelled to Shep as she started tossing the junk from the back of her truck onto the other piles of garbage.

Carl's moving of the pile had exposed the handbag and opened it slightly.

Shep sniffed the bag, stuck his nose inside, and pulled out Henry's penis.

Then with one gulp he ate it and went back to sniffing around.

Now it was certain that Henry's penis would never find its way back to Henry, and to the burial it deserved. Henry was clearly going into the afterlife dickless.

Well, maybe not.

Nine

CONSTANCE FINISHED UNLOADING the truck, got Shep back inside, and headed for home. All the way she left the windows down to clear out the smell of the dump and Shep rode with his head sticking out the window, his tongue hanging out, drool splattering the passenger door.

At home she cleaned up by taking a long shower and tossing her clothes into the washer.

Then she spent a quiet evening listening to the news and all the awful things that had been going on around the city that day.

The next morning, she called her real estate agent, who said there was this great little house where the owner had just died and did she want to take a look? It wasn't officially for sale yet, but the agent knew the attorney who was handling the place and knew it was going to be on the market real soon. Constance could get a real jump on it.

Constance said it sounded a little disrespectful to the dead, but sure, why not, really. The owner of the house was dead, after all, so who would really care. She and Shep piled into the truck and met the agent, Selma, at the house.

The house was a mess, with unwashed dishes and lots of garbage everywhere.

But to Constance it had possibilities.

And the back yard had this great hot tub. Blue, with great tile around it.

The agent didn't mention that the previous owner had died in the hot tub. What Constance didn't know, wouldn't hurt her, the agent figured.

And while they talked about the house, Shep took a shit.

Right beside the hot tub.

Henry's penis had come home.

When Constance moved in she planted a wonderful flower garden beside the hot tub and one flower grew even bigger than all the rest, right from the spot where Shep had shit.

Well, maybe not.

BUTCHERED WHALE

Sometimes a detective can see with more than just his eyes. And sometimes a detective must take steps to stop murders, steps that seem harsh in the cold light of day.

A woman, killed in her own bedroom, brutally skinned like an animal, seems to be just another victim in a ritualized killing. But to one special detective, she plays a much larger roll than victim.

She might very well be a savior.

YOU COULD SAY it wasn't a pretty sight. I never would, but you could say that, and I'm sure it would be the truth. I never say anything about how something looks, because I am blind. But I "see" just fine in other ways.

I can tell you a mile away that there is a dead raccoon rotting in the heat on the side of a road. I can tell you what the last shudder of a common fly with its wings ripped off sounds like. I can even tell you what it feels like to shake a lying man's hand.

But telling you exactly what a dead whale on a red bedspread in a small bedroom *looks* like just isn't possible for me to do.

But I do have enough to visualize it.

I know the bedroom was that of a woman who wore perfume and

164

used Ivory soap to wash her clothes. I know the bedroom has one bed, a dresser to the right of the door, and a window on the street side.

I know the woman is dead on the bedspread.

My partner, J.P. Rancher shuddered beside me, meaning the sight in front of us was just plain ugly. J.P. very seldom shuddered at the sight of a dead whale. But for some reason this one made him shudder.

I knew J.P. almost as well as he knew himself. For instance, this morning, before coming to pick me up, he'd had sex with his girlfriend. He hadn't told me, but he slurred his words slightly, laughed at everything, and just reeked of passion. I may be blind, but I know a happily-screwed man when I smell one.

"That bad, huh?" I asked in response to J.P's reaction.

"Yeah," J.P. said, softly. The last word was more like a sigh than a word.

"Man or woman?" I asked, trying to get him and me back on track. I knew it was a woman, but I had to get him focused as well. We had a job to do.

"Woman," JP said.

"How big?"

"Small, maybe five-one. One hundred and ten pounds. No fat. Nude. She had been a looker..."

"...before this," I said, finishing his sentence. "Standard death?"

"Yeah," J.P. said, "harpoon through the chest, then the hunter skinned and gutted her."

There was bile mixed with blood and fecal matter in the smell. "The hunter must have nicked an intestine. Sloppy work."

"Yeah, real sloppy," J.P said.

"Lamp?"

"Gone," J.P. said. "Looks like it used to be on the bed stand."

"I'll bet the house was tossed as well," I said. "This hunter was a rookie."

"Got it in one," J.P. said. "I'll get all the standard crime boys into action. With someone this new we might get lucky."

I nodded as J.P left my side. My hearing was so good I could have listened to his conversation in the next room, but I knew almost word-for-word what he was going to say. So instead I stood there in the middle of the room and studied everything.

The smell was that of blood and shit and fear.

The room was stuffy, the air still, so clearly the windows were closed tight, with no drafts.

I took a deep breath of the thick air and made myself relax into the place. I used my senses to search out the light smell of breakfast made and cleaned up after hours before.

I imagined the woman, opening the front door and being surprised by a hunter, who shoved her to her bed and shot her with a harpoon. I imagined the skinning, the ceremony of taking the lamp, the final slashing of the skull to destroy the clone link before the hunter left.

But J.P had not mentioned the skull slash. Was this hunter that sloppy?

Of course, I knew there was another thing missing. In all the whale deaths I had investigated, there had always been a clear odor, at least to me, of fish. This room had no such smell.

J.P claimed he could never smell it, but he was a sighted person and he hadn't learned how to use his nose and other senses like I had.

Without even looking, I knew this wasn't a whale that had been killed. The person on that bed, harpooned and skinned, had been human.

I did not smile.

I stood and waited for my partner to come back into the room. I knew better than to move around a crime scene, no matter how good I was at getting around without sight. I needed J.P. to get here and help me outside, and he was still giving orders in the next room to the techs.

Having a human killed in a ritual whale ceremony confused issues greatly. Detectives had to figure out why this poor woman had been targeted as a whale? Had it just been a mistake? Or was this a copy-cat killer by someone who wanted her dead?

Besides the clone chip in the skull behind the left ear, there was no real difference between whales and humans. And the clone chip had been made to look like skull bone on any scan.

So it was impossible to know the difference at a glance. And I believed there really was no difference. Intelligent beings were intelligent beings, but my viewpoint was still in the minority around the world.

Whale intelligence had been first put into cloned human bodies thirty years before in an underground lab in Greenland. The theory was that the twenty scientists in the lab were looking for a way to help save the whales from extinction. I personally think they were just making excuses to justify their working on clones.

The scientists were shocked to learn that whale intelligence could be transferred, unlike human brains, and that the whales were as intelligent as humans. With a human cloned body and training, whales quickly learned a human language and how to function completely in the general population.

And they liked it, at least most whales did. They wanted to stay out of the water, they wanted to keep their fingers, their ability to move around freely on land.

Without telling anyone what they were doing, the scientists in the underground lab worked for years to grow and transfer as many whale intelligences into human cloned bodies as they could. These whales were then sent out all over the world to live normal human lives, with the only drawback being they had to have a certain light every night for a number of hours to stay healthy.

I had been dealing with whale killings for years and I still didn't completely understand the light. But with the hunters, the lights were the real trophies. The skin was the only proof offered to other hunters in the ritual celebration at their lodges. But each lamp was placed in a spot of honor, with the hunters name on it.

It had become illegal to kill whales in human cloned bodies shortly after the news of their existence became public. But arresting humans for killing what many considered to be nothing more than animals was not a popular job. J.P. and I had been doing it for years, and we had gotten used to the names and the anger and the lack of respect that came at us. We were catching killers and that was all that mattered to us.

Over time I started to understand what made humans in general so angry at the whales. It wasn't that they were clones. It was because they were alien in nature and had a chance of living forever.

The early scientists discovered a way to move whale intelligence not only from a whale's body to a human clone, but from one human clone to another. For some reason scientists have yet to figure out how to move human brains from one to another, let alone do it for a second time, so we humans are still stuck with a short hundred years of life, while whales can possibly go on living forever.

A lot of people don't much like that.

By five years ago the anger against whales in general had become so great that there were only a few thousand natural whales left in the oceans. But who knew how many there were living and having children in secret tanks and labs to be put into cloned human bodies.

And like the old days in the south, organizations had been formed to keep the whales in their place, to get rid of the whales if possible. They were called hunting lodges, and they developed their own rituals that they followed with every killing.

I very much wanted to skin every member of those lodges, just as they skinned the whales.

J.P.'s footsteps told me he was headed back toward me.

"We have a problem," I said, lifting an arm in the general direction of the body. "She wasn't a whale."

"What?" J.P. asked.

"Unless whales have managed to get rid of the underlying fish odor, that woman was completely human. Is her skull caved in?"

"Yeah," J.P. said. "Let me check it."

I could sense that J.P had waved for a tech to come into the room to help him, and after a moment a man with a slight after shave habit who had had bacon for breakfast entered the small bedroom.

I knew the guy stared at me for a moment, then turned his breakfast breath away to work with J.P over the body.

"Shit!" J.P said after eight seconds.

"No clone chip, right?" I asked.

"No clone chip. She was human."

"Third one this month," I said. "Detectives with the human division seem to have a problem on their hands."

The tech snorted and said nothing. I liked to use the words "human division" when talking about human crimes, even though J.P. and I were the only members of the "whale division" of the force.

No one much cared that a whale got killed. No real cops moved to close down the hunting lodges. Some cops were even members. But after more and more humans died they were going to care. Of that I had no doubt.

And then, maybe, the whale hunting would be stopped by the decent people of the world. I could only hope, because it was a large sacrifice some people were making to have this change happen.

I didn't know the woman spread out harpooned and skinned in front of me, but she had given her life for the cause of humane treatment for whales. Other humans would do the same until the hunting lodges were a thing of the past, and the law dealt with whale hunters like they did any other sick killer.

"Looks like we're done with this case, partner," I said. We never took cases in which humans were killed. The whale deaths kept us busy enough.

"Sure does," J.P. said. "Let's get out of this mess and let the next detectives in line take the ball."

J.P. touched my elbow and with only slight pressure made sure I made it out of the room and the house without stepping on any evidence. With luck the detectives would catch this killer and string him up.

I got to J.P.'s car and slid in as he talked to the cop we were leaving in charge until the new set of detectives got there.

I was glad that we had not been in that home long enough for me to get to know much about the victim. She had been killed by the stupidity and fear and hatred that had grown in our culture against the whales. I had had very little to do with it.

Granted, I had given her address twelve days ago, a perfectly random address, to someone on the internet who I knew would pass it on as a possible whale home, and then have it passed on again, and then again, through underground meetings in five countries, until it found a hunting lodge in this city and a sick killer who would do the job.

My involvement could never be traced, that much I made sure of. I hadn't done the killing, I had just given out an address.

A random address. There might have been a whale living there. There might have been a human. I didn't know, but I hoped for a human, and again this time I had been right.

Tonight I would start another address for this city floating out there on the underground streams of information about whales. Every night, in a different way, I started addresses in major cities around the country.

The increase in killings of humans thought to be whales was starting to make the national news.

People were starting to get unhappy.

Whale killings were starting to drop off.

So far the deaths were paying off. I would continue until finally enough humans had died to make the hatred and killing stop.

If nothing else, each human death helped remove a killer of whales from the street if the detectives did their jobs. And as far as I was concerned, that seemed only fair.

I wondered what the great hunter who had skinned that woman in there was going to think when he discovered she had been one hundred percent human?

"What are you smiling about?" J.P. asked as he slid in behind the steering wheel and started the car.

"The piece of cheesecake I'm going to buy you at Audry's."

"Oh, man," J.P. said, roughly pushing the car forward and into the light traffic I could hear on the road. "I was hoping you were going to say that. Just keep on smiling until I get us there."

I thought about the hope for the future whales had. I thought about their hope of living as equals with humans, and it did keep me smiling.

Right up to the moment that I picked the next random address.

THE WAITING OF THE WIND

A Buckey the Space Pirate Story

When Buckey the Space Pirate decides to take a creative writing course, of course he turns for help to his best friend, Fred the talking oak tree.

Fred knows the English language better than any human alive. But Fred is still an oak tree, and oak trees do have their quirks when it comes to writing.

First Attempt

I knew the wind was waiting for me. The wind always did. It was my fault for falling in love with the wind. For letting the wind fall in love with me. If I had just worn panties that breezy day in April, this never would have happened. Or jeans instead of that light cotton dress. But it was such a beautiful spring day, the kind of day that makes a person want to feel free, and I wanted to feel completely free.

And the wind noticed.

"WHAT DO YOU think? Nifty opening to the story, huh?"

Fred, the fifteen-foot oak tree, said, "You write well for a space pirate, Buckey."

Oh, oh, not a good sign when an oak tree damns with faint praise.

I could feel the sweat dripping down my back from the heat. I was wearing cutoffs and a tee-shirt to stay cool against the eighty-five degree afternoon temperature and was using what little shade the oak tree gave me as well. But Fred was so darned skinny, I had to move the lawn chair and glass of lemonade every fifteen minutes just to try to stay in his shadow.

And now he clearly didn't like the story I was working on for class.

I had had on my Buckey the Space Pirate science fiction convention costume (sword, plumed hat, and black tights) the first time Fred talked to me.. Or at least the last incarnation of Fred talked to me. So he still called me a space pirate and Buckey, even though that wasn't my name and he knew it.

Fred is a talking oak tree and I'm sort of his dad. But since Fred can travel back along the lines of oak trees in his family for millions of years, I mostly feel like a kid in front of my own kid.

A time-traveling and talking oak tree can make a person feel very small if he wants to.

The previous Fred (who stood in the old park downtown and was cut down because they needed to widen the road) told me how he came to be able to actually talk to humans. On the night before his death he suggested I do the same thing to save him and give him the skill to once again talk to humans. It seemed he was the only oak tree in all of creation that could and if I didn't help him, the skill would die with the chain saws.

So after I was convinced that it just wasn't someone playing a practical joke on me, I used a prophylactic for what it was supposed to be used for, then put a seed from the first Fred in the rubber and planted everything in my mother's backyard.

The new little Fred started talking about a year later and we've been best friends ever since. Which is why I spend so much time in my mother's backyard. I know, weird for a college kid, but at least I don't live in her basement anymore. And since I can't seem to find a girlfriend at the moment, I don't have much else to do.

I took a drink from the lemonade my mom had made for me and glanced back at her house. I had told my mom that I needed to work on a summer school writing project for my creative writing class I was taking, so I might be talking out loud some. The creative writing class in the summer sounded like an easy way to get some credits and get part of the English credits I needed for my degree in history out of my way.

And besides, with what I could learn about history from Fred, I was going to need to learn how to do the books I was going to get rich writing about little-known facts in history. Fred actually showing me history, real history, was why after three years I had switched my major to history from political science.

Today Mom had just shrugged when I said I would be out back. She was getting used to me being in the back yard at all times of the year talking to a tree. I know she worried about me, but at least I wasn't in jail, and as far as she was concerned, that was a victory in its own right.

"Come, on Fred," I said to the oak tree. "It wasn't that bad."

"For a space pirate, I suppose not," Fred said again, his voice sort of surrounding me as it always did. His voice was growing deeper with each month of growth. Pretty soon he would be back to the old depth of voice from the first Fred I met.

I glanced at the spiral notebook in my hand. That first paragraph I had read to him wasn't so bad. I was sort of proud of it to be honest.

"So what's wrong with it?"

"I could illustrate with a limerick," Fred said.

"No limericks," I said, being firm. "Just tell me what's wrong."

Fred loved limericks and most of the time they were just flat rude. Over the last few years I had come to hate them, although I had to admit some of the ones Fred made up stayed with you. And if I let Fred get going on limericks, any real thought of conversation would end completely.

"Besides the anthropomorphism of the wind and the overuse of passive voice, nothing."

"Coming from a talking baby oak tree," I said, "that's an amazing criticism."

"Everyone knows the wind can't talk," Fred said.

"Everyone knows oak trees can't talk either," I said.

But looking at the paper, I knew he had a point about the passive structure. My professor had spent an hour of her time talking on just that alone.

So I turned the page and tried again.

Second Attempt

I knew the wind waited for me. The wind always did. My fault for falling in love with the wind and for letting the wind fall in love with me. I decided against wearing panties under my light dress that breezy day in April. A mistake. But the beautiful spring day opened my mind, made me mad for the desire to be free in all ways. I wanted to feel completely open to everything.

And the wind noticed.

I LOOKED UP at the tender green leaves of the young oak tree shading me from the hot afternoon sun. "Well?"

Fred said nothing.

"You have to admit, no passive verbs in that one. And it's shorter as well."

"Less pain on the reader," Fred said. "Always a good thing."

I knew this conversation wasn't going to go anywhere. Fred seemed to know more about the human language than any human I had ever met. I had no idea why I thought I could write to meet his tastes. After all, I was just a beginner.

But being a sucker for punishment I went on. "So, what's wrong?"

"Setting would be nice," Fred said. "Right now you just have some woman jabbering about getting goosed by a gust of wind. Boring pretty much describes it. But I do have a limerick that might spice up the piece."

"No limericks," I said. "I need to finish this for a grade in this writing class."

"You would be better served to spend your days in your Buckey the Space Pirate costume taking gratuities for saving young damsels in distress. But since you are not likely to take up such a noble occupation, try to write it again and I will listen again."

I nodded and went back to work on the third rewrite of the opening of my story.

Third Attempt

From the top of the rocky cliff of Lover's Leap, I could see out over the green, deep valley below and the river that gave it life. I knew the wind waited for me. The wind always did. My fault for falling in love with the wind, for letting the wind fall in love with me. I decided against wearing panties under my light cotton dress that breezy day in April. A mistake. But the beautiful spring day opened my mind, made me mad for the desire to be free in all ways. I wanted to feel completely open.

And the wind noticed.

Now I stood naked waiting for the wind to take me to the sky so we could be together, drifting over the beautiful green valley and the winding blue river..

"Brooke, no!" Rich shouted from behind me as he climbed the dusty trail toward me.

I READ IT to him again.

"Wow, characters, conflict, and a setting," the little oak tree said. "I'm impressed."

I knew for a fact he wasn't. Oak trees have a level of sarcasm that has few matches in the human race. I suppose that comes from standing in the same place for hundreds of years and letting their minds roam through time. If I had to do that I'd be sarcastic as well.

And completely crazy.

"Come on, Fred. Honestly, I need a grade here. Help me out."

"All right. First, how about better names. In all the fantastic names humans have taken through time, you pick an English woman's name that means stream and a male's name that implies money. Dull. Find names that add layered meaning to your story."

"Says a tree named Fred."

"Short for Friedrich, which means peaceful ruler."

I looked up at the young oak tree. "Why did you shorten it?"

"There was a time in my early years in the downtown park when a German-sounding name was not a welcome thing, so I decided to change it."

"Oh, that's right, you were around in the park for World War Two," I said.

"And The Great War," Fred said. "Besides, would you have listened to me if I said my name was Friedrich?"

"If I remember right, I couldn't shut you up that first time we met."

"I was just trying to entertain your date in my last days."

"By calling one of her body parts, a part I was very interested in exploring, larger than a punt? You call that entertaining?"

I was still mad at him for that.

"I was enjoying myself," the little oak tree said.

The sun seemed to get hotter even through the thin shade from Fred's leaves.

I took a long drink from my lemonade. Most of the ice had melted, which meant I had been out here in the sun more than long enough.

"So if I change the character names, will it pass?"

"Oh, I would think so," Fred said.

"Thank you," I said, closing my notebook and climbing out of my lawn chair.

"But a nice limerick would help you so much more."

"I have to learn how to write on my own," I said. "Not copy down your words. That won't help me at all."

"A Space Pirate with morals," Fred said. "Who would have known? I tell you, saving the fair damsels in distress would be a calling for you."

"Getting a degree in history and getting into a good graduate school is the only calling I care about at the moment."

"Suit yourself," Fred said.

"See you later." I turned for the house.

"Do come back and read me your finished story," Fred said. "I so want to learn how the woman with no underwear used her private regions to fly with the wind like Dumbo. My kind of story."

I just shook my head. As I said, oak trees can be very, very sarcastic. Then behind me Fred started into a limerick.

"There was a woman of Kings
Who ate all three meals of beans..."

"Don't go there!" I said as I walked away. "I can still hear you."

For a moment the little oak tree remained silent. Then as I had almost reached the house, he started into a new limerick.

"There was a woman quite stewed,
whose clothing was found very strewed,
and if I'm not mistaken,
the wind did the takin'
and left her on the rocks most screwed."

As I reached the back porch I shouted back at the young oak tree, "Passive construction, no characters, and setting would be nice."

For the first time in two years, I got the last word on the oak tree.

THE WAR OF POKER

A Poker Boy Story

Poker Boy somehow finds himself facing an imitation of his girlfriend, Patty Ledgerwood.

Within a fraction of a second he somehow saves himself and maybe the world from another war.

Or maybe he helps set up a new war in the future.

I WAS STARTING to figure out that if I wanted a new case or some problem to come up threatening the world and everything I knew, all I had to do was stand in the main lobby of the Las Vegas MGM Grand. Someone, some problem, somehow would find me.

At the moment I really didn't want a new case, but I had learned as a superhero that people needing help or problems needing solving didn't happen when I wanted them to. Annoying, but true.

But even though it might lead to the end of everything I knew, I often spent time in the MGM Grand lobby wearing my black leather coat and black Fedora-like hat that was my superhero uniform, leaning against the same marble pillar, waiting for my girlfriend and sidekick, Patty Ledgerwood, aka Front Desk Girl, to get off work.

That I stood there was common knowledge and also might have

something to do with people and problems being able to find me. Superheroes are not normally regular in their schedules.

But standing and waiting and sometimes getting cases was worth it as long as the world didn't end. I liked watching the crowds and watching Patty work. Her long brown hair, deep brown eyes, and wide smile always made me feel wonderful. To say I was in love would be an understatement.

The only place I spent more time was in poker rooms. But except for the poker room at Spirit Winds casino in the mountains of Oregon near my doublewide trailer, I seldom played poker in the same casino. My job as Poker Boy, a superhero in the gambling universe, was to help those who needed help and take the money at poker tables from those who needed it taken because of their poor play.

Sometimes the two parts of my job crossed and combined, but usually the money part just paid the expenses for the superhero part.

Technically, since I was a superhero in the poker-playing niche of the universe, I should only be solving problems associated around poker and poker rooms. But over the last few years I had managed to gather a team of superheroes around me from different aspects of the world. As a team, we had become known for solving some of the stranger problems to come along, including saving the entire world from tiny bugs one day, stopping an alien invasion on another adventure, and saving Lady Luck herself yet another day.

When the team got to work, things were never dull.

Patty, who was part of that team, was still fifteen minutes away from getting off work when I sensed a problem coming toward me. I call that sense my "tingly-warning bell" superpower. Sometimes, but not always, I know when danger is approaching. It's not the kind of power I can trust like Spider-Man trusts his "Spidey-Sense." I often wished my power was that dependable. But when I feel that shiver and the tingle go down my spine like a drip of ice water, I have learned to pay attention. Danger is close by.

Right at that moment a river of ice was flowing all over my spine and I shivered like someone had turned up the MGM Grand air-conditioning to the Arctic setting.

I swung around to see the most beautiful woman I had ever seen walking toward me with a smile. She had long brown hair that seemed to just glow in the bright lights of the lobby, wide brown eyes, and a perfect smile. She wore the uniform of the MGM front desk crew and wore it better than anyone had a right to wear a simple white blouse and brown slacks.

In fact, the woman walking toward me looked exactly like my girl-friend, Patty.

I glanced around at the front desk wondering how I had managed to miss Patty leaving work.

I hadn't.

Patty was still standing behind the desk working with a customer. Her hair was still tucked up tight on her head. She never let it down until she got off work.

I spun back to the woman walking at me.

It was Patty all right, walking toward me smiling, giving me that "look" with her big brown eyes that could melt every ounce of resistance I had toward anything.

All I could do was stare.

How could there be two Patty Ledgerwoods?

The ice shivers running around on my back finally snapped me out of my shock and I stepped out of time, freezing everyone around me.

The loud sounds of the nearby casino and people talking and background music all vanished instantly.

I loved the ability to do that. I actually couldn't stop time, but I could pull myself out of the flow of time and into an instant so that it appeared to me that time had stopped around me.

I liked to think of it as me being in a bubble outside of time, but that wasn't right exactly either.

Around me kids were frozen in mid-scream, husbands were stopped in mid-look at another woman, bellhops were stopped with a bag halfway onto a cart.

And there were no sounds.

None.

The superpower came in very, very handy and I had learned that when in doubt about anything, I should just get out of the flow of time and give myself some time to think.

I turned toward the front desk again. My girlfriend, Patty, was frozen in mid-sentence behind the front desk of the MGM Grand hotel talking to a woman with a bored-looking husband in bright red shorts. I knew that was Patty. Everything about me could sense that was the woman I loved behind the counter.

From the other direction, the woman who looked just like Patty was frozen in mid-stride about ten steps from where I stood. Her smile looked artificial when frozen like that.

And every sense I had told me she was nothing but danger.

Extreme danger.

I went over and walked around her, studying every detail about her.

She was an exact duplicate of Patty, right down to the tiny mole on her neck.

Same height, same shape, everything.

Creepy didn't begin to describe what I was feeling and I quickly went back to my original position. My damn warning power kept making me shiver like I was fighting upwind through a cold snowstorm in nothing but a swimming suit.

I needed help and I needed it now.

As a superhero, I had learned a long time ago that there were many, many things in the world I did not understand. And with that learning I had lost all fear of just calling for help when there was something I flat didn't understand.

Right now I had no idea what was happening, but I knew it couldn't be good. One Patty Ledgerwood was more than enough for me.

I glanced at the ceiling and shouted "Stan! Need help!"

I have no idea why I look up when I am calling out for Stan, the God of Poker and my immediate boss, but I always do, and he has never failed to show up at once.

And this time was no exception.

He appeared next to me, also out of time. I had no idea how he could do that, jump right into my frozen moment in time and join me, but he had done it in the past so now was not the time to be asking him how. It seemed for the gods, time was a lot easier to deal with than for us mortals and superheroes.

Stan had on a plain pair of brown slacks and a tan, open-collared dress shirt. His brown hair was perfectly combed as always and you could walk by him a hundred times and never notice him. He was a perfect master of disguise and blending in.

He glanced at the woman who looked like Patty walking toward me, then frowned, something I hated when my boss and the God of Poker did it around me.

"That's not Patty," I said. I pointed back at the main desk of the hotel. "That's Patty."

"I know that," he said, only glancing back at the real Patty. He eased toward the imitation Patty slowly and carefully, like trying to sneak up on a sleeping bear.

He was clearly seeing something I was not seeing.

After two steps, he stopped. "We need help. How long can you hold this field?"

"Another half hour," I said, checking in with how I was feeling holding the bubble with me and Stan out of the time stream. I had gotten pretty good at this super power.

Suddenly I could feel that it was slipping.

"Less," I said, now straining to hold the field. "It's slipping."

Stan nodded and focused for a moment.

The field holding us out of time solidified again.

"What caused that?" I asked, trying to catch my breath. It actually felt like I had just run a hundred-meter sprint.

"She did," he said, pointing at the imitation Patty.

Suddenly I could feel the time bubble starting to slip again.

Stan suddenly looked a little panicked and some beads of sweat broke out on his forehead as he too struggled to hold the field.

"She knows what we are doing," Stan said.

I didn't want to know how he knew or how she could know unless she was some god. I didn't want to think about the fact that I had frozen in time a god and she would be angry at me.

Stan moaned and sweat started to run down his neck. I felt like the time bubble I was working to hold now weighed as much as a large truck. No chance I could hold it much longer and as a poker player, there was nothing on the planet more frightening to me than to see the God of Poker sweat and strain.

Stan glanced up at the ceiling. "Burt! Laverne! Help!"

Every ounce of energy I had was going to hold Stan and me out of time at that moment, or I would have just sat down stunned. Stan had just called for Burt, the God of Casino Operations and Lady Luck herself, the most powerful god I had ever met.

Who or what was this Patty imitator and why had she scared me and Stan so much?

Burt and Laverne appeared next to the now sweat-covered Stan. Burt wore a gray, three-piece silk business suit and his short stature made him look more like a mob boss than a major god. Laverne was dressed in a black pants suit with matching jacket and had her hair pulled back tight.

"What is the…"

Then she saw the Patty imitator and Lady Luck herself actually flushed.

Suddenly the pressure was off holding the time bubble as both Burt and Lady Luck took over, giving Stan and me a rest.

My rubbery knees wanted me to slump to the floor and give them a rest, but instead I managed to keep on my feet trying to catch my breath.

"Who is that?" I managed to ask.

"Morrígan," Lady Luck said, walking over around the imitation Patty. "The Phantom Queen as she is often called. And why she is coming to you, Poker Boy, is a mystery."

Now I was officially and formally scared. When Laverne, Lady Luck herself, didn't know something, I knew I was in deep trouble. So I didn't ask the next question on my mind…Who was Morrígan?

"I thought Morrígan was only a myth," Stan said, looking very worried. "Right along with her sisters."

I still had no idea who Morrígan was.

"Nope, all three are real," Burt said, looking very worried. "Just not around much these days."

I am sure I looked worried as well, but that was because I had no idea what was going on and because they were all worried and they were far more powerful than I was.

"After Atlantis," Laverne said, "Morrígan pretty much stayed in the Alps and out of any of the world's problems."

"I heard she was around for the two big wars," Stan said. "After all, she is known as the Goddess of War."

Oh, wow, it was *that* Morrígan who stood there frozen looking like my girlfriend. When a very, very old god started pretending to be your girlfriend, things could not be going well.

Laverne shook her head. "Both wars Morrígan stayed in Switzer-land, neutral."

"What is she doing in Las Vegas?" Burt asked.

And instant later Morrígan, still looking like Patty, moved and smiled at Laverne as she stepped into our frozen time bubble. "You could just ask me," she said.

"That's why I brought you out of time," Laverne said, her voice cold and as hard as I had ever heard Lady Luck sound.

"Nice seeing you again as well," Morrígan said to Laverne.

She might look like Patty, but the voice was nothing like Patty's at all. Patty had a softness to her voice. This imposter sounded harsh, with a coldness in every sentence.

Laverne just stared at Morrígan and the stare was returned in kind. There was clearly no love lost between the two women.

After a moment the woman's appearance shifted. The Patty-look sort of melted and formed into a woman who had long, black hair, a very, very thin face with a long, thin nose, and eyes that were coal black. She had on a white pants suit and was as thin as any supermodel I had ever seen. She towered over all of us because not only was she tall, but she somehow managed to stand on six-inch heels.

Laverne said nothing.

Finally Morrígan smiled at Laverne. "Fine, if you want to be that way, I came to ask a favor of Poker Boy."

Morrígan smiled at me, then went back to staring at Laverne.

I figured if my heart was ever going to explode out of my chest at any point in my life, now was the time. I was stunned I hadn't just fainted dead away under that look. The woman was totally terrifying. I hadn't been this scared in any recent memory. And that was with three of the most powerful gods in existence standing beside me.

"You could have just come to me," Laverne said.

"And you would have agreed?" Morrígan asked, smiling.

"Of course not," Laverne said.

Looks like I was off the hook at least for the moment.

"That's why I had to take a chance on approaching Poker Boy directly," Morrígan said. "But he is as good as his reputation and saw me coming, clearly."

I think I had just been complimented by an enemy of Lady Luck. Not something I would ever want as a poker player.

"So what was the favor?" Laverne asked, her voice perfectly level and very, very cold.

"I wanted him to teach me how to play poker," Morrígan said.

"I assumed as much," Lady Luck said. "Why?"

The idea of teaching that woman anything, let alone poker had my knees weak again. I would rather have five guns pointed at my head than do that.

My warning chill was doing tap dances up and down my spine.

Morrígan laughed, but there was no real humor in the laugh and it brought no smiles to anyone around me. It just made the cold shivers on my spine increase. I was shivering so hard from my danger warning sense, it was lucky my foot wasn't pounding on the ground like an excited dog.

I was going to need to figure out a way to turn that warning signal off when I needed to.

"You might know I have been hanging around with Ares lately," Morrígan said.

I wanted to shout *"The God of War!"* But somehow I managed to stay silent.

"I heard you have been living together since the Cuban Missile Crisis," Laverne said.

"Yeah, he got depressed," Morrígan said, "He was so looking forward to that war. He thought it would have been epic. I've been trying to nurse him back to health."

"I'll bet," Laverne said.

"So we've been playing some poker and I'm tired of losing," she said.

"He cheats," Laverne said flatly. "Get a new deck of cards that he has not touched and see how you do."

Morrígan stood there staring at Laverne for a very, very long moment. Laverne just stared back. For a moment I thought they had stepped outside of the time bubble and were frozen in the instant of time like everyone else in the lobby of the MGM Grand.

Then Morrígan smiled a very mean and angry smile and slowly shook her head. "That bastard."

And then she vanished.

It was as if the sun had come out after weeks of rain and I had won the lottery all in one instant. The cold chills that had been running up and down my back suddenly vanished as well.

"I hate her," Lady Luck said.

"But you might want to let her win some now," Burt said, chuckling.

"Yeah, we'll see," Laverne said.

With that they both vanished.

Stan just stood there shaking his head. Then he laughed and turned to me. "Nice job."

"What did I do?" I said, still feeling stunned.

"You saw her coming," he said. "That's amazing. It's not many people who can see through a Banshee's disguise, let along Morrígan's, the war goddess. And you got out of time without her noticing at first. Impressive against a god that powerful."

"And she's living with Ares? Right?" I asked. "The same Ares of war fame?"

"Yup," Stan said, "as long as they keep themselves entertained with each other and out of the spotlight, the planet is a lot safer."

"Until they get mad at each over a poker game," I said, suddenly feeling less hopeful for the survival of the human race.

"Yeah, until that," Stan said, thinking it was funny now.

"And she and Laverne have issues, clearly?" I asked, trying to get my mind wrapped around what had just happened.

"From way, way back," Stan said, laughing. "A long story I'll tell you about sometime, at least the parts I've heard. It predates me by a few hundred thousand years."

He patted me on the back. "Again, great job. Who knows what kind of problem or major war you just avoided."

"Thanks, I think," I said.

He laughed and vanished.

The pounding sounds of the real world came crashing back in around me as he let go of the bubble outside of time. The fine patrons of the MGM Grand Casino and Hotel were back in motion, laughing, talking, and being very human.

And right now that felt wonderful.

I moved over and leaned against the stone pillar, trying to slow down my racing heart. Patty looked up at me and smiled before going back to helping her customer.

Somehow my poker face allowed her to not notice that I had just escaped an encounter with a very dangerous woman. And who knew what else would have happened if Morrígan had gotten to me.

But how in the world was I going to tell Patty what had just happened in an instant in time right in front of her?

She was never going to believe me.

I turned my gaze to the high ceiling of the lobby. "Stan, can you meet me and Patty at the Diner in thirty minutes? Milkshakes are on me. I need help explaining what just happened. I'm still not sure myself."

I could hear a low, rumbling chuckle echo over the noise of the lobby, then his voice, "Sure thing, kid."

Patty looked up and frowned. She clearly had heard Stan's voice as well.

"Long story," I mouthed at her and she frowned, but went back to work with the customer.

A long story that had only taken an instant to happen.

And a story I had a hunch wasn't over just yet. Morrígan playing poker against Ares just couldn't turn out well. If not this century, then maybe next. That was the nature of the war of a poker game.

Especially now that Morrígan wanted to win.

TWO ROADS, NO CHOICES

The Titanic oceanliner barely escapes disaster when it rams an iceberg on its maiden voyage. Sherlock Holmes and Watson know that. The news covered it.

Then two strangers appear to ask Sherlock Holmes an impossible question: Why didn't the great ocean liner sink?

First published in Sherlock Holmes in Orbit from DAW Books, edited by Mike Resnick and Martin H. Greenberg, and written with permission of the Doyle estate.

One

THE HAND ON my shoulder seemed rough, brusque in its rush to wake me. As I roused myself from the warm comfort of my quilts and rolled to focus on the worried face of Holmes, he said "Dress quickly. And for extreme cold. We have visitors here, possibly to take us for a voyage."

Before my sleep-fogged mind could muster a response, or even a simple question as to where we would be traveling, he turned and left me to the quiet of the late-night hour.

I finished with my toilet and dressed as quickly as I could, for such awakening by Holmes had portrayed in the past a need for haste on a new case. And since my friend had taken very few cases as of late, this new adventure must be extraordinary in nature. That thought had my hands shaking with such excitement that I took two attempts to fasten my vest.

As I emerged into the main room, I found Holmes in his favorite armchair, his fingers in a steeple as was his habit when waiting patiently. He had started a robust fire to take the chill from the room and the orange light flickered across his features.

Across from him sat two strangers and immediately I was struck by their strange dress, the cut of their jackets, and the look of their hair. The one on Holme's left and closest to the door had strikingly blonde hair, green eyes, and a handsome face that showed no scars. He was also clearly the taller of the two, even though they were both sitting. At his feet was a large brown case that had the appearance of being very heavy.

His companion had long, almost shoulder-length brown hair and wore an outer coat that he had opened to the warmth of the fire, revealing on the edges of the coat a form of metal fastener with small teeth running along both sides of the opening. I had read of such a fastener before, but never seen one in use. The man had a dark complexion and seemed to be of Italian or Eastern decent.

I was shocked that Holmes had offered neither of them tea or coffee and was about to correct the oversight when Holmes said, "Oh, good, Watson. Now we can start." He indicated that I should take a chair near the hearth and I did as he instructed.

He turned to the gentlemen as I sat and nodded. "Okay, please explain who you are, why you are here, where you are from, and what you want from me."

Both of the men had been staring at me in a seemingly nervous fashion, as if I were someone they had known for a long time, yet were embarrassed to greet. I knew from what Holmes had said that he had kept them from telling their story, even so much as their names, until I was present. He did that on occasion when he felt the need of a second pair of eyes and ears. Somehow, in a standard Holmes fashion, he must have deduced that they had wanted us to go on a trip and that it would be to a cold climate. Even though I had no idea how he came to such a conclusion, I would wait until later to ask him how he knew such details.

Holmes leaned forward in anticipation and for some odd reason I found myself just able to contain my own excitement.

The short, dark-haired man cleared his throat, glanced at me and then looked directly back at Holmes. "My name is Carl. Doctor Carl Frederick. This is Doctor Henry Serling." He indicated the blonde man, who in turn nodded at both of us.

Doctor Frederick's accent seemed to be American, yet of no region that I was familiar. I would have to ask Holmes later if he knew the regional source.

Doctor Frederick went on. "Slightly over two months ago a new White Star Liner left port from Southampton."

Holmes nodded. "Yes, the RMS. Titanic."

Doctor Frederick nodded. "I'm glad you are familiar with it."

"It would be hard not to be, considering the coverage it received. It seems to be one very magnificent ship. Exceptionally lucky that it did not meet a tragic fate on that first voyage. Even an unsinkable ship meeting an iceberg can sometimes lose the battle."

Doctor Frederick glanced nervously at his companion and then said, "I don't think luck had anything to do with it."

Holmes gave him a very sharp look. "I'm afraid, Doctor, that I do not understand your comment."

Both of our guests seemed almost embarrassed, as if what they were about to say would seen so outrageous, so disgusting that Holmes would toss them into the street. I had seen that look a number of times when a person was about to confess something to Holmes. This time both men stared at their hands, then at the floor, then back at their hands.

The fire crackled and what seemed like a long time passed until finally the blonde Doctor Serling took a deep breath. "Carl, we agreed." His voice was also clearly American, but again very odd.

Doctor Frederick nodded slowly, clearly making a decision. He looked Holmes squarely in the eyes. "The Titanic was supposed to have sunk. Slightly over fifteen hundred lives were lost when it did."

I thought that someone had punched me below the ribs at that moment and I suddenly knew the taste of disgust. It never occurred to me to question that the men were crazy, but their words instantly proved them so and suddenly I felt worried for the safety of Holmes and myself.

But Holmes seemed to take the statement of the possibility of such an immense disaster as a fact. He leaned back in his chair, exhaling slowly, but never taking his gaze from Doctor Frederick. As his friend I could see the thought had him shaken, but he remained composed as always.

The fire popped and flared for a moment as Holmes said in a very cold voice, "Go on."

Again Doctor Frederick glanced at his companion. Then he half shook himself and turned to face Holmes squarely. "We need your help in solving why the Titanic did not sink."

Holmes did not even blink at such an absurd idea and when I started to object he held up his hand and stopped me. "And who might you represent?" he asked. "I assume you are not from owners of the liner or any government agency. What is your interest?"

Doctor Frederick almost laughed. Then he became very serious again. "Our lives. Our very future and that of this time, actually. You see, you will not believe me, but we are from the future. Actually, just over a hundred and two years in the future. But, I'm afraid we are from a future where the Titanic sank."

Holmes nodded. "I assumed you were not of our time from your clothes and your language the moment you stepped into this room. He nodded to Doctor Serling. You are also wearing some form of lens on your eye that I have never seen before."

Doctor Serling smiled and nodded. "They are called contact lenses. They take the place of glasses."

Both visitors seemed taken aback by Holmes calm acceptance of their bold statement that they were from the future. I, on the other hand, was not as willing to take their word. Such fancy imagination was the domain of an early evening of pleasant reading of H. G. Wells, not of the middle of the night on Baker Street.

But Holmes waited for a response. "You have still not answered my question."

Both Doctor's glanced at each other until finally Doctor Frederick seemed to understand Holmes's question. "If you mean our employer, then I suppose that originally would have been the state of California. We were both faculty at the University of Southern California, Physics Department. Our specific research into time travel was funded mostly by the United States government."

Holmes nodded, as if he understood everything they had been saying, as I suppose he might have. "Why the interest in the Titanic?"

"In our time the Titanic, and the night it sank," Doctor Frederick hesitated with that statement, then went on, "are a thing of immense interest. It wasn't until September of 1985 that the wreck of the great ship was found. Since then hundreds of expeditions have been launched to the site of the wreck. It seemed only logical that one of the first time travel expeditions would go back to the night the Titanic sank. Here, let me show you something."

He motioned for Doctor Serling to open the large case and Doctor Frederick extracted a large, colorful book. As he handed the book to Holmes I noticed the word TITANIC stamped on the front cover in red. A beautiful painting of the great liner sailing the open seas filled the cover.

"That book was originally published in 1992. We brought it along as resource material. Little did we imagine that it would be put to this use."

Again the room grew quiet except for the crackling of the fire as Holmes inspected the front and back of the large and obviously heavy book and then opened it and started slowly thumbing through.

"Flip to page 196. That section is about the discovery of the wreck. There are photographs and such."

Holmes did what he was told and then spent the next few minutes moving through the book, his keen eyes missing nothing. I had a great desire to stand and move to his side to look at such a book, but I held my place, as I know Holmes would have wanted me to do. But as the minutes wore on the task of remaining in my chair became very difficult, to say the least.

Finally Holmes closed the book and placed it on the stand beside his chair. "Since it is obvious that a tragedy such as this book portrays would have a large influence on the future, can you tell me what that might be?"

Doctor Frederick shook his head negatively. "I'm afraid not. You see, the future we came from no longer exists. At least to us. The only way possible to move forward in time for us and our machine is to a homing beacon, for lack of a better way to describe it. I could tell you about the future where the ship did sink, but—"

Doctor Serling broke in. "Let me try to explain what has occurred. With every event in history there are two or more possible futures leading from that event. Such as forks in a country road." He glanced at Holmes and Holmes nodded, so he went on. "On the night the Titanic sank the logical two main futures are a future where it did and one where it did not. Of course, there are many other possible futures where only a hundred were killed, or ninety-nine. And depending on who was saved and who wasn't, those lives lost or saved may or may not allow the futures to blend back into one. In our time we call these different worlds parallel dimensions or universes."

I caught myself shaking my head at the insanity of this man's words, but Holmes clearly was giving the man his full attention, so I said and did nothing, even though my instinct was to toss them both into the street.

"So what happened?" Holmes asked. "Did you change the past, causing the Titanic to not sink?"

"No." Both Doctors spoke at the same time and both were emphatic, as if Holmes had asked them if they had committed a mortal sin.

"We arrived, "Doctor Frederick said, "on the Titanic about two minutes before it struck the iceberg, and did nothing but watch. However it quickly became obvious that history had changed. We were unable to return to our time and ended up having to hide in unoccupied cabins until the ship sailed into New York."

"Was it possible," Holmes asked, "that your machine simply moved you over onto a different 'road' as you put it?"

Doctor Serling seemed clearly impressed with Holmes. "We considered that, but we don't think so. If that was the case we feel our homing device would still be functioning. But it isn't. We clearly went back to a fork in the road of history and are now traveling down a different road. Someone or some thing altered our world's history so that the world we came from no longer exists to us."

Holmes nodded. "And you want me to help you find out who altered history. Who stopped this"—he tapped the book—"from happening?"

Both doctors nodded slowly.

Two

"THIS IS BEYOND the imagination," I said, no longer able to hold my tongue. "I have heard some crazy stories in my time but—"

Holmes held up his hand for me to stop and then turned to the gentlemen. "How would you propose I do this task?"

Doctor Frederick pointed to the large case. "In here is the machine that moves us through time. Come back with us to the night of the Titanic hitting the iceberg."

"What?" I said.

But Holmes nodded. "Can you then bring us back to this point?"

Doctor Frederick shook his head negatively. "Not exactly. We can leave a homing package here, but time will flow at the same pace as the time you spend on the ship. If we are there for an hour you will return here in an hour."

Holmes again nodded, then turned to me. "Watson, dampen the fire. And fetch our heaviest coats. We are going for a short trip."

"But you can't really imagine—" For the third time tonight Holmes stopped me with a sharp look and a hand gesture.

"My dear Watson. We have a case at hand." He was clearly seeing something I was missing and willing to let these two have enough rope to prove their insanity.

I sighed rather loudly, but then nodded and did as I was instructed. Holmes and I then donned our coats as Doctor Serling seemed to type on some sort of instrument inside the case, clicking like the sound of a dog scampering across a hardwood floor. Then he placed a small blue-green cube on the table on the top of the large book and nodded for Holmes and myself. "We are ready. Please step close."

Holmes did so immediately and I followed reluctantly. My mind was starting to worry at the possibility of this actually occurring. Yet the thought was so utterly preposterous that I couldn't hold the reality of it.

As I stopped beside Holmes, Doctor Serling tapped a small button inside the case.

For a moment nothing registered. It was as if someone had turned off the lights and the fire and all the sounds and feelings of the world.

Then as quickly as it left the world was back.

In my mind we were still standing like fools bundled against the cold inside the warm Baker Street address. But then Holmes said, "Interesting" and stepped toward the wooden rail to gaze out at the black night.

"What in the devil—" The icy cold wind sucked the words from my mouth. I could not only feel the cold, but smell and taste it. Intense, biting cold mixed with the salty smells of the open sea. I spun around to quickly look in all directions as the wind messed my hair and pulled open my coat sending shivers through my torso. We were clearly on a large ship, somewhere near the bow. The width of the ship was almost that of a city block and a towering wall of metal rose both forward and aft of our position.

"We are on the forward well deck near the starboard side," Doctor Frederick said to Holmes.

Holmes only nodded as his intense gaze took in every detail. I on the other hand fought to keep my late dinner in my stomach. The very fact that we stood here on this cold wooden deck challenged every principle I believed and lived by. I must be dreaming. Holmes had not woken me and any moment this would all be a fleeting memory of a long night of troubled sleep.

Overhead a bell started ringing insistently. I glanced up at the tall pole and could barely see the light from what seemed to be a crow's nest. Words floated down to us through the night air. "Iceberg right ahead."

Doctor Franklin turned to Holmes. "That was lookout Fleet talking to Sixth Officer Moody who is on the bridge." Franklin pointed toward the stern and up. "All right on time."

Holmes only nodded. He seemed to be listening intently to the sounds of the night, the water slapping against the sides of the huge ship, the low rumble of the engines. After a moment he nodded and then leaned out over the rail to watch the iceberg approach.

I moved over beside him and did the same, the cold wind hitting my face and hands with a much harder intensity. Out of the shadow of the well deck, I suddenly realized just how fast the ship had been moving and that realization combined with the blast of cold wind took my breath away.

I stood back for a moment, then again leaned out into the wind, peering into the black where the ship was headed. It took me a moment to understand that the dark shape, darker than the night, as if someone had punched a hole in the air, was a huge wall of ice, far wider and bigger than the ship. Fear twisted my stomach and for a moment I forgot the intense cold on my skin. I could see no way that a ship of this size could turn fast enough to avoid a collision.

Yet I continued to watch with fascination as every moment seemed to stretch. It was a sick fascination, as if watching a horrible fight where someone was being badly hurt, yet unable to turn away.

As my eyes watered and the tears seemed to freeze on my checks, I watched.

Slowly the ship turned, just enough, and just at the last second. The bow somehow slid by the leading edge of ice.

There was a faint rumbling lower in the ship and a distant scraping sound.

The huge gray wall was suddenly beside us and it seemed as if I could reach out and touch the rough ice. Yet I knew that if I did the razor-sharp edges would have cut my hands.

Holmes and I instinctively both took a step away from the rail and watched the mountain slide past the ship. When it was far beyond the stern of the ship and again fading into the black of the night Holmes turned to Doctor Frederick. "So what do you observe is different?"

"Nothing from our three times back here since we became stuck. However, the records we have said that this part of the deck where we are standing was originally covered with ice from the berg as it scraped past."

Holmes nodded.

"So we are only talking a matter of feet," I said, "maybe even inches between saving this ship and having it sink?"

It was Doctor Frederick's turn to nod. "In this world, as I am sure you read in your newspapers, the ship sustained damage, but the water-tight compartments held the ship afloat until it could get to New York. In my universe the damage was too extensive and the watertight compartments did very little."

Behind us ten or twelve hearty men emerged from a door, the yellow light casting a long bright streak across the deck. They were clearly interested in what had happened and why the engines had stopped. They talked loudly among themselves and headed toward both rails to gaze into the night. I again leaned out and looked to the stern. The iceberg was now barely visible, a gray mountain looming in the night.

Holmes turned to Doctor Serling. "Is it possible to see these events again?"

Doctor Serling nodded. "Actually, yes. We can move up, and back in time, to the boat deck."

I looked at Holmes and then at Doctor Serling who was again working in the case. "You mean that we can be up there on the boat deck at the same time we are, or were, here this time watching? I mean —" I stopped. I was totally confused and again my fear returned.

Doctor Frederick nodded and pulled his coat tighter around

himself. "Yes, but there are limits. We have never been able to get close enough to ourselves in experiments to see our earlier, or later, self. But that has not been from lack of trying." He laughed. "Time travel is still new to us. We really can't explain some of the paradoxes. We just know they exist and somehow the universe stops certain things from happening."

"So," Holmes said, pointing up at the leading edge of the boat deck. "I will not be able to go to that position up there and look down at myself here, unless I am, or was, doing it now. Correct?"

I glanced up, but a later version of Holmes was not standing there, much to my relief.

"That would seem to be the rule," Doctor Serling said. "Ready?"

Holmes nodded.

"What about the passengers?" I asked, but to Doctor Serling that question didn't seem to matter.

The cold, the salt-filled air, the feeling of the wooden deck under my feet all went away for a moment.

And suddenly we were standing next to a lifeboat about halfway down the boat deck, again on the starboard side.

Without a moment's hesitation Holmes strode to the starboard side of the ship and looked in the direction of the coming wall of ice.

I glanced around, relieved that no passenger was within sight to witness our arrival. "I have no desire to get used to this mode of travel," I said, pulling my coat around me tightly in a vain attempt to hold out the wind. "How fast is this ship traveling?"

"Over twenty-two knots," Doctor Frederick said.

"Far too fast," I said.

Doctor Frederick only grunted as the alarm bell started its insistent noise from the direction of the bow. He and I moved to join Holmes at the starboard rail leaving Dr. Serling with the heavy case.

Again we watched as the iceberg took its collision course. I found myself unable to take my gaze from that huge, growing mountain. That same sick desire as before kept my gaze frozen into the cold wind until finally, at what seemed to be the last moment, the ship slowly turned, shifting the iceberg to the starboard side of the liner.

With a fairly loud scraping the cold gray wall slipped past. No one said a word this time and again Holmes seemed to be listening.

I, on the other hand, was suffering to again keep my nerves in control. I took a few quick steps back from the towering wall of ice as it slid past. There was something about this entire event that felt ghoulish, as if we were robbing graves. I shook that thought from my mind and instead thought of the warm fire at Baker Street.

Three

THE MOUNTAIN FADED into the distance behind the ship as Holmes stood at the railing, not watching it but instead deep in thought. I had no idea what he might be thinking. I just knew I wanted to be off this ship and back in my warm quilts, if that was not where I was still.

"Once more," Holmes said, turning and moving back over to Doctor Serling. "Only this time could you be somewhere near the bridge?"

Doctor Sterling seemed to think for a minute and then nodded. "Yes, I think I can get us to the boat deck on the port side. That was a deck above where we were on our first visit. That would be close enough for you to move to the port door of the bridge and watch what was happening."

Holmes nodded. "That would be satisfactory."

Serling went to work. A number of first-class passengers now occupied the deck, staring toward the stern after the retreating wall of ice. But Serling and Frederick paid them no attention, as if they were nothing but harmless ghosts.

Serling typed in his case and suddenly the night again vanished.

And just as suddenly returned.

We now stood on the other side of the ship, on an empty boat deck, slightly closer to the bow.

Holmes immediately started toward the door of the bridge. I struggled in vain to remove the thought from my mind that I was not only standing here at this moment, but also at two other places on this same ship. It was enough to make a sane man crazy and I was sure that insanity was where I was heading at a speed faster than the ship.

"You only have one look," Doctor Frederick said. "We won't be able to repeat this again."

Holmes glanced over his shoulder. "I understand perfectly, Doctor."

Just as Holmes stuck his head around the edge of the open bridge door the warning bell rang out through the night air.

Again we watched as the iceberg loomed closer and closer, only to be swept past the starboard side. Being on this side of the deck I felt less threatened by the entire event. Or possibly I was just growing used to it. Another thought I put quickly out of my mind.

Holmes never took his head away from the open door to even once glance at the iceberg. As the ship slowed and drifted in the black waters he turned to us. The look on his face was one that I had never seen before. It was almost as if he had seen a true ghost.

"Holmes, are you all right?" I asked as he rejoined us.

"I need one more time here," he said. "Can you get me close enough to the main engines to watch them during the time of the collision?"

Again Doctor Serling thought for a moment while the cold cut through my coat as if it wasn't there. I had experienced many cold London nights, but none anywhere near as cold as this.

"We'll have to go back five minutes sooner to give you the time," Doctor Serling said. He worked in the case for what seemed to be a long minute.

Then again without warning from him the world and the deck and the cold wind vanished. It would at least be courteous for him to give us a moment to prepare.

This time Doctor Serling had placed us in a fairly narrow hallway lit by electric lamps at intervals along the walls.

I leaned against the polished wood and took a deep breath of the warm, coal-smelling air. It was a relief to be out of the wind and the cold, but the thought of being inside a ship about to hit an iceberg had me on the edge of a slight panic.

"Through there and down the circular stairs," Doctor Serling said, pointing to a wooden door at the end of the hall. "The engine room will be down there. You only have a few minutes."

Holmes nodded and didn't waste a moment striding the distance to the door and disappearing through it.

I opened my coat to allow the warmer air to flow around my torso. Doctor Serling adjusted a dial inside his case and then sat on the carpeted floor. Doctor Frederick just paced.

Finally he stopped and turned to me. "Do you think he can solve this?"

I gave a slight, very half-hearted laugh. "If there is something to solve, I am sure he can. But I do not exactly understand what you are asking of him." I stared at Doctor Frederick and then said quietly, "If you ponder it, I am not sure you understand either."

"We are asking him," Doctor Frederick said, gesturing at the walls around us, "to simply put history right. This ship belongs on the bottom of the Atlantic. It needs to be there for history to return to normal."

I simply watched him as he started his pacing again. I knew it would do no good to remind him of the hundreds of people he said would die tonight if that occurred. In the background we could hear the seemingly distant rumble of the engines and occasionally a noise of a passenger from somewhere nearby. But otherwise the hallway remained silent until a fairly loud scraping and grinding filled the air.

I held onto a smooth edge of wood paneling and took deep, controlled breaths until the noise stopped. The engines dropped silent and then there was only quiet. Again my mind filled in the comparison between the silence of a graveyard, or the silence of the dead of night, before even the birds are moving.

Frederick looked at me and I returned his stare saying nothing.

At the end of the hall the door opened and Holmes rejoined us. "We can go back to Baker Street now," he said, his voice sounding tired and removed of all energy.

I glanced first at Holmes and then at the Doctors as they looked at each other puzzled.

"Did you solve our problem?" Doctor Frederick asked.

Holmes did nothing but shake his head. "The fire would feel comforting against the chill."

After a moment Doctor Serling bent to the case at his feet, made a few adjustments and suddenly the hall was gone, replaced quickly by the familiar surroundings of Baker Street.

Four

WITHOUT REMOVING MY heavy coat I bent to the fire and soon had it roaring again, its yellow flame overpowering the lamps.

I finished and turned to the room. Holmes had removed his coat and was again in his chair. Only it was very clear he was deep in thought. Both our guests understood his mood and both were respecting it. I removed my coat and hung it in its place, then moved back to the chair near the fire. The heat cut into the oppressive cold of the night and the feeling that the ship had been haunted. Haunted by not only our own ghosts, but more by the fact that many people might have died that night. In my years with Holmes and as a doctor I have witnessed many close calls and many deaths. Yet none to my memory had shaken me as much as standing on the deck of that ship tonight.

Holmes stirred and picked up the book beside him. "Does this book have an account of the collision?"

Doctor Frederick nodded and Holmes opened the book and went to work studying and quickly reading. We remained silent and I spent the minutes holding my hands out in front of me so that the cold could be forced out by the warmth of the flames. The memory of being on that ship would, in time, fade into a seemingly bad vision and nothing more.

Finally, Holmes laid the book back down and sighed. "I'm afraid there is nothing I can do to help you gentlemen."

"What?" Dr. Serling said. "You mean you *won't* help us."

"I didn't say that," Holmes said. "I said I *can't*."

"But—" This time it was Dr. Frederick's turn to stop his companion.

"Mr. Holmes," Dr. Frederick said, "Are you saying you do not know what caused the switch in history?"

"Basically, yes. That is what I am saying." Holmes patted the book. "The details outlined here are exactly what occurred on that ship, except, of course, the ship we visited tonight didn't sink. I can think of a thousand factors that would have caused such a difference."

"Such as?" Doctor Serling said. He was not disguising the panic and the fear in his voice at all.

"Such as someone or something turning the iceberg just a fraction of a degree." He made a helpless gesture. "I would not think such a feat possible, yet I did not think travel through time possible until this evening either."

Before either Doctor could say a word Holmes went on. "The switch might have occurred much earlier in the evening. As the Captain ordered the increase in speed, the implementation of the order could have been delayed just a few seconds, which would again allow the iceberg to be in a slightly different position at the time of the collision, thus making the damage lighter."

It was clear that Holmes's words were being understood by our guests. Finally Doctor Serling sighed. "It was a hope. Nothing more."

Doctor Frederick nodded slowly, his shoulders slumping. "A crazy stupid hope, at that."

Doctor Serling stood and moved to Holmes, who also stood. With an extended hand the Doctor said, "I would like to thank you for your attempt and your time. It was generous of you."

Holmes only nodded and shook the Doctor's hand. Then Doctor Serling turned to me as Doctor Frederick moved to shake Holmes's hand.

"Where will you be going?" I asked as he took my extended hand.

"We left a homing beacon in a hotel room in New York. We will return there and do our best to not influence the future too much."

"That seems like a very logical plan of action."

He smiled at me. "It would seem we have very few other options at the moment."

He turned and moved back to the large case as Doctor Frederick shook my hand and then moved over beside the case.

Holmes picked up the large book and handed it to him. "You might want this."

Doctor Frederick shook his head. "Please keep it as a gift. At this point it is nothing more than a work of fiction."

"I will treasure it," Holmes said and tucked the book under his arm.

Doctor Serling nodded, reached inside the case and suddenly they were both gone.

The crackling of the fire was the only sound as I stood staring at the empty place where they had been.

"Quite something, isn't it?" Holmes said.

I turned and watched as Holmes almost dropped into his chair, the exhaustion heavy on his strong shoulders. He laid the book on his lap and stared at it as if it were a monster to be tamed.

I poured us both a hot coffee and a snifter of brandy and then dropped into the chair across from him. He continued to stare at the cover of the book, not even offering his thanks for the drinks.

"It seems," I said, "that the night wore on you as much as it did myself."

Holmes only nodded.

I took a sip of the brandy, letting it warm the deep cold inside. "It is lucky that you did not find the answer to their problem."

Holmes looked up at me and for the first time I saw his eyes, watery and burning with an almost insane gaze. "My dear Watson," he said, his voice low, barely in control, a state that I had never witnessed in Holmes. "I knew exactly what caused the change."

"What!" I almost came out of my chair, my coffee spilling a hot stain down my pants.

He nodded slowly. "I lied to them. Actually the solution was simple." He tapped the book but made no motion to continue.

"Please, Holmes. I must know." I was sitting on the edge of my chair, facing him.

He grunted and then for the first time reached for his brandy. After a long sip he looked me square in the eye. "It is the knowledge of nightmares."

"But they will be my nightmares," I said.

He looked at me and then slowly nodded. "I first read the answer in here. It said that at the time of the sighting of the iceberg the First Officer William Murdock ordered the engines 'full speed astern' and put the helm 'hard to starboard.' Now, such a move would cause the ship to turn to port."

I nodded. I knew enough sailing to understand that basic principle.

"But," Holmes said," putting the engines full speed astern made such a huge ship much more difficult to control and thus the turn was just slightly slower. The ship would then strike the iceberg in a direct manner, thus causing enough damage to cause it to flounder."

"I am at a loss," I said. "Is that what happened? Why did the ship stay afloat?"

"No," Holmes said. "The engines remained full speed ahead, thus giving the ship just a fraction more ability to maneuver, thus allowing it to only graze the iceberg."

"So First Officer Murdock somehow changed his order? But how?"

Holmes shook his head. "No, he ordered full speed astern just as the book says. When I heard him give that order was when I first knew that our guests were correct. That ship should have sunk that night." He took another drink from his brandy.

"That was why you needed to visit the engine room?"

Holmes nodded. "The man on the telegraph between the bridge and the engine room at that moment was not from our time. He ignored the order and thus saved the ship. And changed the future it would seem."

I stared at Holmes. "How could you know he was from a different time?"

"Simple, really. Just as Doctor Serling wore what he called contact lenses, so did the man on the telegraph in the engine room."

I sat staring into my brandy, letting what Holmes had told me sink in. Finally I gathered enough nerve to ask the question I knew Holmes was expecting. "If history really was changed by someone from the future, why didn't you set it right?"

Holmes almost laughed. "I had the opportunity to do so. Remember what Doctor Serling told us about there being more than one future from every decision?"

"Forks in a road," I said.

Again the insanity seemed to burn like a flash fire in Holmes eyes as he fought for control. "We are simply on the branch of the road where I did not stop the person from the future."

He gulped down the last of his brandy, studied the crystal snifter for a moment and then with all the force he had he threw the glass into the fire where it shattered and sent sparks flying.

He leaned back into his chair and closed his eyes. His hands gripped the large book in a death grip, his knuckles white. Softly he said, "On that other road I stopped that man, doomed a great ship, and killed over fifteen hundred human beings in the process. I know that road exists. I know I walked it."

My head was spinning from the very thought of what Holmes had suggested. I took a sip of my brandy and stared at the light reflecting off the shattered fragments of Holmes's glass. "You mean," I finally said, "that on that other world we are sitting talking about how you stopped that man and the deaths it caused?"

Holmes nodded very slowly.

"But you could have never done that." I wanted to shake him, wake him from his crazy thoughts.

He opened his eyes and I saw they were almost empty of energy and life. "My dear Watson. I most certainly could have. And in that other world, on that other road, I most certainly did."

He closed his eyes again and sank farther into his chair, as if a huge weight was pushing him down.

And I finally understood what that weight was. My friend had had the future of the world on his shoulders tonight. More weight than any man should be forced to carry. Even if that man was Sherlock Holmes.

WHO'S HOLDING DONNA NOW?

A game of poker with aliens... never a good idea.

Not that aliens cheat. Not that at all. They know how to win, and they want their winnings when they do win.

No matter the condition of the winnings.

IT WAS AN accident.

Nothing more. A simple accident. I saw the entire thing.

It was awful.

My name is Jacob O'Grady. I own Sandy's Restaurant and Lounge down on twelfth. It's a pretty good-sized place with low, wood-beamed ceilings and more beer signs on the walls than should be allowed in one place. No windows, and a constant smell of lingering smoke.

The polished oak bar had come out of an old saloon from downtown Boise I hear, but never took the time to trace it back. That bar was forty feet long and the center of the place.

I bought the bar six years ago from Sandy's wife after Sandy called some girl a whore. Turned out to be this big cowboy's special girl. The big guy didn't even waste time with Sandy.

Five shots. All hit Sandy.

That guy could shoot. Sort of impressive, actually.

Now I never insult no one. Main rule number one.

I have a lot of main rules. I got to just to stay alive.

Donna was like Sandy. She didn't learn so fast. Now it's too late. Or at least I think it's too late. I honestly don't know for sure.

Donna had long black hair, thick black eyebrows, and just a hint of a moustache along her upper lip. I thought she was good looking, with her long legs, model type figure, and real warm smile. I think the smile was why I hired her.

I suppose I should have warned her right off. But about the time I hired her, I still didn't really believe what was going on. And then after it got started, I was afraid to tell anyone.

Hell, who would have believed me if I would have said that aliens dropped by my bar every night. I'd have been laughed right out of the neighborhood, if not locked up in a funny white suit.

But I had aliens all right.

Three of them.

They looked human, at least on the surface. One seemed older than the other two, maybe in his fifties if he had been human. He had rough skin and dark, intense eyes.

The other two looked to be mid-thirties, also dressed in normal human clothes for men of this area. Jeans, work shirts, work boots. One had a thick, dark moustache and the other had blonde hair.

At first glance, a person couldn't tell they were any different than the other loggers or rock miners that came in here. They dressed the same, drank the same kind of booze, and stayed off to themselves. Damn normal-like. But I could tell they were aliens. I just knew.

I should have warned Donna.

Hell, I didn't know they were going to start playing poker. It fit right in, though, when I thought about it later.

Any night in Sandy's there's at least three poker games going. There's always the high stake in the back room, plus some pretty good smaller games going out in the main room.

The three aliens watched the games real close for about two weeks, drinking just enough to make sure I didn't toss them outside, but not drinking that much as to seem drunk. For all I knew, they couldn't get drunk.

Then one of them asked Donna for a deck.

Tell the truth, I didn't give it a second thought, even though by then

I was pretty convinced they really were aliens, but their money was good and they sure didn't cause any trouble.

Donna gave them the cards. I remember real clearly because it was her second night and I had to show her where the decks of cards were stashed in the second drawer to the right of the cash register on the back bar.

The aliens worked at learning poker for about the next four weeks, never letting anyone join in, just playing their own game over in a corner.

Again, I didn't much care since they paid for their drinks and tipped Donna well.

They didn't ask many questions, but they asked enough around the room that I could figure out they didn't know much to start. But let me tell you, those three aliens were damn fast learners.

Damn fast.

Looking back, it's funny how things just sort of build up. Even them aliens playing cards would have been fine if Donna hadn't taken up with Cutbank Jones.

Cutbank was an odd bird. Long, kind of wiry, and just mean as hell. His eyes were so cold black that it used to make people squirm when he looked across a poker table at them. What Donna saw in him, I don't know. But one night I actually saw her make him smile. Amazing things do happen in Sandy's.

After the first few days, Cutbank came to think he owned Donna. About the only time she got away from him was while she worked. And even then, more times than not, Cutbank would be sitting in on one of the poker games and keeping an eye on her. He never let her get far from sight.

I meant to ask her one night if she needed help avoiding him, but just never got around to it before the night of the big game. I should have, I really should have. Regrets now in hindsight.

The big game started at about nine. The older of the three aliens got up and moved over to a table where Slim, Raymond, Cutbank, and Freddy were playing and bold-like asked if he could sit in.

No one seemed to mind, so after a few hands the other two aliens came over and joined the table, making it seven players.

All of them had the buy-in plus a little, and all seemed to play well, if not mechanical.

Eventually, Jones and Steven joined in when the high stakes game in the backroom got a little slow.

The entire thing made me nervous, but what the hell could I do about it? They were just customers, so I kept my mouth shut and made sure everyone had a drink when they wanted one.

Donna did the serving and the aliens tipped her well.

Cutbank treated her like trash. That not only annoyed me, but most of the men in the game. Donna was well liked. She just had that kind of smile.

For the first few hours, the game went fine and I was beginning to think the evening might just end up being a good one.

Cutbank held his own at the table. He might have been a nasty ass to Donna, but he could play a mean game of seven-card stud.

Both Raymond and Freddy had tapped out and left, with most of their money sitting in front of the three aliens.

An hour later, Slim was gone and not long after that, both Jones and Steven.

That left only Cutbank on one side of the table and the three aliens on the other. Except for a few chips in front of Cutbank, the aliens had it all. And that galled the hell out of Cutbank. I could tell.

So could the few customers remaining in Sandy's.

The hand that started the problem was the hand that Cutbank drew into a straight, King high.

Two of the aliens folded right off, but the older one held on, betting twice what Cutbank had left in front of him, smiling all the time.

The rules in a game in Sandy's is that if you didn't have the money to cover the bet, you lost the hand.

At that point, I never saw a man get so red. For a minute I thought Cutbank was going to jump right across the table at the alien guy. But he didn't.

Being the good player that he was, he first studied his hand, then laid his cards face down in front of him, pushed what was left of his money into the center of the table, and then asked the alien if he could have a moment to cover the rest of his bet.

Standard game policy in Sandy's.

The alien nodded and laid his hand face down on the table in front of him and scooted his chair back.

Again standard action. I had to admit, the alien had learned all the rules.

Cutbank nodded, his face still red, and then turned and scanned the bar. Not a soul there that would loan him a penny, let along the amount needed to cover the alien's bet.

His gaze stopped on Donna. She was standing beside the bar in the waitress station and she squirmed like a worm pinned to a hook.

Cutbank's eyes sort of lit up and he stood quickly and moved over to her.

I knew before he got there that it wouldn't do no good. Donna had had a good night, tip wise and all, but she didn't have anywhere near enough to cover his bet.

And it didn't take Cutbank long to find out.

She said she didn't have enough, but he could have what she did have. He called her something crude and then told her to get out of his way. He grabbed her drink tray and ripped open her money carrier. Maybe twenty bucks in there, plus change. Then he grabbed her and searched her pockets quick-like.

She was smart enough at that moment not to fight him. I'm sure he'd have beat her something awful if she had. Of course, none of the rest of us in Sandy's would have allowed that to happen.

She didn't have the money. As soon as Cutbank realized that, he tossed her roughly against the bar and then slammed his hand against the wall, cussing up a blue streak.

Right at that point, I really didn't blame him for being angry. Hell, I would have been with a hand like his and no money. But then I would have calmed down enough to throw in my hand and walk away.

Most men would.

But not Cutbank.

He went to three of the men in the bar, threatening them if they didn't help him. None of them had enough. He even glanced my way once but then thought better of it. He knew that he might threaten me out of the money tonight, but if he did, he'd never be welcome back in here again.

In a place like Sandy's, there are unwritten rules of the house. Break a rule and every other customer turns into my enforcer.

Cutbank liked Sandy's too much to go doing that.

But it turned out he didn't like Donna that much. He was across the room threatening old man Craig when he turned and saw Donna and the rest of the bar watching him. It was right at that moment that I knew he came up with the idea.

Quickly, he stormed back across the bar and grabbed Donna by the arm and dragged her off into the alcove near the bathroom. From where I was behind the bar I could see Cutbank talking and Donna shaking her head no. Once she tried to pull away from him, but he held her tight.

At that point, if she'd started putting up a fuss, three or four of us would have jumped in. But she didn't.

After a long minute of Cutbank talking real soft but intense at her, Donna's shoulders slumped and she nodded. Then she kept right on nodding. Satisfied, Cutbank pulled her over to the table and sat back down in his chair, leaving her standing beside him.

He smiled real snakelike at the alien and then announced that the other half of his bet would be Donna.

One night with Donna.

Let me tell you that caused a stir in the bar.

I wanted to object, but then remembered Sandy and how he had ended up and my main rule of not getting in the middle of something not my business.

Donna might work for me, but she had made herself Cutbank's woman and anything she did on her own time was her business. If she wanted help, all she had to do was ask and everyone in the bar would jump to help.

But she was just standing there, so no one moved.

The alien was as surprised as the rest of the room. He glanced up at Donna and then back at Cutbank. Then he asked Cutbank to repeat what he had just said.

Cutbank did.

Then the alien did what any self-respecting man would do in that kind of poker game. He looked up at Donna and asked her if she agreed.

Right about then, I guess Donna had another chance to get out. If she'd have said no, not a person in the bar would have let her leave with Cutbank. She hesitated, but it wasn't a long hesitation before she said it was all right with her. Whatever Cutbank wanted.

The alien nodded and told Cutbank he accepted his call. Then the alien turned over his down cards.

Full house, queens over sevens.

Donna turned almost white as Cutbank slammed his cards into the pile of money and told the alien to deal the cards.

As the older alien pulled the money and the cards toward him, he asked just what Cutbank intended to wager.

Cutbank indicated Donna and again the alien looked up at Donna for her confirmation.

Donna nodded real slow.

Real slow.

All three aliens nodded in agreement and then they spent the next half minute or so discussing what a night with Donna was worth on the poker table.

I could tell that Cutbank was getting a little crazy right at that point. His voice was higher, his gestures quick and angry. I wanted to stop the game, close the bar and just go home and take a hot shower to wash off the stink of men like Cutbank and the women who let themselves be used. But another one of the unwritten rules of Sandy's was that no one ever interrupted a game. What went on in a game was between the men in the game and no one else.

So I stayed behind the bar and wiped out the same glass ten times.

The next hand was even sadder.

Cutbank again had a damn good hand. This time he had the full house, kings over sixes. Any respectable player would bet damn near the limit on that hand in seven-card stud.

Only this time, Donna was the limit.

The older alien that held the marker for one night with Donna dropped out early, but the other two stayed in. One of the aliens had four sevens.

Unbelievable hand.

Enough to make anyone crazy.

And that's what it did to Cutbank. Again he slammed his cards and his fist down on the table. Now his face was red and I could see clearly that he was sweating.

Donna looked as if she might faint.

But somehow Cutbank held his composure long enough to indicate another hand.

And once again Cutbank had a good hand. Three queens.

The two aliens who already owned nights with Donna dropped out when it came time to push forward their money. But the one with the moustache stayed in.

The alien had a straight, ten high.

That was all Cutbank could take.

He took one long look at the alien's cards, his face getting redder and redder, then slammed himself back and away from the table while reaching inside his coat. He yelled something about cheating and the next instant a forty-five was in his hand and swinging up at the aliens.

He never had a chance.

Quick as anything I have ever seen, all three aliens had small devices in their hands aimed at Cutbank.

The little guns (or whatever they were) looked like pocket calculators and made high-pitched whining sounds.

Cutbank staggered back under the blows of whatever the three aliens where aiming at him. His forty-five went off, the sound of the shot echoing around and around the room.

His shot, knocked off line by the aliens fire, hit Donna square in the chest sending her flying backwards into a table and then crashing sideways onto the wood floor.

Cutbank ended up slumped against the bathroom wall, very dead, but without a mark on him.

The alien with the moustache went quickly to inspect Cutbank while the other two and the rest of us gathered around Donna.

She too was obviously dead. Her pretty face was contorted into an expression of surprise. Blood formed a large pool under her, soaking her clothes, and giving the room a sick, copper smell that seemed to overwhelm the always-present smoke smell.

Quickly, the older alien said something in a language that sounded something like Spanish and Chinese rolled into one. The one with a moustache picked up Cutbank's forty-five and pocketed it while the blonde alien man attached a small box to Donna's arm.

I objected, telling them that they shouldn't touch anything until the police arrived. Murder was a serious thing, even if it was self-defense.

The older alien just shrugged.

He said that they had each won a night with Donna and they were going to take their winnings. I was going to object a little more strenuously, but suddenly I caught a glimpse of one of those little calculator guns they had used on Cutbank and I thought better of it.

I guess everyone in the place at that moment thought better of it, because no one jumped in and tried to stop them.

Donna's body just sort of floated up off the ground until it was about waist high and then hovered there until the older alien expertly used Donna's foot to push her ahead of him out the front door while the blonde alien held the door open.

The one with the moustache followed and then the blonde alien just sort of nodded to the room and pulled the door closed behind all four of them.

Right at that moment, you could have heard a baby cry clear across town.

There were nine of us left and not a one said anything.

Finally, after I turned around and saw the big red puddle of blood and Cutbank very dead against the wall, I broke the silence by telling someone to please call the police while I made myself, and whoever else wanted one, a drink.

Of course, the police didn't buy the fact that three men just sort of zapped Cutbank and then floated Donna out, even with all of us telling somewhat close to the same story.

They did an autopsy on Cutbank and ruled that he had died of a heart attack. Made sense to me since there wasn't a mark on him. They didn't know what to do about the blood on the floor, so they didn't do anything and I mopped it up.

That all happened three days ago and now it's time to head to work. Tonight will be the forth night since they took Donna.

I don't know what to expect when I open up Sandy's. Sometimes I think Donna is just going to come walking back in the door live as can be.

And then sometimes I think that they just might dump her three-day-rotted body off after doing what they pleased with her for three nights.

That thought makes me sick, but it could happen. Sometimes you just never know.

I don't like to think that, so that's one of the reasons I've been covering for Donna the last three nights and holding her job open.

I can always hope.

AMBASSADOR TO THE PROMISED LAND

First contact with an alien race brings complications. And troubles.

Especially when the first contact occurs under a dining room table at a Christmas dinner. And especially in front of the promised land.

I wanted to bring this goofy little Christmas story back into the light since it was first published in the anthology First Contact *edited by Larry Segriff and Martin H. Greenberg from DAW Books in 1997. The anthology came out and vanished without a trace. I felt disappointed at that, since I really had a fond feeling for this light Christmas story.*

Now it's back, like that second piece of pie you knew you shouldn't have eaten.

THIS CHRISTMAS EVE I met an alien, or maybe a ghost, and saw the Promised Land. Sort of like a bad Dickens nightmare, only it happened for real, right in the front formal dining room of my neighbors, Dotty and Harvey Jones.

My wife, Amelia, Amy for short, thinks the entire ghost/alien incident can be clearly explained. Now understand that Amy always says that, and more times than not, she's right. Her parents conceived her while on a vacation to the south Pacific, so they named her after Amelia Earhart, thinking that maybe she might be the reincarnation of the famous flyer. This start in life made Amy the most practical, down-to-earth woman I have ever met. She also hated to fly.

On the way back from the emergency room Amy said my alien/ghost incident was a combination of too much eggnog and the knock on the head I got when I looked up Dotty Jones's skirt while reaching for my napkin under the table at the annual Christmas Eve neighborhood dinner.

I didn't argue with her. But just for the record, it was before I hit my head, while I was reaching for my napkin and after looking up Dotty's skirt, that I had the ghost/alien incident.

However, Amy was right about the eggnog. I had drunk even more this year than the year before.

To my defense, I actually hadn't been trying to look up Dotty's skirt, even though her skirt was the shortest red thing I had ever seen, and ex-dancer Dotty most surely was worth looking at.

Granted I had been staring across the table at her all during dinner as her husband Harvey talked and talked and talked about his car dealership. Besides the eggnog, ham and sweet yams, she was the only interesting thing happening.

Pam and Howard McDonnell from two houses down hadn't said two words since dinner started, and Walter and Wendy Clark who had the house on the other side of mine looked as bored as I felt.

During most of dinner Dotty had been smiling back at me when Amy wasn't looking, laughing at any word I managed to get in edgewise in her husband's monologue. But I never once thought about dropping my napkin so I could look up her skirt.

To be honest, the idea just never crossed my mind.

No, I dropped my napkin like anyone might drop one at a Christmas Eve neighborhood dinner. I was reaching for a second helping of ham and the red cloth thing just slipped off my lap. It happens.

It has happened to me before. Even once in a really fancy restaurant I dropped one.

No big deal.

I did the normal thing required in good social settings such as Dotty and Harvey's formal dining room. I scooted my chair back slightly, and went under the festive holiday tablecloth to retrieve the napkin.

There, I came face to face, or make that face to legs, with Dotty's lower half.

She had legs that, from my perspective of head-under-the-tablecloth, clearly belonged in Playboy or Cosmopolitan. Now I'm a normal red-blooded American male, and any normal red-blooded American male would hesitate when faced with a vision as clear and pure as those legs.

And I did.

I hesitated.

And hesitated.

And hesitated.

There was no time passage for me under that table. I had left this plane of existence and gone on, drifting in a timeless place that existed only under that holiday dining table, in that close space between me and those legs.

I had no name, no reason, no pride.

It was like getting drunk back in high school.

Or the time Linda, my first girlfriend, let me slip my hand under her bra.

Or the time in college when I took mushrooms and ended up staring intently for hours at the design on a bathroom wallpaper.

This was like all those times, only more so.

Now, at age forty, I no longer did drugs. I had a great job in city hall, a wife of 14 years, two kids in junior high, and a three-bedroom house in a subdivision. I hadn't had a mind-altering experience in a long, long time.

Too damn long.

So I hesitated.

I forgot who I was, where I was, why I was even living.

I doubt I even took a breath.

I doubt I would have been able to take a breath.

But there was no doubt I had totally forgot about my napkin.

Then two things happened that changed the entire experience.

First, Dotty uncrossed her legs.

Now, from the perspective of my mind-altered state, this took about six wonderful and glorious years of slow motion.

It was a pure cinematic moment.

My camera-like gaze followed the line of her ankle.

The line of her calf.

The shape of her knee.

And then beyond.

Beyond to a place I should never have gone.

A place I had no intention of ever going. But I went because I was faced with the challenge.

And when challenged, any red-blooded American male will step up and face his challenger.

She uncrossed her legs, so I looked.

And I saw the promised land.

The gates of heaven stared me in the face.

I heard the Hallelujah Chorus.

Dotty wasn't wearing underwear.

Now, I swear, Dotty showing me the promised land broke the illusion. I came back to real time, the last bite of ham choking in my throat.

Seeing such a sight, under normal circumstances, would have sent me out from under the tablecloth, back into my chair with a red face and a giant desire to sprint for home.

But normal circumstances were not to be. There was this second thing that happened.

At that moment an alien, or ghost, or whatever he was, decided to make a trip into my reality, or to my planet, right there under the table with me, while I faced the promised land and a new religion, all on Christmas Eve.

The alien/ghost guy stood about sixteen inches high, his bald head barely coming up to Dotty's right knee. He was naked as the day he was born, tinted pure white like any ghost on television, and I could see right through him like a clear plastic shower curtain.

Now again an event such as a short, naked, see-through white guy appearing under a table would have sent me back into my chair, and then maybe right down the street to a local bar to try to drown the memory.

But I couldn't move.

Not a muscle below my shoulders.

I fought and fought for all of ten seconds, but I just couldn't budge or even feel the rest of my body.

My mind screamed "Practical Joke!" as I panicked, fighting to move.

But after another long ten seconds of panic, a little voice in my head said, "Calm down. This is not normal."

Sometimes little voices can be so damn smart.

But I calmed down anyway, and without once looking at the little ghost/alien man, or the promised land, (avoidance is a good thing sometimes) I looked around under the table.

From what I could tell from my position (bent over double, head under the tablecloth) no one around me was moving either. Harvey's constant talking had suddenly stopped. In fact all sound had stopped from everywhere the moment the little guy appeared. I had never heard it this quiet in this neighborhood in the ten years Amy and I had lived next door. I could actually hear my own breathing.

Amy's legs beside me were not moving, still crossed. But that was nothing unusual. She could sit like that for hours and never uncross her legs. I swore she had no blood flow at times.

Harvey's right leg was frozen in mid tap. Wendy's legs were crossed and also frozen in position, her brown pant leg riding up above her sock enough to show me she hadn't shaved her legs in a few weeks, a piece of information I didn't really want to know.

And Dotty's legs were being held in the open position, leaving just about exactly nothing about the promised land to my imagination.

The short, white, naked, see-through guy did a full turn surveying his surroundings as I stared at him. He looked like a normal male, except for being very short, as pure white as a ghost, and transparent. Maybe he was a ghost. Maybe he was a ghost Dotty and Harvey had been hiding. Knowing them, anything was possible.

Or maybe he was an angel who made a break from heaven when Dotty opened her legs and showed me the pearly gates. But if that was the case, why wasn't he making fast time away from her? I sure wanted to at that moment.

Maybe this was a bad movie and he was my conscious? Maybe he was here to punish me for looking up Dotty's skirt?

There was just no way of telling. Somehow I managed to keep the panic down to a dull roar in my head.

The little guy stopped looking around, then said something in a high, Mickey Mouse-like voice in a language that I might have guessed to be Latin, if Latin wasn't a dead language.

With that he got a little less glowing white, and a little more solid, as if he'd been fine-tuned a little. I could see through him still, but not as clearly.

He again said something in the strange language into the air, then made a nodding motion to himself. Then he turned to face me.

Surprise.

I managed not to panic completely again, but I swear my stomach had left my body. Up until that moment I wasn't sure he even realized that the head part of me wasn't as frozen in place as the rest of the body parts he could see. Obviously he did.

He looked me right in the eye and asked in a high, squeaky voice, in English. "Human?"

He actually wanted an answer.

Now I had never been asked a question before while in full-blown panic. It was just another first among many this Christmas Eve.

I took a deep breath, then managed to reply. "I think so. But at this moment I wouldn't put money on it." My voice sounded very weird in the complete silence of the world under the table.

He nodded, turned and said some more quick Latin-like mouse-words into the air, then faced me again. "Greetings. We are pleased."

"Hello to you, too," I said, sort of getting miffed. Panic had always turned almost immediately to anger for me, and this time was no exception.

"Now that we have that out of the way," I said, "would you mind telling me what's happening? And who you are? And what you're doing under Harvey and Dotty's formal dining room table?"

That got him confused, which was just damn fine with me. If I was confused, he was going to be confused right along with me.

He turned back to look into the air, said a few more quick words in his strange Latin, then faced me again. "Too fast," he said slowly. "Computers cannot translate."

Wonderful. The little white guy had computers. I should have expected as much. This had to be a prank by some computer nerd somewhere. Maybe the Wilson kid from down the block. He was always doing this sort of thing. I'd just play along until it ended. I nodded as best I could.

"Un-der-stand," I said.

The little guy listened for a moment to the thin air, then smiled, showing me a mouthful of sharp, pointed teeth. "Good."

"Who are you?" I asked. I'd have pointed at him, but my arms were no longer in use.

After he listened for a moment, he said, "I am friendly. Who are you?"

"I am confused," I said and with that the little white translucent guy smiled real big and nodded happily.

Now that we were formally introduced, I wanted some answers. "Where are you from?" I asked while he was still nodding.

After the customary pause to check the air beside him, he said, "Spattcha. I am from Spattcha."

Okay, that made sense to me. I could tell we were getting someplace now. I wasn't sure exactly where, but if it got me out from under this table, it would be a good place. I glanced at the promised land over the guy's shoulder, then asked, "Where is Spattcha?"

"Cannot see it from here," he said.

"To be honest," I said, "I'm seeing a lot more under this table than I ever expected to see, so you might be surprised."

Somewhere, no doubt, some computer nerd was laughing himself silly. But my little voice didn't believe what I was thinking about this being a joke. My little voice said I should be taking this translucent guy seriously, since he could freeze bodies and make all sound go away. But taking a sixteen inch white, translucent, naked man under a dining room table seriously was damn hard.

The short guy looked puzzled as he listened to thin air, then glanced around at his location. Now granted, his location must have looked damn strange to him. It looked damn strange to me, and I knew what I was looking at. Eight pairs of legs under the tablecloth, plus one head and a naked short guy. Weird by any measurement.

The short guy pointed at Amy's legs. "Human?"

"All but four days a month," I said.

That seemed to confuse the little guy even more, so he turned and pointed at Dotty's legs. Only he actually pointed at the promised land. "Human?"

"No," I said. "Fantasy, mixed with divorce, unemployment, and a drunken death." Of course as I said all that I was looking at where he was pointing. What red-blooded American male wouldn't?

He listened to the thin air, then shook his head. "Our language computer is having problem."

"I can understand that," I said.

He listened, then frowned.

I was getting nowhere fast. And at that point I wanted to be moving anywhere that wasn't under Dotty's formal dining room table. "I have a simple question?" I said slowly.

After a moment he said, "I will answer question."

"Why is nothing moving around me?"

The short guy waited for a moment, then smiled like a contestant on a game show who could give the right answer to a question. "I am projection through space/time. Other humans still move, only very slowly. Time pass slowly here."

"And I can see and talk to you because...?"

The little guy consulted with the thin air for almost a full three seconds, then said, "you are inside my time/space influence. It was a good happening, to talk to a human. We only planned to look around."

He glanced at the air again, then turned to face me fully. "Little time left. I must do the event."

"Event?" I said, wishing like hell I could stand up straight and run. Or even feel my body enough to know that someday I might again stand up straight.

The little translucent guy nodded. "Event. I proud. I bring humans welcome."

He stepped forward and stared me right in the eye, smiling, his sharp teeth looking damn dangerous, even though I could see through them.

I didn't say anything, because, to be honest, I had no idea what to say. And again the panic had gotten my brain locked down tight.

After a moment he looked confused, looked off into thin air for a consult with his thin air friends, then turned back to face me. "Did you not understand?" he said slowly. "I bring welcome. My people. Your people."

Suddenly I understood. The little guy wanted me to represent my country and all the rest of the world and the entire damn human race, while bent over double, head under a holiday tablecloth, staring up my hostess's skirt.

It would be a challenge, but I was up for it.

"Welcome from all of us humans," I said.

He smiled real big as soon as his computer translated.

"Our people," he said. "We be friends some day."

"You will be returning?" I asked. Suddenly the thought of this little guy popping in and out all the time had me more frightened than I wanted to think about.

"Return," he said. "Need vast power. Right conditions. Your planet must circle your sun two hundred and eleven times first."

I hope I didn't show the relief I felt. "We will be waiting," I said.

The little guy flickered from pale white to bright white like an old television set going bad. "Must go now," he said. "Much information to study before next time."

"Don't stay up too late," I said.

The little guy frowned, then flickered and was gone.

Suddenly Harvey was talking again.

And Dotty was still moving those legs apart.

And I could feel my body again.

Then the worst thing possible happened. Amy, my wife in the real world above the table, tapped me on the back to see if I was all right.

Now I had just seen an alien, or a ghost, or whatever he was. And come face to face with the promised land. My panic was still way too close to the surface and I didn't need Amy tapping me on the back right at that moment.

But she did.

A simple, solid little tap.

But my reaction wasn't so simple. It was as if she had punched the "on" switch and every muscle in my body decided to move at once.

Now, even though I didn't, it must be remembered I was face to face with Dotty's legs at this point, bent over in my chair, tablecloth over my head.

So when Amy tapped me and every muscle in my body suddenly fired, I came up straight, the back of my head smashing into the underside of the formal dining table.

Dishes scattered, ham was tossed into the air, and people yelled.

But it wasn't over yet.

Intense pain made my entire body jerk, sending my chair smashing backwards into a glass corner table that held a big ugly plant.

I went down like a log, flat onto Harvey and Dotty's green shag.

Now granted, right at that moment I suppose I could have said I saw God, too. God would have been a nice addition to the evening I was having. But instead I'm fairly certain that all I saw was a bunch of swirling blue and purple and red lights clouding my vision. I doubt very much if those lights were God. More likely they were just revenge for me looking in on his promised land.

The next thing I remember I came to, still on the floor, but someone had dragged me out beside the table and turned me face up.

The light was beyond bright, and my head felt hollow and empty with someone ringing a loud bell inside it.

Amy was crouched beside me, holding a cloth to the back of my head and looking worried.

Harvey was swearing about how I broke his glass table, and Dotty stood over me, smiling, her long legs showing the way directly up into the dark, where I knew only trouble waited.

Luckily for me the emergency room was slow on Christmas Eve and we got out in just under two hours.

On the way home I tried to tell Amy about the alien without telling her about the promised land part. I even told her about the moment where I had represented the entire human race. After all, shouldn't she be proud of me? I had been the first human to ever talk to an alien. In two hundred and eleven years the world would know the truth when the aliens returned and I would be famous.

But being the down-to-earth Amelia Earhart namesake that I married, Amy just laughed, as if she was seeing right through me like I had seen through the little guy under the table.

After pulling into our driveway and parking, she patted me on the leg and suggested that I not tell anyone about my adventure with my alien friend.

Then she laughed again and told me that a bad headache and hallucinations were what I deserved for drinking too much eggnog and trying to look up Dotty's skirt.

Even though the lump on my head hurt something awful at that moment, I was smart enough to keep my mouth shut. Probably the only smart thing I had done all night.

JUKEBOX GIFTS

A Jukebox Story

A bar, five friends, and a very special jukebox that lets you time travel back to a memory for the length of the song.

What could go wrong with giving such a special trip and the gift of a second chance to each of your closest friends?

First published in The Magazine of Fantasy and Science Fiction *way back in 1994, this story kicked off my Jukebox Series of stories, even though the first real Jukebox Story was published in* Night Cry Magazine *in the 1980s.*

For those wondering, the Jukebox Stores are tied to the Thunder Mountain series of novels.

One

THE STEREO BEHIND THE BAR was playing soft Christmas songs as I clicked the lock to the front entrance of the Garden Lounge and flicked off the outside light. I could feel the cold of the night through the wood door and the heat of the room surrounding me. I took a deep breath. Christmas Eve was finally here.

I could see the entire lounge and the backs of my four best friends sitting at the bar. I had never been much into decorating with Christmas stuff, and this year was no different. My only nod to the season was a small Christmas candle for each table and booth. Some customer had tied a red ribbon on one of the plants over the middle booth, and the Coors driver had put up a Christmas poster declaring Coors to be the official beer of Christmas. The candles still flickered on the empty tables, but the rest of the bar looked normal. Dark brown wood walls, dark brown carpet, an old oak bar, and my friends. The most important part was the friends. My four best friends' lives were as empty as mine. Tonight, on the first Christmas Eve since I bought the bar, I was going to give them a chance to change that. That was my present to them. It was going to be an interesting night.

"All right, Stout," Carl said, twisting his huge frame around on his bar stool so that he could face me as I wound my way back across the room between the empty tables and chairs. "Just what's such a big secret that you kick out that young couple and lock the door at seven o'clock on Christmas Eve?"

I laughed. Carl always got right to the point. With big Carl you always knew exactly where you stood.

"Yeah," Jess said from his usual place at the oak bar beside the waitress station, "What's so damned important you don't want the four of us to even get off our stools?" Jess was the short one of the crowd. When he stood next to Carl the top of Jess's head barely reached Carl's neck. Jess loved to play practical jokes on Carl. Carl hated it.

"This," I said as I pulled the custom-made, felt cover off the old Wurlitzer jukebox and, with a flourish, dropped the cloth over the planter and into the empty front booth. My stomach did a tap dance from nerves as all four of my best customers whistled and applauded, the sound echoing in the furniture- and plant-filled room.

David, my closest friend in the entire world, downed the last of his scotch-rocks and swirled the ice around in the glass with a tinkling sound. Then, with his paralyzed right hand, he pushed the glass, napkin and all, to the inside edge of the bar. "So after hiding that jukebox in the storage room for the last ten months, we're finally going to get to hear it play?"

"You guessed it." I ran my shaking fingers over the cold smoothness of the chrome and polished glass. I had carefully typed onto labels the names of over sixty Christmas songs, then taped them next to the red buttons. Somewhere in this jukebox I hoped there would be a special song for each man. A song that would trigger a memory and a ride into the past. My Christmas present to each of them.

I took a deep breath and headed behind the bar. "I hope," I said, keeping my voice upbeat, "that it will be a little more than just a song. You see, that jukebox is all that I have left from the first time I owned a bar. Since I've owned the Garden Lounge, it has never been played."

Jess, his dress shirt open to the third button and his tie hanging loose around his neck, spun his bar napkin on top of his glass. "So why tonight?"

"Because a year ago on Christmas Eve I made the decision to buy the Garden Lounge, and try again."

"And I'm glad you did," David said, lifting his drink in his good left hand in a toast.

"Here, here," Fred said, raising his drink high above his head and spilling part of it into his red hair. "Where else could we enjoy a few hours of Christmas Eve before going home to be bored."

All four men raised their glasses in agreement as I laughed and joined them with a sip of the sweet eggnog I always drank on Christmas Eve. No booze, just eggnog.

"It's been a good year," I said, "especially with friends like you. That's why I've decided to give each of you a really special present."

"Oh, to hell with the present," Jess said. "How about another drink? I've got a wife to face and knowing her, she ain't going to be happy that I'm not home yet."

"Is she ever happy?" David asked.

Jess shook his head slowly. "And I wonder why I drink." He slid his glass down the bar at me as he always did at least once a night. I caught it and tipped it upside down in the dirty glass rack.

"I'll fix everyone a last Christmas drink as you open the first part of your presents." I reached into the drawer under the cash register and pulled out four small packages. Each was the size of a ring box wrapped in red paper and tied with a green ribbon.

"Awful little," Fred said as I slid one in front of each man and then put four special Christmas glasses up on the mat over the ice. I'd had the name of each man etched on the glass.

"You know what they say about small packages," Jess said, twisting the package first one way, then the other while inspecting it. "But knowing Radley, the size will be a good indication."

"You just wait," I said.

"Great glasses," David said, noticing them for the first time. "They part of the present?"

"Part of the evening," I said. I let each man inspect his own empty glass before I filled it. The names were etched in gold leaf over the logo of the Garden Lounge. I'd had them done to remember the night. I hoped I would have more than a few glasses left when it was all over.

Carl was the first to get his present unwrapped. "You were right, Jess. It's a quarter." He held it up for everyone to see. "Looks like old Radley here is giving us a clue that we should tip more."

I laughed as I filled his glass with ice. "No. It's a trip, not a tip." I finished pouring his drink and slid it in front of him. "Since you unwrapped yours so fast, you get to go first." I nodded at the jukebox. "But there are rules."

"There seem to be a lot of rules around here tonight," Fred said. Everyone laughed.

I held up a hand for them to stop. "Trust me. This will be a special night."

"So give me the rules," Carl said.

I leaned on the dishwasher behind the bar so no one could see that I was shaking. "On that jukebox is every damn Christmas song I could find. Pick one that reminds you of a major point in your life — some *thing* or *time* or *event* that changed your life. After you punch the button, but before the music starts, tell us what the song reminds you of."

Carl shook his head. "You know, Stout. You've gone and flipped out."

"Sometimes I think so, too," I said. I wasn't kidding him. Sometimes I really did think so.

"Tonight seems to be ample proof," David said, holding up the quarter.

"Just trust me, that is a very special jukebox. Try it and I'll think you'll discover what I mean."

Carl shrugged, took a large gulp out of his special glass and set it carefully back on the napkin. "What the hell. I've played stranger games."

"So have I," Jess said. "I remember once with a girl named Donna. She loved to—" David hit him on the shoulder to make him stop as Carl twisted off his stool and moved over to the jukebox to study the songs.

I watched as he bent over the machine to read the list. At six-two, two hundred and fifty pounds, Carl was all muscle, with hands that looked like he was going to crush a glass at any moment. A carpenter in the real world outside the walls of the Garden Lounge, his small business sometimes employed four or five workers. Mostly he built houses, although his big project this year had been Doc Harris's new office. That had taken him seven months and helped him on the financial side. He had never married and no one could get much information about his past out of him. He had no hobbies that I knew of, and winter or summer I had never seen him dressed in anything other than work pants and plaid shirts. He kept his graying black hair cropped short and never wore a hat, no matter how hard it was raining.

After a moment bent over the jukebox, Carl's large shoulders slumped, almost as if someone had put a heavy weight square in the middle of his back. With effort he stood, turned around and faced the bar. His face was pale, his dark eyes a little glazed. "Found one. Now what?"

I took a deep breath. It was too late to back out now. These were my friends.

"Put the quarter in and pick the song." My voice was shaking and David looked at me. He knew me better than anyone and he could tell something was bothering me.

I took a deep breath and went on. "Before the song starts tell us the memory the song brings back."

Carl shrugged and dropped the quarter into the slot. The quiet in the Garden seemed to almost ring as he slowly punched the buttons for his song. "Anything else?" he asked as the jukebox clicked and the mechanism moved to find the record.

"Just state what the song reminds you of. And remember, you only have the length of the song — usually about two and a half minutes. Okay?"

Carl shrugged. "Why?"

"You'll know why in a moment. But remember that. It might be important. Now tell us the memory."

He glanced at the jukebox and then quietly said, "This song reminds me of the night my mother almost died."

I thought my heart had stopped. This wasn't what I had planned. Why did he have to pick a memory like that? This was Christmas Eve. Most people would have memories of good times. Times they wanted to relive. Damn, it was too late now. "Two and a half minutes, Carl," I managed to choke out. "Remember that."

He glanced over at me with a frown as "I'm Dreaming of a White Christmas" started. Then he was gone, back into his memory.

Two

THE URINE AND DISINFECTANT smells of the nursing home washed over Carl like a wave over a child on the beach. He grabbed the door frame and held on, feeling dizzy, confused. A moment before he had been standing in front of the jukebox at the Garden Lounge, playing a stupid game that Radley Stout, the owner of the bar, had insisted on playing. Carl had that memory firmly placed in his mind, as well as the memories of the last twenty years.

Yet he also had fresh memories of driving to the nursing home this Christmas Eve. Memories of wishing he could go back to college, wishing he could do something to put Mother out of her pain and suffering. And a very clear, very fresh memory of his decision to help her die with some dignity as she had asked.

It had been a Sunday afternoon, right after the second stroke. She had not only asked, she had begged him to help her if another stroke took her mind and left her body alive. That had been her worst fear. Yet he hadn't done anything. The part of his mind that remembered the Garden Lounge knew that she had suffered three more strokes. He had been too afraid.

He squeezed the doorframe until his hand hurt. Christmas music played softly down the hall. "I'm Dreaming of a White Christmas," the same song he had just punched up on the jukebox at the Garden Lounge. How...? This made no sense.

He forced himself to take a deep breath and look around. There was a white-haired nurse sitting behind the counter at the nurse's station. His mother was in her bed across the small room. Slight, wasted remains of the woman she had once been, she no longer recognized him or anyone else from her life. Most of the time she sat in a wheelchair and just drooled, her head hanging limp.

The doctors had said she would never recover from the series of strokes.

She would spend the next five years in that bed and chair. He would grow to hate this room, hate his own fear, hate his own inability to do something to help her.

He glanced over at his own hand against the doorframe. It was his hand all right, only young. No scar where the broken window cut it last year. No deep tan from being outside for so long. He was somehow in his young body, his old memories combined with his young ones. He felt dizzy with the conflicting memories and thoughts. His mouth was dry. He could really use a drink.

From down the hall the song reached its halfway point and Carl felt panic filling his mind. Radley Stout and that damn jukebox of his had given him a second chance. An opportunity to do what he had always wished he had done. Now he was wasting it by doing what he had done the first time.

Nothing.

He took a deep, almost sobbing breath. This time would be different. He checked the hall and then moved across the room and around to the other side of his mother's bed. She smelled of urine. The nurses would change her diapers many times in the next five years, and many times he would be forced to help.

"This is what you wanted, Mom." He swallowed the bile trying to force its way up into his mouth. "I'm doing what you asked."

He pulled the edge of the pillow up and over her face, pressing it hard against her mouth and nose.

"I love you, Mom," he said, softly. "I've learned to be strong. I hope you would be proud of me."

She struggled, trying to twist her head from side to side. But he held on, wanting to be sick, wanting to let go, wanting to let her breathe, but not wanting her to suffer day after day for five long years.

Finally the tension in her body eased and her head became heavy in his hands. Very heavy.

He gently stroked her soft hair as he held the pillow in place for another fifteen seconds. Then he eased his mother's head back into a more comfortable position.

He stood up straight and took a deep breath, never taking his gaze from the face of his dead mother. A feeling of sadness filled him at the same time as a lightness, as if a great weight had been lifted from his shoulders.

"Thanks, Stout," he said out loud as the last faint chords of the song died and took his future memories with it.

Three

AS THE LAST FEW NOTES of the Bing Crosby song faded into the carpet and booths of the Garden Lounge, the air shimmered as if a heat wave had passed though the room. None of the plants moved. And I felt no heat. But I knew what it meant.

I glanced around the room. Fred was sitting where Carl had sat, and the planter that Carl had built for me under the east window was gone, replaced with two chairs. Carl wasn't coming back, that much was clear.

During the song I had calmed the other three men down, explained that Carl had gone back into a memory. Then, on the excuse of Carl needing a drink when he returned, I took his glass and moved over to the jukebox. I had stood there with one hand on the cool chrome of the jukebox for the last half of the song.

I glanced down at the glass with Carl's name in my hand. So it had worked. Anything I held as I touched the jukebox stayed in this time line after the switch. Good. And because I was touching the jukebox, I still remembered Carl. Carl had changed something in his past and his new future no longer brought him to the Garden Lounge. I hoped it was a good new future for him.

I studied the jukebox to see if anything had changed. Damned if I knew how it worked. I had just taken it from storage in my old bar and fixed it, put a favorite record in, and the next thing I knew I had found myself facing my old girlfriend, Jenny, in my young body.

Scared me so bad all I did was sit there and stare at her. I had wanted to be with her more than anything else, but I had not had the courage or the desire to ask her to stay with me. On our third year of being together she had gone back to college while I stayed in our hometown to work. That semester she met someone else, and by Christmas she was married to him.

The song I had played on the jukebox had been our song. It had been playing the afternoon I had a chance to stop her leaving. And that was where the jukebox took me and left me for the entire length of the song.

The next day I played the song again and the same thing happened again. I did nothing but sit and stare at her.

I didn't play another song on the jukebox until I had all the possibilities figured out, including what would happen if I changed something, as Carl obviously had done.

"What the hell are you doing over there?" David said, twisting his custom drinking glass in his good hand.

"Yeah," Jess said. "You going to tell us what we're supposed to do with these quarters?" He flipped it, caught it and turned it over on the bar. "Heads."

"Play a song," I said. None of them remembered Carl or my explanation of where he had gone or anything he had done, which included playing the last song. He had never existed for them because they had not been touching the jukebox.

I moved back around the bar, dumped the remainder of Carl's drink out and set the glass carefully on the back bar.

"Who's Carl?" David asked.

"Just another friend I wanted to give a glass to."

"So how come you want us to play a song?" Jess asked.

I took a long drink of my eggnog and let the richness coat my dry throat. I was going to miss Carl. I just hoped he was happy. Maybe sometime over the next few days I would look up his name in the phone book. Maybe he had stayed around town. He would never remember me, but it would be nice to see him again and see how things ended up for him.

"You all right?" David asked. All three men were staring at me.

"Yeah, I'm fine. I was just thinking about how songs are like time machines. When you hear one it takes you back to some special moment when the song was playing."

I pointed at the little boxes and the quarters. "Those are for your memory trips. Fred. Why don't you try it? But you've got to follow my rules."

"More damn rules, huh?" Fred said. "Can I at least get off my bar stool or do I have to toss the quarter at the machine from here?"

I tried to laugh but it came out so poorly that David again looked at me with a questioning look. "Go pick out a Christmas song that reminds you of something in your past. Then after you've selected it, stand beside the machine and tell us the memory."

Fred picked up the quarter from the bar and swung around. "I think I can handle that."

"I'll bet that's not what your ex-wife would say," Jess said.

Everyone laughed, and that started the nightly joking about Fred's ex-wife. She was well known to the group because it seemed at times that was all Fred could talk about. Her name was Alice and she and Fred had gotten married young, had one child, and gotten divorced in an ugly fashion about ten years before.

Fred was tall and thin, with about twenty pounds of extra weight around his stomach. He used to have bright red hair that was now sun-bleached because he worked for the city streets department. He said that almost a quarter of his salary every month went to paying child support, even though his ex-wife very seldom let him see his daughter. He claimed he loved his daughter, and one Saturday had brought her in for all of us to meet. Sandy had bright red hair like her father.

"Got one," Fred said as he dropped the quarter into the slot and quickly punched two buttons.

"So what's the memory?" I asked. My stomach felt weak. Was I going to lose Fred, too? Maybe I shouldn't warn him that he only had the time of the song, that if he wanted to change anything, he would have to do it fast.

"The first time I got laid," he said, smiling. "The night Sandy came to be."

God, what was I doing to my friends? What kind of presents were these?

"Stout," David said. "You all right? You're as pale as a ghost."

I nodded and looked up at Fred. "You only have the time of the song. Remember that. Just over two minutes."

Jess laughed. "More than enough time for Fred to get laid, from what I hear."

Fred had taken a step toward Jess when the Gene Autry song started and Fred vanished from the bar.

Four

THE SNOW BLEW HARD against Fred's face as he dodged across the rush of pedestrians on the busy sidewalk and in the front door of Abraham's Drug Store. The bell over the door jingled as he entered. The store smelled clean, with a faint background of medicine. The tile floor looked slick from polish.

Old man Abraham was behind the druggist's counter in his white smock. Judy, the clerk, was at the cash register waiting on a heavyset man who was buying cough syrup. In the background the song, "Rudolf the Red-nosed Reindeer" played. That was the same song he had punched up a moment before on the Garden Lounge jukebox. How the hell had Radley Stout done this? What was going on?

Fred glanced down at himself. He was young, dressed in his high school clothes. How could that be? Only a moment before, he had been in the Garden Lounge, drinking, eighteen years in the future. This was some practical joke. He'd get Jess for this. And Stout.

He was about to turn and head back into the storm when the younger memories that were mixed with the older ones reminded him of why he was here. He had come to the drugstore to buy a rubber. A condom.

He was on his way to Alice's house. Her parents were at a Christmas party and would be gone for a long time. He and Alice would start out on the couch watching television and work their way naked to the floor. It would be their first time and because he had chickened out and not bought the rubber on the way to her house, she had gotten pregnant and they had gotten married right out of high school. Sandy had followed three months later.

He grabbed hold of the doorframe, then touched a bottle of hair oil on a nearby shelf. Everything felt real. Damned if he knew what was going on.

He turned back to face old man Abrahams who was now watching him. It was no wonder he had chickened out the first time. He had bought condoms hundreds of times in the last twenty years, but right now he felt afraid. But what the hell could the old man do to him? Fred shook his head. He didn't want to think about that.

He took a deep breath and moved up to the counter.

"Can I help you?" Abrahams said, staring down from his high perch. The guy looked like a cross between God and his dad.

"I'd..." His voice broke and he cleared his throat and tried to lower the pitch to a more normal range. "I'd like to buy a..." He glanced quickly around. Judy was watching him and smiling. He'd had a crush on her for years. It was no wonder his younger self had chickened out.

"Well, young man?"

Fred turned back to face Abrahams. He could feel his face getting hot. If he didn't ask now, Alice would get pregnant and they would end up married. That had turned out to be a fate much worse than asking one simple question. Much, much worse. All those years of shouting and the hate and the ugliness their marriage had been. The only slightly good thing had been Sandy. But who knew how screwed up she was going to be because of the ugly marriage he and Alice had had.

He looked up at Abrahams. "I'd...I'd like to buy a condom." There. He had done it.

Old man Abrahams had the good sense not to laugh. But Fred could tell he was holding back a smile. "Well, son, they come in packages of three or six or twelve."

"Six," he said quickly. No point in having to go through this too often. But a dozen would seem like bragging.

Abrahams nodded and rummaged behind the counter. "Now, which brand would you like?"

At that Judy giggled and Fred could feel his face and neck burning. His younger self wanted to flee the store. He'd never be able to face her.

But his older memories kept him there. "I... I... I don't care. Your best."

Again Abrahams nodded. "That would be Trojans." He slid the box across the counter. "Pay Judy."

Damn him. He was doing this on purpose. He had a register. He could take the money. Again Judy giggled as Fred picked up the box and turned. At that very moment he noticed that the song was almost over and he knew without a doubt that his face was as red as Rudolf's nose.

He pulled a five-dollar bill out of his pocket and tossed it on the counter. "Keep the change," he said to Judy and, without looking at her, he sprinted for the front door and the snow beyond. At least now he had the choice to have Sandy or not. He'd have to give this some serious thought.

As the door slammed shut and the song ended, the memories of the choice, Sandy, the marriage to Alice, and the next twenty years faded and were gone.

Five

WHEN THE LOUNGE finished shimmering I let go of the jukebox and moved around behind the bar. Carefully I dumped what was left of Fred's drink and placed his glass beside Carl's on the back bar. I hadn't felt this tired in years. I looked at the two glasses. "Good luck, guys," I said softly. "I hope life is better for both of you." But now I only had two friends left in the bar. I could stop this at any time, while there was still someone left to talk to.

"So what are we supposed to do with these quarters?" Jess asked. "I got to get home before that bitch of a wife chews my head off."

I glanced at Jess and then at David. He was looking worried. "You play a song. That's all." I motioned at the jukebox. "But find one that has a strong memory with it." I took a deep breath. I might as well give him a real present. "Maybe even one that was during the time that you met your wife."

Jess laughed. "Why the hell would I want to do that?"

"Trust me," I said. "Just find a song." I dropped down onto the counter behind the bar and concentrated on taking deep breaths and not thinking about Carl and Fred.

"You all right? David asked. I looked up into his worried face. What would I have done over the last few years without David's friendship? What was I going to do without it over the next few years if I let him play a song?

"Just suddenly got tired. Nothing big." I stood and moved to pour myself another eggnog and watch Jess pick over the tunes. Jess was the best joker. He said he needed the practical jokes to keep his sanity with his bitch of a wife. But when asked why he didn't just leave her, he always said marrying her was his mistake and he would live with it. That was what he had been taught. Then he would make a joke and change the subject.

"Found one," Jess said. He held up the quarter. "You want me to play it?"

"Yeah. But after you select the song tell Dave and me what memory it reminds you of."

Jess dropped the quarter into the slot and punched two buttons to start the jukebox. "You remember the song, 'Snoopy Versus the Red Baron?'"

David and I nodded.

"That was playing the moment I asked my wife to marry me. Figures, doesn't it?"

David laughed.

But I didn't. I knew I was going to lose Jess also. "Remember that you only have the length of the song. Not one second longer. All right?"

Jess shrugged and started back toward the bar. "Whatever you..."

The song started and he vanished.

"What the hell?" David said, standing and heading toward the jukebox.

I picked up Jess's mostly empty glass and moved around toward the jukebox, too.

David glanced at the two glasses on the back bar and then at the glass I held. Then he looked over to where Jess had been. "You want to explain exactly what the *hell* is going on here?"

I nodded, too tired to argue. "But come on over and touch the jukebox. It's the only way you're going to remember."

Six

SNOOPY AND THE RED BARON were just starting to go at it on Jess's '65 Ford car radio as Jess found himself face to face with Mary, his soon-to-be bitch-of-a-wife.

"What the...?"

"Is something wrong, Jess, honey?" Mary said, her hand stroking his arm up and down and up and down. She looked more beautiful than he had ever remembered, and she smelled wonderfully fresh, as if she had been outside in the country all day. But he knew the look and the smell wouldn't last long. Six months after they were married she would gain fifty pounds and a few years later she would level out a hundred over her marriage weight. But now, in this dream or whatever it was, she looked sexy and very trim in her low-cut blue dress.

Jess pulled back away from her and looked around. This was his car all right. The same one he had sold in '71. The same one that he and Mary had first made love in. He rubbed his hands along the steering wheel to make sure it felt solid. They were parked just down the tree-lined street from Mary's house.

So how had Stout pulled this off? This had to be some kind of dream or hallucination. That was it. Stout had hypnotized him and he was still sitting in the Garden Lounge while they laughed at him. He'd get them for this.

Mary scooted over closer to him and rubbed his leg real nice, getting the reaction in his crotch she wanted. "Were you going to ask me something?" she said, looking up at him with her large brown eyes.

"That I was," he said. It was a clear memory that in this exact situation he had asked her to marry him. He knew that's what his younger self had been planning to do. He was currently a second-year law student, and he remembered his classes that Friday morning real well. Yet he also remembered sitting having a Christmas Eve drink with his friends at the Garden Lounge twenty some years in the future. Strange. Too damn strange.

On the radio the Red Baron shot down Snoopy. Stout had said Jess only had the length of the song. Whatever was going on, it was halfway over. Mary rubbed Jess's leg and waited. Waited, knowing what the question would be. Waited, knowing that she had led him right to where she wanted him.

Well, this time around she would get a surprise, because dream or no dream, this was going to be fun. Hell, after all the years with her, he deserved a little fun.

"I wanted to ask you," Jess said, then paused, trying not to smile.

The Red Baron and Snoopy drank a Christmas toast.

"Yes," Mary said, her voice low and sexy. She had been one beautiful woman on the outside. That had kept him blind to all the ugliness that was just under the surface. Blind until it was too late.

"I wanted to ask you if it would be all right if I slept around with a few other women? You know, sew a few wild oats before I settle down?"

That did it. The sultry look drained from her face like wet makeup, to be replaced by the bitch look he had grown so familiar with. "What did you say?" she asked, her voice low and mean and controlled. He knew that voice real well, too.

He smiled, easing toward her, trying to act romantic. "I was just thinking that for a few years, maybe five or ten, we could have an open relationship. I'd love to sleep with a few other women. It would be good for us. Honest. You know, free love and all." He moved as if to kiss her and she backed away across the seat.

"Wouldn't you like sleeping with other men? Then after we've both got a little more experience we could live together for a few years. Trying on the old shoes, as the saying goes." Jess knew that would get her. She had said a hundred times how much she hated the thought of living together. For her it was marriage or nothing. Damn it was hard keeping a straight face. He was going to thank Stout for this one. Best Christmas present he had ever had.

"You're sick!" she screamed. "Sick! Sick! Sick!"

Jess tried to look innocent and sad.

On the radio Snoopy flew off singing about Christmas cheer as Mary rammed against the car door, opened it and ran up the sidewalk.

"Thank you, Radley Stout. I've been dreaming about doing that for years."

The song ended.

And so did the dreams.

Seven

I MOVED SLOWLY around behind the bar, dumped out the remainder of Jess's drink and set his glass beside the others on the back bar.

"Got quite a collection there," David said as he moved over to take his stool. "So Carl and Fred were friends of mine in another time line?"

I took a long hard drink of my eggnog and then nodded.

"Jess," David said, "was sent back by the jukebox to his memory and he changed something that moved his life in another direction. And with that new direction he didn't end up coming in here. Right? And he would have no memory of ever being in here because he hasn't been."

Again I nodded and finished off the drink.

David picked up the quarter in front of him and glanced over at the jukebox. "You know this is a wish that everyone has had at one time or another? How come you've never done it?"

"Oh, I did. Actually twice when I first discovered what the jukebox could do. But I didn't change anything. Too afraid, I guess. And, I suppose, not that unhappy with this life." I nodded at the three empty glasses. "That is until tonight."

David took a sip of his drink and looked at his name on the glass. "So you gave the gift of a second chance to your friends for Christmas."

I laughed. "Seemed like a good idea at the time. But I didn't expect to lose everyone. Not exactly sure what I expected, to be honest with you"

"I'm still here."

I glanced over at my best friend. He worked as a vice president of a local bank and enjoyed flying his small plane on the weekend. But back twenty-some years ago he and his new wife, Elaine, had been driving home from a Christmas party. David was scheduled to finish flight school that next spring. He had a dream of flying for the airlines.

That night David had had a little too much to drink and the car missed a slick corner and plowed into an embankment. Elaine was killed and David lost most of the use of his right hand. End of flight school. End of dream.

I reached out and slid the quarter at David. "Your turn."

David shook his head. "No chance. There's no way I'm leaving you after what you've done for Jess and those two other guys." He pointed at the glasses lined up on the back bar.

I laughed a laugh that sounded bitter even to my ears. "I don't know what exactly I've done except change their life in some fashion. I can only hope it is for the better. But you I *do* know the jukebox can help." I reached across the bar and patted his ruined right hand. "Go back to before the crash and save Elaine. And yourself."

David jerked as if he had never thought of the possibility.

"You saw it work," I said. "If nothing else, give it a try. You don't have to change anything. Just go back and see Elaine again. It's not a one-way trip if you don't change anything."

He looked dazed. "If I don't change..."

I nodded and picked up the quarter and placed it in his good left hand. "Go say hello to your wife."

Still looking dazed, he slowly stood and moved toward the jukebox. "Is it really possible?"

"Yes," I said. "Now pick the right song."

He nodded and turned to study the song list. His tie hung loose in front of him, his right hand useless against the glass of the jukebox.

My stomach hurt and I downed a little more eggnog. I knew that once he saw Elaine he would be unable to stop from changing the past. I was going to lose my best friend. But maybe someday I would see him again, striding through an airport in his pilot's uniform. That alone would be worth it.

"Found the song," he said and turned to look at me.

"Then go for it," I said.

He paused, as if he wanted to say something. Then he turned and dropped the quarter into the machine and punched the two buttons.

"State the memory," I said. "Got to follow the rules, you know."

He smiled. "This song reminds me of the night my wife died."

I nodded. "Good luck. And say hello to Elaine for me."

"I will," he said." And I'll be back."

"In case you're not, I'll be holding onto your glass and the jukebox."

He smiled. "Thanks." The song started and he vanished.

Eight

A LIGHT SNOW KEPT the old Ford's windshield wipers busy as David and Elaine headed down the gravel country road toward the lights of the city.

"Silent Night" was playing on the portable radio on the seat between them. She was singing along, her voice pure and clear, even though a little drunk. The party, just south of town in the foothills, had been a good one and they had stayed far later than they planned.

David looked over at his wife of six months. She had dark brown hair that flowed long and straight down her back. Her eyes were a dark green and her face lightly wrinkled with laugh lines. While David was in school she worked at a dress shop. Her desire was to someday design clothes, and he knew she would be, would have been, good at it.

"Son of a bitch," he said out loud. "Stout was right."

"Who was right?" Elaine said, then went back to singing and watching the beautiful wooded countryside flash by through the snow.

David glanced once more at her and then back at the road. He couldn't let her die. Stout had known that.

David braked the car to a quick stop on the side of the road. He turned off the car, yanked the keys out of the ignition and got out. Then as hard as he could, he tossed the keys into the woods. In the silence of the night he could hear them catch brush as they landed.

That was his only set. Now there would be no way he could drive again tonight.

"David," Elaine said, getting out of the car and coming around to him. "What are you doing?"

"Saving our lives," he said. He grabbed her and held her tight, relishing in the feeling of her against him after such a long time. He had never remarried because there had never been anyone again he felt this way about. No one woman who had felt this good.

The faint sounds of "Silent Night" drifted from the portable radio in the car. The song was about half over. He didn't have much time.

"Are you all right?" Elaine asked. "Why did you throw the..."

"I'm fine. Like I said, I was just saving our lives. But now, before that song ends, I need to save a friendship. A very important friendship to me. And I'm going to need your help."

Nine

I LET MY HAND SLIP off the jukebox as the last strains of the song faded into the empty Garden Lounge. David's glass was in my hand and I looked down at it, feeling its heavy weight.

David must have stopped the wreck.

"Well, Stout," I said to myself out loud just to hear some noise. "Looks as if you've gone and done it now."

I moved slowly around behind the bar and set David's glass beside the other three, name out. "I'm going to have to find some special place for these." I laughed. "To remind me of another life that never was."

The silence seemed to echo in the room. It was going to be a very long, very quiet Christmas.

I refilled my glass of eggnog and moved around to what had been David's favorite stool. The jukebox seemed to call to me. "Come play me, Mr. Radley Stout. Come and see your old girlfriend again. Ask her to marry you. What would it hurt?"

"No," I said, loud enough to echo between the empty tables and booths. I squarely faced the glasses on the back bar and held up my mug in a toast.

"Merry Christmas, my friends."

Then I added softly, "Wherever you are."

The empty glasses didn't return my toast, so I went ahead and drank alone. I had the sneaking feeling I was going to be doing that for a while.

I had finished the eggnog and was about to start closing down when someone knocked on the front door.

"I'm closed," I yelled. "Merry Christmas." I was in no mood for visitors now.

But the person knocked again. "All right, all right. Hang on a minute." I went around to the back bar and, being careful to not look at the four glasses lined up there like so many tombstones, retrieved the keys and headed for the front door.

As I unlocked it and swung it open I heard, "Merry Christmas, Mr. Radley Stout."

David and a woman about his same age stood arm in arm facing the door. He wore an airline overcoat and she had on a nice leather jacket. "David," I said. "How...?"

He unhooked himself from the woman's arm and extended a perfectly healthy right hand for me to shake. "Your hand," I said as I shook it. "You didn't...?" Again I stopped. There was no way he could know about the wreck and his lame hand if it hadn't happened. And in this world it hadn't.

"This is my wife, Elaine," he said.

"I don't know what to say," I took her hand. I felt as if I was shaking the hand of a ghost. "Please come in." I stepped back, the feeling of shock washing over me.

David and Elaine moved into the bar. Both of them walked directly to the jukebox.

"But how could you remember?" I asked moving up beside them.

"He doesn't," Elaine said, laughing with a tense sort of laugh. David only nodded and then turned to face me.

"Christmas Eve, twenty years ago, Elaine said I suddenly called out the name 'Stout,' then stopped the car. I then proceeded to toss the car keys into the trees. For what crazy reason, I have no idea."

I laughed. "I do. Pretty smart thinking if you want to make sure you can't drive that night."

"But why would I want to do that?" David said. "And how would you know anything about it? This entire thing has been driving me nuts for two decades."

I waved my hand. "I'll try to explain in a minute. For now please go on."

Elaine reached into her purse, pulled out a few tattered pieces of paper, and handed them to me. "For the next minute after he tossed the keys into the brush, David madly wrote this while repeating your name and the name of this bar over and over again so that I would remember it. He made me promise that no matter what he claimed he didn't remember, we would come to this bar on this Christmas Eve at this time to meet you. Not one minute before or one minute after."

David looked at me and shrugged. "Dammed if I can remember why. It was as if I was possessed."

"In a way, you were," I said.

"You know what else he said?" Elaine asked. She looked at David and he motioned for her to go ahead. "He said it was his Christmas present to you."

David looked at me. "Did it work?"

I nodded, afraid to say anything. But I could feel the smile trying to break out of the sides of my face. And after a moment all three of us were laughing just because I was smiling so hard. I was going to enjoy these new friends.

I motioned for them to take a seat at the bar. "Boy have I got a story to tell you." I scampered like a kid around behind the bar and grabbed the glass with his name on it.

"And for you, David," I said as I held the glass up for them to see. "A very special Christmas present and a toast to friendship."

SANTA'S SNACK

A mystery story about a grown man, an attorney, alone on Christmas Eve, who can't allow himself to believe in Santa Claus.

But someone keeps eating the cookies. Every year.

Just as it happened in his childhood. Maybe Santa Claus really does exist.

Or maybe, just maybe, this skeptic needs to understand where the jolly fat man lives.

One

THE FAT OLD BASTARD ate the whole thing. Again.

I was twenty-seven years old, a lawyer in a big downtown firm, and lived alone in my parent's old Victorian house. I didn't believe in Santa Claus.

Yet again this Christmas morning, every crumb of the dozen sugar cookies I had left on one of Mom's best plates, every drop of the milk, was gone.

Just like every Christmas Eve for the last twenty years, the cookies and milk had disappeared at some time during the night.

"Got you this time," I said, staring at the empty plate.

For three years I'd been trying to catch the person eating the cookies, and for three years I had failed. But this Christmas this joke was going to end.

I turned and headed for the hidden cameras I had had installed around the room. Six of them, two on the shelves behind the couch, one on each side of the stone fireplace, one over the entrance, and one over the big bay window near where the Christmas tree sat. Nothing could have moved in the living room last night without me knowing about it.

Back when I was a kid I used to believe Santa actually ate the snack, but then when I learned that Santa didn't exist, I figured Dad did it.

And I had believed that for years.

One year, when I was home from law school for Christmas, before my parents were both killed by that damned drunk driver, I had asked Mom why she kept putting out the cookies and milk.

"Tradition," she had said, smiling at me as she slid the dozen sugar cookies onto the coffee table. It was always sugar cookies, with white frosting and some sprinkles. I loved the things, always had, still did. Every year as a kid I ate those cookies from two days before Christmas and a week after. Those cookies had been as much a part of Christmas for me as the presents and the tree.

My mom's answer of tradition had been enough of an answer for me that year. It sort of made sense in a Christmas fashion. My mom had been big into traditions, and I had to admit, I liked a few of them myself.

The next morning those cookies she had put out for tradition's sake were gone, just like always. I figured Dad must really enjoy his Christmas Eve midnight snack.

Then, on the Christmas Eve after I moved back in after their deaths, I found myself alone and remembering all the wonderful Christmases in the big old house. I really missed my parents, missed my mom's laugh, my dad's snoring from down the hall. And tomorrow I was going to miss waking up to the wonderful smells of my mom cooking a Christmas turkey. I knew this first Christmas was going to be rough, but I didn't expect it to be this hard.

Twice during the evening I put on my coat to leave and find a bar, and twice I stopped before going out the door. I think the problem was that I had made the house look a little too much like they were still here. I had put up a tree, in the same spot they always did, using the same decorations Mom used.

Traditions died hard in my family, of that there was no doubt.

I was sitting, staring at the tree when it suddenly dawned on me I had missed one tradition.

The cookies.

The coffee table looked empty without Mom's offering for Santa. Without the cookies there, it sort of made the room seem even emptier than it felt.

So being in a sentimental and sad mood, and wanting to not break any traditions of my parents so soon after their deaths, and wanting any excuse to get out of the house for even a few minutes, I went out and got some store-bought sugar cookies and some milk. Then on the same plate as she always used, I put out her offering.

It made me laugh at myself for going to such lengths to do such a silly thing, but for a while the room felt right, felt like a Christmas Eve like the old days.

I figured it was going to be sad in the morning when the cookies were still there and I finally got my answer as to who had eaten the cookies every year.

But the cookies and milk were gone the next morning.

I stood there in my bathrobe, the tree lights not even turned on, staring at the empty plate, totally freaked out. My stomach twisted in a combination of fear and excitement. More than likely some friend was pulling a trick on me, trying to cheer me up or something.

It spooked me, yet for an instant I believed in the magic of the moment, in the excitement of the holiday, in the tradition itself. Then the law school training took over and I started looking for how it had happened.

I checked the doors and windows. Nothing was open and nothing had been disturbed. And over the next few days I asked every one of my friends if they had eaten the cookies. They responded with varied looks of worry, followed by laughter.

Just like when I was a kid, the only logical explanation was that Santa ate the cookies and drank the milk, but there was no Santa.

And Dad was dead.

So there was no explanation.

Two

THE NEXT YEAR I put out the cookies and milk again, feeling damned silly again. I figured I had imagined the cookies gone last year, but just in case, this year I planned on sitting in the living room during the night. No one was going to pull some dumb stunt on me this year.

Somewhere along the way, more than likely during the sixth boring Christmas special, like a bad cliché, I fell asleep. When I woke up, the cookies and milk were again gone.

I ran like a mad man around the house checking every window, every door. No one had gotten in. I had even put on the security chains on both my doors.

Yet the damn cookies were gone again.

It couldn't have happened, yet it had.

That kind of puzzle will drive a logical-thinking lawyer nuts. Again I asked my friends, and again got laughs and head shakes.

I spent the week between Christmas and New Years doing nothing but walking around inside and outside my house, looking for any way anyone might be getting in. I even went up on the roof and checked for an attic entrance. But I knew the big old house, had grown up in it, and there just wasn't a way inside that I didn't know about.

Those damned missing cookies ate at me the entire year.

The next year on Christmas Eve I made sure the glass was completely clean, and I used gloves to fill it and place it on the table with the cookies. And I did my best to again stay awake, without luck.

When the milk and cookies were gone again the next morning, and I got finished running around the house checking every window, every door for the tenth time, I went back to the empty plate and glass. I remember saying, "Got you now."

I carefully took the glass to a friend of mine who had some crime lab experience. Even though it was Christmas morning, as a favor for what must have seemed a very disturbed friend, he dusted the glass for fingerprints and found none.

Someone had drunk the milk without leaving a trace.

So now, finally, this year, I was going to know exactly how this trick was pulled off. This year I had the hidden cameras recording every inch of the living room and the offering of cookies and milk on the coffee table near the old stone fireplace.

And again the cookies and milk were gone in the morning, just like every year.

I played the recording back. The camera was focused clearly on the table and Santa's snack. I fast-forwarded to a point where suddenly the cookies were gone, then rewound to a minute before the moment and played the tape.

Nothing. One minute the cookies were there, the next instant they were gone.

It was exactly the same way on the other recordings from the other cameras. It took me a good half day of walking around my house, afraid to even touch the empty plate on the coffee table, before it dawned on me to check the time counter on the recordings.

No time was missing from any of the recordings. The cookies and milk had just vanished in what seemed like an instant.

That made no sense.

But nothing about the missing cookies made logical sense, and with no hard answers coming, all I could do was wait until the next Christmas and try something else.

But during that year my life changed.

I met Brin, a wonderful brunette woman with deep brown eyes and a swimmer's body. Brin was an attorney as well, working for the city, and had a six-year-old child named Zack from a previous marriage. We dated, going slow at first, then as we slowly fell in love everything changed.

We were married right after Thanksgiving, and by the time Christmas rolled around, she and Zack were living with me in my big old Victorian house. For the first time since my parents had died, it actually felt like a home again.

We did all the Christmas things, cutting down our own tree, putting presents under it, buying stuff for each other and Zack from Santa. And we even made sugar cookies together, although I swear more icing got on us than on the cookies.

Then, without me realizing it, it was Christmas Eve.

I had never told Brin about my crazy obsession of the last number of Christmas Eves. It just never came up. And I didn't see much point in telling her now. If the cookies disappeared again, we'd talk about it in the morning.

But for now it was Christmas Eve. The cameras were long gone, the tree was in a slightly different place closer to the window, and I hadn't even had the time to come up with a way to try to catch my cookie thief.

"My mom had a tradition," I said as I came out of the kitchen carrying a plate of the sugar cookies and a glass of milk. Brin was on the couch and Zack was on the floor, staring at the presents under the tree. I had built a small fire in the fireplace and it added a comfortable glow and warmth to the room.

"What's that?" Brin asked.

"We have to leave a snack for Santa."

Brin laughed and kissed me as Zack got excited, begging his mother to let him stay up and see Santa.

"Trust me," I told him, "Santa doesn't want to be seen. I know, I've tried."

"So did I," Brin said, kissing me on the cheek. "Three straight years."

"Then why can't I try?" Zack asked.

"Maybe next year," Brin said, laughing.

Three

AFTER ZACK HAD GONE off to bed, Brin and I spent a few hours watching television, getting the last of the presents under the tree, and then we went off to bed.

Around four in the morning I awoke. For some reason I thought I had heard a noise down in the living room, so I went to investigate. The room was dark except for a few embers left from the fire, so I turned on the tree lights and looked around.

Nothing. And the cookies were still there, along with the milk. For some reason, that surprised me.

The lights of the tree were beautiful, the reds and oranges and greens casting wonderful shadows around the room. I dropped down on the couch and put my feet up beside the cookies, just letting myself stare at the tree and feel the wonderful calm and happiness that went along with the evening.

There was life in the big old house again. I just hoped my parents were watching from somewhere and smiling at the moment.

"Waiting for Santa?" Brin asked as she came into the room and joined me on the couch, her white bathrobe tucked under her for extra warmth.

"Just enjoying the moment," I said. "It's great having you and Zack here."

"It's great being here," she said, snuggling against me. "It feels like we're a family."

"We are," I said as she snuggled against me.

We sat there for the longest time, staring at the wonderful lights, enjoying the moment.

I wondered how many times my parents must have done the same thing. Maybe this was part of the tradition my mom had talked about.

Maybe it was the power of that tradition that had carried through the years, maybe bringing them back over the last few Christmas Eves to eat the cookies I left out for them.

But now the cookies and the milk and playing Santa was our tradition, mine and Brin's.

I leaned forward and picked up the plate, offering a cookie to Brin. "Have a cookie, Santa?"

She laughed and took one.

"You know," she said, "I always knew my mom and dad were Santa. I just never expected to some day become one myself."

I took a cookie and put the plate back. "I know what you mean."

Over the next hour we talked, we laughed, we sat quietly staring at the lights of the tree. By the time we started out of the room to go back to bed, the cookie plate was almost empty, with only one cookie remaining.

Then, just before I reached to turn off the lights, I noticed the one last cookie was now gone.

"Ate Santa's last cookie, huh?" I asked Brin.

Brin turned, waiting for me in the doorway to the hall. "Not me. Five was my limit. See you in bed." She headed down the hallway.

I turned and stared at the empty plate again, just as I had done for the past four years.

Then suddenly Mom and Dad were standing beside the tree, smiling at me as if I were Zack's age, opening presents.

I wanted to call for Brin to turn around, see if she saw them too, but I didn't. This was just between me and my parents.

Mom smiled, Dad smiled, and then he held up the last cookie as if to say thanks.

I nodded a welcome and smiled as well.

Then as he bit into the cookie, they faded and were gone.

I stood there staring at the space where they had been, feeling content for the first time since they had died. I missed them, sure, but for some reason, for the first time I was at peace with losing them.

I flipped off the tree lights and headed for bed, just as I am sure Dad had done for years and years, his stomach full from the cookies and milk.

The next morning Zack stood staring wide-eyed at the empty cookie plate. I knew exactly what he was thinking, because at his age I had thought the same thing.

Santa hadn't forgotten him.

I had to wonder why, during the previous four years, I hadn't thought that same thing. Why hadn't I just accepted the fact that the cookies being gone proved I hadn't been forgotten. Alone, the idea hadn't seemed logical, but now, with a wonderful family around me on Christmas morning, it seemed perfectly right.

Santa always got a snack.

He hadn't forgotten to come to this house. It was a tradition.

SPRINKLE ON A MEMORY

When murder matters more than the cookie.

Red sugar sparkles on white cookie icing. Blood drops on a snowdrift. Who would have thought that decorating Christmas cookies would remind him of a murder he may or may not have done.

Reality, dream, or memory: Only murder matters.

First published in Ellery Queen's Mystery Magazine *in 2005, I really wanted to give this story life yet again.*

One

RED SUGAR SPARKLES on white cookie icing.

Blood drops on a snowdrift.

Who would have thought that decorating Christmas cookies with my kid would remind me of a murder. A murder I had no real memory of doing, yet I had no doubt I had done.

I could bring back a few details. The feel of the cold of the night air, the white of the snow under the light from my car's headlights, and the smell of hot blood from the woman's throat. I have a memory of her blood spraying, just like all my victim's blood did. Her blood had left red dots all over the snow bank. Why hadn't I remembered her, or that night, or the blood on the snow before now?

Had I killed too many? Or maybe she was one I had yet to kill.

"You all right, Dad?" my daughter, Jennifer, asked.

My mind snapped out of the vision, or the memory, and came back to the kitchen table. The bright-lit room smelled of baking cookies and felt too warm by a few degrees.

I was sitting at our tablecloth-covered oak table, across from my daughter, Jennifer. My wife, Lisa, was taking another batch out of the oven. Decorating cookies had been a tradition in our family since before Jennifer was born. I always enjoyed it. It made it feel like the Christmas season.

I had my hand poised over a cookie, the few bits of red sprinkles still in my hand, the rest on the white icing.

Like blood drops on snow.

"Changed my mind," I said, smiling at Jennifer. "I think this one needs green."

"You're strange, Dad," Jennifer said, laughing and shaking her head before going back to work on getting the exact right color on an angel cookie.

My wife Lisa laughed also, but it was a fond laugh. For some reason she loved me and all my quirks. Why such a beautiful, brown-haired, brown-eyed smart woman would love me, I had no idea. But I was very glad she did.

Neither she nor Jennifer had any idea about my little hobby, as I thought of my killing. Everyone in the city, I was sure, had heard of me. I was what the newspapers and police called "The Foothills Killer." I got the nickname because I always dumped my victims up in the foothills above the city of Boise.

I picked up the bottle of green sugar sparkles and started to put them on the half-decorated cookie. But again the red specks on the white frosting distracted me, brought back a memory I clearly had been holding back for a long time.

Blood splatters on the snow.

I remembered the woman now. It was my first kill, my first wife, actually, long before Lisa.

Her name was Stephanie, and we had met in college. She had been tall, blonde, with green eyes. Everything about her shouted sex, and I remember liking that the most about her.

For some reason Stephanie and I had been arguing the night I killed her. The police had never found her body, and never would. I had buried her up in the Boise National Forest, deep, very deep, and then killed our dog Harvey and buried him two feet above her, so anyone digging would find the dog bones and stop.

Since she had no parents or close family, I told friends she had taken Harvey and left me for New York City. She had always talked about going to New York to try to break into acting in the theater, and every friend we had knew that we fought all the time. So her leaving me was no surprise to anyone.

I acted upset, angry, then upset again.

Everyone bought my little hurt-husband play-acting.

And after some time had passed, I got a divorce and people stopped asking about her.

That was over twenty years and thirty-five other kills ago. And not once during that time had anyone even questioned me about any of the deaths. I was that good, and that careful. The Foothills Killer had the police stumped.

Now I was happily married, had a wonderful daughter, and taught school in a local high school. I even was an assistant coach on the football team. I only killed once or twice a year, always in my private storage building near the river that I had bought to store sports equipment.

Only Stephanie had been killed out in the open, where I couldn't control every detail. In the storage building, I controlled the details, controlled the mess, even had a shower to wash up in, along with a washer and dryer to clean my clothes. With gloves and hot water I washed down every woman I killed, then stood them up to dry. I always left them nude, never left any trace of myself on them, and dumped them by keeping my van on the pavement of a well-traveled road in the foothills.

I also changed vans every year.

So why now, sitting in my kitchen, did seeing red specks on a cookie take me back to the memory of that first murder? I hadn't thought of Stephanie for a decade.

Suddenly around the cookie I could feel the wonderful kitchen, the image of Lisa, slipping away. I tried to hold onto it, but I couldn't.

Two

THE FRESH SMELL of baking cookies was still around me, but now instead of a covered oak dining table, I was sitting at a Formica kitchen table. The room around me was smaller, clearly less expensive.

"Jason!" my wife demanded, glaring at me from across the room. "Are you all right?"

I glanced up into Stephanie's face, the face of the woman I had thought about killing for twenty-five years.

"Fine," I said. "Just day-dreaming."

Stephanie snorted and shook her head, clearly disgusted. "Wow, that's a surprise."

She always complained that I never seemed to be there, never talked to her, never wanted to touch her anymore. The truth was that she was right. I was always off daydreaming, imaging a life where I had killed her.

I glanced around, wondering what had happened to me? How I had become this weak person?

I had the memories of Lisa and Jennifer, yet I knew that in reality Stephanie and I had gotten married right out of college, had two children, one named Craig and one named Leslie. Both kids were now off at college and would be coming home in the next day or so.

Stephanie had wanted us to decorate cookies like we always did, so the kids would have some.

"Make it feel like Christmas," she had said.

I had agreed because it was just easier to agree with Stephanie than fight her. I had learned that long ago.

The cookie in front of me had white frosting with red sparkles, just like I imagined the snow would have after I cut Stephanie's neck. For twenty years I had imagined killing Stephanie, imagined doing my dream job of teaching high school.

I also imagined killing dozens of other women I had met in my corporate job, women like Stephanie who deserved to be killed and hung naked to dry.

But instead of acting, I simply did nothing.

That was the story of my life it seemed. I only dreamed of acting while doing nothing. And by doing nothing, I got nowhere. I agreed with my wife, worked my boring job, and came home to the same old bitching. Somehow I had lost the person I might have become.

All I had left was my daydreams.

I stared at the white icing on the cookie, letting the red specks become something besides sugar as I imagined killing Stephanie, slicing her throat, letting her blood spurt out over the snow.

Three

"JASON," LISA SAID, putting her hand on my shoulder as I stared at the cookie. "Can I get you something?"

"Yeah, Dad, take a break," Jennifer said. "You're acting even stranger than normal."

The memory of cutting Stephanie's neck, of killing all those other women was there again.

"I'm fine," I said. I glanced up at my beautiful Lisa. "Honest. I was just thinking how lucky I am to be here with you two."

"Oh, weird," Jennifer said.

Lisa laughed and kissed me. "I'm glad you're here too." She gave me a wonderful hug and went to get another batch out of the oven.

I looked around the kitchen, at my perfect family, at the wonderful, rich-textured room filled with the smell of fresh-baked sugar cookies. I had made a life for myself with Lisa. Not Stephanie. And it was in this life where I wanted to live.

I stared at the cookie with the red sprinkles, remembering how wonderful it had felt to cut Stephanie's neck and watch the blood spray.

Then I took another cookie, put white frosting on it, and again put the red sprinkles on it, just to remind myself how lucky I had it.

THE OLD GIRLFRIEND OF DOOM

A Poker Boy Story

Even superheroes can't always save the girl.

As one of the greatest superheroes in all of the Gambling Universe, Poker Boy does everything he can to help, but when the damsel in distress refuses to be rescued from her own deadly breasts, what's a superhero to do?

"The Old Girlfriend of Doom" was first published in the anthology Crime Spells *in February 2009 from Daw Books, edited by Loren L. Coleman and Martin H. Greenberg.*

One

SOMETIMES EVEN SUPERHEROES can't save the day, or the girl, or the dog, and that fact is even sadder when the girl is one of the superhero's old girlfriends.

Honest, Poker Boy, and just about every superhero, once had a childhood, a life as a young adult, without powers. I only discovered my Poker Boy super abilities later in life, after I had lived a fairly regular life until the age of twenty-nine. Little did I know that some day I would put on the black leather jacket and the fedora-like hat and become Poker Boy, savior of blind women, lost husbands, and dogs.

It was Christmas Eve, a holiday for me just about like every other one. I was home, alone, in my double-wide mobile home that I had bought twenty years ago with the money from my winnings in a poker tournament. The green couch and chairs had come with it, and so far I had seen no reason to replace the perfectly good, but dog-ugly furniture. As a national-level poker player, I had more than enough money in a dozen accounts to buy a nice home, and nice furniture, but since I was in poker rooms and hotels more than I was here, what was the point?

Besides I spent most of my time with Patty Ledgerwood, aka Front Desk Girl, in her apartment in Las Vegas. She was working tonight, pulling a double shift, so we had no plans until later in the week.

I was watching some lame Christmas program on television and eating a TV dinner with fried chicken and the really good cherry desert. I had about two hours to get to the casino to sign up for the poker tournament, and I was enjoying the quiet, to be honest.

Then there was knock on my door.

As Poker Boy, I very seldom have the people who need help come to me, but there have been exceptions. And since I wasn't expecting any company, I figured right off this was one of those exceptions.

I opened the front door of my double-wide mobile home and saw my old girlfriend, Julie Down, standing there on the other side of the screen door. Of course, right at that moment I didn't know it was Julie. All I could see was that it was some woman about my age with a nice smile and an over-built chest.

"Hi," Julie said, smiling at me as I stood there, hand on the wooden door, staring at her through the screen.

Now I have a great memory for faces across poker tables. I can tell you the moment a person sits down if I have played with them before, the style of their play, and their poker tells. I won't remember their names, but I know the important stuff and how to take their money.

With old girlfriends, from the life before I became the superhero Poker Boy, I am lucky to even remember going out with them, let alone things like their names, or if we slept together. I assume that any old girlfriend coming to find me years later is someone I must have slept with.

On top of my bad memory, Julie didn't look like the Julie of old. Granted, I'm forty-nine in human years, and Julie and I were an item back twenty-five years before, when she was only twenty. But that said, she just didn't look the same. Not even close.

Julie of old had long blonde hair that had touched the top of her butt. I remember I used to love lying in bed and watching that hair flow over her back as she walked naked around the bedroom. This Julie standing in front of me had tight, short graying hair, curled in a style that made her look older and very business-like.

Julie of old was rail thin, with no real breasts to speak of, and no body fat at all.

This Julie had filled out, as all of us have. She wasn't fat, but she wasn't that light and rail thin either. And she had had a boob job at some point. Or one hell of a growth spurt focused only on her chest. The white blouse she now wore under her open suede jacket made sure that everyone could see the growth spurts and the lace bra trying to hold back the progress.

"Hi," I said in return, at that point not yet knowing who the hell I was talking to. I wished at that moment that I had my black leather jacket and hat on, and was closer to a casino. Then I could use my super powers to help me figure out exactly what this woman wanted to sell me.

Or wanted me to do.

"You don't remember me, do you?" she said.

Okay, I have to admit that those words are the worst words any guy can ever hear from some strange woman standing at his door. I didn't have a clue who she was, yet she remembered me well enough to track me down.

A guy is never allowed to forget a woman.

Ever.

I glanced at her boobs, and since they were new since the last time I saw this woman, they didn't help. And her face rang a sort of bell when I looked right at her, and into her eyes, but not much of a bell. Actually, sort of a faint ding, like an oven timer going off in another room.

If I hadn't been a superhero, who didn't lie unless it was to save a life, or rescue a dog, I would have just laughed and said, "Sure I do, come on in." And then tried to figure out who she was through the conversation.

But she had asked me a direct question, and being a superhero, I couldn't lie. So instead I said, "I can't really see you very well in this light. Come on in."

I honestly couldn't really see her that well in the porch light and through the screen door, so I didn't lie. I just bought a little needed time.

As I swung open the screen door to let her come inside, she let me off the hook.

"It's me, Julie."

For a moment, as she stepped past me, leading into the room with those new growth spurts on her chest, I couldn't remember any Julies in my life either. Especially Julie with a chest the size of the Rockies.

"Julie Down," she said, ending all torture.

"Oh, my god, Julie," I said, "what a great surprise."

Actually I sounded happy mostly because she had let me out of the trap, and not because I was actually glad to see her. The last time we had spoken, she had called me a lazy bum, said I would amount to nothing, and that I should get a life. Or at least a reason for living and breathing.

Actually, at the point she left me, I was a lazy bum, and I really did need a life, but I wouldn't find that life until a number of years later when I became Poker Boy.

In all, I think we dated seven months, or more accurately, had sex for seven months. I don't remember much else in the relationship with her.

After I gave her the required hug, with her growth spurts holding us apart, she stepped back and studied me, then my abode, like a meat inspector looking over a side of beef.

"You look like you're doing well for yourself," she said.

Even without my super powers I knew that was a lie. I was living in an old mobile home, with old, ugly furniture and a half-eaten TV dinner on the coffee table. I looked like, on the surface, the same guy she had gotten mad at twenty-five years before. If I had not had my Poker Boy identity, and a lot of money in different banks from all my poker winnings, I would have been ashamed that an old girlfriend saw me living like this. But superhero status, and large bank accounts tend to make a guy not care, and I didn't really care what she thought.

"Actually," I said, "I'm doing very well. Can I get you something to drink? Diet Coke and water are the options."

She laughed, a high, soft sound I remembered from our past. Her laugh had been one of the things that had attracted me to her back then. That, and sex.

Now I just wanted to know what she wanted. And the only way I was going to be able to do that with my super powers was get my coat and hat on, and get back into a casino.

My super powers don't work a great distance from a casino. They are powered by the energy of a casino, like a flashlight is powered by a battery. My black leather coat and hat seemed to focus the energy from the casino and make me into Poker Boy.

"Wait," I said, "I have another idea. Let me buy you dinner and a drink at the casino." I pointed to my partially eaten TV dinner. "That just isn't doing it for me."

"That sounds great," she said.

No doubt she was clearly relieved to get out of the old mobile home.

Two

FIFTEEN MINUTES of very, very small talk later, we were seated in the fine dining restaurant at the casino. I had my leather coat and hat on, and was in full Poker Boy power mode.

I knew with a quick scan with my Ultra-Intuition Power that she needed help. Poker Boy's help, actually, which was interesting that she had found me.

My Ultra-Intuition Power is my most used power. With a focused glance, I can tell what a person needs, what they might say next, or even their next action. The information comes to me by "little voice messenger" and I have learned to listen.

I could list all my super powers right now, but that would be a dull monologue, not worth the time since there are so many. Some of the powers I haven't even named.

"Thank you," she said to me after we were settled at a table and the waiter was off getting our drink orders.

"For what?" I asked.

"For being so welcoming, especially on Christmas Eve."

"Poker players are never much for Christmas," I said, shrugging. "The ones with the families miss days and sometimes weeks of play. The rest of us just continue on and mostly don't notice."

"You have no family?" she asked. "And you play poker for a living?" She sounded actually impressed about the second part.

"Right on both counts," I said. "How about you?"

She sighed, and then for the next twenty minutes, through drinks, appetizers, and into the main course, she told me about her family, her parents being sick, her brother being stupid, her last two husbands being abusive.

I wanted to ask her when the growth spurt on her chest had happened, but refrained. Some things you just don't ask a woman, I have learned, and that's one of them.

Suddenly, she stopped talking, afraid to tell me about something. She had been fairly graphic about her past husbands, what they had done to her. Some of it I couldn't believe she would just tell a stranger like me. Granted, we had a past, but after not seeing this woman for over twenty-five years, I was still a stranger.

She studied her salmon, forked it a few times, studied it some more, forked it again, all the time trying to say something. Whatever was now stopping her must be really something. It was, more than likely, the reason she had looked me up.

I used my Ultra-Intuition Power on her again, but could only see blackness.

Deep, deep blackness.

Not good, not good at all.

I needed another super power to help her out, get her to tell me her problem. I focused across the table at her, leaning forward, clicking my mind into a friendly, giving mode. A moment later I felt the super power click on.

Empathy Super Power to the rescue.

I could make her feel better: I could make her trust me. My Empathy Super Power sort of radiated good feelings to another person, so it really wasn't empathy, by the standard dictionary definition, but Empathy Super Power was the only thing I could think to call it. I had tried Feel Better Super Power, but that had seemed silly. And so did Trust Me Super Power. So until I could come up with a better name, it was called my Empathy Super Power.

She looked up at me, her gaze holding mine. "I just feel like I can talk to you, and that you'll understand."

Empathy Super Power working just fine.

"I will," I said, easing my hand across the table between the water glasses and salt shaker to touch her hand.

Touch always made my Empathy Super Power even stronger.

"What's bothering you?" I asked.

She looked embarrassed for a moment, then took a deep breath and blurted out her problem.

"Aliens are trying to steal my breasts."

Three

I KNEW THERE WERE NO SUCH THINGS as aliens, at least at the moment on the planet. There had been in the past, and I am sure there would be again. They visited all the time. But right now none of them were around that I knew of.

But there were many, many other things that normal people confused with aliens. And there was an entire dark world that existed along with the light world we all lived in. It was against creatures from that dark world that I, and other superheroes, fought so often.

"Aliens?" I asked, keeping my touch on her arm and my super Empathy power turned on. "What do these aliens look like? Have you seen them?"

She nodded. "Gray, short, with long fingers and little round-shaped mouths."

"Big heads?" I asked.

"Yeah," she said, staring into my eyes. "Big for their bodies."

I could feel my stomach twist. She was in even more trouble than I had thought.

"And they want your breasts?"

She nodded.

I sat back, pulling my hand away and shutting off the super power. "You're not dealing with aliens. Those are Silicon Suckers."

"Silicon Suckers?" she asked. "How do you know that?"

"I've had to deal with them a couple of times over the years," I said. "They're not a nice bunch, and you clearly have something they want, or they wouldn't be showing themselves to you."

I knew exactly what they wanted, but I was going to have to work into telling her what it was.

Silicon Suckers are a race of intelligent creatures that have existed on Earth far, far longer than human beings. They live in the deserts, burrow deep under the sand, and have the ability to change their appearance and blend with about anything. In this country, Phoenix, New Mexico, and Las Vegas areas have the most trouble with them.

"Silicon Suckers?" she said. "My breasts are silicon implants." She was clearly starting to understand what the little guys were after.

I almost said, "Really, I hadn't noticed." But I stopped myself before that gaffe and instead just nodded. Then I moved to the next question.

"Where have you been living?"

"Vegas," she said. "I've been working as a blackjack dealer at Circus Circus for the last six years, since I left Bastard Husband #2."

"Good for you," I said, actually impressed. I knew how hard, and how special it was to become a dealer on the strip. "When did you have the implants put in?"

"Twenty years ago," she said. "I did it between Bastard Husband #1 and Bastard Husband #2. But I upgraded them six months ago, and that's when the gray aliens started showing up."

"Oh, oh," I said. "Dr. Doubleday did the upgrade. Right?"

She looked at me as if I had lost my mind, then nodded. "How did you know that?"

Actually, I wasn't reading her mind or using any other super power. I had dealt with Silicon Suckers for a friend of a friend in Vegas five months before, on an adventure that also rescued three dogs. On that trip, I had discovered that Dr. Doubleday had been using a very special silicon mix taken from pure natural sand and then refined down into a very special silicon gel.

The problem was the sand he had been using was from a sacred Silicon Suckers burial site. Julie, my old girlfriend sitting across the table from me, had a real problem. She had dead Silicon Suckers for breasts.

Four

"I KNOW BECAUSE one of the things I do is help people as I travel around the country playing poker," I said.

"I know," she said. "I've heard about you. Some people call you Poker Boy."

Since she clearly looked as if she didn't believe what she had just said, I let it pass and went on. "I helped a previous client of Dr. Doubleday. I assume you tried to go back to him after the Silicon

Suckers started showing up and playing with your breasts. And I bet you found him missing."

Now Julie was looking at me as if I was an alien.

I knew for a fact that Dr. Doubleday had given his life for trying to improve his craft and find the most perfect silicon implants. After what he had done to the Silicon Suckers sacred resting place, many of us in the superhero world thought he got off light by only being killed. His body will never be found. More than likely parts of Dr. Doubleday are tinting car windows everywhere.

"How did you know he wasn't there?" she asked.

"Doubleday is dead," I said. "Killed by the Silicon Suckers."

She sat there in silence, first staring at me, then down at her salmon. Finally she said, "Let's assume that I believe what you're saying."

"No weirder than thinking aliens are trying to steal your breasts."

She shrugged. "True. So what do I do?"

I put another bite of steak in my mouth, savored the flavor for a moment. There was only one answer to her question.

"If you're going to want to live, you have to give them your implants back."

"I'm not going to do that!" she said, her hands going to the monsters on her chest as if to protect the big girls.

I kept eating, staying calm. "You have no choice. If you don't have the money, I can pay for an exchange operation for the silicon implants you have now. All they want is those implants. They don't want you to be flat chested."

There was no chance at that point that the rest of her salmon was going to be eaten. She scooted the plate away and stared at me.

"I was *not* flat chested before I had the implants," she said. "You know, you're totally nuts."

I wanted to remind her that she had come to me for help. That she thought aliens were trying to take her boobs, but I didn't. Instead I just gave her the rest of the information, calmly and slowly, keeping my voice level.

"The creatures you are having trouble with are not aliens, but they are after the special silicon Dr. Doubleday used in those implants. If you have the implants removed, I'll be glad to help you give them to the Silicon Suckers in a special exchange ceremony. You give them back what they want and you'll always be an honored guest in their sand castles."

She stared at me like she was seeing me for the first time.

"Sand castles?"

"That's what they call their homes. I've been in a few of them outside of Tucson and Las Vegas. Big, but very dusty and dry."

She stared at me again, then shook her head slowly from side to side.

"I knew better than to come to you," she said. "Even with Suzy's recommendation, I knew better."

She stood and thrust her chest out so far I was afraid she was going to go head-first into my steak. Somehow, she managed to remain standing, although she cast a very dark shadow over the table as her breasts pulled an eclipse on the overhead light.

"These are mine and I paid good money for them," she said, loudly, indicating what did not need to be indicated. "And I'm not letting any little gray alien suckers take them."

The guy at a table against the wall choked, then coughed, clearly trying not to laugh.

"Your choice," I said. "But I'm doing all right with money and I would be glad to pay for replacements. Remember that. No strings attached. You can even make them bigger if you want."

"I'll give it some thought," she said.

"Don't take too long to decide," I said, staring up at her over the monster mountain range between us. "Silicon Suckers are not creatures to be played with. The only way they know how to get into a human body is through the anus, and trust me, taking those silicon implants out that way will not be fun. And more than likely fatal."

She sputtered, started to say something more, sputtered again.

I didn't blame her.

Finally she managed to get those sacred and very dead Silicon Suckers on her chest turned toward the door. Then, with one last withering glance at me, she stormed out.

The guy against the wall was laughing so hard I thought he would go face down in his soup.

For me, it really wasn't a laughing matter. She was in mortal danger.

I wanted to run after her and stop her, but I knew, for a fact, there was nothing I could do at this point. I certainly wasn't going to force her to have an operation. A woman's choice of what to do, or not do, with her body was not something a man, or a superhero, should get involved with. She was going to have to make that choice for herself.

For some reason that I didn't completely understand, Julie's entire self-image must have been tied up in what the Silicon Suckers wanted back. And replacements might not be enough to matter to her.

I wished I understood Julie's side. I did understand the Sucker's side.

The guy against the wall finally coughed a few times, shook his head, and went back to eating. I stared at my steak for a moment, thinking over anything I might still do to help her. Without butting in on her rights to do with her own body as she saw fit, there wasn't much.

She had come to me for help, then refused it. As those of us in the Superhero business know, there are times you just can't help.

Five

I FINISHED MY STEAK, and just barely made it into the poker room in time for the seven o'clock tournament.

I won the thing and put the money in a jar on my kitchen counter, saved for Julie's operation. But I had a hunch she would never call me, because after the tournament, on the way home from the casino, I found a German shepherd in the ditch beside the road. It had been hit by a car, but was still alive.

I rushed it to the local vet, but the dog died on Christmas morning.

On good adventures, I save people and dogs. I couldn't save the dog, so I had a hunch I hadn't saved the person either in this one.

But that didn't stop me from trying some more.

I tracked down Julie and called her the day after Christmas with the hopes of trying to convince her to change out the breast implants. She heard my voice and hung up.

I called a few friends I knew in Vegas who could be trusted to go talk to her. Both of them said she got rude and angry at them the moment they brought up the subject, or my name.

Julie had made her decision, and by all the gambling gods, she was sticking with it.

Somehow, I had to convince her to change that decision.

I had to keep trying.

That's what superheroes did, usually against all odds and at some cost and danger to their own lives. And trying to convince any woman to change her mind always had danger involved.

So throwing all caution to the wind, I jumped on a plane and headed for Vegas. Besides, I wanted to spend some time with Patty and get her opinion on all this.

Julie wouldn't see me, and had me removed from the Circus Circus when I went up to her blackjack table and sat down. Even my Empathy Super Power couldn't cut through the anger, although it made the guard very nice and apologetic for escorting me to the door.

Since the direct approach hadn't worked, I headed out into the desert, to where I knew the Silicon Suckers had a pretty good-sized village. It was impossible to see unless you knew exactly what you were looking for, and I did. The entrance to this one was hidden right under a billboard beside the highway.

The entrance led to a huge underground cavern cut out of the sand and rock and filled with castle-like buildings. I was welcomed into their castles, as I knew I would be, since I had helped them recover one of Dr. Doubleday's mistakes.

The main leader of this band clicked at me in Silicon Sucker language, and I used what I called my Understand Most Anything Super Power to talk with him, asking him for more time to convince Julie to get their sacred dead off her chest.

He clicked that he would give me two full moons, or something that meant two months.

I thanked him, backed from his castle in a show of respect, and went back to Vegas.

Patty told me what I had feared, that there was nothing I could do unless Julie decided for herself.

I left the message on Julie's answering machine that I had the money for the exchange, had contacted the best doctor in Vegas to do the job, and had prepaid for it. All she had to do was show up. I left the time and date and address of the doctor, the most famous and expensive in Vegas, hoping that might convince her to change her mind.

Nothing. She missed the appointment.

So I pulled some strings in the Casino Gods area of the superhero world, and got the Blackjack God named Danny to talk to her pit boss at work.

That didn't work.

I talked to her friends, even called her mother, then I set up another appointment for her with the great doctor.

Again she missed it.

So one last time, with Danny, the God of Blackjack keeping the pit boss busy at another table, I went in to talk to her.

She was shuffling and didn't see me coming.

When I slid the doctor's business card with a third appointment written on it across the table toward her, she glanced up, the anger in her eyes almost knocking me back a step.

"Why are you insisting in meddling in my life?" she demanded, ignoring the stares from the older couple sitting at the table.

"Because you are in real danger," I said, using every convincing power I could use in my super power collection. With this much energy turned on at a poker table, I could have convinced a world-class player I had a pair of deuces instead of aces.

Julie, on the other hand, was a little tougher. She just glared at me, so I went on.

"I have enough money to help. You won't ever see me again, but please, just do this. It's paid for."

She stared at me as I radiated super levels of good will and empathy and convincing. My superhero powers were on full tilt right at that moment, and for a second I thought she was faltering a little.

"I'm being honest with you," I said. "Your life is in danger. Please just do it, either with this appointment or on your own. It's your life, I know, and your body, but I care about your life."

Then I turned and walked away.

There was nothing else I could do.

I spent the night with Patty trying to sleep, then got back on the plane and went home.

I finally heard three months later that they had found her body face down in the desert, as flat-chested as the day she had come into the world.

I think back and wonder at times what more I might have done to convince her I knew what I was talking about. More than likely nothing. She needed to believe I was still the loser she left for abusive husband hell all those years before.

She needed to believe that those special breasts made her a better person. For her, a certain self-image was more important than life itself.

For me, Poker Boy, I have my hat, my leather coat, and my super powers. What more could I want out of life?

Nothing, except maybe winning every time. But even the best superheroes have to lose once-in-a-while. I learned that lesson on the poker tables, and with Julie.

Still, you have to feel bad for a person like Julie, caught in a self-image nightmare.

And besides, pulling those sacred suckers out of her ass just had to have hurt.

I'M HER DEAD HUSBAND

Sometimes ten years with the woman of your dreams might be better than no years. But who wins? You or the woman?

A story of love, dedication, and living a lifetime when faced with reality.

I wrote this story a few years back and never mailed it out, at least to my memory or my scattered records. I really like it, liked it when I wrote it. Not sure why it never got sent anywhere, but now it finds a home here.

One

TALL GLASS, ICE, PEACH SCHNAPPS, orange juice, red straw, and a thin slice of orange.

I finished the Fuzzy Navel and slid it toward the woman across the polished wood bar. "Two-fifty," I said, using my bar towel to wipe water spots off the surface.

I was always wiping up something. This bar might be a smoke-filled dive, but as long as I worked here it was at least going to be a clean, smoke-filled dive.

She dug in her large brown purse, obviously unused to paying for a drink. The older balding guy beside her was making no move for his wallet. He hadn't said a word, but he stood beside her as if they were together.

After bartending for ten years, since my last year in college, I knew, at a glance, which people belonged in a bar and which didn't. But way back on my first night I would have bet anything this lady didn't belong in The Continental Lounge.

And I would have been right.

The older guy she was with was another story. He looked vaguely familiar and a bunch washed out, as if he had spent half his life drinking. I wouldn't have been surprised to see him sliding drunk off of any bar stool in town.

I watched her while she dug for the money. Her dark red hair was conservatively fixed close to her head and pulled back tight. She kept her elbows tucked against her sides, as if opening them up might let everyone know she had tits. She wore a white dress blouse with all but the very top button done up tight. I figured normally she'd have them all buttoned, but tonight she was being daring.

Being in here proved it.

I glanced again at the guy beside her. His face rang bells in my head, but I'd be damned if I could exactly place him. Trying to made my stomach churn.

He was older than her by a good fifteen years and was within a combs length of not having a hair left on his head. He wore what I call the comfortable style: Open necked sweater, no shirt, and soft looking slacks. He looked just plain wrong standing beside the redhead.

Then, while I was looking directly at him, he did the weirdest damn thing. The old dude, just plain as could be, reached down and grabbed her ass.

The woman didn't even flinch and I shook my head.

The things you see in bars never ceased to amaze me. She laid two bucks on the bar mat and went back to searching through her purse for change. Women who looked for exact change in a bar were no-tippers. Guaranteed. Amazing how cheap some people could be.

Of course, with her I doubted if she knew any better. Yet she stood there letting some old guy grab her ass.

Go figure.

I was still waiting and she was still digging when the bald dude reached up and placed his hand on her left tit. He didn't squeeze or nothing. Just held it there.

Again she didn't seem to notice.

"Wait 'til you get outside, would you?" I said to the guy.

He looked up at me and smiled. "So I'm right," he said, taking his hand off her tit. "It's the time."

He looked at me real carefully. "But I almost didn't recognize—"

He stopped as she found two quarters and laid them next to the bills.

"I don't know what you're right about," I said. "But don't do that kind of shit at my bar."

"Excuse me?" she said, looking up at me for the first time.

I noticed she had huge brown eyes. Puppy eyes, too big for her thin face. She didn't strike me to be the type to let some jerk grab a quick feel in public.

"Just talking to your friend there." I nodded in the old guy's direction.

She took a quick glance his way, then looked up at me. Her eyes seemed even bigger, and her face had turned a sick white under the light layer of makeup. "You can see him?"

I glanced over at the guy. He was just looking at me, half smiling.

These two were beyond the college weirdos we got in here on a Friday night.

"Two-fifty," I said, counting the money out loud as I scooped it off the bar and put it in the cash drawer. "Thanks."

I started pretending to work at something in the well. Rule number one when it came to strange customers. Ignore them. After a while they usually went and bothered someone else.

"No," the woman said again, reaching across the bar and touching my shoulder. "Please tell me if you can see him."

"Come off it, lady. Of course I can see him. And don't make believe you couldn't feel his hand on your boob, either."

At that, she got real red and her face went from white to a bright pink that sort of blended right up into her dark red hair.

The guy laughed. "Now you've done it."

The woman whirled and shouted at the empty air about three feet to the guys left, "Keep your hands to yourself and leave me alone!"

She grabbed her drink, stalked over to a table and sat down with such force I thought the chair was going to give way.

Wow. One mad woman.

The older guy was laughing, leaning back with his hands tucked into pants pockets.

"I'm her dead husband," he said as if that would explain everything. "But she was fiery like that when I was alive."

Again he laughed as if he had said something funny. "By the way, my name is Dave."

Full moon. That was it. All the crazies hit the bars on a full moon. Documented fact. This Dave guy proved there must be a full moon out tonight, because he was as crazy as they came. I went back to wiping at the bottles in my well, hoping he'd just move away.

But he didn't. Instead, he moved over closer. "Don't believe me, do you?"

"Sure I do," I said.

Second rule when dealing with a nut case. Agree with them and they smile and go away.

"But you don't," he said. "I can tell. And I seem to remember I didn't either. Which means you didn't. Which..." He waved at the air. "Oh, never mind. Here. Touch my arm and I'll prove it to you."

I glanced up. He had his arm stuck straight out over the bar and was holding it there waiting for me to touch it.

Third rule. Humor them. I reached up to touch his arm just above the jacket sleeve.

My hand went right through.

"Christ," I said, yanking my hand back.

"See. Ghost all the way."

I reached out to touch his shoulder.

He let me.

My hand went right though his chest and I couldn't feel a thing. Nothing. Just like I was sticking my hand out in the air.

I pulled my hand back and glanced at it. Nothing wrong. Hell, now I needed a drink. These idiots were starting to make me see things. Not a good sign.

Especially so early in the night.

"Bet you can't touch my leg, either," the guy said.

"No thanks," I said. Then I purposefully laughed. It probably sounded strained. "Tell me how you did it. You really had me going there."

"It's easy," he said. "First you die. Then you find someone who can see you."

"Cute," I said. "Real cute. You want something to drink?"

"Yes, but no thanks," he said. "I'm afraid I couldn't pick it up if you made it for me."

To prove his point, he reached out and stuck his hand through the fruit tray sitting on the bar. Then, for a final show, he put his hand right through a bottle of limejuice sitting beside the tray. I could see his sleeve inside the bottle, tinted green.

He pulled his hand out and held it up. "Believe me now?"

I didn't know what to think. Part of me wanted to turn and run for the back room as fast as my little shoes could hit the floor. But another part of me was real curious. The part that kills cats won over the part that wanted to take a coffee break.

"I'm not sure," I said. "What exactly do you want me to believe?"

"That I'm a ghost."

"Then the answer is no," I said. "What else would you like me to believe?"

"How do you explain that you can't touch me?"

I shrugged real obviously. "I don't do explanations. I make drinks. Besides, there are a lot of people in here I can't touch. Your wife, for instance."

I pointed in her general direction. She was staring at me. I waved. She looked flustered and turned back to watch the jukebox and the one lone couple dancing in front of it.

"Hell, go ahead," the guy said. "She's single. I've been dead a year now. She's starting to forget me. Soon she won't even remember that I exist."

Rule number four with crazy customers. If the first three rules don't work, be rude to them. That always does it.

"Is she good in bed?" I asked. "Wouldn't want to go wasting my time with some skirt who won't even get on top. Know what I mean?"

But the old guy didn't flinch. He gazed over at his wife and got this faraway look, like he was remembering the first time he got to first base at the old drive in. Then his eyes sort of misted over and I had a twinge of guilt. But only a twinge.

"She used to be real good," he said, after a moment. "When she wanted to be. No one better. You'll like that."

"I'll what?" I shook my head. This guy had gone way beyond crazy and he was towing me along as if I were a damn trailer. No more.

"Look, if you don't want a drink, why don't you move along. All right?"

"God, I've forgotten," he said, "just how——"

"Can you really see him?" The wife had gotten up and stormed back over to the bar. "I can't believe he followed me here."

"Lady, I really don't know what you're talking about."

"Tell her I still love her," the old guy said. "But that I'm leaving now."

The red head was staring at me as if she hadn't heard a thing the old man said, waiting for me to say something.

"He said he's leaving now," I told her, playing along with their stupid game.

"Is he gone?" she asked, looking around.

"No," I said, glancing at him.

The old guy shrugged. "I can't leave. I'm sort of tied to her. Got to stay close. But I guess I could go outside."

She looked in the direction I had glanced, then back at me. "Tell him I'm leaving. And tell him thanks for spoiling my evening."

She slammed her drink down on the bar in front of me and headed for the door with short, quick steps.

"Looks like we're leaving," he said. "Next time she'll be alone."

"Sure she——"

Right in the middle of my snappy answer, he faded and disappeared faster than a puff of smoke on a windy day.

"Shit," I said and leaned over the bar to check out the floor where he had been standing. Nothing but stains and cigarette burns in the carpet. That did it.

I grabbed a highball glass and poured myself a good solid double shot of well bourbon. I added two ice cubes and a splash of soda, then headed for the back room. I needed a break. It was going to be one damn long night.

Two

TWO NIGHTS LATER, during the slow time between the business drunks from happy hour and the regular night drinkers, she dropped back into the bar. The ghost guy had been right. She was alone.

I was cutting lime wedges, getting ready for what promised to be a steady night. She came through the door, paused a moment to let her eyes adjust to the dim light, then came over to the bar and sat down on the end stool.

"Hi," she said, almost too softly for me to hear over the song on the jukebox. "Remember me?"

"Sure do," I said, sliding a bar napkin in front of her. "Figure out your problem with that guy?"

I glanced quickly around the bar. He wasn't anywhere to be seen.

She slowly moved the napkin back and forth in front of her real self-conscious like, as if she almost didn't remember. Finally she said, "I'd rather not talk about him."

"Can't say as I blame you," I said, making my voice sound as cheery as I could. "He was a strange bird, that one. What can I get for you to drink?"

She looked up at me with those huge eyes of hers and smiled a soft thank you smile. "I'll try a Fuzzy Navel. I heard they were good."

I don't know if it was right at that moment that I fell for her, or if it was sometime over the next few hours as she sat at the bar and laughed at my stupid jokes. But I know that it was right at that moment that I started noticing how really pretty she was.

About halfway though the evening I finally got around to asking her name.

"Alice," she said. "Alice Rule? What's yours?"

I didn't want to tell her, on account my name was the same as the strange dude who called himself her dead husband. So instead of Dave, I said David. She didn't even flinch. She said she liked that name. Said it was strong and showed character. Maybe it was at that moment that I fell in love.

Hell, I don't know.

Before she left, I asked her out for lunch the next day and she said yes without even a moment's hesitation. She said she worked as a buyer for a local department store and I could pick her up there.

We had lunch together the next few days and every night she came into the bar to sit and talk. After a while the place started to seem empty without her sitting on that end stool.

After a week, the regulars were really starting to take a liking to her. That convinced me even more that she was really someone special.

I'd served some of those folks for years. I knew and trusted their judgment. When they liked a person, it meant something. They really liked Alice and made her feel welcome and safe.

On my night off, six nights after we met, she took me to her apartment to cook me dinner.

The place was a small, tidy, warm one bedroom, with pictures of parents and one sister on the wall, a white fluff-ball of a cat, and a couch that was so soft, you didn't want to get up.

A single woman's perfect apartment.

Dinner was the best chicken I had ever tasted and later she served a perfectly chilled white wine. I didn't have to come back for breakfast and I didn't get much sleep.

Thinking back now, it was odd that not once during that week did we talk about the guy she yelled at the first night. I don't remember, but I suppose I figured it would come up sooner or later and was happy to have it later.

Hell, I had a few things in my past I didn't much like, including an ex wife I wasn't real excited about.

It wasn't until two full weeks from the day I first saw her that the strange guy appeared again. She was sitting on her normal stool, talking to Wilber, the retired truck driver who was one of the old time regulars. They were laughing about something and I was staring at her from the other end of the bar, thinking about how young and healthy she was looking, when I noticed out of the corner of my eye a slight movement.

I glanced around and there was the bald guy, Dave, sitting at the bar across from me.

He hadn't come in. I knew that. I had been facing that front door and no one had come through it since Wilber. So just how the hell had he gotten in?

I started to ask him, but he held up his hand and put his finger to his lips for me to be quiet.

"Don't let her know I'm here," he said. "I wanted to see how things were going. Got tired sitting out front all these nights."

"Siting out front?"

Little stabs of jealousy cut at my stomach.

He motioned for me to turn my back so Alice and Wilber wouldn't see me talking. "They can't see me," he said. "But they can see you talking."

"We going to start that shit again?"

But I said it so Alice couldn't see me. I stood with my back to her and pretended to be working on something in the well. She was far enough down the bar she couldn't hear me over the jukebox.

"Let me prove I'm a ghost once and for all," the bald guy said.

He stood up. "I'll show you. Then, when you believe me, maybe we can talk." He walked right through the bar, then through the back bar and disappeared into the mirrors behind the call liquors.

"David?" Alice called out as I stared at the mirrors. "Everything all right?"

"Sure is," I said, scooting quickly along the bar until I was in front of her and Wilber. "Just working on getting ready for the night."

I straightened her drink, then gave her hand a squeeze, proud of the fact that I kept my hand from shaking.

She smiled at me. I felt almost guilty for not telling her what was going on. But at the same time, I wasn't sure exactly what I was seeing. And I didn't want to go losing her, scaring her off by being a nut case.

The bald guy came walking out of the mirrors, back through the bar, and sat down on the end stool.

"Need another drink here?" I asked Alice and Wilber, forcing myself to not stare in the bald guy's direction.

Both said no, so I gave Alice's hand another little squeeze and went back to the ghost. He'd made a believer out of me with the walk through the bar routine.

But what the hell did he want?

"Looks like everything is progressing as I remembered it," he said as I moved back into position by the well with my back to Alice.

"You remembered it?" I asked. "You lost me. In fact, you being here has me damn confused, to say the least. Who the hell are you?"

I had a bunch more questions for him, but figured that would be enough to start.

He laughed. "My name is Dave. I'm Alice's dead husband. I told you that. Although, from how young she's starting to look, I doubt if she will remember me. I've been staying outside lately, away from her."

He glanced down the bar at her. She lives forever, you know. So do you, so do I, only in a different sort of way than her."

I shook my head and laughed. "Hold on one damn minute. Past you name, I didn't follow a word of that."

It was his turn to laugh. "I doubt if you'd believe much more. I know I wouldn't have. Just enjoy while you can."

"Enjoy what?"

"Alice," he said, softly. "The next ten years."

He gazed in her direction and sighed, then glanced back at me. "I only wanted to remind you I was here. You'll understand when your time comes. Maybe you can break the cycle."

"Wait—"

He was gone again. Not even a cloud of smoke. I glanced over the bar at the empty stool, then grabbed a glass and filled it with ice.

Time for me to have a drink.

A very large drink.

Three

THAT NIGHT AT MY PLACE I almost got up the nerve to ask Alice about the bald guy. But it had been a long night, I was tired, and Alice was in a "playful" mood, so the question never got asked.

The next day it just didn't seem as important somehow. Not that I forgot about it. I didn't. It was just never the right moment. And after the ghost didn't show up for a while, there seemed to be little point in asking.

Alice spent a lot of nights sitting on her end barstool and over the next month I found out a lot about her past. But not one word was ever said about being married. In fact, her history filled in solid all the way from high school to the night she came into the bar the first time. There didn't seem to be any time that she could have been married. But why would a ghost lie to me? Made no sense.

Two months after we met, we started talking about getting married. She liked the idea.

I liked the idea.

We'd do it and then she'd help me go back to school, finish the master's degree and get a real job.

Of course, by the time we started making those kind of plans I was head over heels in love and not questioning anything. The truth of the matter was, I wasn't thinking about it. I plain didn't want to.

Six months from the day we first met, we were married in the Methodist church downtown, the big one with the huge colored windows and the ten-step altar. We had to climb all ten of those suckers and I was so nervous, I almost didn't make it.

Alice held me up.

Before the service, while I was standing in the front of the church waiting for Alice to come flowing down the center aisle, I thought I saw the bald guy in the balcony above the entrance.

He was wearing the same clothes he had on in the bar. He waved, gave me the thumbs up sign, and then disappeared when the music started.

I didn't understand.

Four

TEN YEARS AND TWO DAYS LATER, I died.

And then I understood.

The doctors told Alice it was a massive coronary arrest.

I was forty-one.

The moment I found myself sitting next to her in the hospital waiting room, listening to the news of my death, wanting to comfort her, hold her, I knew I was the bald guy.

As best I can let me explain what I think happened. If Alice had been the one to have died, I don't think I could have survived. We shared everything. We were more in love the last day then the day we were married.

Not that we didn't have our troubles. Turned out that Alice had one hell of a temper. There was no getting in her way when she was mad. I had a drinking problem that almost split us up three years into things. But she helped me though the drinking and I usually laughed at her temper.

Until I died, I didn't really realize how totally dedicated to me Alice was. Obsessed might be a better term. I figured that the first time around, her total dedication was why I got stuck here, couldn't move on into the next life until her attention was turned to someone else.

And that's why she went back.

Back into the past, her past, my past, dragging me with her until she again found me and married me. Her love held me near her like a dog on a leash.

And all those years I hadn't really noticed.

In fact, I'd enjoyed it.

But it isn't anywhere near as much fun now that I'm dead. And somehow, someway, I have to break the cycle.

After the funeral, she had holed up in our house and wouldn't go or do anything. She didn't eat and was losing weight really fast. I figured she was trying to kill herself so that she could join me. Even though I wanted to break the cycle, I couldn't take the thought of her doing that.

That's when I let her see me for the first time.

Scared her something awful.

I guess those first few times I still didn't have the hang of being a ghost. Making yourself visible is no easy task. You'll discover it takes a lot of real concentration and energy. I suppose I looked sort of watery and not all there.

I couldn't tell.

Like Vampires, mirrors don't work for ghosts.

Maybe it was my reappearing that started her returning to the past. At first, she wouldn't admit that I was even there. If I'd have stopped then, stayed invisible, I might have allowed her to get through her grief and on with her life.

But my showing up, trying to get her to eat kept her in our past. The more I was there, the more she regressed. I could feel the years drifting, coming unstuck.

She didn't like me only being a ghost. She wanted me to touch her, hold her or even talk to her for longer than a few minutes at a time.

She wanted me back, alive, the way I had been the day she met me.

That's you. You're me. Now do you understand why I've been telling you all this? Don't talk to her when she comes back into the bar in two days. I'm not strong enough to break the cycle on this end except by telling you this story.

After years of marriage, you'll understand.

But you can end it. Don't let the next cycle start.

At that moment Alice stood up from the table near the jukebox and stormed back over to the bar. "Can you really see him?" she demanded. "I can't believe he followed me here."

I glanced over at the old balding guy who claimed to be my ghost and who had told me the wildest bar story I had ever heard, then back into her huge brown eyes.

"See who?"

She looked puzzled for a moment, then smiled.

She took a long drink off her glass and set it empty on the bar. "What did you call that drink?"

"Fuzzy Navel," I said, sliding the empty over the bar and into the dish rack.

She walked down the bar and pulled out the end stool. "I think I'll have another. I always heard they were good."

The old guy sighed and then vanished without so much as a pop or a wisp of smoke. I saw him again sitting in the balcony of the church the day Alice and I were married.

And it was a wonderful ten years.

OUR SLAYING SONG TONIGHT

A Jukebox Story

Sometimes the special jukebox in the Garden Lounge does more than take a person back to a memory. Sometimes it brings a memory to the bar.

And when that memory shows a murder, Stout and the rest must risk their lives to do the right thing.

One

THE GARDEN LOUNGE functioned like a big family room for a lot of people. Comfortable described it. Earth-tone brown carpet, old-fashioned tables and booths, and no windows to let in the troubles of the outside world. The only way in and out for the people who came for friendship and relaxation was the wooden front door.

And, on Christmas Eve, the old Wurlitzer.

The jukebox sat against the wall beside the long oak bar like a king in a place of honor. Four special crystal drinking glasses with names etched on them over the Garden Lounge logo were in a handmade glass case above the old music machine. A large fern hung from the ceiling beside the jukebox, almost seeming to protect it from the stares of the customers.

The jukebox always sat unplugged and dark. The room's music

came from a stereo hidden behind the oak bar. The jukebox was decoration only, except for Christmas Eve. And even on Christmas Eve I was the only one allowed to plug it in. It was just too dangerous any other way. On this particular Christmas Eve there were only four customers to witness the third annual playing of the jukebox.

"Well, Stout?" Carl said. "Is it time?"

I glanced over at Carl. At six-two, two hundred and fifty pounds, Carl had more muscle than two other normal men. And his hands were so huge that his friends figured that women were afraid to get near him. He had never married, never had children. He spent his interest and his energy on a thriving construction business.

The other two there at the moment were David and his wife, Elaine. David was a pilot for a major airline and only allowed himself to drink on Christmas Eve. He had been my best friend before the jukebox had taken him away two years ago and changed his life. Since he came back with his wife, Elaine, we had again become close friends.

Elaine was a beautiful woman in her early forties, with long brown hair that streamed straight down her back and bright green eyes that caused everyone to ask if she wore contacts. She loved David with every part of her soul.

"All right," I said. I guess it's time."

I moved around the end of the bar and unlocked the glass case above the jukebox, then pulled out a glass with David's name on it and another one with Carl's name. I gazed at the other two glasses and the names of Jess and Fred before closing back up the case. Jess and Fred were old friends I missed seeing. I just hoped that when they left the Garden two years ago on Christmas Eve, they found good new homes. Every year I wished they would drop in to say hi. But they didn't know I was here, or remember the Garden and the time they spent here. So far only David and Carl had found their way back.

I moved around behind the bar, washed out the glasses, and filled them with their owner's regular drinks. Bourbon and water for Carl. Rum and eggnog for David. Vodka tonic in a normal glass for Elaine. And then for me I poured myself a mug of warm eggnog without any booze and held the mug up in a toast.

"To friends," I said, "both here and apart."

"I'll drink to that," Carl said and we all raised our glasses and drank.

"Now, I said, putting my mug down on the bar and pulling out a package from beside the cooler, "for the traditional playing of the jukebox this year I have something special."

Everyone laughed. I supposed that playing a time-traveling jukebox would be considered special enough for most. But I had a hunch that I had something even more special.

I unwrapped the package and held up the record.

"So what's so unique about this?" David asked as I handed the record to him and he turned it over to read the title. "It's just *Jingle Bells*." He shrugged and handed the record to Elaine.

"Before I tell you, I need to know if any of you have any strong memories tied to this song." I first glanced at Carl.

He shook his head. "Just feelings of being a kid and having fun. Nothing strong."

"Good. How about you, Elaine?"

"Same thing as Carl. For me this song has sort of always just been there."

I looked at David and he shook his head no.

"You sure?" I asked.

"Nothing that comes to mind," he said. "Which means we aren't going anywhere. Right?"

"That's what I was hoping for," I said. "This song has just always been there for me, too. With no distinct memories attached to it."

"So what makes it so special?" Carl asked, looking at the record and then handing it back across the bar to me.

"Well, with a jukebox that can physically take a person back in time to the memory that the song brings up, wouldn't you think that the *only* record in the jukebox when I found it was special?"

"You're kidding?" Elaine said.

I shook my head. "Not kidding. Remember I told you I found the old jukebox covered in a back hall of the first bar I tried to run. Well, when I went broke and took the old jukebox out just before the bank padlocked the doors on me, this was the only record in it at the time. It was hidden in a small folder inside the back door. The record and the insides of the jukebox were so covered with dust that when I started fixing the thing up, I missed seeing this record and instead put in one of my own. That was how I discovered that the jukebox sent people back to their memories. I ended up sitting staring at Jenny, my old girlfriend.

I held up the old record and looked at it. "I have never played this record."

"Which is why you asked us about our memories with this song. You're going to play it. Right?"

I raised my mug in another toast. "That's right. And tonight, unlike some Christmas Eves in the past, I'd like my best friends to walk out the front door at the end of the night, not through a memory and a jukebox."

Everyone laughed and drank to my toast. Then I went around, opened up the jukebox, and dropped in the record.

"Ready?" I asked as I shut the top and reached to plug in the jukebox.

"Fire away," Carl said.

"You're not really expecting anything, are you?" David asked.

I shrugged. "Not really sure what to expect. I have a feeling there is something special about this record. And combined with that jukebox, your guess is as good as mine. It is curious that this was the only record in there. I assume that the jukebox's previous owner knew what it could do. This may be nothing more than the song that had memories attached to it for him or her."

"And that owner went back, changed the past, and never got to the point where he owned the jukebox in his new future. Right?"

I shrugged. "One theory. Shall I punch it up and see?"

"Why not?" David said.

So I punched E-34, the slot I had put the record in, and stepped away from the jukebox and back around behind the bar.

What did happen was something I never would have guessed.

Two

AS THE SONG STARTED, two men shimmered into being in front of the jukebox. The jukebox had never brought anyone *to* the Garden before. Only took them away, into their past memories.

One of men was an elderly gentleman wearing an apron and carrying a towel. He had thick silver hair and a worried expression on his face. I knew immediately from the way he was dressed that he was a bartender somewhere in the late fifties or early sixties.

The other man was almost a boy, with red hair, ragged overalls that hung loose on his thin frame, and a red plaid work shirt with stained elbows. With both hands he clutched a large revolver pointed at the old bartender.

We all instantly jumped and Elaine said something about the Holy Mother. Carl started toward the scene.

"No," I said. "I don't think they're really here."

Carl stopped and we all stared.

I was right. Our movements and the sound of our voices didn't alter the scene we were watching in the slightest. It was as if we were watching them through a one-way window.

"Money!" the boy demanded, waving the gun in the direction to the right of the bartender. His voice seemed distant, almost from down a long tunnel. Yet it was clear. "Just reach into that cash box and pull out a handful."

"Nope," the bartender said, wiping his hands on the towel. "You're going to have to take it yourself if you want it. That money is my money and I ain't giving it away to no child with a gun."

"I could shoot you," the kid said, poking the gun forward at the bartender's stomach.

"But you won't," the bartender said. "will you Billy? In fact, if you give me that gun right now I might not even..."

Just then the kid...Billy...seemed to be startled by something behind him that none of us could hear. He turned and as he did the old man reached out and took hold of the gun.

"It's my daddy's gun," Billy said, fighting to pull the gun back away from the bartender. "You can't..."

The explosion seemed almost too loud for one gun.

Too loud for a vision.

Way too loud for the song playing on the jukebox.

The explosion echoed around and around the bar as we watched the bartender grab his stomach and stagger back against the jukebox. His hitting it didn't disturb the record playing Jingle Bells.

Billy just stood there, holding the gun in both hands, staring as the old bartender slid down the jukebox into a sitting position on the floor, his back against the machine. Blood flooded out from the hole in his apron, turning the white cloth dark.

As the record ended, the old bartender took a deep breath and died.

Three

THE LAST NOTES of Jingle Bells echoed around above the empty booths and tables as the two figures faded from the Garden Lounge.

After the sound of the struggle and the shot, the complete silence of the empty bar seemed the loudest of all.

"Holy shit," Carl said as he sat back down on his stool and took a long drink from his glass.

"I feel like I want to be sick," David said as he too sat down heavily on his stool. Elaine's face was pure white and she just stood there staring at the jukebox as if it might explode at any moment.

I knew how David felt. My stomach was clamped up into a tight knot and my hands were shaking as I tried to get my mug to my lips to get some of the eggnog to my completely dry mouth.

I had no idea what I had expected, but it certainly wasn't a murder.

"You sure know how to throw a Christmas Eve party," Carl said.

David tried to laugh and Elaine just hiccupped and climbed back up on her stool and put her head down on the bar.

"Christmas Eves tend to be that way around here," I said. "Maybe we'll just skip it next year."

"I'll drink to that," Carl said. And did.

David also took a long swallow from his glass and looked across the bar at me, then over at the jukebox. "So now what are we going to do?"

"I know what I'm going to do." I moved quickly around the bar, pulled the plug on the jukebox and then took the record out. It felt odd touching the record, as if I was holding some person's casket. Carefully I put the record back in the bag I had kept it in all these years. I stood the bag on the back bar and went back to my friends who had been watching.

"You think it was the murder that gave the jukebox its powers?" Elaine asked, sitting up and shaking her head slightly as if it might help put away what she had just seen.

I shrugged. "I don't think so, but I really have no idea. There are electronic parts in that thing that are not in any regular jukebox. I have always thought that what that thing could do was just mechanical. Besides that record hasn't been anywhere near that jukebox since I fixed it."

"So maybe," David said, "those two...ghosts, I guess you could call them, are attached to the song. Or more likely, that record." He pointed at the bag. "And obviously the jukebox."

"But why?" Carl asked. "And how? Makes no sense."

"Maybe we should play it again," Elaine said, "even though I don't want to. Maybe we could try to stop the murder."

"I doubt we could," I said. "It looks like it happened a long time ago. I think Carl is right. This makes no sense. But does a jukebox-time-machine make sense either? Yet there it sits. I think the best thing we can do is just let the record and the machine alone until we get more information."

"I'll drink to that," Carl said and raised his glass.

"That's what you said before the floor show started," David said. "Remember?"

Carl shuddered. "I got to stop saying that."

Four

IT TOOK ME most of the next year to dig out all the information about what we had seen that night. The murder had occurred in 1959, in a bar called Danny's in a little town in the northern part of the state. The bartender was the owner of the place, Danny Kline, and his murderer was nineteen year-old Billy Webster. Two witnesses had come in just in time to see Billy grab some money from the cash box and run out the back. They found him two days later on a bus headed south, and the trial was quick and without much doubt as to the outcome.

Initially Billy was sentenced to the gas chamber, but after four years on death row, his sentence was commuted to life in prison. It wasn't until I was reading the account in the old newspaper file about his new sentence that I decided what I would do. Maybe Elaine had been right. Maybe we should try to stop it.

Christmas Eve this year was going to be interesting again.

Five

FOR A CHANGE, I had strung Christmas lights around the bar to make it feel more festive. And I had even put up a tree in one corner so that now the bar not only smelled of smoke and stale beer, but it had a faint pine scent. I sort of enjoyed that.

"So what's the big surprise you have been hinting at this year?" Carl asked as I opened the glass case above the jukebox and pulled down two of the special glasses. "Because if it's anything like last year, I think I'm going to just head for home."

"I'll go with Carl," Elaine said. "My stomach didn't settle down for a week last year. And I've got a turkey to cook tomorrow that I'd like to taste."

I laughed and moved back to the well to make everyone their drink. "Nothing to worry about, I hope."

"Sounds threatening to me," Carl said.

I just laughed, but I think David could tell by the way he looked at me that I really was worried. Not so much worried about what I had planned working. But more about the final results. What I was going to do might give away the Garden and everything else, including our lives.

I finished making the drinks and raised my mug of eggnog in a toast. "To friends – and doing the right thing."

"I'll drink to that," Carl said, and this year everyone laughed.

I took a drink and set my mug back on the bar. "We have a special guest this Christmas Eve. He's in my office right now waiting for us to finish our toast. You've all seen him before, but none of you have met him." I smiled at their puzzled frowns and went down the bar to my office door.

"Bill, come on out."

Elaine gasped at the name and Carl said, "I'll be a son-of-a-bitch." as the balding, gray-haired Billy Webster opened the office door and walked over to my side. Twenty-eight years in prison had been hard on him. He had obvious scars and he limped slightly off his left leg. He had a beer-gut stomach and deep, sad eyes. In the two years since his parole he had worked as a janitor for the Elk's Lodge. He nodded to everyone as I did introductions.

"Stout," David said, "are you thinking what I think you are thinking?"

I nodded. "Seemed like a good idea to me."

"But if it works," David said, "and the old bartender stays alive and keeps the jukebox, then you may not be here. Did you think about that?"

I just tried to smile.

"And did you think about the chance that we would be gone, and that would mean..." He turned to look at Elaine and she nodded that she understood. It was because of the jukebox three years earlier that David had been able to go back and save her from dying in a car wreck. If the jukebox wasn't in the Garden Lounge for me to send David back, Elaine would be dead.

"But there is a real good chance it won't work out that way," I said. "And Elaine will be as alive as she is now and all of us will be right here, drinking. Besides, if we hold onto the jukebox when the song ends and the world switches, we remember the old timeline. That's how I remembered you two when you didn't come back."

"But you don't know if Elaine will stay for sure, do you?"

My stomach felt cramped and my hands were sweating. "No, I don't."

Billy cleared his throat. "I came here because you said you might be able to help me. I'm just kind of wondering what this is all about."

"It's about taking one hell of a chance," David said.

"It is at that," I said. "But not for you, Bill. The chance is ours. What we need you to do is simple. There was a song playing on a jukebox when you shot old Danny. Remember?"

Bill nodded.

I picked up the sack from the back bar and pulled out the record. "And this was the song. Right?" I held the label and title up for him to see.

Bill again nodded, this time real slowly. There was a shocked look on his face as he stared at the old record. Then he looked up at me. "How did you know? There is no way that anyone could have..."

"Too long a story to explain right now. But if you would just trust me, I think you may have a miracle handed to you this Christmas evening."

"I don't believe much in miracles," he said, still staring at the record.

"Well," I said, glancing over at where David and Elaine sat with worried expressions. "I do. So you are just going to have to trust me."

God, if I said that one more time I wasn't going to believe it either. I just wished I felt as sure of what I was doing as I sounded.

I led Bill down the bar to the jukebox, opened up the lid and put the record in its place. Then I reached around back of the jukebox and plugged it in.

The colored lights flickered on and a slight hum and the smell of burning dust came from behind the jukebox. I reached into my pocket and pulled out a quarter and handed it to Bill. "Your miracle," I said.

He looked at the quarter and then at me. "You're nuts, you know. I knew I shouldn't have come here." He started toward the front door.

"Wait," I said. "Everyone wants a chance to go back and correct their mistakes. Don't you?"

Bill stopped and turned back to face me. "Of course I do. I wished it every day for twenty-eight long years. But I ain't no fool and damned if I will be taken for one. What is done is done. And that is the way it is and should be."

"Sometimes that is the truth and sometimes not." I said. "I'm just offering you a chance to make up your own mind. Nothing more. It is up to you to take it."

"Mr. Stout, I personally think you are as crazy as they come and I met some crazy ones behind the walls." He glanced down at the quarter in his hand. "But I suppose you have got me this far, I might as well finish your damn game and let you all get your laughs."

I only hoped we would be laughing when this was over.

He moved back to the jukebox and dropped the quarter in.

"All you have to do," I said. "is punch E-34 and think about the night you killed Danny. But give us just a second."

I quickly hurried around behind the bar and slipped industrial strength ear-plugs to everyone sitting there. "Put these on and think of playing golf or snow skiing or something different when the song starts. Otherwise you'll end up back last Christmas Eve."

"No chance," Elaine said and stuffed the earplugs hard into her ears. "But are we going to see that scene again this year?"

I shrugged. "Don't know. With Bill here anything is possible, I suppose." I nodded to Bill. "Go ahead."

He shook his head in disgust and turned to the jukebox. Carefully he punched up E-34 as I did everything I could do to think about the last round of golf I played.

It worked. The only one of us who disappeared out of the bar that Christmas Eve was Bill Webster. As the song started, he blinked twice and then, with a sad frown on his face, he was gone.

And the murder scene did not show up again.

For that I was grateful.

Six

I MOTIONED FOR EVERYONE to grab their drink and move over to the jukebox. I could barely hear the song through the plugs so I watched down through the glass until the record was almost over. Then I motioned for everyone to touch the jukebox. I knew without a doubt that Billy would not kill Danny if he had a second chance. But what I didn't know was how Danny being alive would change the history of the jukebox.

If the history of the jukebox did change and I never found it in the back hallway of my first bar, would we be here now, holding onto the jukebox or not?

I didn't really know.

I tried to smile at David beside me, but he was focused on Elaine, as if his pure mental energy would keep her there. I hoped beyond hope that it would.

Carl was standing near the back of the jukebox, with one hand on the chrome and the other on his drink. As the song ended he raised his glass in a toast motion.

The air around the jukebox shimmered.

And Bill appeared.

I thought for a moment I was going to faint.

He looked over at the bar where we had been sitting and then turned around and faced our stunned faces. He had come back. How the hell had he done that?

I pulled the earplugs out as fast as I could, but David had beat me to the question. "What happened?"

Bill smiled and then laughed a low, almost mean laugh. "I shot the son-of-a-bitch again."

"What?" was all I could manage to say as both David and Elaine backed away from him.

Again Bill laughed, only this time I could tell he was thinking back to what had just happened. "You know, Mr. Stout, I just didn't believe you until I found myself standing there with my daddy's big heavy gun in my hand pointed at old Danny."

"But why did you shoot him again?" I asked. "If you knew where it would take you?"

Bill shrugged. "At first I didn't think I would. But I kept the gun pointed at him and just sort of stood there and listened to that damn song and looked at old Danny and thought. I thought about how I had killed him the first time and about how I had paid my debt. And I thought about the little apartment I have now and my job down at the Elks Club cleaning up."

He faced me directly. "And you know something, I'm a hell of a lot happier now than I was then. My old man was beating me all the time. I was holding Danny up for enough money to get out of town and away from my daddy and his big fists. Well, killing Danny did that for me too. It got me away from that son-of-a-bitch and his fists. He never hit me once after that."

Carl just shook his head and I moved over to a stool and sat down.

"So you shot Danny again?" Elaine asked.

"Yes ma'am," Bill said. "As far as I am concerned, he was dead thirty years ago, so I really wasn't shooting anyone new or alive. But, I did remember what Stout and David here were arguing about. I remember Stout said something about that if I didn't shoot Danny, you might die and he might lose this bar. Now that would be killing somebody new and I just couldn't do that."

Both Elaine and David just stared at Bill with their mouths slightly open.

Bill stepped toward me. "I'd like to thank you for a real nice gift, even though it didn't work out. Not that I pretend to understand exactly how you did it. But as they say on the TV, it is the thought that counts."

He reached out and shook my hand. "Maybe I'll stop by sometime for a drink," he said and then laughed. "But only if you promise me one thing."

I felt more lost than I had in years, so all I could do was nod.

"Promise me you won't play that song while I'm here?"

Finally his words got through the shock I had felt when I saw him reappear. I started to laugh and he joined in and so did Carl and David and Elaine.

"I'll do one better than that," I said after a moment. I stood and leaned over the jukebox and unplugged it, Then I opened the top and took out the old record and with a quick flick of the wrist smashed the record over the edge of the planter beside the jukebox.

"How's that?" I asked.

Bill laughed. "Looks as if you got yourself a new customer."

Both Elaine and David applauded and Carl said, "I'll drink to that."

It took both David and me to stop Elaine from hitting him.

SIGHED THE SNAKE

A Poker Boy Story

Poker Boy saved the world a number of times, but never from an alien. With the help of his sidekick, Front Desk Girl and Laverne, Lady Luck herself, Poker Boy must do battle with an alien snake across the only battlefield Poker Boy knows: a poker table.

The stakes are higher than in the original Garden of Eden.

To make matters worse, Poker Boy hates snakes.

One

"POKER BOY, the aliens are back."

Stan, the God of Poker, said those exact words to me as I sat in his office next to my sidekick and girlfriend, Patty, aka Front Desk Girl.

His office, glass-walled and floating invisible somewhere high above the Las Vegas strip, had felt cool and comfortable when we had entered from a hidden door at the MGM Grand Casino. The view just took your breath away as Las Vegas stretched out below, surrounded by desert and then mountains in the distance. The walls were invisible, so it felt as if Stan had put office furniture on a floating carpet. Only pictures of great poker players on the walls lined out where the room started and the air outside ended.

As we got seated, a United Airlines jet passed silently to our west, just below us, headed for the airport. I could only imagine what the passengers I could see through the window on that jet would have thought if suddenly Stan's office had become visible out their windows, with Patty and me sitting in front of his desk.

Sometimes Stan kept his office dark and dingy, like a back room at an old, downtown casino, straight out of the mob days. That was when he was in a bad mood or things were threatening. When he let it float above the city, as it was now, you knew Stan was feeling pretty darned good about life with the Gambling Gods.

But his casual statement about the aliens returning rocked me, and I studied his smiling face. Even with my black leather superhero jacket and Fedora-like superhero hat on, I didn't have the power to get a read on Stan. No one could get a read on the God of Poker, which was why he had the job. So I reverted to the most logical way to get an answer. I asked him.

"This makes you happy, the aliens being back?"

Patty had sat forward in her seat at the comment from Stan, her long brown hair flowing over her white blouse and dress slacks, her new uniform for work. She had just recently taken a job as customer relations at the MGM Grand Casino and Hotel, and we had been having lunch in the nifty little Greek place just off the downstairs promenade when Stan called us.

When I'm in Vegas, Patty and I not only work cases together, we are an item. Actually, she's my only item whether I'm in Vegas or not, but I haven't figured out a way to tell her that just yet. As Poker Boy, I'm not known for being a ladies' man, or for having just one woman in my life either. I wasn't sure how she would react, but knowing Patty, she probably already knew. She seemed to sense things about me before I did. I figured it was one of her many superpowers. Thank heavens she didn't play poker.

"Actually," Stan said, "not so much happy as satisfied. I won the pool."

"The pool?" Patty asked, glancing at me with those wonderful brown eyes of hers before looking back at Stan.

"We had a pool as to when they would return," Stan said, his smile getting bigger. "I got it to within a month. We started the pool the day after they left."

"They've been gone since the late 1950s," I said. "I'm impressed."

Stan smiled even larger. "Thanks."

"So, why are we here?" Patty asked, shaking her head and sitting back. She worked the hotel side of the gambling industry. And even though she was a superhero working under Laverne, Lady Luck herself, Patty sometimes just didn't understand the nature of a gambler's need to bet on things. The Gambling Gods had bets running all the time for one thing or another. It was what they did. The alien pool was no surprise to me.

"We need you two to make contact with their representative, find out what they are planning, that sort of thing. Right now he's sitting in a 2-4 no-limit game at the MGM Grand."

"Not over at the Bellagio, huh? I wonder why." I would have figured the aliens could afford the higher stakes.

"Not a clue," Stan said.

Now it was making sense to me. I hadn't been a superhero long enough to have met the aliens the last time they visited the planet, but from what I understood, they loved to gamble, which was why the Gambling Gods ended up being their major contact with the planet Earth. The world governments at the time had hated that, but in the end, had to live with it. I doubted anyone in the current world governments had even been briefed that aliens actually existed, let alone the Gambling Gods. The gods, and the superheroes like Patty and me, tended to stay under the radar as much as we could.

"Is the alien any good at poker?" I asked, smiling at Stan.

Stan laughed. "Not a clue. He's new. Go find out."

The wonderful view from Stan's office faded, and Patty and I moved from sitting in front of Stan's desk to walking down the hallway toward the MGM Grand's poker room. Always took a second for the mind to adjust when Stan did that.

Two

THE POKER ROOM at the MGM Grand had been remodeled a few years back, and now was in the shape of an hourglass. It usually had a good ten games going at any one time, and ran daily tournaments that were pretty popular around town. They catered mostly to tourists, with a few local pros working the room. The big money and high-stakes games had moved over to the Bellagio a number of years back, but the MGM still had a loyal following and they spread a good game and ran a tight room.

"So, what do we do now?" Patty asked, clearly worried about meeting a real-life alien.

"Stop at the counter and stay close until I figure out what the guy wants. I'm going to take us in as much undercover as I can manage."

I had no idea why I was taking those precautions. It just felt right, and as a superhero and a poker player, I had learned a long time ago to trust that feeling.

Patty reached over and squeezed my hand, then let go, which was a good thing. I always found it hard to concentrate when Patty was touching any part of me. Some parts more than others.

As we neared the room, I brought up my Don't-Pay-Attention-To-Me superpower and covered both of us. Someday I was going to have to give that superpower a better name, but describing the effect it had seemed as good as any name for the moment.

I got a rack of five-dollar chips from the front counter and moved toward the 2-4 no-limit table against one drab-colored wall. Four men and two women sat around the table. The two women were clearly together, clearly from some Midwestern state, and pretending to be in over their heads. They didn't even notice me.

The guy in the number four chair was a local pro named Dan, and he managed to see through my cloak and nod as I sat down. Dan stood no more than five feet tall, and usually wore a dress shirt and tan jacket that made him look more like an accountant taking a break from the office than a professional poker player. But I knew he was as sharp and mean as they came and made good money every day at this table. I had no intention of tangling with him.

The other two men were tourists, both with drinks in front of them, and both more interested in the women than in playing poker. That left the guy wearing a snakeskin cowboy hat, sunglasses, and a western shirt, sitting in the seat to the right of the dealer. The weirdest thing about the guy was his tiny nose and almost complete lack of chin. It was as if his face just sort of blended down into his neck and into his black shirt collar.

I sat down in the chair directly across the table from him and slipped the five hundred in chips out of my rack, stacking them neatly as he watched.

He lowered his sunglasses just enough to show me his dark, black eyes, then grinned without showing any teeth. "Poker Boy, I presume."

Dan jerked at the mention of my name, then just stared at me. Clearly, my reputation had gotten ahead of me. I ignored Dan and focused on the alien.

I got nothing, no read, no sense of any emotion at all.

I dug deep and put my best superhero Poker Boy poker-read on him, getting almost nothing but a strange, dark feel. That was getting me nowhere.

"I don't think I have had the pleasure," I said in return.

"Just call me Snake," the alien said, his voice as close to a hiss as I could imagine a human voice sounding.

I hated snakes. I didn't mention that to him. More than likely, he knew. Instead, I just nodded.

I folded the first two cards the dealer fired my way without looking, then watched as Snake glanced at his and folded as well. He had very thin hair sticking out from under his hat that looked combed back over a dark scalp, and he also clearly had a dandruff problem, since flakes kept falling on his black shirt.

"It's been a long time," I said, aiming at him as much of my Make-Them-Relax superpower as I dared use. "At least fifty years."

"Nah, that wasn't my people," Snake said, again grinning under his sunglasses without really opening his mouth. His leather-like skin sort of moved in waves up his neck to his mouth and then back down and I thought for a moment I heard a faint rustling sound. "We haven't been here for a good ten centuries at least."

Oh, crap! Stan wasn't going to be happy with that information. More than likely it meant he hadn't won the pool after all. And he hadn't told me that there was more than one alien race out there.

I felt my stomach tighten into a tiny fist. I hoped like hell Stan and Lady Luck were listening in on this. And I hoped like hell I had managed to keep my best poker face on when Snake told me he was with a different alien race than we were expecting.

"So, what brings you to our little corner of the poker universe?" I asked, forcing myself to stay as calm as possible.

"Why does anyone come to Las Vegas?" Snake asked, glancing at the two women who were ignoring our conversation and flirting with the two men. One of the women had just pulled the last pot and both were laughing about their luck. I had a hunch they were better than just lucky and this flatlander hick routine was just a ruse to take money. And the two guys were going to be more than happy to give it to them.

Dan, the pro, was just shaking his head at their antics and mostly watching me and Snake. I would wager he wasn't real pleased at how his favorite table had shaped up today.

"So," I said, keeping my attention focused on the alien, "you came across vast distances in space to vacation, gamble, drink, and have sex?"

He nodded, glancing at the two cards the dealer had just given him. "That pretty much describes it."

He put a chip on his cards and again sort-of smiled at me, the rustling of his dry skin clearly loud enough to hear this time. It sent shivers down my back. Did I mention that I really, *really* hated snakes? Especially snakes with a bad dandruff problem.

He raised a smooth hundred and Dan folded at once.

"But mostly," Snake said, again pulling down his sunglasses just enough for me to see the pitch black eyes behind them, "I'm here to see if I can beat the best poker player in the game. You up for a little heads-up action, Poker Boy?"

Now, I had to admit that having the alien call me the best player in the game stroked my ego just a little. I knew I was good, but I didn't think of myself as the best by a long ways.

"What did you have in mind?" I asked as I glanced at my cards and flipped the low pair of fours back at the dealer. Any two cards that would cause that kind of raise from Snake had a small pair beat from the start.

"We each start with a million in chips," Snake said. "When one of us has them all, he wins. Blinds level at five hundred, one thousand."

Every sense in my body, and a couple of my superpowers as well, were screaming there was more to this than a simple game for a million bucks.

"So, what would you do with my million, assuming you won it?" Actually, it would be the Gambling Gods' money, not mine. I was fairly rich, but not rich enough to risk a million against some alien.

Snake smiled again without opening his mouth. Again his skin made that dry rustling sound and I tried not to show the shiver that was running up my back. This guy could really be helped by a little lotion.

The dealer flipped me a pair of tens this time around, and I folded them like they were a seven-deuce off. No point in actually playing at this point in the conversation. One of the women giggled and raised and both of the suckers staring at her chest called. Dan and Snake both folded.

Snake reached down under the table and pulled up a golden apple, placing it on the rail in front of him. "I assume you don't remember this."

I stared at the apple for a moment. The thing shone in the casino lights, begging for someone to take a bite out of it. My stomach clamped up so tight, I could hardly breathe. I was talking with a member of the alien race that had caused the legend of Adam and Eve. It sure had been a while since they had been here.

A very, very long time, actually.

"Plucked right from the Tree of Knowledge, I bet," I said, keeping my calm exterior as poker-faced as I could, pretending to not really care.

Snake's thin, eyebrows raised above the top edge of his sunglasses. I had surprised him, and for the first time, my poker sense told me this alien had a weakness.

"I am impressed," Snake said. "I was led to understand that your race in general had no long-term memory, that you destroyed your past, or worshipped it for monetary gain."

"For the most part you're right," I said. "But you still haven't told me what the real bet is."

Snake tapped the apple with a long finger. "Contained in the apple is the design and basics for a good dozen major inventions that would forward your race into the stars." He touched the thing again. "Anti-gravity, time control, teleportation. It's all in here."

I didn't mention to him that the Gambling Gods already had all of those things and humanity would discover them in their own sweet time. I wanted to see exactly what he was after in return.

"Nice," I said. "Worth a million I would say."

Snake shook his head, the rustling so loud this time that even one of the guys staring at the women's chest looked around.

"Your money means nothing to me," Snake said.

"I assumed as much," I said, glancing over at where Patty stood near the main desk. Her eyes were wide and now Stan and Laverne were standing beside her. Clearly they were listening.

I gave Snake the old poker stare. "So what do you want in return if you win?"

"Political sanctuary," Snake said. "And twenty of your acres of land with a privacy dome over it so I can build my own climate-controlled garden to live in."

"And if I win?" I asked.

"You get the information in the apple and I will leave the planet and never return."

I glanced at the poker front desk where Patty now stood alone. Clearly Stan and Lady Luck had heard and were off doing what they needed to do.

"Give me fifteen minutes to talk to my boss, and I'll see what I can do," I said, pushing my chair back and standing.

Snake put the apple away and nodded, glancing down at his new cards. "I'll be right here."

I motioned for the dealer to watch my chips and deal me out, pushed my current cards back at the dealer without looking at them, and headed toward Patty.

Three

WE WERE TEN PACES down the hall away from the poker room when we suddenly found ourselves in Lady Luck's big office. Stan was pacing in front of Laverne's desk, and she was tapping her fingers, staring at a blank screen on the wall beside her desk.

After a moment an alien that looked exactly like the guy sitting in the poker room came on the screen. Only this guy wasn't hiding his snake-like body with four arms and two legs. He was also golden colored, with streaks of red and blue and bright orange along two sides. I had no idea how large he was compared to the guy downstairs, but he seemed much, much larger on the screen.

Who knew that alien life in the universe would develop from snakes as well as monkeys?

"Laverne," the snake said in perfect British English. "It is always a great pleasure."

"The pleasure is all mine, Commander," Laverne said, bowing slightly.

I just stared, more than likely my mouth open. Not often you see Lady Luck herself bowing to anyone.

"I was expecting your call," Commander said. "I assume you have encountered the Lacit fugitive."

"He is sitting in one of our poker rooms as we speak," Laverne said. "He has challenged Poker Boy to a wager: an apple's-worth of knowledge against political sanctuary in a heads-up game of no-limit poker."

Commander shook his head. "They do love that old apple trick. Their entire race seems to never tire of it. They cause more damage to young cultures than any other race."

"I'll take your word for that," Lady Luck said.

Commander frowned and glanced around at something off screen before going on. "We are not scheduled to arrive for another seventeen of your hours. You would do us a great favor by stalling him without giving him political sanctuary. We have been chasing this fugitive for a great deal of your time."

"What will he do if we don't agree to his challenge?" Laverne asked.

"More than likely flee, *after* doing some very permanent damage to your culture. A couple of those apples in the wrong hands would have a very destructive result on your young culture I am afraid."

Laverne glanced around at me. "Can you keep him playing long enough, Poker Boy?"

I glanced at the golden snake on the screen, then at Lady Luck. "I can, with a little help."

"Come in undetected," Laverne said, turning back to Commander. "Your fugitive will be waiting for you at a poker table in Las Vegas."

"Thank you," the big golden snake said, and the screen went dark.

I sure hated snakes.

Lady Luck turned to me. "What kind of help do you need?"

I glanced at Patty, then back at Laverne. "Can you, without Snake noticing, slow down the time in the casino while we play? Make the seventeen hours actually seem more like four or five? I can hold an all-in player for that long, but not a lot longer I'm afraid."

Laverne and Stan both nodded, clearly understanding what I was asking for. Patty just looked puzzled, so to make sure we were all on the same page, I explained to her what I was thinking.

"The Snake has nothing really to lose, so in a no-limit game, he can just shove in all his chips at any given point. Without me facing him in a one-hand showdown, he can just whittle me down slowly as I keep folding. My problem is that I don't dare win or lose. My assignment isn't to beat Snake, it is to play him for a long time, to a draw. Much, much harder thing to do."

"I get it," Patty said, nodding.

"Let's just hope he came to play," Stan said. "I'll set it up in a private room at the MGM. Give me five minutes."

With that Stan vanished.

"Good luck," Laverne said, her face tight and not smiling.

The big office of the head of all the Gambling Gods faded and Patty and I were left standing in the hallway outside of the MGM Grand poker room.

"I really hate it when Lady Luck wishes me good luck," I said, shaking my head.

"Yeah," Patty said. "That's got to worry you. Means she can't really help you much."

"Great," I said, taking a deep breath. I was used to winning, not playing someone to a draw.

"Ready," Stan said, appearing beside us. He indicated a door off to one side of the poker room.

Patty leaned over and kissed me on the cheek, which for a quick second made me forget about how much I hated snakes and remember how much I really liked her. "Luck," she said.

"It will be interesting, if nothing else," I said, smiling at her. I glanced at Stan. "Think you can slow things down a little?"

"We'll see what we can do," Stan said. "But if he starts to notice, we'll back off and you'll be on your own."

"Just keep the snakebite kit handy," I said, then turned and walked toward the table where the alien sat.

Four

"PRIVATE ROOM," I said as I got near the alien, indicating the door. "Chips are being set up. You have yourself a bet."

"Perfect," the alien said, smiling again, rustling his dry skin.

I indicated that the pit boss should cash in our real chips and bring them to us, then led the way into the private room.

A poker table filled the center of the meeting room, and an MGM Grand dealer was sitting ready. Two large stacks of chips of varied denominations were stacked in front of the third chair and the seventh chair, facing each other.

I indicated that Snake should pick and he took the three chair while I shut the door behind us.

I sat down and then pointed upward. "We're being recorded and watched by two casino employees to ensure no problems."

"Understandable," he said. Then he smiled again and even from the length of the table I saw dandruff float down onto his narrow shoulders.

As Stan said, luckily, Snake had come to actually play. So, for the first hour, we traded hands back and forth, pretty much ending up level. I would raise and he would fold, he would raise and I would fold. We saw maybe a dozen flops total, with one or the other of us betting and the other folding. Not the kind of match the television folks would be happy with. In fact, on television, the first hour would mostly be edited right out.

I held a slight advantage of less than eighty thousand going into the second hour, not enough to count in this kind of game.

About ten minutes into the second hour, I caught a pair of kings on the button and raised it twenty thousand. Snake smiled and reraised another fifty. I smooth called and we went to the flop.

A third king hit the flop, but there was also an ace and ten, rainbow, meaning all suits.

Snake, with a rustling sound moved another fifty thousand into the pot.

A smallish bet, which might mean he wanted me to call. I didn't like the feel of it.

I sat back and stared at the board, trying my best to get a read on Snake's hand. More than likely he had aces and had me dead. I doubted he would have reraised with Jack/Queen to give him the straight. And if he had ace/king, I had him dead with two pair.

But the key was, I didn't want to win this pot. If I folded now, I would still be slightly ahead, but I had to fold perfectly, showing him I had a read on him, to keep him under control and playing light.

So, like any good poker player, I went into acting mode. I always figured there should be an Academy Award for poker table acting. Those of us who are pros can act with the best of them. It's also why some damn fine actors become good poker players. They already have part of the skill down solid.

"Let me see if I have this right," I said, smiling at Snake and leaning forward. "You reraised me before the flop, not large, but large enough. Now, with the ace on the board, you come out betting, again not huge, but strong enough to make it interesting. Why do I feel like I'm being suckered into this pot?"

He again lowered his sunglasses and I could see his dark eyes under the lip of his cowboy hat. "You trying to get a read on me, Poker Boy?"

I laughed. "Oh, I already have that," I lied. "You're sitting there with a pair of aces in your hand and trying to sucker me in like I'm one of those rank players out there. Maybe next time."

I flipped my pocket kings toward the dealer, face-up so he could see them.

He stared at my kings for a moment as the dealer scooped them up and then the sound of snakeskin rustling filled the room. Oh, oh, I had made him mad. That snakebite kit might not be such a bad idea after all. I had been right about his aces.

He flipped his two cards to the dealer without showing them to me and started stacking the chips from the pot as the rustling slowly faded.

Why couldn't the aliens have been badgers, or gophers, or even alligators? Anything but snakes.

Five

FOR THE NEXT HALF HOUR, Snake shed a lot of dandruff and folded almost everything, and I gained chips on him, slowly working it up so that I had a couple hundred thousand extra on him, enough to fold some hands without being in any danger. If I hadn't been playing an alien snake, I would have said that my play had Snake snake-bit.

But I said nothing. I just hoped time outside of this room was moving a lot faster than it was in this room.

Finally, around the beginning of the second hour, Snake seemed to shake himself, a rustling sound that sent dandruff flying everywhere. I had no idea how much dandruff would be covering the table, the chips, everything, if he hadn't been wearing that cowboy hat. I just hoped the snake he made the cowboy hat from hadn't been a relative.

Or another poker player.

Two hands later, he raised and I folded.

For the next fifteen hands straight, he raised and I folded. He clearly had changed strategy and I was looking tight and weak to him with my play now.

"What's wrong, Poker Boy?" Snake asked as I folded yet another hand. "Afraid to play?"

"No cards," I again lied. Poker players lie a lot to other poker players. Actually, I had folded six perfectly playable hands to his raises. I just didn't see any point in mixing it up yet, since I was still a good hundred and fifty thousand ahead of him and was in no hurry at all.

Three more hands he raised and I folded, then with him raising ten thousand, I looked down and saw the worst hand in poker. Seven/deuce off-suit. So I reraised him fifty thousand.

He stared at me from behind those sunglasses, his face ringed with a coat of dandruff white, then finally folded.

I flipped my cards again face up so he could see my bluff. "Got tired of the bad cards. Decided to play a couple."

The rustling filled the room again and the dandruff flew as Snake shuddered and got even angrier. At this point, he had to know he was way outclassed in this game and that I had a complete read on him, even though I didn't really. One of two things would be his reaction. He would settle into slow, steady play, or he would get even more aggressive.

Luckily, after a small dandruff storm, he settled down and stopped raising every hand, and we went back to exchanging blinds with small raises as we had done the first hour.

In that style of play, with me not having any ability to sense him at all, or his hands, he was dangerous in the long run. But it would take a long time for him to wear me down, and that's what I needed to have happen.

Finally, just under four hours into the game, we had a hand that television announcers would love. I had ace/queen and raised thirty thousand.

He flat called and we went to the flop. I put him on a pair, or maybe a weak ace such as ace/nine. At that point I was fairly certain we were going in mostly even.

Flop came out ace and two eights. I had two pair, aces and eights, but I didn't much like that flop.

He bet out forty thousand and this time I called him.

The next card was a third eight, filling me up. But again, I hated that card more than I wanted to admit. We were either going to tie if he also had an ace, or I was beat with my full house against his quads if he had the forth ace.

He checked.

I checked right behind him.

Dandruff flew, telling me he wanted me to bet. It seemed his tell was his bad skin problem. He had the eights.

The last card was a worthless rag, and he bet out another forty grand, just enough to keep me in. I called him, since I would still be up slightly even losing the pot, and he rolled over ace eight.

I rolled over my ace/queen and Snake said "Nice hand," as the dealer shoved him the chips."

"Nice bet," I said.

So after four hours of play, we were still almost even. So far, I had managed to do what I needed to do.

Six

B Y THE END OF HOUR FIVE, I was a hundred grand behind, all from small pots, and Snake's shirt was almost pure white from the dandruff.

By the end of hour six, I was two hundred thousand behind, and Snake had settled into the pattern that I knew from the beginning would wear me down. In a game where winning and losing were an option, I would have ended this hours ago. It had already gone on a lot longer than I had thought possible.

And I thought the same thing by the end of hour seven. I had pressured him into folding a few hands, being clear that he was beaten, but he had gotten me to fold even more, and now my chips were just over six hundred thousand.

"Be nice to my chips," I said, smiling at him. "They are about to come back my way. I can feel the cards turning."

He just grinned and rustled his skin and shed even more dandruff. "We shall see, Poker Boy. We shall see."

My comment had the desired effect and he started raising regularly again, forcing his play, and for a good dozen hands, I folded everything, pretending to get angry at the cards for not turning, even though I was seeing some perfectly good playable hands.

Then, on the button, I looked down at pocket rockets. Two wonderful red aces.

"It's about damn time," I said, and raised a smooth forty thousand. My comment, of course, would tell any decent poker player I really *didn't* have a strong hand. He just called and sat back in his chair.

Not a good sign. He had a monster hand as well.

Flop came ace/queen/jack, rainbow. He bet out forty thousand, the same bet I had made and I flat called him with my three aces. And then I sat back.

"Interesting," Snake said, looking over the top of his sunglasses at me with his dark eyes.

I said nothing and the turn came a ten. If he had ace/king, he had just hit his straight and I was beat.

Before he could reach for his chips I said, "I wouldn't bet much on that straight until you see the river."

His hand froze over his chips, letting me know I had figured his hand perfectly. And by speaking up, I had told him exactly what I had as well. His straight was the best hand, but I had to get any one of one ace, three queens, three jacks, or three tens to win the hand and two kings to tie him with a straight of my own. Twelve outs were a lot of outs.

At that moment, a shimmering went through the air and I had the sense that a bunch of hours suddenly passed. The door to the room opened and two large, gold-colored, snake-like men walked through, followed by Laverne and Stan and Patty.

In a hissing language I had no desire to learn, the two golden-snake men moved over behind Snake and made him stand, sending dandruff everywhere like a faint snowstorm.

Snake glanced at the cards and then up at me. "Nicely played, Poker Boy. A match I will always remember."

"As will I," I said. But not because of the poker, but I didn't say that.

"Any chance we can see that river card?" Snake asked.

I nodded to the dealer and he flipped the last card over. Another ten.

I rolled over my aces full.

"I guess it wasn't meant to be," Snake said.

A moment later the three aliens vanished.

"Nice job, again, Poker Boy," Laverne said, smiling at me. Then she, too, vanished.

I can't begin to say, as a poker player, how much I liked having Lady Luck smile at me.

Stan smiled as well. "We owe you one for that." Then he was gone.

Patty kissed me, and for a second I forgot all about snakes, poker, and Lady Luck as I enjoyed the feel of Front Desk Girl welcoming me back to the real world.

"Have I ever told you," Patty said as we turned and headed for the door, "how much I hate snakes."

"Oh, after about five hours of playing poker with one, you get used to them."

She laughed. "You up for a wonderful dinner, on me?"

"I think I need a shower first," I said as we walked arm-in-arm down the hallway.

"Oh, I like that idea, too," Patty said, hugging me even closer. "I'll scrub."

"Only if you use a lot of shampoo," I said. "Dandruff shampoo."

VARIATIONS OF A SCREAM

Each of us face reality in our own ways. Each of us do what we can do.

Elizabeth Beven, in this biting little story, faces her new reality in the only way she can.

This story fits with many of the nursing home stories I wrote.

THREE A.M.

ELIZABETH BEVEN, EIGHTY-FIVE, sat at a small manual type-writer and picked at the keys with a paced rhythm like a slow drip from a faucet.

Every night she trickled words onto a page in the form of a letter, folded the page with shaking hands, addressed an envelope, and left both letter and envelope together on the top of her typewriter before returning to bed.

The nurse always mailed the letter the next morning before Elizabeth was dressed.

For the past two years Elizabeth had written a letter every night.

Her routine was always the same.

She awoke at 2:30, after four hours sleep, took fifteen minutes to get from her bed into her wheelchair, to the toilet, and then to the typewriter. Writing a letter made her tired and then she could sleep until morning.

Tonight, the letter was to her daughter, Mary.

Mary lived in the city below the nursing home with her husband Greg and two children, Matt and Martha. Mary said she enjoyed getting the letters from her mother, even though she stopped by the nursing home twice a week.

Elizabeth also wrote to her son, Bill, who lived out in California. But she only wrote him once a week and saved doing his letter for the nights when she felt exceptionally awake. Sometimes, she would even add to his letter during the day, but she never told her daughter.

Tonight, the letter was to Mary.

Mary,

Today, as most days, there is very little news to relay. This morning, Mrs. Robinson—you remember her, two doors north down the hall—fell and broke her hip. She's in the hospital downtown now.

My cold I thought was getting never came on. The nurse gave me something for it yesterday, but I didn't take it because it would have made me too tired to write a letter to Bill last night. You know how I get tired every time they give me a pill.

That's all the news. Mostly nothing happens. We sit here and wait for someone to die and then, when they do, somebody else takes their place.

Oh, by the way, would you please do me a favor and bring—

An intense flash of white light suddenly filled the room, startling Elizabeth and causing her to jerk backwards.

Her wheelchair rolled slightly away from the desk as the room rumbled and shook.

She pulled her robe tightly across her with one hand and held onto her chair with the other.

The long curtains over the sliding glass door danced and jerked like puppets on strings.

She could hear glass breaking down the hall and people shouting and screaming.

The floor of the room shook her right up through the wheels of her chair as she bit her lip and held on.

The lights flickered once, came on bright, then went out, leaving only the faint light coming though her curtains. But even in the dark, she could see the letter to Mary as it rattled and fluttered.

The typewriter vibrated sideways toward the edge of her small desk. She wanted to reach out and save it, but didn't dare let go of her chair.

Finally, with almost an audible sigh, the shaking and rumbling stopped. Her typewriter perched on the edge of her desk, threatening to fall at any moment. She quickly moved forward and pushed it back into place.

Noise from the hall replaced the rumbling.

She turned her chair toward the door. Loud running footsteps went past as she reached the handle and held on to it while backing her chair away. Finally, when the door was open far enough for her chair to pass through, she moved forward into the hall.

The hall was empty to the left. A weak, emergency light cast a faint shadow off the tile floor. She could hear a few of the residents calling out for help, but there was no movement.

To the left was a different story.

Emergency lights flooded the nurse's station like spotlights over a stage. One aide was frantically rummaging through drawers behind the desk.

As Elizabeth watched, the night nurse and another aide came running from the medical supply room, their arms full of packages.

The nurse shouted "Quickly!" and all three of them ran in the direction of the front door.

Elizabeth heard the front door slam.

Again, only the noise of the few residents calling out disturbed the night. The empty, bright light of the nurse's station made her shiver.

She turned her chair back into the familiar surroundings of her room.

She stopped in front of her typewriter and tried to think. Maybe there had been an accident out in the front parking lot and everyone was rushing to help. That would make sense.

She would be able to see that from her patio which overlooked the front lawn, parking lot, and the city in the valley below.

She went to the curtains and pulled them halfway open.

Then she unlatched the lock on the sliding glass door, slid it open, and rolled herself out onto the small patio.

It took a moment to realize what she was seeing.

In the distant valley below, the city was burning. Fire seemed to be everywhere, coloring huge clouds of smoke with orange light.

A few of the houses that lined the street below also burned, the crackling of the flames loud against the hills.

In the distance, Elizabeth could hear a woman screaming. Dozens of people milled in the street, watching, running, shouting.

Elizabeth glanced around at what she could see of the nursing home. It seemed to have survived without much damage. She could see a window broken, but nothing more.

She turned her attention back to the city.

On clear nights, she used to imagine that she could see Mary's house through the trees that shaded the downtown area. On nice evenings she would sit and stare out over the city, imagining what it was like at Mary's house that evening with the two grandchildren playing.

She loved to spend time at Mary's house. But, except for holidays, there never seemed to be much chance. Still, she felt lucky to have raised two such fine children. She had always hoped she would live long enough to see her grandchildren grown.

Now the area around Mary's house was nothing but fire.

The entire city was fire, smoke, and orange light.

Carefully, she wheeled herself to the edge of her patio, folded her hands in her lap and watched the flames.

Later, the chill from the night air forced her into movement.

She took one last look at the street below the nursing home. People still moved. A few gathered around a body on the street.

She watched only a moment, then turned and moved back through the door to her desk.

The orange light from the door gave her just enough light to reread her letter to Mary as she held the paper straight up with shaking hands.

After a short moment, she began to type.

Oh, by the way, would you do me a favor and bring my gray sweater. The nights are starting to get a little chilly and you know how I love to sit on my patio.

That's all for now. Hope to see you soon.

Your loving mother.

She signed the letter, addressed an envelope, and very carefully laid both on the typewriter.

CUTTING DOWN FRED

A Buckey the Space Pirate Story

One fine summer night Buckey the Space Pirate takes his girlfriend for a little excitement to a local park. He hoped for a sexual adventure and ended up meeting Fred, a talking oak tree.

With a talking oak tree, adventure and bad limericks never end.

First published in Dinosaur Fantastic edited by Mike Resnick and Martin H. Greenberg. The book came out from DAW Books in 1993.

The origin story for Fred, the time-traveling and talking oak tree.

One

I TRIED TO MAKE LOVE under Fred for the first time on a warm October evening two years ago.

It was right in the middle of Big John's annual Halloween bash, the very same party that keeps three square city blocks of the city up all night. My current girlfriend, Annie, was in one of her moods, none of which I ever figured out. So when I suggested, after six very fast and hot dances, that we go somewhere cool, take off some costumes and really get hot, she laughed and said she would love to.

But she wanted to go somewhere new. She said she was tired of my apartment and "those old squeaky bed springs." She wanted to be daring. "Really live," was the way I think she put it.

So we ended up under Fred.

We left the party with a wave at Big John and headed downtown. I was wearing my Buckey the Space Pirate costume, with the white tights, white cape, lace shirt, saber, and plumed white hat. Most people thought I looked like one of the Three Musketeers, but what the hell did they know about space pirates, anyway?

Annie had on her Queen of the Alien Warlords' costume made up of black tights, high black boots, and lots of chains over a very open-necked blouse. On her head she wore this three-foot tall jeweled head-dress that gave the entire costume a feeling of power. The only problem was that she kept forgetting to duck when going through doors.

I didn't exactly know what Annie had in mind when she said "daring," but I figured Russell Park might fit. And it was close by. I didn't feel like walking too far dressed as Buckey, especially in this part of the city.

Russell Park was the second oldest park in the city. I'd been there a few times, mostly passing through. It was one of those places where old people sat around on the benches and watched the young mothers ignore their children. It measured a half a block wide, a block long, and was filled with benches, small patches of grass, and big old oak trees. But it didn't smell much like a park because there just wasn't enough green to hold back the smells of the city.

We ended up under one of the biggest trees in the park, tucked off in one corner, near a hedge and a wooden bench that looked like no one had sat on it since the First World War. There I hoped we would have the least chance of getting seen, yet give Annie the thrill she needed.

To say Annie was thrilled would have been putting it lightly. She liked the idea of making love out in the open. In the two months we'd gone out she said we'd never done anything this much "fun."

"My dear Queen Annie," I said, taking my plumed hat off and bowing deeply at the waist while sweeping the hat along the grass. "Will this place of repose suit a lady of your stature?" She always loved it when I went formal on her.

"You have done well, faithful servant," she said, smiling. Then she reached up, took off her headdress, and sat it against the base of the tree. Then the chains came over her head, then the blouse. She was working on taking off the tights before I had enough common sense to start getting undressed too.

She was totally nude and lying on the grass by the time I had gotten my boots and saber off. So instead of finishing undressing, I went to work, kissing that soft skin, starting at her right ear and working my way down. I was doing my best to not miss a spot on that beautiful body, when this deep voice came out of nowhere.

"There was a young lady from Hunt
Whose body could take a small punt.
Her mother said, 'Annie,
It matches your fanny,
Which never was that of a runt.'"

I thought my heart was going to explode right out of my chest.

I expected to look up and see a policeman standing there with a big nightstick, slapping it into his palm as he smiled down at us. We were going to end up in jail. I just knew it. Mom would never understand.

So from between her legs I glanced quickly around. No one. At least in sight.

"What did you mean by that?" Annie said, pushing me away and sitting up. "That seemed like a pretty crude thing to say, especially when you were doing what you were doing. And just what the hell is a punt?"

"I didn't—"

"It's a flat-bottomed boat that is propelled by thrusts from a pole," the voice said.

Annie glanced quickly around, then stood up and stared down at me, hands on her hips. "I don't think I like you anymore," she said and pulled on her black tights.

"But I didn't say anything," I pleaded.

"Then who did," she asked. "And you know, if you were any bigger than a pencil, you wouldn't think I was so large."

"A pencil?" I said. "But—"

She pulled her blouse quickly on, grabbed the chains and headdress and stormed off with me still there on the grass trying to get my boots back on. "But— But— But—" I said over and over as she disappeared through an opening in the hedge.

"There was a young fellow of Buckingham
Wrote a treatise on girls and on fucking them.
A learned Parsee
Taught him Gamahuchee,
So he added a chapter on sucking them."

"Who's there?" I quickly turned around, but couldn't see anyone. The deep baritone voice sounded like it had come from right beside me. "Come out, damn you!"

I pulled on my boots and saber and checked behind the trunk of the old tree, then in the hedges, and then in the branches of the tree itself. No one. In fact, the entire little park looked completely deserted.

"Aren't you even curious," the voice asked. Again it sounded as if it was coming from right beside my head. I spun around, then checked my shirt for hidden microphones someone might have slipped in at the party. Nothing.

"All right," I said. "I give up. What's the joke?"

"Oh, no joke," the voice said. "But I wonder if you are curious as to what Gamahuchee means. Most people would be."

"Who's talking?" I shouted at the dimly lit park. This was getting damned annoying. It was going to take me a week to calm Annie down, if she would even talk to me again.

"I'll tell you who I am if you first ask me what Gamahuchee means."

"Oh, for hell's sake," I checked once more in the limbs of the tree, in the hedge, and around the trunk. Just one old oak tree. No one anywhere near.

Finally, I gave up and sat down. "All right, what the hell does Gamahuchee mean?"

"No one is really sure," the voice said.

"Great," I said. "You—"

"But it is thought to have a Japanese derivation, and in the context of the limerick, it refers to oragenitalism. Or, in more current terminology, oral sex."

"I could have figured out as much," I said. "If I really gave a shit. Now would you please tell me who the hell you are? And where you are so you can laugh and I can kill you?"

"I am the tree you now repose under. I refer to myself as Fred. I am

320

sure you would not like to hear the story of how I came to acquire that name, even though it *is* quite interesting."

"You're right," I said, looking up into the thick green leaves of the tree. "I wouldn't. And I don't buy this for a minute. Where's the speaker hidden?"

"I am really the tree," the voice said, sadly. "Why don't you believe me? Dressed as you are, I had hoped you at least would believe me."

"Well I don't!" I shouted up into the tree. "And there's not a damned thing wrong with how I'm dressed." I felt immediately stupid for shouting. Somewhere, someone was laughing their fool head off and I was playing along. I stood and headed for the entrance to the park. A joke was a joke. But Buckey the Space Pirate had let this one go too far.

Two

BY THE NEXT AFTERNOON, no one had come up to me and laughed at how much they had got me. And Annie didn't show one sign of talking to me no matter how much I pounded on her door. The only way she was going to ever speak to me again was if I proved to her that it wasn't me who had accused her of being able to do strange things with boats.

If I uncovered whoever the joker was, I could prove to her it wasn't me. So that evening I found myself back down at the park under the old tree.

"You look much more normal for these times dressed as you are today," the voice said as I walked up. I had on a tee shirt and Levi's. "Would you like to hear another limerick?"

"Whoever you are," I said as calmly as I could. "Please show yourself."

"I am showing myself. I'm shading you from the sun. What more do you want? Don't you like my limericks. I have one I made up for a young couple back thirty, maybe forty years ago. I was much smaller then and they were one of the first who used my shelter for the purpose that you were using it for yesterday. I feel it is one of my best limericks. And by the way, my name is Fred."

"Fred. Sure. You told me." I moved slowly around the tree trying to humor the voice while spotting exactly where the speaker was hidden.

"You know you could have at least waited until we finished. And I'm not buying this talking tree line. I know someone's behind all this and when I find out who, I— I—"

"Do what you like," the voice said. "I won't be around much longer for you to believe or not believe."

"Sure." I searched through some high grass near a sprinkler head. "You're just going to pull up roots and walk away. Right?"

"Hardly," Fred said.

"All right then," I said and went back to searching the trunk, feeling for any loose bark. "Why don't you tell me, for starters, how you can talk. Some witch cast a spell over you or something?"

"I suppose it could be called magic," Fred said. "But I prefer to think of it as the miracle of life. Actually us trees are much more intelligent than you humans think and have very long memories."

"Sure. Sure. All from the miracle of life." I said, as sarcastically as I could make my voice sound. "So how'd that get you a voice?"

"I don't actually know. I don't actually have vocal cords as you do, but I can project my thoughts to make humans hear the thoughts as a voice. You see, ninety-seven years ago, a sailor visited a brothel here in this fine city. The man used a prophylactic. It was disposed of in the alley outside of the brothel and a very young girl found it a short time later. She took an acorn from my mother, put it in the sperm and planted the entire thing here. The young girl watered me carefully for the first two years until she died, ran over by a wagon right in front of me. Poor child. Of course, there was nothing I could have done."

I had kept looking the entire time he had been talking and still hadn't found one hint of any speaker, microphone, or wiring. The voice seemed to come from everywhere around the tree and inside my head at the same time. "You don't really expect me to believe that?" I said.

"You asked," Fred said. "Would you like to hear another limerick? I know all of the good old ones."

"Not just yet." I had come to the realization that this stunt was so well done that I was going to get nowhere unless I played along. Eventually whoever was behind it would slip up. "Say, why don't you tell me how you came to do limericks?"

"If you stood in one place for almost a hundred years, you'd do limericks, too."

With that I granted he had a point. I studied the tree for a foothold. The speaker was probably hidden in the limbs somewhere and I was going to have to climb up there to find it. Best thing to do was keep humoring the voice while being quiet while climbing the tree. "What's this about you not having much longer?"

"Tomorrow, to be exact," Fred said. "That's why I decided to talk to you. Do you realize that I have only talked to seven people in one hundred years. I look back and find that fact most amazing."

"What's going to happen?" I picked my way carefully up the bark like a rock climber going up a sheer face. Finally I got my arms around the lowest limb and pulled myself up.

"See the stakes in the grass?" Fred said. "The ones with the orange ribbons on them?"

I looked back down through the branches. "Sure." They were scattered across this corner of the park. I hadn't noticed them last night with Annie.

"I overheard workmen talking about widening the road. I'm scheduled for the chain saws tomorrow."

"You're kidding?" I finished checking out the limb I was on and climbed higher where I could see the stakes better. They did show a pattern that looked like the street was going to be wider right through the big tree.

"I am afraid I am not kidding," Fred said, his voice almost too faint for me to hear. Then he got suddenly louder. "But, that is life. Or death. And please do be careful. I've had fifteen children and three adults fall out of my limbs. It is always so painful an occurrence. Actually, the first person who fell out of my limbs was killed by a dinosaur. It was a very sad experience since his wife was standing nearby in the park at the time and never really understood what happened."

"A what?"

"A dinosaur. Actually a Pterosaurs angry that he was there. You know that Pterosaurs were large flying reptiles that..."

"Now you have gone too far. First you expect me to believe you are a talking tree and then you expect me to believe that you have been around since the dinosaurs. There were no men during that time. That much I remember from grade school. And you said you were not even a hundred years old."

"You are quite right," Fred said. But we oak trees have family memories that go back, for lack of a better way of putting it, to our roots, which incidentally, were in the early Cretaceous period in this part of the world."

"Fine," I said, glancing down at the ground below, wondering when the funny farm wagon was going to come and take me away for talking to myself in a tree.

"I can tell you do not believe me."

"No shit," I said. "I am still looking for the microphone so I can get this joke over."

"Please hold onto a limb and I will take you back. Do you have a favorite dinosaur you would like to see?"

"Yeah, sure," I said and started down. "And next you will be telling me I can ride a Triceratops if I want."

Fred laughed softly. "Not hardly, but I can certainly show you why you wouldn't want to ride one."

Three

AROUND ME the air suddenly shimmered and the branches of the oak seemed to move and sway, as if there was a slight earthquake shaking the roots. I grabbed tight around a limb and held on as I was suddenly hit by a wave of hot and very humid air that smelled of swamp and fresh greenery.

Below me there was a crashing of brush and again the tree seemed to shake. Through the shaking leaves I could see that the city was gone. There was nothing except trees and brush. And below me was the ugliest, most scarred-up Triceratops I could ever imagine.

"Hold on," the voice of Fred inside my head said as the dinosaur bumped into the tree and then started using it to scratch itself. I thought I was on a ride at a carnival.

The dinosaur bumped the tree and I bounced among the limbs. Then the Triceratops backed off, looked at the tree and hit it again.

As I held on for dear life I heard Fred's voice in my head. "See why you wouldn't want to ride one?"

Somehow, as the dinosaur took aim once more on the base of the tree I managed to scream, "Get me out of here!"

And I was back in the tree in the park.

A tree that wasn't moving.

I looked slowly around to make sure that I was where I seemed to be, then carefully pulled my fingers out of the grooves they had dug into the bark.

"Pretty amazing beasts, weren't they?"

I took a deep shuddering breath and let it out. "How did you do that?"

"How do you walk around and drink water without roots? It is just a part of what we are. We can move our conscious minds back and forth through our ancestors and through time. I guess it makes up for not being able to move in real time. You didn't actually leave the park, but I took your mind back with mine. Fun, huh? Now, would you like to hear another limerick now? I have one about a dinosaur."

"No. Thanks." I gave one more quick look to make sure the city was where it should be and there was no Triceratops lurking behind the hedge, then climbed down. Once I was back on the ground I walked quickly around the tree, then sat down.

"You seem upset," Fred said.

"That ride you gave me was really something. I am not saying that I believe you, but can you take me to any time at all?"

"Sure," Fred said. And to almost any place as long as the oak at the location is, as we say, in my family tree."

I groaned.

"Sorry," Fred said. "But," his voice suddenly sounding sad. "I am afraid that today will be the last day for you to experience any other time, so we should make the best of it."

I climbed back to my feet and walked along the line of stakes in the grass. They did start at the corner and go inside the edge of the tree. "Just for the sake of argument," I said, "is there something I can do for you? I doubt that I could stop the street from being widened, but—"

"Oh, my dear man," Fred said quickly. "It is so kind of you to ask. I was hoping you would. I have studied the problem at some length and I feel the only solution would be to repeat the process from which I came."

"What?" I asked. I had lost whatever Fred was talking about halfway through.

"In other words," Fred said, "get a rubber, ejaculate into it, put one of my seeds in the resulting solution, and plant it. Very simple, really."

"No way! You must think I was born yesterday?" Now at least I was starting to see the joke. I didn't know how they had pulled off the voice and the dinosaur schtick, but someone was having a great laugh on this one and I wasn't going to play along any more.

"I'm afraid I do not know when you were born," Fred said. "But I got here by exactly the method I told you. I have watched it happening. I have studied the event many times and I fear it may be my only chance of survival."

"Sure." I made one more quick check of the tree, then studied the stakes. I had to admit it was sure one elaborate gag. And it looked like the only way I was going to get to the prankster was go along and get it over with. Then I could prove to Annie that I didn't say anything and get back on her "good" side.

"All right," I said. "I'll bring back the part of the deal you need from me. Where will I find a seed from you?"

"I will drop an acorn that is ready to sprout," Fred said. "And thank you."

"No problem," I said.

I made one more quick check around the area of Fred to make sure no one was hiding in the bushes laughing their fool heads off, then headed for Annie's house in hopes of her giving me a helping hand. She still wouldn't talk to me or even let me explain what I was trying to do. Not that I really blamed her. So I went back to my place and did it myself. I was back at the tree in an hour.

I checked quickly around to make sure no one was watching, then held the rubber up. "Here you go."

An acorn hit the grass right at my feet. I picked it up, looked at it, then stuck it inside the rubber. "Got any place special you think I should plant it?" I asked, checking the area of the branches it fell from to make sure there was no one sitting up there.

"Anywhere that will be safe," Fred said.

"I'll be back tomorrow morning early." As I headed for the park gate, I heard Fred start into a limerick about a girl from Troy.

Four

I TOOK MY "PACKAGE" to mom's house in the suburbs and planted it off to one side in her back yard. She didn't care. As far as she was concerned, I was always doing strange things. And she hadn't even seen me in my Buckey the Space Pirate costume.

I staked out where I planted the seed. I told mom it was a special seed for an exotic tree and needed really special care. She liked that.

I made it back to the park by ten the next morning, but I was way too late. The old tree was in a hundred pieces piled in neat stacks. I watched while the workmen used chain saws on what was left, but I couldn't take it for very long. Even though I knew the entire thing had just been a joke, I couldn't shake the feeling of pain and sadness coming from that wood.

I never did get back with Annie. She wouldn't have anything to do with me. And no one ever came forward and laughed at me about jacking off into a rubber and then planting it. If it was a practical joke, or a hidden camera stunt, I never found out about it. Seems to me that I would have, too. I don't understand why someone would go to all that trouble without pulling the final "gotcha?"

Since I never uncovered the joke, every time I visited Mom I found myself checking on the spot where I had planted the tree. Nothing. Over the winter I pretty much forgot about it.

It wasn't until the following May, while I was mowing Mom's lawn, that I almost ran over the little oak tree. I spent an entire hour cleaning the weeds and grass away from it, then putting up a solid, two-foot-high wire fence around it. It felt kind of funny to know that my sperm had worked as fertilizer for a tree.

I checked back on the little tree all through that summer and fall, telling myself I was crazy each time I did, but yet doing it anyhow. It became one of those little obsessions a person has that they can't explain. I sure in hell made no attempt to tell anyone. Mom loved it. Said she'd never had so much help on the yard.

It wasn't until the following May that something finally happened. I was carefully mowing around the now almost four-foot tall baby oak tree when I heard this high, child-like voice. At first I thought it was something going wrong with the mower, but after I turned the engine off, I heard:

"A bather whose clothing was strewed
By waves that left her quite nude,
Saw a man come along
And unless I am wrong
You expect this line to be crude."

I sat down hard on the grass. I couldn't believe it. I was either going completely crazy, or it had worked. I had actually planted a tree with my sperm that grew and could talk. No way. That was just too stupid. Just like before, I figured it was either a joke or I had imagined it.

"You know," the little voice said from what seemed like the direction of the little tree. "I have this strange desire to do things to a woman dressed in a costume."

I stretched out on the grass with my face real close to the small trunk of the tree.

"Fred?"

"Hi, Dad," the little tree said. "You want to hear a limerick? Or maybe go see a dinosaur?"

DADDY IS AN UNDERTAKER

A Poker Boy Story

What's a girl to do when Daddy wants her dead?

Mortuary Dan, otherwise known as Death himself, just happens to be her father.

Poker Boy and his team must help the only daughter of Death understand that she might not really die as she turns twenty-one.

Even though she will.

Sort of....

One

I USUALLY FIND THE PEOPLE I'm going to help by accident. Most of us superheroes do, or we are told to help someone by one of our bosses.

But this time, my sidekick and girlfriend, Patty Ledgerwood, aka Front Desk Girl brought me a person who really needed help.

And I do mean a lot of help if she planned on staying alive more than another few hours.

Actually, Patty sent my boss, Stan, the God of Poker, to get me.

It was a dark and rainy Oregon Saturday night in March. I was dressed and watching a rerun of an old Star Trek show starring the bald actor whose name I can never remember. In an hour or so, I planned on heading over to the casino near the doublewide trailer I called home. I never went near the casino too early on a weekend night, because the players were new and fresh and hadn't had enough drinks.

I always gave the Saturday players a few hours, and then went over to take the money that they were willing to give to me across the poker table. Even though I was a superhero, I still had to make a living, and playing poker was my way of doing it.

"Knock, knock. Poker Boy, need to talk," the voice-without-a-body said from the middle of the air in my living room, interrupting a scene with an alien with a forehead problem and some sort of sticky paste-like substance.

I knew the voice. Stan had only been to my home once before for only a second. It wasn't like him to be polite and actually knock.

"I'm decent," I said, standing and heading for my superhero costume on the hook by the door. I had on tennis shoes, jeans, and a white Polo shirt, but my costume was my black leather coat and black Fedora-like hat that I never took off in a casino. It helped funnel the power of the casino to me. If Stan was coming to talk to me, I knew I was going to need the costume very quickly.

Stan appeared in the middle of my living room and glanced first at the old television, then the remains of my T.V. dinner on the scarred coffee table, then around at the old 1970s furniture and green shag carpet that had come with the doublewide when it was new.

"We clearly don't pay you enough," Stan said, disgusted at what he saw.

"You don't pay me anything," I said as I slipped on my coat and hat.

"Oh, yeah, there's that," Stan said. "But I know for a fact you have enough in your bank accounts to buy a dozen mansions in every state in the country, with enough left over for a castle in Britain."

I shrugged. He was right. In about fifty accounts in fifty different banks, I had a vast amount of money. And a ton of investments that seemed to be doing real well when I bothered to check on them. I had won a lot of tournaments and just didn't spend much money after taxes every year.

"I like it here," I said. "Keeps me humble."

"Oh, yeah, Poker Boy humble," Stan said, laughing. "I bet Patty doesn't come over often,"

With that he had a point. We always stayed at her wonderful place in Vegas. She had only seen my home once and never come back. Maybe Stan was right, it might be time to upgrade some. When I had the time.

And besides, Patty thought I was a broke gambler. Maybe at some point I should get around to telling her about my money. Not a conversation I was looking forward to.

"To what do I owe this visit?" I asked the God of Poker.

"Just doing a favor for your girlfriend," Stan said. "She needs your help on a case and she asked me to come get you. Guess there isn't enough time for you to fly commercial." Stan just shook his head at my old doublewide. "You know, you could afford a few private jets as well."

"Or you could teach me the jumping-around-in-space skill," I said. "Or is that only for gods?"

He shrugged. "Maybe when you're done helping Patty."

I was actually surprised at that. I didn't know I might be able to actually teleport around the world. Of course, I still didn't know what half my powers were. I was still pretty new at this superhero stuff.

The next moment I was in the crowded lobby of the MGM Grand.

The noise of the casino and the hundreds of guests in the lobby slammed into me. But at the same time I could feel the energy coming from the casino through my coat and hat, making me feel extra alive.

Patty was standing in front of the desk, talking to a woman with longish blonde hair. Patty glanced over, saw me, and smiled.

Like normal, her smile melted a part of me and got other parts all agitated in a very good way. She had the ability to do that to me with just a look. Her long brown hair was pulled back and she was dressed in the standard MGM front desk uniform of white shirt and black slacks and MGM vest. She made it look great.

She was a stunningly attractive woman. What she saw in me was anyone's guess.

I made my way through the crowd and luggage over to her and she gave me a hug. "Thanks for coming."

"Anytime," I said, and I meant it.

"Thanks, Stan," Patty said to the air.

"More than welcome," Stan said without showing himself.

The young woman with Patty sort of looked around for the voice, but before she could say anything Patty said, "Lisa, this is Poker Boy."

I turned on my what I called my "Charming Power" for lack of a better name. It helped put people I was trying to help in a more relaxed and talkative mood. I shook her firm hand. "Very nice meeting you."

Lisa looked like an odd imitation of an American flag, with a red, white and blue outfit that included a too-tight skirt. It really wasn't a flattering look on her. Up close I could tell she couldn't be more than twenty-two, and more than likely she would get carded everywhere she went in this town.

Plus she had on way too much makeup. Her eyelashes seemed to extend halfway into the big lobby.

She smiled, but the smile didn't reach her dark eyes. I could tell that something was very wrong in her life.

"Tell him what's bothering you," Patty said, patting Lisa's arm gently in support.

As a superhero in the world of hospitality, Patty could calm the most upset person and make them feel good about anything. It was one of her many superpowers.

Lisa nodded, took a deep breath, and then in a deep southern accent she said, "My daddy is an undertaker."

I waited for her to keep going, but she seemed to think that was enough explanation of her problem.

Finally I said, "Yes, go on. What's happening?"

"No, you don't see do you?" Lisa said, clearly about to break into tears that I was sure would run black from all the makeup. "I'm turning twenty-one in four hours, and my daddy is an undertaker."

I looked puzzled and was about to try a tell-me-the-truth power on her when Patty said softly to me, "Capitalize the word *Undertaker.*"

I opened my mouth to say something, then the realization hit me: the young woman in front of me was the child of an *Undertaker*, the most feared branch of all the deities.

That wasn't possible.

Undertakers never had children.

I had never heard of an Undertaker having a kid, and of all the rumors about Undertakers, the worst rumor was that their kids never lived past the first moment of their twenty-first birthday!

Now I saw the problem.

"Which one of the twelve is your father?" I asked softly, almost afraid to hear the answer. There were only twelve, one per month. It seems the twelve of them took turns being Death for the month.

"They call him Mortuary Dan," Lisa said.

Patty's face went white, and I felt like the chicken TV dinner I had eaten was about to make another showing in the lobby of the MGM Grand.

"I'm assuming you want to live longer than four more hours?" I asked, getting right to the point as I tried to get my stomach back under control.

The worst part of the kid rumor was that their own fathers took them.

The Undertakers took everyone at one point or another, except for maybe the gods, who seemed to live a very long time. And some super-heroes as well. Patty had been a superhero for about a hundred years before I became one. I'm not aging now and so far we've never talked much about what happened in those hundred years before I was born.

"I would like to live longer," she said. "Much longer. Can you help me?"

Usually I just say that I can help the person, give them encouragement, make them feel something positive. But all I said to Lisa was, "We can try."

But what Patty and I could do against an Undertaker was beyond me. Especially Mortuary Dan, the oldest of all the Undertakers. He was the worst, the nastiest of the twelve from what I had heard. All twelve were nasty people. Dealing with the dead and dying every day, day after day, would do that to a person. It was no wonder they only worked one month at a time. I had no idea what they did the other eleven months of the year. I honestly didn't want to know.

Somehow, to save this woman, we had to stop Death himself.

The big problem was that Death was her father.

Two

I TOOK A DEEP BREATH and tried to pull my thoughts together. Somehow, we had to stop the tradition of not letting a child of an Undertaker live longer than the first moment of their twenty-first birthday.

I had no idea at all why such a stupid rule existed.

"Has your father ever talked to you about this?" I asked Lisa.

She shook her head.

"Do you have a place to stay here in Vegas?" I asked.

Lisa nodded. "I came here to enjoy my last night, then when checking in, I broke down in front of Patty and told her the entire story."

"Tell you what, Lisa, go ahead and go to your room, have a nice relaxing bath, then meet us down here in two hours if we haven't contacted you first. We need to do some work and you might as well enjoy the time it's going to take us."

"I'll upgrade you to a nice suite," Patty said, nodding to me and gently turning Lisa around toward the front desk before the Daughter of Death could object.

I pulled out my phone and called Screamer and had him meet us at our normal place downtown in fifteen minutes. Then I called The Smoke, the fourth member of my team, a human who could turn into a wolf when he wanted. He was out of town and working a case in the Canadian woods. There was no way he could make it in time, and I could tell he felt bad. I assured him that missing this one was a very good idea.

Then, as Patty got Lisa headed toward the elevators and turned to join me, I shouted into the noise and crowds of the large lobby, "Stan! Need some help!"

Around me the room froze except for Patty, as Stan took us out of time and appeared beside me. Everyone else just stopped in the instant of time. I had the power to do that as well, but Stan was better at it than I was.

"I thought I might be getting a call when I saw who needed help. You know the rumor is that she's going to be dead in a few hours by her own father's hand."

"That's what we need help with. We want to try to stop that."

Stan just laughed long and hard, choking before catching his breath. His laugh echoed in the quiet of the frozen huge lobby.

Patty and I didn't join him.

After a moment he said, "You two are serious, aren't you?"

Patty and I both nodded. "I don't even understand why a rule like that exists," I said.

"Because it does," Stan said.

"Why?" Patty asked. "How did it get started? Maybe if we knew that, we might be able to figure a way around it."

Stan shrugged. "I honestly don't know. It's just been a rule for the few children of Undertakers for as long as I have been around. Although, to be honest, no Undertaker has had a child except for Lisa in all my years. She's the only one."

I wanted to ask Stan how long that was, but decided it was a question for another time.

"Would Laverne know the reason behind all of this?" I asked, not really believing I had asked that question. Laverne was Lady Luck herself, one of the most powerful of all the gods. Patty and Screamer and I had saved her once, but that doesn't mean lowly superheroes like me and Patty and Screamer can bother her at every whim. But I was hoping that Stan might ask Burt, the God of Casino Operations; and if he didn't know, maybe Burt would ask Lady Luck.

"I don't know if she does or not," Stan said. "You meeting the rest of your team at The Diner?"

I nodded. "The Smoke is busy in Canada, but Screamer will be there."

"I'll see what I can do," Stan said. "I'll meet you at The Diner as soon as I get some information. You know, you two worry me sometimes, screwing with things you shouldn't screw with."

Both of us nodded at that. What could we say?

He vanished, letting us slip back into normal time as he did. Around us the movement and the noise filled the air again, slamming around us like a stream moving around rocks.

"Sorry to get you into this," Patty said, looking worried as we turned and headed for the parking garage.

"Any excuse to spend time with you is great by me."

She laughed. "Silly, you never need an excuse, you know that."

For a moment I actually forgot that we were going up against an Undertaker, Death himself, to try to save Death's daughter.

Three

FIFTEEN MINUTES LATER I told the problem to Screamer, a super-hero with the power to read other people's minds and transfer thoughts.

We were sitting at a large table in The Diner, a hole-in-the-wall little restaurant decorated with pretend 1960s stuff. It was on a side street downtown, and a woman named Madge was our normal wait-ress. She always wore her uniform three sizes too small, and it was a chore to not stare when she had to pick anything up.

If you *did* stare, you ended up having nightmares for a week about exploding humans. Or at least I always did.

We had started going to The Diner when the team first formed and we had to fight the Slots of Saturn. And for every mission since, we met here to talk and plan and drink the fantastic milkshakes.

Madge had just set down our milkshakes when Screamer said he was very worried about even thinking of going up against an Under-taker. "Superheroes can live a long time, but we do die. We can be killed."

That was a thought I didn't want to think about at all.

Suddenly the sounds from the street stopped, and Madge froze in mid-stride back toward the lunch counter in the back.

A moment later Laverne showed up with a thin man dressed only in a loud-colored bathing suit and a white towel. I had no idea who he was, but he wasn't looking happy.

Stan appeared a moment later, smiled a sheepish grin, and sat down without a word at a nearby table to watch the fireworks.

"You know, Laverne," the man said, "I could have gotten at least two more waves in before sunset."

"Sorry, Dan," Laverne said, shaking her head.

Dan's bathing suit changed to a dark, silk business suit with his tie perfectly in place and a blue shirt under it that seemed like it belonged on a surfer.

Then Laverne said, "But after the month is over, you're going to have a lot of time to surf all you want."

Dan smiled, and an image of a skeleton face sort of flashed over his face. "You got that right."

All three of us at the table had slid back away from the front edge where Laverne and Dan were pulling up chairs and talking. I had zero doubt I was about to meet the most feared Undertaker of them all, Mortuary Dan.

Dan sat down and then glanced at us, nodding. "I see, Laverne, that you have your top superhero team together here, minus one. What can I do to help?"

Laverne glanced at the milkshake in front of Patty.

Patty nodded that it was all right for Laverne to take a drink and slid it to Lady Luck. After a sip, Laverne smiled, then turned to Dan with a serious expression. "You need to talk to your daughter."

"Why?" Dan asked. "I'm going to see her in just under four hours."

Wow, this guy was cold, even for Death.

"She doesn't know what's going to happen," Laverne said.

"That's silly," Dan said, taking Screamer's untouched milkshake and sipping it. "Wow! These are darned fine milkshakes. I can see why you guys meet here."

I think I nodded, but damned if I was going to say anything.

"She doesn't know, Dan," Laverne said, again sipping on the milkshake. "All she knows are the rumors handed down over centuries. You know she's the first kid of any Undertaker since the Dark Ages."

Dan nodded and made a large dent in the milkshake. "Yeah, those were tough times. It's been easier since."

The four of us just sat and listened to the two major gods talk and drink our milkshakes. As superheroes, what else could we do?

"She thinks she's going to die," Laverne said.

"Technically, she is," Dan said, slurping the milkshake and somehow managing to not get any on his silk suit.

"She contacted Poker Boy and his team to try to figure out a way to stop it."

Dan set the milkshake glass down hard, then turned and looked me directly in the eye. His face seemed to flash back and forth between skin and skeleton, and it had to be the most frightening thing I had ever seen. "What do you say to her?"

I sputtered, then dug down and managed to apply some calming skills from my years playing poker and said, "We told her we would find out what was happening."

He looked at me for a moment, than shook his head. "You don't know either, do you?"

Laverne laughed. "Dan, remember how long it has been since any of you had a kid. None of the younger superheroes or gods know anything more than the tradition of Undertakers killing their children."

He looked at Laverne, then back at me and my team. "So you are telling me, Lisa doesn't know what's going to happen in a few hours?"

"She believes she's going to die, sir," I said. "She's terrified."

Dan slammed his fist on the table, rocking all the milkshake glasses.

If we hadn't been between time and frozen, that would have brought Madge running.

Dan's face went to complete skeleton, then he pushed his chair back and stood. "I knew I shouldn't have trusted her mother to raise her."

I desperately wanted to ask who Lisa's mother was, but smartly kept my mouth shut. When Death himself was pissed off, making him even angrier wasn't a good plan toward a long life.

Mortuary Dan paced for a moment, and even Laverne let him go, drinking the rest of Patty's milkshake with a slight smile on her face.

Finally Dan stopped and turned back to the table. "Anyone have any ideas what I should do?"

I didn't have a clue what the problem was, other than the legend that he had to kill his daughter in a few hours – and he didn't seem to be denying that at all.

I glanced at Patty. Her face was white and she was leaning back toward me. Screamer just seemed stunned.

Stan, in the other booth, had his God of Poker face on, and I couldn't even begin to get a read on what he was thinking or feeling.

"You need to talk to your daughter," Laverne said softly. "Before midnight. She needs to know and understand what's going to happen."

"Oh," Dan said, clearly disgusted as he started to pace again. "She's going to be so scared of me now, she won't listen. And she needs to know."

"Yes, she does," Laverne said, her voice softer and more compassionate than I had ever heard from Lady Luck.

I wanted to raise my hand like a kid in class and ask just what the adults in the room were talking about, but again my common sense got the best of me and I kept my mouth shut.

Dan kept pacing, clearly thinking, and after a moment Laverne looked over at me and Patty and Screamer. "I think Dan needs your help," she said.

Okay, at that moment you could have knocked me down with a slight breeze. Lady Luck just told us that Death needed our help.

Dan stopped and stared at the table, clearly as puzzled as I was, which made me feel only a slight bit better.

"Can you four," Laverne asked, nodding to us and Stan, "get Lisa and bring her here and help her father tell her what is going to happen tonight? She needs to be kept calm. Very calm."

Laverne just stared at me and Patty. After a moment we both nodded, starting to understand what we needed to do.

"And she needs to learn vast amounts of information from her father in a very short time." She glanced at Screamer who just turned white at the idea.

"I see where you are going, Laverne," Dan said, stepping back to the table and looking at me and my team. "Would you help me help my daughter through the transition?"

I couldn't take it any longer, I had to ask something, so I asked the most pressing question of the thousands I had spinning in my mind.

"What transition?"

"At midnight," Dan said, "Lisa will change from being a mere mortal to being an immortal god. An Undertaker. I'm retiring to surf in Hawaii. She's taking my spot, the first female Undertaker. I start her training at midnight tonight."

Four

IN MY FEW SHORT YEARS of being a superhero, I had never been so scared of an assignment. Somehow the three of us, with Stan's help, needed to link up a god, Death himself, and his daughter in an out-of-time link so that he could have the time to talk to her. And we needed to help her understand what was coming, and that it was all right that she was going to die.

Or sort of die, anyway.

If we screwed this up, none of us might live to see the end of the year.

If that long.

I had a hunch Mortuary Dan wouldn't think twice about just moving us on to the next place, wherever or whatever that was.

Stan gave me and Patty a lift to pick up Lisa.

When we appeared in her suite, she was still dressed in the same red, white, and blue outfit and was sitting on the couch. Clearly she had been sitting there since she arrived.

When she saw us, she jumped and rolled up over the back of the couch to get it between her and us.

I glanced at Patty. "She doesn't know anything at all about gods and superheroes, does she?"

"Not much I discovered," Patty said.

"How did you do that?" Lisa asked.

"I've been wondering the same thing," I said, glancing at Stan, who just shrugged. "We've got some good news for you," I continued, as Patty and I started working to calm her down with all the calming powers we had between us.

"You do?" she asked, clearly relaxing and even starting to smile, forgetting that we had just appeared out of nowhere in front of her.

"You're not going to die at midnight," I said, fibbing a little. She actually wasn't going to die. She just wasn't going to be mortal anymore.

A slight detail.

"But there's one condition," Patty said. "You need to talk to your dad. And your dad wants us there with you for support."

Lisa started shaking her head back and forth and I could feel the panic starting to gain intensity.

I dug deep and Patty and I joined hands and hit her with every calming power we had. And I have to say, that was considerable. We could have put a bull moose to sleep.

Lisa calmed some.

"It's only to talk," I said. "He needs to tell you where the rumor is coming from and why it exists. He said your mother should have taught you all of this."

"All she said was that my daddy is an Undertaker – the Grim Reaper."

"Well, he sort of is," I said. "And a pretty fine surfer, from what I gather."

"My father surfs?" Lisa asked, calming even more under the intense push of calming powers from me and Patty.

"Eleven months a year that's about all he does," Patty said, smiling.

Lisa finally stopped shaking her head and stared first at me, then at Stan. "Who exactly are you people?"

"I am known as Poker Boy. I am at the rank of superhero in the Gambling Gods universe, which basically means I do a lot of the chores the gods don't want to do."

She nodded, so I went on.

"This is Patty, also known as Front Desk Girl. She is a superhero working for the Gods of Hospitality."

I pointed at Stan. "This is my direct boss, Stan, the God of Poker.

It is our boss, Lady Luck, known as Laverne, who convinced your father that he needed to talk to you and help you understand this different world before anything could happen tonight."

"But I still might die tonight?" Lisa said, the panic starting to build again even against the onslaught of calming that Patty and I were directing toward her.

"Oh, trust me," I said, "at ten minutes after midnight tonight, you'll be talking to me just fine. And you could talk to me any time you wanted after that. I promise."

"As do I," Patty said, nodding. "You just need to have a conversation with your father first, to understand everything that's going on."

Lisa clearly calmed with our promise. Then she laughed. "My mom hated what my dad did for a living, and never wanted him to come around. And she said his world was full of nutcakes. If I believe who you say you are, I guess she was right."

"Oh, trust me," I said, "as a person fairly new to this world as well, it's crazier than you can even imagine."

Lisa smiled and took a deep breath. "All right, let's go see my father."

A moment later the four of us were standing in The Diner.

Both Dan and Laverne were halfway through two more milkshakes, sitting in the booth with Screamer sitting in the middle looking slightly panicked. Madge was moving around, shaking her head as she sometimes did when she had to wait on us.

Mortuary Dan stood, his human face staying firmly in place, and stepped toward his daughter. "Hi, Lisa. It's wonderful to see you again. You've become a beautiful woman."

Lisa smiled and stepped into the hug of Death. "Hi, Daddy."

Five

WE LET LISA AND HER FATHER TALK.

After a few minutes, Dan turned to all of us, with Madge standing right there beside the table. "We need to start all this. Lisa has a lot to learn about her old man. Madge, would you put up the closed sign and keep those milkshakes coming for all of us? To do this right, we're going to need the energy."

Madge nodded. "I'll be glad to, Dan. Lisa, what kind do you like?"

"Chocolate," Lisa said.

"You got it, dear," Madge said, turning to close the front door as Patty and Screamer and I stared.

"Madge is a superhero in Food and Beverage," Laverne said, clearly trying not to laugh. "I thought you all knew that."

I shook my head and glanced around at Stan, who just smiled and shrugged. He had known, just hadn't bothered to tell any of the rest of us.

Laverne took one more long drink from her milkshake, then stood. "I'll be back a little later."

She vanished leaving us all alone with Mortuary Dan and his daughter.

Dan pointed to the spot where Screamer sat in the back of the booth. "Poker Boy, you and Patty sit back there. Lisa, you sit on one side of the booth, I'll sit facing you so we can talk directly, and Screamer, you sit on a chair at the head of the booth so you can touch both of us."

Dan glanced over at Stan. "Keep us out of time for about forty-five minutes the first time. We'll adjust from there. And help everyone with energy when needed."

Stan nodded.

I thought my heart was going to pound out of my chest. In the back of the restaurant Madge had the milkshake blenders going full speed, filling the restaurant with the whining sound. It didn't begin to cover the sound of my heart.

I could feel Lisa suddenly starting to get upset again, so Patty and I both sent calming powers at her as we slid into position, our legs touching for extra support.

I don't know how we could calm anyone down, as worried as we were ourselves, but for some reason our calming powers weren't hooked to how we were feeling. Luckily.

"What's going to happen?" Lisa asked, clearly afraid to take her position in the booth.

"Screamer here is going to hook our thoughts up so I can help you learn faster all the things your mother didn't teach you over the last twenty-plus years. And that way you can get to know me, the real me."

"You can do that?" Lisa asked, staring at Screamer.

"I can," he said, turning to face where she stood. "It's my power. You can trust me, it will be painless. Odd and a little confusing at times, but painless, I promise you. It will be exactly as your dad said, and the connection will help you learn very quickly what is a rumor and what is the truth."

"And I will be very careful to ease you into all of this," Dan said.

I was very glad he said that. I couldn't imagine suddenly knowing all at once all the things I had learned in my short five years being a superhero. But Lisa had no choice. She had to learn a lot and very quickly. There was only three hours to go until midnight.

"Ready, daughter?" Dan asked, smiling, and not showing his skeleton face at all.

Patty and I hit her with as much calming as we dared, and Lisa nodded. Then she slowly slid into position beside me in the booth.

I scooted closer to Patty to make sure I wasn't touching Lisa. Last thing I wanted to do was be included in the conversation they would have in their heads while Screamer held them together. But if I touched her, I would be automatically included, just as if Patty touched Dan on the other side.

The booth suddenly felt very, very small.

"I guess so," Lisa said.

Dan glanced at us and nodded, then nodded to Screamer.

Patty and I ramped up every bit of calming we could as Stan dropped us between time, killing all the sound in the restaurant and from the streets.

Screamer touched Lisa, then laid a hand gently on Mortuary Dan's arm.

For a moment, I thought we were going to have to calm Screamer down as well; but then he nodded and sat back and closed his eyes.

Lisa's eyes got huge and she was fidgeting some. I motioned for Stan to help, and he boosted both Patty's and my calming power.

Lisa calmed slightly. I was stunned she wasn't so calm she was asleep. The woman had a very, very powerful mind. No wonder Laverne wanted us all to help Dan with this.

And why Dan wanted the help. He and Laverne both knew how powerful the child of a god would be to deal with.

Screamer kept his eyes closed, and Dan and Lisa just stared at each other. I slowly motioned for Stan to back off and he did, then Patty and I pulled back slightly, only increasing when we could sense Lisa getting upset.

Forty-five minutes later in out-of-time time, Stan said, "Break."

Screamer pulled his hands away and Stan dropped the room back into real time. The sounds of Madge working on the milkshakes hit all of us hard.

Patty and I kept our concentration firmly on Lisa, who seemed to close her eyes, then open them and look at her father again as if she was seeing him for the first time.

No one said a word.

Then Lisa said, "So I'm not going to die, I'm going to become immortal at midnight."

Dan nodded. "For all intents and purposes, yes."

Lisa nodded, then said, "I have to use the restroom."

"I'll go with you," Patty said.

And wow was I glad she said that, since I had no idea how I was going to make it through more hours without visiting the restroom myself.

"I'll be right back," Dan said and vanished.

Stan also vanished.

"You all right?" I asked Screamer. I had no idea what it would be like inside of Death's mind, and I was very glad I didn't have to find out.

"I'm fine, actually. Dan is keeping me and Lisa blocked from most of his mind, just showing Lisa what she needs to see to get started. But this isn't going to be a short process."

"That slow?" I asked.

He nodded. Then he and I both headed for the rest rooms in the back, meeting Madge with a tray full of shakes.

"Don't tell me you all are leaving again?" she asked.

"Just a break," I said. "But I have a hunch that by the time this is over, you're going to wish we had left."

"Anything going on with both Laverne and Mortuary Dan, I suppose you might be right."

She went to put our milkshakes on the table as I just kept on, shaking my head at all the surprises I was getting on a simple Saturday night.

Six

IT TOOK NINE HOURS of actual lesson time spread over six

different sessions in just over three hours of real time before Lisa finally seemed to know what she was getting into and was ready.

It was five minutes until midnight.

Patty and I had stopped helping keep Lisa calm about three lessons back. Stan had asked me on the last break to help him keep up the out-of-time shield, since he was getting tired and Screamer needed some help with energy as well from him.

So for most of the last hour of lesson time, with Stan spelling me every ten minutes, I held up the shield that kept us out of real time.

As we dropped back into real time and Screamer moved away from the two he had kept connected for almost nine hours, everyone climbed out of the booth. I felt as if I had sat in that booth for most of my life.

Laverne appeared, smiling. She and Dan moved off to one side for a moment as Patty and I stayed with Lisa.

"Amazing stuff I was born into," Lisa said. "I wish someone had told me about this last year so I wouldn't have been so worried for so long, but thanks to all of you, this didn't catch me by surprise now."

"Good," Patty said. "Knowledge is far, far more powerful than rumors."

"But only slightly less scary," Lisa said.

Suddenly, around the restaurant, other people began to pop in, almost none of them anyone I knew, until the place was very crowded with only an open circle in the middle of the floor where a table used to be.

Stan stepped over beside us and whispered. "The other eleven Undertakers have arrived, plus a number of top gods from all the deities. This is a real event."

Stan and Screamer and Patty and I sort of moved back against the edge of the booth to allow the really powerful to take their places around the center.

"Are you ready to join me, daughter?" Dan asked, stepping into the circle in the center of the crowd.

Lisa smiled at us, then turned and stepped forward. "I am."

"Thirty seconds," Laverne said.

Dan indicated that Lisa should kneel in front of him and she did.

"Thank you all for joining this special occasion," Dan said, his face now a complete skeleton, even though his hands and business suit looked perfectly pressed and in order. "We are here to welcome to our ranks the first new Undertaker in centuries. And the first woman to ever hold that position."

"Five seconds," Laverne said.

Dan reached out both hands and placed them over Lisa's head. Then as the clock ticked midnight, Lisa seemed to slump slightly, then something bright and shining and very yellow filled the air around her.

After a moment the yellow light all went inside of her, like she was a giant sponge soaking up water.

After a long pause, she opened her eyes and smiled.

Everyone cheered.

I didn't know what to think. I didn't think I could feel so relieved in all my life.

"May I introduce you to the newest god?" Dan said, extending an arm to his daughter to help her off her knees. "My daughter Lisa. An Undertaker."

The entire room cheered, then calmed as Lisa looked around, smiling, nodding at many people she now clearly knew somehow.

Then she looked at us and said simply, "Thank you, Poker Boy, Screamer, Stan, and Patty. And most of all Laverne, who loaned my father such a wonderful team to help me through this transition. I will be forever grateful to you all."

Everyone cheered.

And I did as well, and just kept smiling.

Somehow we had managed to save yet another person. And that always felt great.

But it felt even better to have Death herself grateful to you.

It just didn't get any better than that.

GUS

Imagine the past masters of the game of golf getting a chance to play the top players of the 1980s.

Imagine a ghost golfer gag getting a little out of hand.

There's all that and more in this crazy story. This is the first publication of "Gus" anywhere.

July 17ᵗʰ, 1986

Dear Bill,

Thought I'd better write you real quick like and tell you what's going on. Since it was your crazy idea that started this mess, I figure you just might have a way to get rid of Gus.

You remember Gus, don't you? That was the name you suggested. You know, the idea for the invisible golfer?

Gus?

I'm sure you remember. It was in your Christmas letter. You said, Wouldn't it be funny if someone got one of those new remote controlled golf carts (not the ride-in kind, but one like a pull cart, only with a quiet little motor and a remote control switch) and hooked up a tape player in an empty bag with all the sounds of a golfer pulling a club out of the bag, hitting a ball, and putting the club back in the bag?

Then, from a hidden spot, someone could drive the empty bag and cart up near some unsuspecting golfer, stop the bag and start the tape. After the imaginary shot was hit and the imaginary club put away, the bag would head up the fairway as if pulled by an invisible golfer chasing an invisible ball.

That's exactly what you said because I went back and got your Christmas card.

"Funny as hell," you also said.

Well, like a damn fool, I agreed with you. I've got to stop doing that. Every time I've gone along with one of your crazy ideas, it's gotten me in trouble.

Remember that belly dancer? I'm still sending her checks.

Anyway, stupid old me followed your instructions and rigged up one of those remote controlled carts with a tape player in the bag. It took me a good month to learn how to steer the thing so that I wouldn't run it into trees. Did all my practicing in the back yard so no one would know about it over at the course. I'd stand up in the kitchen window and steer it around and around the back yard. Even chased my dog with it once. Scared hell out of the poor thing.

Alice thought I had flipped totally until I told her it was your idea. Then she just shook her head.

Mostly she wasn't real happy with me spending that much money. Just the empty bag alone cost sixty bucks. She's on one of those kicks lately about saving every penny for retirement. She scares me with that kind of talk. Hell, I'm only forty. I got a few good years left in me, don't I? Besides, I'm still technically recovering from "the accident." You spend all your accident money, yet?

Anyhow, it was two Saturdays ago that I finally had enough courage, matched with good weather, to give the cart its first run on the course. I picked hole number fifteen.

You know, the par five that runs along the edge of the river. I figured I could hide down in the trees alongside the fairway and steer Gus from there. My intended first victim was Carl Stevens, a new member at the club, just down from Boston.

I think I introduced you to Carl last time you were here. Tall guy, skinny, bald, always wears yellow. He usually gets a real early start and plays alone. I figured he'd be out on fifteen by about eight-thirty. So I was there at eight.

I hid the cart over behind the pump house and got down in the trees where I could see the tee. Old Carl came off fourteen green ten minutes later, walking fast, head down, not looking real happy.

Just as he reached the tee, I sent the cart in motion, bringing it around from behind the pump house and up toward the tee box. Carl didn't even see it coming until it was almost up to the tee.

I guess I didn't tell you. I added one little feature to your idea. Instead of just having the sounds of the clubs, I added a few lines of talking.

You were right about one thing. The entire gag was damn funny.

The look on Carl's face when that empty cart pulled up and stopped beside the tee box was almost more than I could stand. I bit my lip to keep from laughing and started the tape. I had used my own voice on the tape and talked through a tennis ball can to disguise it.

Sounded really strange.

Almost spooky.

"Excuse me," my tennis can voice said, "Would you mind if I play through?"

At that point I had recorded the very clear sound of clubs rattling and then one club being withdrawn.

"Nice weather, huh?"

I could see Carl's head nodding in stunned agreement with the voice on the tape. He just stood there and listened to the sound of a ball being hit. He even glanced down the fairway to see if he could see the ball. I damn near fell over laughing, let me tell you.

"Damn slice," the tape said, followed by the sound of a club being put back in the bag. I started the cart just as the tape said, "Thanks again."

I steered the cart down the fairway to the right and then off into the trees like the owner of the thing was looking for a sliced ball.

Poor Carl. He looked almost white, standing there.

Finally, after I had the cart and bag out of sight, he teed up his ball and topped it down the fairway. I waited until he was completely out of sight around the dogleg before I moved the cart from where I had steered it behind the maintenance shed.

As fast as I could, I got the cart back in my car and headed up toward the clubhouse. I wanted to be there when Carl came in and had his usual breakfast in the coffee shop.

I've got to hand you one thing. At that point, I was laughing. In fact, I didn't know if I was going to be able to keep a straight face around Carl.

I got myself a stool at the lunch counter just as Carl came in from the back nine. He dropped down into a chair at an empty table and just sat there shaking his head. Besides Carl and me, there were only about a dozen other men in the coffee shop.

Perfect for part two of my plan.

"What's the matter," Doris asked Carl as she slid a glass of water in front of him. "Bad morning?" Doris is the normal Saturday waitress in the coffee shop. All the guys like her, even though she talks too much and doesn't know a thing about golf.

Carl shook his head no. "Just saw the damndest thing," he said, almost to himself. "Out on fifteen."

"Oh oh," I said loud enough for Carl to hear, "Gus is back."

"What?" Carl said, looking over at me.

"Oh, nothing," I said, waving off his question as if it didn't matter. "What'd you see?"

I swung around on my stool to face him.

At this point five or six of the other men were listening, but Carl was now talking to both me and Doris.

"This pull cart with an empty bag on it came up on the tee and —" He shook his head. "No, this sounds so stupid, I can't even tell anyone."

"And this voice asks to play through," I said, acting real serious.

"Yeah," Carl said, nodding his head like a toy in the back window of a car. "That's exactly right. How'd you know?"

"That's Gus, the course ghost. You fellows remember hearing about Gus, don't you?"

I turned to the table of three Saturday morning regulars. I had learned a long time ago that if you directly ask a group of men a question that puts them on the spot and has a yes or no answer, they will usually nod their head in a vague yes.

I suppose it's just easier than looking stupid in front of their friends by not knowing some obvious sounding piece of information. This time, two of them nodded while the other just looked at me blankly.

I turned back to Carl. "You just had a run in with the course ghost, that's all. I'll even bet he sliced his shot into the right trees. Right?"

"How'd you know?" Carl's face was again white.

"He's been hitting that same shot for eighty years," I said. "Ever since the course was built. I've seen him twice. Lucky for you he didn't ask you to play along."

"No, he just asked to play through," Carl said.

"Lucky for you, right guys?"

This time five men in the room nodded, and one even said I sure was right.

"Why?" Carl asked.

"Well, the last time Gus was around a lot was back in the middle thirties. Almost exactly fifty years ago, now that I think about it, since this is nineteen-eighty-three. The stories go that he usually just did what you saw this morning. But one Saturday, he asked to join this twosome. They both knew about Gus and the story goes that they said yes just for the hell of it."

Carl nodded so I went on.

"The three of them played off down the fairway and no one has ever seen those two men since. Of course, there have been lots of reports of people sighting them playing early in the morning when the dew is still fresh on the greens. In fact, you know when you're out there real early and there's footprints already in the dew around the flag?"

"Yeah," Carl said. "Happens all the time, but I never see who's ahead of me."

"Take a guess," I said and took a long sip of the coffee Doris had brought me. I didn't want to tell him those footprints were really made by the green's keeper changing the pins every morning. What he didn't know wouldn't hurt him.

"Oh," was all he said.

"You think maybe this means Gus is coming back?" one of the other men asked.

I shrugged, fighting like hell to keep a completely serious face. "Maybe. All I know is that I'm certainly not going to get near that empty bag if I see it."

I tossed Doris some money for the coffee and headed out the door before I exploded trying to contain myself.

And the rest of the week I just kept laughing. Gus was the talk of the club. Most of the members didn't really buy into the tall tale. But people talked about it. Carl even got invited to join a regular group on Saturday mornings so he wouldn't have to play out there alone.

For me, I couldn't leave well enough alone.

The following Saturday, I got down to the course real early, had Gus hidden behind the pump house, and me down in the trees way before anyone was around.

Forty minutes later, Steven Forbes and Franklin Jones came off fourteen green and headed for fifteen tee. You haven't met them. They work for a law office downtown and play golf a few times a week. I had heard them laughing about Gus Wednesday afternoon in the bar. I also had heard Thomas Sullivan, a regular member, warn them to stay away from the ghost cart if they saw it. Just in case.

Well, Bill, your idea worked twice. I ran the cart up beside them just as Franklin was teeing up his ball. Startled him so much that he stepped back and tripped over the tee marker.

I ran through the entire tape and had the cart headed down the fairway before either of them even thought to move. Damn that was funny. My side hurt from laughing without making a sound.

Again, I hid the cart over behind the old maintenance shed. That's where I think I made my mistake. You see, I left the cart there while I went up to the clubhouse to listen to the fun. And when I went back down an hour later to get it, there were just too many people around to get it over to the road and into my car without being seen.

So I had to come up with something fast or blow the entire gag. I don't know if you noticed the old white house sitting off to the side of sixteen, way back in the trees. It's been abandoned for years and there was talk at one time among the men's association about turning it into a club, but nothing has ever been done.

I decided to hide Gus there until there were fewer people on the course. I put him down in the fruit cellar of the house and tossed some old newspapers over the bag. No one had been down there in years. A great hiding place. In fact, at the time, I was really happy I found the spot. Beat hell out of lifting it in and out of the trunk of my car.

Monday I was sitting in the coffee shop, after playing with my usual group, when Hector, the assistant pro, came in. He'd been about three groups behind us. He started in about how he and three guys had just seen Gus. Only this time Gus was playing sixteen and had hooked the ball.

Let me tell you, I scrambled out of there and down to the old house faster than I had moved in years. I sure didn't like the thought of just anyone messing around with Gus. I planned on using him for my own golf cart when the joke was done.

Well, you guessed it.

Gus was gone.

I searched everywhere, but couldn't find a clue as to who took him. I even walked the golf course and sat out beside fifteen for a few hours in hopes that whoever had taken him would strike again.

I looked all day Tuesday, too.

Nothing.

Wednesday (yesterday) Gus found me.

Gus and his friend, Horton, that is.

This is where I'm hoping you might have an idea or two. You see, normally on Wednesdays I have my match with the "Cold Crew." That's what we call those of us who play golf most of our lives instead of working like our wives think we should.

I was playing with old Doc Rule, Howard Erickson, and Scott Golden. We were out on twelve, the short par three, when Gus and this other empty bag come up onto the tee box. Let me tell you, I was one scared fellow right at that moment. And trust me, I wouldn't have believed it if I hadn't seen it myself.

Why?

Because the other empty bag was a carry bag. And some invisible person or thing was carrying it about three feet off the ground and the shoulder strap was full of something that I could see the trees through.

Gus excused himself and asked very nicely if they could play through.

Bill, it wasn't my tennis can voice that asked. No sir. It was just as spooky as my made up voice, but it wasn't mine. And it didn't come from the bag.

At that point the empty carry bag dropped to the ground with the sounds of clubs rattling.

After a moment there was a sound of a golf ball being hit.

"Nice shot, Horton," a voice said from the area of Gus.

"Thanks, Gus," a slightly higher voice said from the tee box.

You could have knocked me down with the old proverbial feather.

All four of us just stood and watched, or listened would be a better way of putting it, as Gus hit his shot and then the two bags headed up toward the green.

Just before they reached the green, though, both bags just sort of faded away.

Now I'm not kidding.

Remember, twelve is a short par three. Those two bags vanished not more than eighty yards in front of me, right out in plain sight in the middle of the fairway.

One moment they were there, the next, bingo, they were gone.

Well, we waited an extra long time just to make sure they were off the green, then tried to finish our round. Ruined the day, though.

And back in the clubhouse, I learned that we weren't the only ones to see Gus and Horton. They had played through three other groups as well.

Bill, any idea as to just what the hell is going on?

Or any ideas as to what I might do to get rid of Gus and Horton and maybe even get my cart back? You know more about this stuff than I do. I've really gone and gotten the club and myself into a mess, this time.

People are getting scared and if word of this gets out, it will close down the course. If that happened, there would be no way I could talk Alice into letting me buy another membership.

Please send any ideas you might have as soon as possible. Hope you are well.

Say hello to that beautiful wife of yours for me.

Desperately,
Fred

Dear Fred,

I looked up the name Horton in one of my golf reference books and it just so happened there was a great golfer back in the early part of the century named Horton. Horton Smith, to be exact.

Track Gus and his Horton friend down and find out if it really is the same Horton. If it is, I've got an idea or two that just might work.

In response to your question, my "accident" money is holding out just fine. But in about five years we might have to try that again.

What do you say?

Say hi to Alice for me.

Keep it hooking,
  Bill

Dear Bill,

Are you kidding? Just how the hell am I supposed to find out the last name of a ghost?

The situation is getting worse. Gus and Horton were seen three times yesterday. And this morning I heard that they played through a group of women, and on women's day, to boot. And there was a third bag with them. They called that bag "Harry."

Hoping for help,
  Fred

p.s. Repeating the "accident" might just get some folks a little suspicious, don't you think?

Dear Fred,

Simply walk up to the ghosts and ask them.

And while you're at it, ask Harry if his last name is Vardon.

And if it is, see if you can get me some lessons.

Slicing is part of life,
  Bill

Dear Bill,

Damn it, I'm serious. This is a real mess down here.

Now a forth golfing ghost has joined the group. At this rate, they're going to be holding tournaments. So be serious, would you?

I need help.

I figured that it wouldn't hurt to try your suggestion about finding out their names, since they do seem to talk a lot between themselves and they do ask everyone very politely if they can play through, even though no one has ever seen them finish a complete hole.

I told Hector, the assistant pro, your idea about talking to the ghosts, but I didn't mention the names. He thought it might work and agreed to play a few rounds with me to see if we could spot the invisible foursome.

They found us on the seventh tee. Gus, plus three carry bags, all floating three feet in the air as if slung over invisible shoulders.

"Mind if we play through?" a voice said from the direction of Gus.

"Not at all," I stammered out after a moment of shock.

And let me tell you, seeing those four empty bags and hearing the normal sounds of four golfers on a tee box, is a shocking thing.

"Wondering if you'd answer a question or two?" I said after a moment of swallowing hard to get the courage.

"Sure thing," Gus said. "Harry, you're up."

"Is that the Harry Vardon?" I asked.

"Sure is," a voice laughed from between the tee markers.

"Harry's reputation always did beat him to a course," another voice said from near one of the carry bags laying on the ground.

I waited for the laughter from the four invisible men to subside slightly before I asked my next question.

"Is Horton Smith also here?"

"Sure am," a high voice said.

"Who's your fourth?" I asked.

"Well, you know me," the voice said from beside my trick pull cart. "So I guess you must mean Bobby."

"Bobby?" I asked.

"Not Bobby Jones?" Hector blurted out.

"That's right, son," another voice said. "Now can we stop all this gabbing and let Harry get on with his shot. We don't have all day, you know."

Hector and I stood there in silence and listened to the sounds of four men laughing and hitting shots.

"Thanks again," the voice said from beside my trick cart after they had all hit. And with that, all four bags started off the tee box and down the fairway. They vanished about a hundred yards off the tee.

They had played through three other groups that we know of by the time we got into the clubhouse.

Bill, the course just can't take much more of this. People are afraid of going out to play. Men's league has been canceled this week. And sooner or later, someone at some newspaper is going to start believing all this and then where will we be? I'll be without any place to play, that's where. And that means staying home with Alice all day and you know how I'd feel about that.

I don't see how knowing they are the ghosts of three great golfers does any damn good at all. We sure can't stand around and watch them. But send any ideas you might have. It was your idea that started all this mess.

Besides, no one here can seem to come up with anything other than shooting at the bags. And so far, calmer heads have held those trigger happy fools off. Luckily, very few really staunch Catholics have seen the foursome so far. Otherwise, we'd have priests doing exorcisms on the putting green.

Damn. Why do I ever listen to your fool ideas?

Although, I must admit, the accident idea worked out real well.

Waiting impatiently,
Fred

TELEGRAM

Fred STOP Tournament brilliant idea STOP Will solve your problem and make us rich STOP Flying in tomorrow at ten STOP Please pick me up STOP Bill

Article from the local Monday newspaper.

MODERNS WIN BIG IN MATCH OF THE CENTURY

For years, golf historians have asked the question, "Who was better? The great players from the past or today's superstars?"

Yesterday, in one of the most bizarre golf matches ever played, that question might or might not have been answered by the resounding victory of Nickalas, Travino, and Palmer over the supposed ghosts of Bobby Jones, Harry Vardon, and Horton Smith in the controversial tournament billed as "The Match of the Century."

"Thrilled," Nickalas said, when asked how he felt after the match. "How else could I feel?"

Travino and Palmer seemed equally excited to be taking part.

When asked if he thought the entire match was serious, Travino replied, "Would I be here if I didn't?"

But to many, the question of the day was, "Is this all a giant hoax?" Three of today's great players didn't act like it was. All three dropped commitments to the Greater Sunshine Open and put on an exhibition of golf at its finest.

Consequently, "The Match of the Century" between the modern day greats and history's finest was never even close.

Travino led the elite field with a superb eight under 64. Nickalas followed with a brilliant 66 and Palmer with a 69. Harry Vardon led the "Ghost Team" with a 72, followed by Smith with a 74 and Jones with a 75.

When asked by reporters near the last hole why they were having troubles, Harry Vardon answered, "The courses are tougher today. I haven't been back long enough to get the feel of them. Back in my day," he said, "the greens were like postage stamps and hard as rocks. Different kind of golf."

Horton Smith, said to be the best putter ever in the game, had trouble even getting to the greens. "The holes are a lot longer. And there's a bunch more sand," he said. "Makes it more interesting, that's for sure."

Horton Smith found sand traps an even dozen times in the eighteen-hole match.

The match, the brainchild of Fred Henning and Bill Addison, was set up on the Shadow Acres Country Club after the sudden unexplained appearance of the three golfing greats. Or, more accurately put, the appearance of their bags and voices.

Hundreds of unanswered questions surround yesterday's match, such as why the bags appeared, but not the clubs or the men. Or how could the ghosts hit visible new balls with invisible old clubs? When asked just exactly what they were playing for, and why, all six contestants stuck to "No Comment."

And all six just laughed when asked if this would become an annual event.

However, they had no trouble talking about everything else, so the gallery and the viewers at home were treated to an eighteen-hole history lesson on the early days of golf.

It seems that most of the questions will never be answered. It doesn't seem to matter. "The Match of the Century" now joins the three ghosts as part of history.

But one thing is for certain, regardless of whether you believe in ghosts or think somehow the entire day was a setup, "The Match of the Century" at Shadow Acres Country Club was a day the game of golf will not soon forget.

Dear Bill,

Thought you might be interested in the enclosed article. It came out in the morning paper the day you left. Didn't know if you saw it or not, as busy as you were.

You know, over the last few weeks I've been thinking a lot about what happened. And the more I think about it, the more amazed I become. The best way to describe what we pulled off was a miracle.

No, a serious of miracles.

For example, in all the craziness those three weeks before the match, I never did ask you just how you got Lee Travino to fly in and meet the ghostly foursome.

But somehow you did. Amazing.

And the way you talked the club into putting up perpetual memberships and complete playing right-of-way as prizes for the ghosts is beyond me. Who else but you would realize that the one thing the ghosts would enjoy more than anything was never having to ask to go through another group again.

And then talking the ghosts of three of the top players in history into wagering that prize versus finding a new place to play in a match against the three best players of modern times.

Brilliant.

Nothing short.

But we forgot one thing. Gus. He was seen yesterday down on sixteen again. He's still got my bag and cart and now he seems to not be real happy. He even yelled at one woman to get the hell out of his way so he could play a decent round of golf.

Did you talk to him while you were here? I sure didn't. Hell, I still don't know who he is. Or was. I'm going to go down and try to talk to him. But I don't know exactly how that's going to work.

Any ideas this time?

Let me know if the movie deal goes. Always can use more money. Alice is happy about what we got from television rights and stuff, but she's still clamping down hard on every penny. I suppose someday I will thank her for that.

Someday.

At least the match keeps us from thinking about another accident for a few more years.

Your friend in the money,

Fred

Dear Fred,

Just got back and opened your letter. The movie deal looks like it's a for sure. We'll make another bundle on that when it happens. And there's talk about a book. Not bad, huh?

Sorry I didn't tell you about Gus. I feel sort of bad about this, since I forgot all about Gus. There were just so many details that had to be looked after. Sorry.

I did get a quick chance right at the beginning to talk to Gus. Remember that first day after I arrived when we walked down seventeen fairway with them. You were talking to Horton about the match and I was talking to Gus. I found out his real name was Lawrence Meadows. He used to own the old white house down off sixteen that you stored the cart and bag in. In fact, his body is buried in the fruit cellar.

And he was the one who brought back Smith, Jones, and Vardon. He said he just wanted someone to play a few rounds with.

I did promise him a few things, but now I think it might be too late. You had better get down there and talk to him if you can.

Again, sorry I forgot.

Happy digging,
Bill

Dear Bill,

Not damn funny.

Not by a long sight.

Me and the sheriff found the skeleton in the mud and clay in the old fruit cellar. Right exactly where you said it would be.

I told the sheriff you told me where the body was, and he now wants to know if you would please tell him exactly who killed the poor guy and buried him there sixty years ago. There was a bullet hole in the skull.

Leaving that fun little "chore" up to me would have made me real mad at you if not for the fact that in the same mail as your letter I got a very, very large check.

Alice likes you more every day.

Maybe next week she might even let me phone you instead of write.

However, I still got Gus, or whatever his name is, to contend with. The members are not real happy he's still around and some of them are starting to blame me. I finally caught up with him down on number three yesterday and he said I was supposed to play with him and had gone back on my side of the deal.

Just what the hell is he talking about? I'm not going to go around playing golf with any damn ghost. No way. Even if the entire PGA tour does it.

And if you told him I would, you get your ass down here right now and play with him yourself.

Waiting with muddy shoes,
Fred

Dear Fred,

Glad you found the body.

Gus, or I guess his name was Lawrence, never told me he had been killed. But you could always ask him who done it next time you play with him. You see, that really was the deal.

Sorry I forgot to ask you, but you're supposed to play golf with Gus every Monday morning or he's going to bring a bunch more golfers back. He said he'd just stick his invisible old clubs in your bag so no one has to know he's there.

I feel really bad about mentioning this before, but you know how busy it was. Besides, what could be wrong with playing golf with Gus? He told me he was a pretty good player in his day. He just might give you a run for your money.

Just be careful with what you bet.

Money from the movie deal should be heading your way this next week.

Have fun,
    Bill

Dear Bill,

Go to hell.

There's no damn way I'm going to play golf every Monday with a ghost. You better think of something fast. If I get booted out of this club because of you, I just might think about telling a few certain people about your little "vacation" last year.

You remember the one, don't you?

Think quick,
    Fred

Dear Fred,

I don't understand why you are so upset. You play golf all the time, anyway. I sure didn't think anything would be wrong with playing just one round a week with Gus.

Give it a try. You might like it.

And it certainly will solve your problem with the club.

By the way, I got the money for the movie deal. Your half is enclosed. Now, wasn't that worth it?

Wishing you luck,
Bill

Dear Bill,

Boy was I mad when I sent you that last letter.

Wow.

In fact, I was so mad, I came up with an idea all my own.

I went marching down to the club and spent the entire afternoon looking for Gus. Finally spotted him on ten tee, getting ready to go out on the back nine. I told him my idea and he liked it. So now I have played twice with Gus.

And you know what, you were right. Gus is a pretty good golfer.

Today I got your letter and the check. Made Alice real happy. We even went out for dinner tonight. I don't know if my heart can take many more shocks like that one.

She even suggested it. Thanks.

That much money means we don't ever have to think about another accident. I like that.

I still haven't been able to talk Gus into telling me who killed him. He said it just doesn't matter anymore. It was a long time ago. For some reason, the sheriff still thinks it matters. He's going to send someone to talk to you next week.

You know, that money you sent calmed me down some. I'm not anywhere near as mad at you as I was.

And that brings up a problem I suppose I should tell you about. Maybe you, since you got me into this mess, can help me with it. You see, I think Gus cheats.

That's right, I think a ghost cheats at golf.

Think about it. With an invisible ball, it's damn hard to tell exactly what his score is on any given hole. I'm not always close enough to hear every shot. And who the hell knows if he's improving his lies. He might even be kicking the ball. I tried to get him to use some of my balls, like you had them do for the match, but he says he doesn't want to take the chance anyone will see them and discover he's still around. He says that's part of the deal I made with him.

He's right.

It is part of the deal. And it's got the Country Club off my back. You see, for me to play with him, I figured it had to be worth my while.

So I made him a little side bet. You know, just like all golfers do. Just like you had them do in the Match.

What are we playing for? Good question. Remember now, I was really mad at you when I made this deal.

I feel bad about this, especially after all the money you made us. But after all, you did tell Gus I would play with him without asking me first. So I feel bad, but not too bad.

If I win, it's simple. Gus tells me where some buried treasure is. He says there's lots of it around the area. In fact, he hinted he even knew where the Lost Dutchman Mine is. He said ghosts just know those sorts of things.

What am I giving him if he wins? He made me promise I wouldn't tell you. Just trust me that it is very important to you that I win.

Very, very important.

Remember, I was really mad at you when I came up with this idea. And I'm sure I would win, too.

If Gus wouldn't cheat.

You'd better think fast.

Losing, but smiling, your friend,
    Fred

THE LAST BURP OF A VERY GOOD WOMAN

Mary did her best in her small restaurant to keep everything just perfect. She swept and cleaned constantly and didn't much like crude behavior near her.

And everyone knew of her bad stomach.

But now even a handful of Tums couldn't help Mary do what she needed to do to move forward.

MARY, THE OWNER and only cook at Mary's Cafe on the old highway, was a prude, plain and simple. No one in Idaho City, the closest town to the north, would ever think of swearing or saying anything crude at all in Mary's. No one who actually knew Mary was sure just how often she cleaned the place, but bets were that it was at least three times a day. She always wore a plaid dress, proper shoes, and a towel tucked into her white apron. Mary seemed to constantly be wiping her hands on that towel.

People in the valley liked Mary's place, and liked Mary, but in the backwoods Idaho valley there just weren't that many people. Not anywhere near enough to support a restaurant. Yet somehow Mary kept open Mary's Cafe, selling a sandwich or soup to the occasional tourist who stopped there thinking that the pristine little place with wooden booths, table cloths, and the ancient cash register were all just part of some "local mountain charm."

When I first met Mary, more than fifteen years ago now, she was a thin woman, with clear blue eyes, a wide, welcoming grin, and a temper that flared into a frown and nothing more. Normally her skin was pale, accentuated by the bright colors of the plaid dresses she always wore. But when she got angry a bright red flush took over her face and made her skin splotchy, like she had some bad sickness.

I was about Mary's age, pushing the wrong side of sixty like it was a heavy wheelbarrow too full of my life to move. Why I thought of her as a friend I'll never know, but I did, and she sometimes beamed a little when she saw me. My wife had died eight years ago of the cancer, and her husband was long gone and she never mentioned him. Just like me she had had no children, and considering what a prude she was, that didn't surprise me.

Up here in the Idaho wilds, where the snow was six foot deep in the winter and the dust three inches thick in the summer, we sort of leaned on each other. And to be honest, I liked that. And I liked her.

The last day of July started out just like any other day, with the highway running logging trucks off the Sand Creek section down to the mill below Idaho City. All of the drivers knew Mary, knew Mary's place, but just never had the time or the thought of stopping. Those big trucks, even loaded, roared by at upwards of forty, leaving large clouds of dust to cover everything in the narrow valley behind them. After a few weeks of no rain and dust from the trucks going and coming, everything around Mary's place looked gray.

Even when I went through the front door and banged it closed, I sent a thin cloud of dust into the air.

Mary during the summer was always in a constant battle with the dust, and since the logging started, this summer was even worse. Since there were no cars in the gravel parking area, I expected her to be madly dusting some part of the restaurant.

But when I went in Mary was sitting at the counter, her head down, like it was too heavy for her neck to hold up right. I moved up beside her and sat down. I hadn't seen her sit at the counter in all the years I had known her. Usually when she rested she sat at the table near the old jukebox, waiting for a customer to come in, or trying to get up enough energy to clean something.

She always tried to keep a fresh pot of coffee going to keep the smell nice in the place, but today the restaurant just felt hot and dusty.

Mary's Cafe never felt hot and dusty. I knew right then that something was wrong.

"You need to kick up the air conditioning a little," I said.

She didn't move or even say anything, so I asked, "You all right?"

She still didn't move so I did something that never would have occurred to me with Mary at any other time. I touched her shoulder.

She sort of tipped real slowly and went over sideways.

Now at my age I don't move real fast, and I didn't move fast enough to catch her as she tumbled to the floor, hitting with a sick thumping sound.

I went to one knee and moved her gently over so I could see into her face. The moment I touched her I knew it wouldn't matter. She was cold and dead, her eyes open and staring at nothing.

"Shit, Mary," I said, swearing in a place that I had never spoken a swear word in before. "What happened?"

I wasn't expecting an answer, but I half expected Mary to sit up and just scold me for using foul language.

But I think she might even find it in her heart to excuse my one swear word. I was seeing the only friend I had in these damn woods laying dead on the old tile floor. The idea of Mary being dead just sort of took my breath away.

I made her look a little more comfortable even though I knew it made no difference at all to her. And I felt odd not taking her off the floor, because Mary would have never spent any time on the floor. But I left her there anyway, because I would have felt even odder touching her to pick her up and move her.

I went into the back and got her best tablecloth that she kept stored there for special occasions. I figured her passing on was about as special as it got.

As I put the tablecloth over her face I heard her voice from behind me. "Real nice of you."

I spun around to see her sitting there at her table by the old jukebox, just like she always did.

I stared at her, then back at the body under the tablecloth on the floor. My old brain was just not working today it seemed.

"Wish you hadn't used my good tablecloth though," she said. "One of the old white ones would have worked just fine. Now you've gone and got that one dusty from the floor."

This time I slowly looked up at where she sat at the table. She was there all right. Or more likely, her ghost was there. The ghost was wearing the same exact thing the body was. And the ghost was talking to me.

At that moment, to be honest, I thought my old heart might just up and stop.

"You're dead," I said.

Not a real bright thing to say, but under the circumstances, it was the only thing I was thinking about.

"No kidding," she said, sort of smiling at me like she always did when she humored me. "Hurt like all get out for a minute. I must have burst a few blood vessels in my head."

She pointed at the counter. "The headache came on so fast that I sat down there at the counter and don't remember another thing until you started covering my body with my best tablecloth."

I glanced at the body, then back at her sitting at the table.

"So," I said, glancing once more at the body and then moving over and sitting at my normal spot at the counter on the end where I could talk to her sitting at the table. "How come you haven't, you know, passed on yet?"

"I don't honestly know," she said, shaking her head and looking very puzzled as if I had asked the most difficult question ever thought up. "Maybe it takes a while for the next life to find me way up here in the mountains."

"Could be," I said. No chance I was going to argue with a ghost, so just agreeing seemed to be my best choice.

She smiled at me. I always enjoyed when she smiled at me. I missed the companionship of a woman, and Mary was the closest thing I ever got to that now. Or had been.

"Maybe I'm doomed for all eternity to sit and talk to you."

She was still smiling, letting me know she was joking. Mary's jokes were always light and very seldom funny.

"So you're not upset at dying?" I asked, glancing back to make sure her body was still right there on the floor where I'd left it.

"Of course I'm upset," she said, shaking her head at me. "I had been looking forward to cleaning up after another day of dust from the logging trucks, and sitting in this place for ten hours without more than five or six customers."

"Oh," I said. I said that a lot with Mary, especially when she tried to be sarcastic.

She patted her chest lightly with her age-worn right hand. "I think I have heartburn. And my stomach's acting up again."

I stared at her for a moment, not really understanding what she had said.

"Would you mind getting me that bottle of Tums back there by the Coke machine. For some reason I don't think I can leave this spot." She shrugged. "Not sure why I know that. Just do."

I got up and grabbed the bottle of Tums and sort of eased myself toward the table where Mary's ghost sat.

"Don't be worrying about me biting you," she said, smiling. "I have never heard of a ghost biting anyone, have you?"

I couldn't say that I had, but I still didn't much like taking any chances. I slid the bottle onto the table and moved back to my stool.

I needed to be calling Sheriff Andrews about Mary. It would take him a good half hour to get up here from Idaho City as it was, but instead I sat down. Even though she was a ghost, talking to her was a lot better than not talking to her, especially when this might be the last time I could ever do it.

Mary tried to pick up the bottle of Tums and her hand went right through it. She tried twice more before saying, "I suppose that's not going to work."

"Heartburn that bad?" I asked.

"Like a bad case of chilly," she said, pressing her chest. "I don't know what I'm going to do if this gets any worse."

Suddenly she just up and burped.

A good one, too. It echoed around the empty restaurant.

I stared at her in complete shock as she turned bright red and covered her mouth. In all my years I could have never imagined Mary letting out a belch like that.

I started to laugh and she just got redder.

But she was also lighter, more see-through, more ghost-like.

"Oh, please pardon me," she said. "I don't know what's come over me."

"You being dead might be a fairly large part of the problem."

I didn't tell her the burp had changed her as well. She was just too embarrassed to stand any other news. And clearly, from the way her hand pressed against her stomach, the heartburn was still bothering her.

"I need to be calling the sheriff," I said. "Mind if I use your phone?"

She pointed to the antique dial phone on the back wall. "Be my guest. I don't think I'm going to be worrying about the bill at this point."

I moved around the counter and toward the phone as she burped again.

I pretended not to notice, but when I glanced back at her she had gotten a little lighter, a little more see-through.

I spent the next minute telling the sheriff about finding Mary, and promising I would stay right where I was until he got there.

I hung up the phone and looked back at Mary, who was considerably lighter still. She must have been burping those little hiccup-like burps that tight women like Mary used in polite company.

Just as I was sitting back down she covered her mouth and gave out another little one, her face getting even redder.

"I'm really sorry I'm burping like this," she said. "Guess death just isn't good on the stomach, and you know how uneasy my stomach can be at times."

Everyone in the valley, and even some of the tourists who stopped by, knew about Mary's stomach, and all her problems with the doctors down in Boise, and how they wouldn't do anything for her to help. The worst fear many locals in the valley had was being trapped in Mary's place for dinner when she didn't have a tourist or two. Then all you heard about was her stomach problems.

She covered her mouth again and burped lightly. Again she sort of faded a little.

Finally, after a few more small burps, she sort of stared at her hand for a moment and then shrugged. "Guess I'm slowly going on to the next life."

"One burp at a time," I said.

She frowned. "What do you mean?"

"Every time you burp you get a little lighter."

"That's not possible," she said, shaking her head. "I just have a horrible case of heartburn is all."

"You want to say anything about impossible?" I asked. I pointed at her body on the floor. "I'm sitting here talking to you while your body is stretched out on the tile. I know for a fact *that* isn't possible either."

She nodded. "I suppose that's true, but I just don't see how my burping is moving me any closer to heaven."

"A good belch can sometimes be heaven," I said, then instantly regretted being so crude to Mary.

"I suppose," she said, actually seeming to think about what I had said.

I could tell she was in some pretty intense discomfort, and no matter how hard she tried, after a moment she covered her mouth with a see-through hand and burped softly again.

Again she faded a little more.

"You know," I said, "maybe this burping is just God's way of having people get the last of their earthly bodies out of their system before moving on. Sort of a letting go of the pressure thing."

Mary looked at me and then half nodded. "I suppose, but it just doesn't seem right that the stomach problems I had all during my life would go with me into the next."

"Maybe they're not," I said. "Maybe that heartburn you're feeling is the old problems wanting to leave you. Maybe a few more good belches and you'll be free to move on into the next world."

As crazy at it sounded, I actually seemed to be making sense to Mary.

"So you think I should just go ahead and let it all out?" she asked, clearly uncomfortable with the idea.

"I'm the only one here, and I won't think any the less of you if you do. A couple of good belches and off you go to heaven."

Even as a ghost, Mary's face turned bright red with my comment. But I could tell the pain in her stomach was getting worse and she was thinking about it.

Finally she nodded and took a deep breath and looked at me. "You've always been a wonderful friend. If this works and I move on, I just wanted you to know that."

I could feel a little moisture sort of building up in my eyes with her statement. I swallowed and then said, "You've been a great friend to me. The valley is going to seem empty without you."

She nodded, a tear in her eye.

Then she sort of squared her shoulders, took a deep breath, and without even covering her mouth, let out the longest and loudest belch I had heard outside of the army.

I wanted to cheer her.

For an instant there, before she disappeared completely, while that huge rolling belch came out of her mouth, she seemed so free, so unencumbered by all the rules she had lived by.

She had finally let go.

As the last memory of her belch echoed through the insides of her diner, I suddenly understood that she was gone.

Really gone.

Only her body remained behind me on the floor.

I put my head down on the counter top and just sat there, trying not to think about how empty my future was going to be. She had been my best friend, a prudish woman who strived to always do everything just right, keep everything clean, keep me on the straight and narrow, yet she was still a good friend.

I had to admit that it was ironic that Mary, a woman who had owned and run a restaurant her entire life, went out in a burp.

Granted, it was one hell of a burp.

I stared at the empty chair at the table where Mary always sat. I was going to miss her more than I could imagine. She had been a very good woman.

Not a great woman, just a very good one.

But I still had no doubt they had heard that burp all the way to heaven.

A VANILLA THREE-WAY WITH A CHERRY

When the ghost of Marilyn Monroe joins you and your girlfriend for a milkshake with a cherry on top, things change in a relationship, sometimes for the better. Especially when your girlfriend thinks she just might be Norma Jean.

One

SOMEONE HAD HUNG a framed, black-and-white photo of Marilyn Monroe right over the diner's only urinal. The picture was about a quarter life-sized, which made her a *very* dominating presence. The bathroom was the standard restaurant bathroom, with a tile floor, metal stall, and painted walls. It was as clean as I had ever seen a bathroom, no graffiti anywhere.

Only Marilyn's picture.

In the photo Marilyn had turned her shoulders sideways, keeping her face straight and looking over her shoulder. She was wearing a low-cut black evening gown. Real low cut, actually, with the old fifties-style bra cups that looked so sharp they could poke out a guy's eye if he went in at the wrong angle.

The points on those breasts were right at head level as I stood at the urinal, and for half the piss I couldn't look at anything else.

Then I glanced up.

Marilyn's face was framed by light, almost angel-like. She stared down at me, sort of smiling, as if she had known when the picture was taken that some guy would be holding his dick while staring at her tits.

I almost couldn't finish the job I was there to do.

And, to be honest, after looking into Marilyn's eyes, I had trouble looking back at her breasts. It just didn't seem respectful, even though those points were right there in front of me, and she was long dead.

So I kept my neck cranked upward, staring at her perfect face, that I-know-what-you-are-doing-smile, those dark eyes. I have no idea how long I stood there, penis flapping in the air-conditioning, just staring at her. I don't even know what I was thinking. I had never been attracted to Marilyn before.

Finally, I realized I was finished and managed to pull away from the picture, get myself zipped up, hands washed, and headed out the door.

"You all right, baby doll?" Betty asked as I slid back into the booth, her gum popping as it often did when she was flustered. Clearly I had been in there with Marilyn for a long time.

Betty and I had been dating for five months, from the moment she had come into my garage to have her classic T-Bird's transmission fixed. Betty loved anything about the fifties. She kept her blonde hair in the old flipped up way, and often wore fifties-style blouses, poodle skirts, and shoes with white socks. When she dressed like that it made her look one hell of a lot younger than her twenty-eight years.

And hotter.

She also loved *Happy Days* on television, and any movie set in the fifties, no matter how stupid. I know, because we had watched a bunch of them.

This diner, "The Fifties Place," was her favorite restaurant, with its Elvis pictures on the wall, Wurlitzer bubble jukebox, and bright red vinyl booths. But tonight was the first time the Marilyn picture had been in the bathroom. I was pretty sure I would have noticed it before.

The diner seemed busier than it had been when I had gone into the bathroom. And the waitress had already brought us the vanilla milkshake we had ordered just as I left to pee.

What the hell had happened to the time? People had always said that Marilyn had a strange effect on men, but this was getting silly. It was just a damn picture.

I pulled my thoughts back out of the men's room and focused on the table in front of me and at the three milkshakes.

"Three?"

The servings in this place were so big, we usually ordered only one shake, and an extra glass to pour the rest of the shake out of the tin mixing cup. But this time we had three vanilla shakes on the table, all in the nifty glasses. The top of the tall, heavy, glasses was wider than the bottom, which tapered down to a glass base.

The waitress had added whipped cream to the top of all of them, and two of the shakes still had their red cherries perched on top. Only the cherry from the glass in front of Betty was missing. She loved the things, so I had no doubt that cherry had given its life over her thick, full lips.

"They needed the mixing cup," Betty said, "so the waitress just poured it all in glasses and gave us extra whipped cream."

I nodded, just staring at the three milkshakes. Maybe I should offer one to Marilyn.

Betty reached a hand forward and touched my arm. "Baby?"

I looked into her deep brown eyes and saw the worry there. I hadn't gotten past second base with her in six months, because, as she said, "Good girls don't do that sort of thing." Maybe if she thought I was sick or something, I might get a little nursing.

I instantly decided against that idea. Betty liked the image of guys from the fifties who were macho types, with their cigarettes rolled up in their tee-shirts, who fought over their girls at drive-in movies. Sick played no part in any image Betty had of me, I was sure of that.

"Fine," I said, smiling at her. "Just got staring at a new picture of Marilyn in the bathroom. Can't make myself believe how much you look like her."

Betty's face turned red and she smiled like I had just promised her a meeting with James Dean. "You really think so?"

"I sure do," I said, squeezing her hand. Actually, she sort of had a passing resemblance, but not much else. And her chest was half the size of Marilyn's, even without the pointed bra.

"You'll be my Joe DiMaggio?" she asked.

I wanted to say sure, if you let me slide into third base tonight, but instead just smiled and said, "Not sure if I can live up to that guy, but why not try?"

Betty loved humility in her man, and I could be as humble as was needed.

Suddenly her smiling face turned serious. "I've got an important question to ask you."

"Go ahead."

"Can I have your cherry?"

I almost blurted out, *I thought that I was supposed to ask that question.* Somehow I managed to say instead, "Which one?"

She laughed at that.

I slid the milkshake closest to me toward her and she took the red cherry, holding it over her mouth for a moment before letting it go.

"I'll drink this one," I said, pulling back my cherry-less shake and putting a straw in it.

Then I put a straw in the third glass and slid it over to the seat beside me. "We'll save that one for Marilyn."

Betty smiled again. "You think she might join us?"

"Depends on if she can get out of the men's room in time," I said.

Betty actually laughed at the lame joke.

Two

BETTY STARTED TALKING about a coming dance she wanted me to go to with her, and I got to nodding and thinking of Marilyn and that amazing look on her face.

Then the hamburgers came. I took the onions off of mine because Betty did the same, and sometime later tonight I hoped to be kissing Betty, and I didn't want onion breath spoiling the moment.

It was during my first bite that Betty said, "Not fair. You ate Marilyn's cherry."

I glanced at where the third shake sat. She was right, the cherry was gone, and the glass looked like someone had taken a good drink from it.

"I thought you didn't like the cherries," Betty said.

"I don't," I said, looking closer at Marilyn's shake without touching it. "The cherry must have just sunk when the whipped cream melted."

"Maybe Marilyn ate it."

Betty was looking at the shake and I had no doubt she was half serious. I just shook my head and went back to eating my burger.

But three bites later the level of the third milkshake was lower still, and there was no sign of the missing bright red cherry.

I hadn't touched the thing, and I knew Betty hadn't reached across the table and drank any of it. In fact, she was still staring at it, her eyes wide, her burger forgotten.

"What?" I asked.

"Marilyn," Betty whispered, not so much that she didn't want anyone to hear, but like she was in shock. Her face was white, her eyes round.

I glanced at the third milkshake on the table beside me. Again some more of it was gone. I was about to say something about the hole in the bottom of the glass when I caught a slight movement out of the corner of my eye.

Then I saw her.

Marilyn.

Sitting right *there* in the booth beside me, between me and the wall, leaning forward and sipping on the milkshake. She had on the same black, low-cut dress that she wore in the picture, so when she bent forward, everything about her sort of became skin. Beautiful, soft, pink skin. Not ghost-like at all.

Betty leaned over the table and grabbed my hand so hard I thought she was going to break it.

"You see her?" she whispered.

"Yeah," I said, not believing what my eyes were telling me.

Marilyn finished the shake, sucking the last of it from the straw with a slurping sound. Then she turned to me and Betty, putting a hand on my leg.

I kid you not, she touched me, softly, yet with overtones of sex like I had never felt before.

Betty kept hold of my hand.

Marilyn Monroe rubbed my leg.

"That was wonderful," Marilyn said, her voice almost a sigh, just like she had done in a bunch of her movies. "I haven't had a good vanilla milkshake in years. Thank you."

"My—my pleasure," I managed to say, even though my voice was screaming that I was dreaming, that I was still standing in the bathroom staring at her picture.

Marilyn squeezed my leg and laughed. Then she turned to Betty, leaving her hand on my thigh.

"Your boyfriend's right, Betty. You do look a little like me, in my Norma Jean days."

For a moment I thought Betty would just faint away. She clearly was having trouble breathing. Finally she managed to say, "Thanks."

Marilyn gave me one of her famous sideways glances that said more with one look than a million words could get across.

And then she went to rubbing my leg, up and down, up and down.

I was definitely more up than down at that moment.

I had to be dreaming.

I swore I was dreaming. But right at that moment, to be honest, I didn't care that I was or wasn't dreaming. I was going to enjoy it all.

Marilyn looked back at Betty. "You know the difference between Norma Jean and Marilyn?"

Betty managed to shake her head.

"Illusion," Marilyn said. "I'm an illusion, what men think they want in a woman. Marilyn is the sexual side of Norma Jean. Marilyn got famous, Norma Jean didn't."

Okay, now I knew this had gone too far. An illusion of Marilyn telling us she was an illusion. If it hadn't been for the hand stroking my leg, I would have laughed.

"Norma Jean was real," Marilyn said. "You're real, Betty. But you have a Marilyn side in you as well. Let it out to play, if you get my meaning."

Oh, god, I had died and gone to heaven. Marilyn Monroe was giving my girlfriend sex advice while giving me a hard on.

Marilyn smiled at Betty with that smile that only girls know the meaning of.

Betty smiled and nodded back at Marilyn.

I smiled as Marilyn's hand moved up my leg a little more.

"Thanks for the shake," Marilyn said.

Then with one last squeeze, very high up my thigh, she vanished.

Three

SUDDENLY THE NOISE from the diner came flooding back in, as if Marilyn being there had stopped it. A kid was crying two booths over, Buddy Holly doing his most famous song on the jukebox, and the waitress was talking to the people in the booth behind Betty.

It was as if the world had stopped for a few minutes, and I had been holding my breath.

I let out a deep sigh and looked around. It seemed no one had noticed Marilyn.

No one but me and Betty.

And my dick. It had most definitely noticed Marilyn's hand rubbing my leg.

Betty was still just sitting there, staring at where Marilyn had been, holding my hand across the table as if she was about to slip over the edge of a cliff.

Finally, as someone knocked over a glass of water three booths over, I asked, "You all right?"

Betty took a moment, then with what looked like a force of will, pulled her gaze from where Marilyn had been and looked into my eyes.

"Did that just happen?"

"I'm not sure what just happened." I pointed at the empty milk-shake glass. "But someone drank that thing."

Betty nodded, staring at the empty place beside me. Then she said softly, "Marilyn."

"One hell of an illusion," I said.

"Maybe," Betty said. "Maybe not."

We both sat there for a moment in silence, Betty still holding my hand. Then suddenly she said, "I want to see that picture in the bath-room." She stood and pulled me up behind her.

"In the men's room?" I asked. Betty had always struck me as the biggest prude to live in the new century. Imagining her going into a men's room just didn't seem possible.

"You make sure no one's in there first," Betty said.

We moved over to the door of the men's room and I poked my head inside. "Anyone in here?"

My voice echoed, so I turned to Betty and said, "Clear."

Betty pushed past me and stopped in the very center of the bath-room, with me still standing holding the door open.

"Where is it?" she asked.

"Over the urinal," I said, but the moment I said that I knew the picture, just like the Marilyn beside me in the booth, was gone. There was no way Betty would have missed seeing that picture.

I let the door close and moved to stand beside her, staring at the blank wall.

"It was right there," I said. "Honest."

Betty took my hand and laughed. "I know it was."

As she pulled me out of the men's room and we headed back to the table, the waitress gave us a dirty look. All I could do was shrug.

We finished our burgers and shakes, talking about Marilyn and what she had said, as if it really hadn't been an illusion, that she had just joined us from the land of the dead to share a vanilla milkshake.

After I had paid the bill, we left all three empty milkshake glasses together, touching in the center of the table, straws bent outward in three different directions.

And that night, back at my apartment, the Betty I had known for six months added a Marilyn side to her personality.

I have no idea if it was an illusion or not, but to be honest, I didn't care.

LIVING TIME

A Poker Boy Story

In a casino in Oregon, Poker Boy beats a man fair-and-square at the poker table while a stranger watches, a stranger who knows too much about Poker Boy and his job.

It turns out that much of Poker Boy's future rested on that one hand of cards.

A classic Poker Boy story with true heart.

One

I SAT UNDER THE GAZE of some idiot who had watched too much poker on television as he stared at me like he knew what he was doing. I have no idea what he was looking for, and I had no doubt he didn't know either, but he kept it up, trying to decide if he should toss in his last two hundred bucks and call my bet.

He had on a heavy wool sweater and had taped one side of his glasses with white tape. The longer he stared at me, the more he sweated. He was in the third chair and I was in the sixth. The two men between us had both scooted their chairs back to stay out of the way of the showdown.

Around us the Spirit Winds Casino poker room was doing a good business for ten o'clock on a Thursday night in the middle of January.

Five tables were going, including two no-limit tables and from the looks of it there was a waiting list on the board.

The noises from the slots and blackjack tables filtered into the room like a steady background of white noise and two of the televisions in the corners were on, both showing different professional basketball games.

A couple players were sitting at empty tables just watching the games.

I had two more hours before I needed to jump from the Oregon mountains to Las Vegas using my new teleportation power to pick up my girlfriend, Patty Ledgerwood, aka Front Desk Girl, from her job at the MGM Grand Hotel on the Strip. So I was enjoying a friendly game picking up a few hundred here and there along the way.

In two hours it had been a profitable night, a large part because of the guy staring at me. He had started with almost a grand and was down to his last two hundred of the two racks of five-dollar chips he had sat down with.

Outside the Casino the night felt like it would snow at any moment and the wind was biting and cold. In Vegas the temperature would be in the low fifties at midnight when I picked up Patty.

At some point I was going to just move to Vegas, buy or build a place there. But I still liked this casino and the area around it and considered this casino my home casino, even though I didn't spend much time these days in my doublewide trailer a few miles from here.

In fact, I couldn't remember the last night I had slept there. It hadn't been since Patty and I got more serious and I learned how to teleport. And that had been a good six months.

Down the table the guy just kept watching me, sweating, trying to decide what to do. I had a pair of aces down and there was an ace and two deuces on the board with a king. I doubted he had a pair of deuces in his hand, otherwise he would have called me at once and laughed while flipping his cards over.

More than likely he had the 4th ace and a bad kicker. He might have a king and was wondering if I had an ace. Either way I had him beat and beat badly.

I smiled at him, tipping back my black Fedora-like hat.

"Anything I can tell you?" I asked him, smiling.

The dealer frowned, but said nothing.

The guy just shook his head, checked his cards again, then went back to staring at me.

The more he sweated and stared, the more I stared to sense the guy had a problem larger than this hand. He was playing with money he couldn't afford to lose. I had figured that much out earlier, and now I was about to take his last few hundred. The sweat on his forehead was for a lot more than just a hand and a couple hundred dollars. To this guy, he thought he was betting his entire life.

And at a poker table, that never worked out well. Poker could be a very cruel game, especially when you shouldn't be playing.

He stared and stared, the sweat beading on his forehead and his eyes slits behind his broken glasses. More than likely he had read some stupid book on poker tells and was trying to watch me for one. So I decided to give him a tell from the first chapter.

I leaned forward, pretending to want to flip my cards over and show him. The book said that if a player acted strong, they had a weak hand. I honestly didn't care if he called me or not. I just wanted the stupid hand over.

He smiled. "You don't have it," he said. "You're bluffing."

He pushed in his last two hundred bucks and then waited for me to flip over my cards. If he had flipped his cards over I might have mucked and just given him the hand and the money, but he didn't.

I flipped over my two aces and his face went pale.

"Might want to read that book again," I said as the dealer shoved the pile of chips my way.

The guy beside the loser on the end of the table just shook his head. "You should know better than to mess with Poker Boy."

I glanced at the guy again, pretending I wasn't upset that he knew my superhero name. But I was.

The dealer glanced at me, then went back to gathering the cards to shuffle.

I didn't like it that someone had used my superhero name here, in my home casino. I didn't like it at all.

I had a read on the guy from his play over the last two hours. Strong player, cautious, no real tells. He was someone to be very careful with. More than likely he was a pro. Of the chips that had come across the table in the last two hours, I had a large number of them and he had the rest.

He wore a tan Izod golf shirt and had put his ski parka on a hook beside the door. He had brown short hair and brown eyes and a slightly hooked nose. He looked to be about thirty, but I could be off in either direction by a decade.

He looked to be about my height at six foot. But he looked stronger, with wider, football-player-like shoulders and neck.

He was nothing exceptional and except for his play, he had stayed under my radar for the two hours he had been at the table. I had just not paid him much attention.

Impressive.

"Have we met?" I asked as I stacked the chips, knowing for a fact that we had never met before. I did not forget a face. I had trouble with names, but never a face. That was part of my superpowers. And as a poker player, I know I would have remembered him from his play.

"Nope," the guy said, smiling. "Stan sent me."

My stomach flipped, but I kept stacking my chips trying to get some sort of read on the situation.

The loser beside him finally decided he was done and shoved his chair back, clearly angry at his loss.

"I hope you two are proud of yourselves," he said looking at me, then at the guy I had been talking to. "I know collusion when I see it."

The guy I had been talking to who claimed Stan had sent him reached over casually and just touched the arm of the guy. "We're just having a friendly game here," he said. "Nothing out of the ordinary, I can promise you."

The guy sort of stood there for a moment, then shook his head and laughed. "Yeah, I know that. Just sort of mad at my own stupid play."

Wow! The guy had some powers! I was stunned.

"Actually," the guy said to the angry man, "you are a pretty damn fine player. You just ran into the best tonight."

The guy nodded. "Thanks, appreciate that." He looked at me, smiled and said, "Nice playing with you."

Then the guy walked off as I stared at the guy who knew my name. I felt I should follow the guy out to see what he planned to do after his loss, but at that moment I was more concerned with the guy across from me who knew my name.

"You said Stan sent you?" I asked. "Which Stan?"

"Your boss of course," the guy said, smiling.

Two

I INSTANTLY TOOK THE TWO OF US out of time, freezing everyone else in the room. All the sounds of the casino vanished and everyone stayed in place, stuck between two moments in time.

Except the two of us.

"Wow, nifty trick," the guy said, his eyes large as he looked around. "I hope I can learn how to do that someday."

"Stan!" I shouted at the ceiling as I stood and moved a few steps away from the poker table.

A moment later Stan, the God of Poker, appeared in front of me. He was wearing his normal tan slacks, tan shirt and sweater and he was smiling.

"Good," he said to me. "I see you've met The Kid. How'd he do?"

"What do you mean by that?"

Stan smiled and looked at the chips in front of both of our chairs. "Doesn't look like he got much of your money."

"He's a fine player," I said. "I just want to know how he knows me and you?"

"I'm right here, guys," The Kid said, waving his hand.

Stan laughed. "He's the new recruit. So how did he do?"

"Besides blurting out my name in front of an entire table, and mentioning your name, and being way too old to be called kid, he played decent poker."

Stan looked at The Kid and shook his head. "You never say another superhero's name out loud in front of regular people."

"Sorry," The Kid said, actually looking worried and sheepish. "I didn't know."

Stan laughed and waved it off. "You'll learn."

I couldn't begin to count the times Stan had used those same words with me in my first few years as a superhero. And now that I was actually looking at The Kid, he did look a lot younger than my first take on his age. At most he was twenty-five. It was a nifty trick being able to shift his age appearance like that. I would have to learn it.

"New recruit?" I asked Stan. "Working for you?"

"Yup," Stan said, smiling. "Laverne approved it and everything. She said you and your team are doing more work for all of the gods and I needed the help with just poker."

"I told you that last week," I said, smiling at him.

I walked over to The Kid and stuck out my hand as he stood from the table. "Nice meeting you, Kid."

"The honor is all mine, Poker Boy," The Kid said, smiling and shaking my hand like I was a rock star. "You are the smoothest player I have ever had the honor to sit with."

"You ain't half bad yourself," I said. "And nice job staying hidden as long as you did."

"Thanks," he said, beaming.

I remembered in my early years how important it was to have someone tell me I did something right. Hell, after ten years now, it was still important. I doubt it would ever get old.

Then I got serious as I turned back to Stan. "I can handle it from here," I said. "We have some work to do."

"Give him time," Stan said to me. "Don't push too hard."

"I promise," I said.

Stan vanished and I turned back to The Kid. "Come with me. We have a problem to clean up."

The kid looked puzzled, but followed me through the frozen people and the silence of the casino.

"This is just creepy," he said, staring at a woman chewing on a large hotdog, her mouth open and full of half-eaten bun.

About halfway across the casino I found who I was looking for. The guy who had been at the table on that last hand. I had taken the last of his money.

"Did you sense any problem with this guy?" I asked The Kid.

"He was desperate, playing with important money. That's why I tried to calm him some."

"And you did fine with that, but my sense is that what you did won't be enough. I may be wrong, but if I'm not, I want to make sure nothing goes too wrong."

The Kid looked puzzled, but only nodded.

"Now, let's get back to the table so I can put us in real time again. Follow my lead."

Three

WHEN WE WERE BOTH SEATED, I put us back into the natural flow of time. The sounds of the casino smashed into us.

"Let's go talk," I said to The Kid and pushed my chair back.

"Glad to," he said. Then to the dealer he said, "We'll be right back."

The dealer nodded and began dealing to the other six at the table.

The Kid stayed with me as we left the poker room.

"Dead camera area here," I said and jumped us to a dead camera area in the parking lot.

The Kid looked stunned. "Wow, do I have a lot to learn."

"Give it time," I said, heading toward the front door of the casino.

A moment later the guy who had tried to get a read on me came out of the front door and turned to the left toward one of the parking lots. When he got there, he climbed into an old Ford that looked like it had seen its better days.

Then he just sat behind the wheel as if he had no place to go.

More than likely, if my sense of him was right, he didn't.

The Kid and I stood off to one side near a truck so we could watch him and not be seen. I had on my black leather coat and hat that was my superhero uniform, but I could still feel the cold wind. The Kid was in a short-sleeved golf shirt and he was shaking already.

"You might want to learn to always wear a jacket of some sort in a poker room," I said. "Both for sitting under air-conditioning and for this job."

"I'll remember that," he said, his teeth almost chattering.

"Where you from?" I asked.

"Southern California," he said.

"You want to go back in for your coat?"

He shook his head. "I'll make it."

At that moment the guy in the car moved. But he didn't go to turn on his car. Instead, he reached over to his glove box and opened it and pulled out what looked to be a pistol of some type.

"Shit, he's going to off himself," The Kid said, starting to run at the car.

I jumped us out of time again, then called for The Kid to hold on. He stopped and waited for me.

"I really need to learn how to do that," he said.

Then he followed me over to the car as I opened the car door, took the gun from the guy's hand, unloaded the clip, made sure there was no round anywhere in the gun, then put the gun back in the guy's hand, closed the door and indicated that The Kid should follow me away from the car.

"You were sure right about the guy," he said. "How did you know?"

"Just reading people," I said.

We got back to where we had been and I let us go back into the flow of time. The wind again hit us hard and The Kid shivered.

"Follow my lead completely," I said and he nodded as we started back toward the guy's car.

He didn't see us coming. He just kept staring at the gun in his hands until I knocked on the window and startled him.

He tried to hide the gun by dropping it on the floor before he opened the car door and stepped out into the cold.

"Yeah," he said. "So you two really are together."

"Not really," I said. "In fact, we just met tonight at the table, but we were both worried about you."

"You are the only people on the planet who are," he said, the sarcasm clear in his voice. "Thanks."

He was in even worse shape than I thought.

I turned on what I call my "empathy-power" and directed it at the guy. And also the power I call "tell-me-the-truth." With both of those powers directed at the poor guy, he had no choice but to tell me what was going on like I was a trusted counselor he had poured his heart out to for years.

"So how bad is it?" I asked. "What's happening?"

"No job, my wife left me six months ago, I'm homeless, and you took the last of my money. I don't even have gas money to get off this stupid mountain and back to Portland. That's how bad."

"That's bad," I said, nodding.

Beside me The Kid nodded, but said nothing.

"So what did you do for a living?" I asked.

He laughed. "What every other unemployed person around this area did. I worked construction. Actually, I had my own construction business, had a dozen guys working for me, building some of the best custom homes in Oregon. Bobby C. Davis Construction."

He said the name of his business with pride and I suddenly had a great idea to help this guy not put the barrel of that gun in his mouth.

I laughed. "Great meeting you," I said and extended my hand. "I'm Gary Barnes."

Gary Barnes was one of my fake names I used in the real world when I had to. Actually, everyone around this casino called me Gary and my doublewide trailer a couple miles away was under that name as well.

The kid stepped forward to shake the guy's hand. "I'm Roger Stevens," he said.

I had a hunch that was a made-up name by The Kid as well.

"Bob Davis," the guy said, now even more puzzled.

I kept the empathy power turned on high and focused at him and then also turned on my "trust-me" power. This poor guy was putty in my hands, especially in his depressed condition. Luckily, I only used my powers for good.

"I actually looked for your business a few months back," I said, lying through my teeth. I was a poker player. Lying was part of our job description. "I've been wanting to build a custom home on some property I have near here, a big, beautiful custom home, and your firm was recommended to me a number of times."

"Really?" he asked, smiling. Then his mood turned again. "See how quality work turns out?" He pointed at the old car he was driving. "I sold my rig and most of my tools to get living money and money to pay my child support. I hoped to win enough tonight to make next month's payment and get a little apartment. That went well as you know."

"How old are your children?" The Kid asked, expertly moving the subject from the guy's loss to something better.

The guy seemed to melt at the mention of them. "Six and eight," he said.

"I think they would rather have their father than money," I said.

He shrugged, but I could tell he wasn't so sure.

Four

"TELL YOU WHAT, BOB," I said. "How about you go to work for me and my girlfriend and build us the house of our dreams?" I sure hoped Patty had some idea of what would make a good custom home. I didn't.

He looked at me and then smiled, but shook his head. "I don't have the tools or even a truck or a place to stay."

"None of that's a problem," I said, laughing. "I need someone with your skill. I've got a doublewide close to here that I'm not using that you can live in for free, and I'll fund you for a new truck and tools. Besides that, I'll put you on a regular salary for as long as it takes to build the house. And from what Patty and I want, that might take some time. All custom."

We all three stood there in the cold wind as he stared at me, again trying to get a read on me.

Luckily, this time it didn't take as long as at the poker table.

"Are you for real?" he asked. "You can't really be scamming me. I've got nothing more anyone could take."

"I'm not kidding," I said. "I was hoping to hire someone with your skill to build me a house here and from the looks of your situation, I can get you cheaper than you used to charge. A good deal for me."

With that he laughed. "Yeah, a bunch cheaper, to be honest."

"Do we have a deal?" I asked, extending my hand. "You come to work for me and build me the best damn place you can. And maybe by the time you're done, the economy will have turned a little and you can ramp your business back up. Or come down to Vegas and help me build a house there after you're done here."

He hesitated for only a moment, looking me right in the eyes, and then he nodded and shook my hand, smiling. "We have a deal. Thanks. You need to know you just saved my life."

"Actually," I said, waving off his thank you. "You just saved me from moving away from a place I love. But we have to make one more agreement."

"What's that?" he asked, looking suddenly worried.

"You won't come in here while you work for me to do anything but have dinner. You're a fine poker player, but you need to play for the right reasons."

"Deal," he said, smiling. "And after we get the house done, maybe you can give me some lessons."

"That I can do," I said, smiling.

I handed him a few hundred dollars and pointed at the gas station and grocery across the highway. "This is an advance. I'm going to go cash out my chips. You need to get some gas and some food to stock a fridge for later and breakfast. There's not a damn thing in that doublewide. Meet me back here in twenty minutes."

"Got it, boss," he said, smiling, the look of desperation now completely gone from his eyes, replaced with a glimmer of hope.

Halfway back across the cold parking lot, The Kid finally broke his silence. "That felt great helping him like that. Is that what it's like being a superhero?"

"Sometimes, yeah, it is. On the good nights."

We walked a little ways in silence again before he asked the next question.

"You really wanted to build a house up here?"

I laughed. "I hadn't actually thought of it until tonight. But I own some nice land on hills around here as well as my doublewide. And Patty, my girlfriend, won't stay up here with me because my place is so shabby. So I might as well build a house with her help so she'll come up here at times."

"You like it here that much?" The Kid asked as we got close to the front doors.

"I do," I said.

"So you saved a man's life and helped yourself at the same time. You are good. Both at poker and at life."

"Is there much difference?" I asked, repeating a phrase that Stan once said to me when I was starting out.

"Not when you play them both the way you do," The Kid said, holding the front door of the Casino open for me.

And that was one of the nicest things anyone had said to me in a long time. I was going to like this kid.

ALSO BY DEAN WESLEY SMITH

THUNDER MOUNTAIN STORIES:

Stand for Home

Last Car for This Time

The Cavern

The House at Thunder Rock

SEEDERS UNIVERSE NOVELS:

Dust and Kisses: A Seeders Universe Prequel Novel

Against Time

Sector Justice

Morning Song

The High Edge

Star Mist

Star Rain

Star Fall

Starburst

SEEDERS UNIVERSE STORIES:

Remember Me to Your Children

A Matter for a Future Year

A Bad Patch of Humanity

Dreaming Large

Pilgrim Hugh Incidents:

The Case of Pilgrim Hugh: Five Strange Detective Short Stories

The Case of the Intrusive Furniture

The Case of the Dog-Bit Arm

The Case of the Lost Treasure

The Case of the Man Who Saw

The Case of the Dead Lady Blues

Miss Smallwood's Goodies

DOC HILL THRILLERS:

Dead Money

Mary Jo Assassin Novels:

Death Takes a Partner

Death Takes a Diamond

MARY JO ASSASSIN STORIES:

Death in the Morning

The Remodeling of a Life

Make Myself Just One More

MARBLE GRANT STORIES:

A Lady in Heat: A Marble Grant Story

A Look at His Heart: A Marble Grant Story

OTHER SHORT STORIES:

The Big Tick of Time

Long Shadow

The Matchbox Agenda

Out of Coffee Experience

Sleeping with the Goddess

If Sex is All a Dream, Then Who Cleans Up the Mess

Love with the Proper Napkin

Neighborhood

Remember

A Bubble for a Minute

Waiting for the Coin to Drop

A Pinch of How Rosie Lived

In Case of Emergency

The Mouth that Walked

A Pathetic Fallacy

As the Robot Rubs

Music in Time

The Tragic Tale of a Man in a Duster

Skiing the Graveyard of Souls

Marriage in Six Floors

Well, Maybe Not

Butchered Whale on a Red Bedspread

Two Roads, No Choices

Who's Holding Donna Now

Ambassador to the Promised Land

Santa's Snack

Sprinkle on a Memory

I'm Her Dead Husband

Variations of a Scream

Gus

The Last Burp of a Very Good Woman

A Vanilla Three-Way With a Cherry

Nostalgia 101

A Life in Whoopees

Between Showers

Squatter's Rights on the Street of Broken Men

After the Dance

Mated from the Morgue

Me and Beans and Great Big Melons

Don't Rust on Me Now

Shopping Cart Lover

Iron Eyebrows: A Romance with Too Much Hair

Mom's Paradox

The Keeper of the Morals

My Socks Rolled Down

The Romance Novel Challenge

In the Shade of the Slowboat Man

It's a Story About a Guy Who…

Standing in Line at the Intersection

Husband Dummies

On Top of the Dead

The Yellow of the Flickering Past

Cheerleader Revelation

Dead Post Bumper

Clicking Sticks

Peter the Hermit

In Search of the Perfect Orgasm

The Life and Death of Fortune Cookie Tyrant

Tumbling Down the Nighttime

Growing Pains of the Dead

The Call of the Track Ahead

Dinner on a Flying Saucer

The Great Alien Vibration

Cold Comfort

For the Delusion that Waited

The Face in the Fullness of Time

Playing in the Street

Best Eaten on a Slow Tuesday

Here to Stay on the Edge

The Stone Slept Here

To Remember a Single Minute

Something Wasted On

A Parker House Roll

The Thickness of a Warp

Unlocked Gate

Last Man Out

Shadow in the City

Another Damn Deal

Habit

Smile

The Last Short Putt of a Fearful Man

Keep Hoping for a New Tomorrow

The Wait

ABOUT THE AUTHOR

Considered one of the most prolific writers working in modern fiction, *USA Today* bestselling writer Dean Wesley Smith published almost two hundred novels in forty years, and hundreds and hundreds of short stories across many genres.

At the moment he produces novels in several major series, including the time travel Thunder Mountain novels set in the Old West, the galaxy-spanning Seeders Universe series, the urban fantasy Ghost of a Chance series, a superhero series starring Poker Boy, and a mystery series featuring the retired detectives of the Cold Poker Gang.

His monthly magazine, *Smith's Monthly*, which consists of only his own fiction, premiered in October 2013 and offers readers more than 70,000 words per issue, including a new and original novel every month.

During his career, Dean also wrote a couple dozen *Star Trek* novels, the only two original *Men in Black* novels, Spider-Man and X-Men novels, plus novels set in gaming and television worlds. Writing with his wife Kristine Kathryn Rusch under the name Kathryn Wesley, he wrote the novel for the NBC miniseries The Tenth Kingdom and other books for *Hallmark Hall of Fame* movies.

He wrote novels under dozens of pen names in the worlds of comic books and movies, including novelizations of almost a dozen films, from *The Final Fantasy* to *Steel* to *Rundown*.

Dean also worked as a fiction editor off and on, starting at Pulphouse Publishing, then at *VB Tech Journal*, then Pocket Books, and now at WMG Publishing, where he and Kristine Kathryn Rusch serve as series editors for the acclaimed *Fiction River* anthology series, which launched in 2013. In 2018, WMG Publishing Inc. launched the first issue of the reincarnated *Pulphouse Fiction Magazine*, with Dean reprising his role as editor.

For more information about Dean's books and ongoing projects, please visit his website at www.deanwesleysmith.com and sign up for his newsletter.

www.ingramcontent.com/pod-product-compliance
Lightning Source LLC
Chambersburg PA
CBHW021952120726
47898CB00001BA/114